INFAMOUS

JENNY HOLIDAY

Infamous

Copyright © 2017 by Jenny Holiday

Cover art: L.C. Chase, lcchase.com/design.htm

Editors: Sarah Lyons and Chris Muldoon

ISBN: 978-0-9950927-8-5

Second edition, March, 2018

Also available in e-book (ISBN: 978-0-9950927-9-2)

CHAPTER ONE

At the last second, Jesse changed his mind and sat next to the hot guy instead of the middle-aged businesswoman.

It was a breach of the rules. Jesse had been taking the Sunday afternoon Montreal-to-Toronto train once a month for the past four years, and he had a system, a well-honed methodology developed from painful trial and error.

And by *painful*, he meant, for example, *five hours trapped next to a young mother holding a teething baby.*

Most people liked to rush onto the train as soon as possible, and they aggressively went after empty rows, seating themselves alone. But this route always sold out. Since the train was going to fill, it was smarter to hang back a bit, to bide his time and get onto a car that looked like it was about half-full. That way, he could choose his seatmate, whereas all those hasty people alone in two-seater rows had to resign themselves to a journey with whoever happened to plop down next to them.

No, it was infinitely preferable to be in control of one's own destiny.

And Jesse was nothing if not in control of his destiny.

So whenever Jesse got on a train, the first thing he always did was start profiling the hell out of potential seatmates.

Middle-aged women were the best. Even better if they looked like they were traveling on business. If they *also* wore wedding rings? Jackpot. Women in general tended not to initiate conversation and left him to pass the time in peace, the aforementioned mother-of-teether being emblematic of an exceptional subcategory: mothers desperately in need of adult conversation.

Another subcategory to avoid regardless of gender? The elderly, God bless them, were not ideal seatmates.

Neither were teenagers, the ultimate undesirables. They were starting to recognize him. Some people in their twenties and thirties did too, but they usually couldn't remember from where—or if they did, it sparked a brief conversation and then they picked up on his not-so-subtle cues and left him alone. But if a teenaged girl recognized him, he was doomed. He generally didn't like to think of teenagers as the band's target demographic, but you never had any idea what the record label was going to do with your stuff. Before you knew it, you'd be appearing on Spotify playlists called "teen heartbreak" or some shit.

He was beginning to think it was time to arrange alternate transportation for his monthly trips back from Montreal. Things were happening faster on the career front than he'd anticipated. By the time he was on the cover of *Rolling Stone*, he wasn't going to be taking the train anymore anyway. And what do they say? "Start as you mean to go on"?

Today, he ambled down the aisle, scanning the rows until he spied the perfect target: midforties, hair blown out into a perfect dark-brown helmet, business suit, laptop already fired up.

As he approached, he surveyed the rest of the car. The row

across from the businesswoman was occupied by a man reading a book. He was dressed in an aqua button-down shirt and dark jeans. Salt-and-pepper hair, which was clearly premature—the guy couldn't have been more than thirty-five—swooshed back into a messy pompadour that was shorter on the sides. His most prominent facial feature was a chiseled jaw dusted with a few days' worth of beard growth that was more salt than pepper.

Well, shit. A baby silver fox.

The poor bastard would probably end up with some clingy woman sitting next to him, projecting all her hopes onto him for the duration of the trip.

Jesse should do a good deed and sit next to him.

He usually tried to ignore men who weren't obviously working on something. You never knew with men. It was harder to make snap judgments about them. Sometimes they kept to themselves, but sometimes the newspaper they'd seemed so engrossed in would turn out to be a prop and they'd want to buddy up with you.

Someone was coming up the aisle behind him. Jesse was holding everyone up.

The woman was safer. Infinitely safer.

He set his bag down on the seat next to the man.

Jesse rummaged through it to pull out the items he'd need during the trip—phone, bottle of water, the latest issues of *Billboard* and *Rolling Stone*. It was hard not to sigh over the talentless, manufactured boy band on the cover of the latter. But he would have his turn someday.

As he reached up to stash his bag on the overhead shelf, the man looked up and caught his eye.

Jesse nodded as he sat. The man's eyes were striking—a kind of light brown flecked with gold, bright enough to be visible behind his black horn-rimmed glasses. The silver hair and the almost-gold eyes were a weird but compelling combination, like clashing jewelry.

The man gave a slight smile and said, "Hey," before returning his attention to his book. A second later, though, his phone dinged. He picked it up and eyed the screen. Jesse watched him key in his passcode and read a long text. His eyes seemed to darken in real time, becoming a little less gold, like the sun dimming. He dropped the phone carelessly into the seat pocket in front of him, closed his eyes, and mouthed, *Fuck.*

Some part of Jesse's brain could sense some other part of his brain gearing up to speak.

Don't do it.

They had a five-hour journey ahead of them.

Don't do it.

"Everything okay?"

Damn it.

The man's eyes flew open as the rational part Jesse's brain railed at the mouth-controlling part, which had apparently gone rogue.

"Sorry," Jesse said, and what was he *doing*? This way lay ruin. Or at least the possibility of an excruciatingly tedious five hours, because who knew if he'd been brainwashed by this guy's good looks? "You just seemed…upset all of a sudden."

The man opened his mouth, then closed it, like maybe he was at war with himself too.

"Sorry," said Jesse again, which was weird because *Spin's* review of the band's last record had called it "unapologetic," and never had Jesse been more satisfied with an adjective. "I'll leave you alone."

You know the best way to leave someone alone? Leave them the fuck alone.

"I'm a doctor," the man said, kind of woodenly, like he was

4

trying out this talking thing for the first time. His voice was all gravel and velvet, which should have been a contradiction, but apparently a guy with silver hair and gold eyes didn't have to hew to the rules that governed the rest of the slobs in the world. "A pediatrician. I have a patient who got some bad news."

"Yeah?" Jesse prompted, because suddenly, he could no longer imagine anything he'd like to do more for the next five hours than listen to Baby Silver Fox talk about his job. Also: what the hell?

"He needs a new liver. We were testing his brother as a possible donor." He looked out the window at the passing scenery as he spoke. "It was this kid's best hope. That was one of the nurses texting with the news that the brother is not a match. Now he's got to sit around on the waiting list biding time—and time isn't something this kid has a ton of." He ran his hands through his hair, scraping his fingers against his scalp in frustration as he turned his attention back to Jesse. "Sorry. That was probably a longer answer than you wanted."

Christ. That put things into perspective, didn't it? Here Jesse was, his biggest problem that he wasn't making enough money to fly back from Montreal after his visits with his sister but he was starting to be recognized on the train. "You know what? I'll be right back." He popped up and hunted down the porter, who hadn't begun food and beverage service yet and, by dangling an enormous tip, managed to procure two tiny bottles of whiskey.

When he plunked them down on Baby Silver Fox's tray, it occurred to him that maybe whiskey wasn't the best answer to *liver problems*, but the man grinned and said, "It's noon somewhere?"

"Exactly," said Jesse, a fierce sort of satisfaction lodging in his chest at the idea that he'd made this man smile. "Nothing like a little midmorning whiskey to take your mind off your problems." He twisted open one of the bottles and handed it over, belatedly wishing he'd gotten something classier than whiskey. This guy probably drank martinis.

"Thanks." Baby Silver Fox clinked his bottle against Jesse's and then took a sip.

He wasn't sure what to say. "So you're a pediatrician? That must be rewarding." As soon as it was out, though, he regretted it. *The guy tells you a kid is on the verge of death, and you say, "How rewarding"?* "On the whole, I mean. Making kids well," he added, because why stop while he was behind?

"I wish. Most of the kids I see are really sick. I work at Toronto Children's Hospital. I'm a hospitalist. You know what that is? Most people don't."

"I would be one of those people."

"It's sort of like a general practitioner, but for patients in the hospital. I oversee their care—many of them are being seen by lots of different kinds of specialists and technicians. I make sure everything is integrated optimally and…" He trailed off and sighed.

"And that kids who need new livers get them?" Jesse finished softly.

Baby Silver Fox—make that *Dr.* Baby Silver Fox—rolled his eyes like he was disgusted with himself. "In theory."

"Hey, now. It's not your fault this kid's brother wasn't a match."

"I know. I'm just… I don't know. I moved to Toronto from Montreal three months ago. I thought about changing things up when I decided I was going to move—joining a regular pediatric practice. Giving out vaccines and fixing tummy trouble and referring on the hard cases. You'd think stuff like this would get easier, but it doesn't."

"I don't imagine dying kids ever gets easy."

The doctor made a vague noise of agreement. "Sometimes I wonder what I was thinking. The point of moving was to make a fresh start. And here I am doing the exact same thing I was doing in Montreal…and, Jesus, listen to me. I don't even know you, and it's like I think you're my therapist or something." He held up his now-empty bottle. "I'm a bit of a lightweight, I'm afraid. And also a chatty drunk, so…"

"Hey, it's okay." And, amazingly, it was. This was exactly the kind of conversation he normally bent over backward to avoid, but somehow, this time, with this guy, he wanted to know more.

"Let's change the subject," said the man. "What about you? What brought you to Montreal? Or is Montreal home?"

"Nope, headed home to Toronto. I'm in a band. We have a monthly gig in Montreal."

"A band that travels by VIA Rail?" He smiled. "You guys should make a commercial."

"No, the gig's on Friday, and the rest of the band heads back afterward in a couple of vans. My sister and her son live in Montreal, though, so I usually spend the weekend with them and make my own way home on Sunday."

"Would I know your work?"

"I doubt it."

"Try me."

"The band's called Jesse and the Joyride."

"Alas, I don't think I know it. Are you Jesse?"

"Yep. Jesse Jamison." He stuck out his hand.

"Hunter Wyatt."

Hunter Wyatt's hand was soft. Or maybe it was only Jesse's guitar-induced calluses that made it seem so.

Jesse held on a heartbeat too long, lulled for a moment by the rocking of the train and the warm flesh against his own.

Hunter quirked a smile as he pulled away. "It's not every

day you meet a rock star on the train. Especially a rock star taking the train because he's so dedicated to his sister. You're a regular saint."

"I'm not a saint. Or a rock star, for that matter." *Yet.* "But, yeah, it's just me and my sister and my nephew—he's three. Our parents are gone. My sister's had a rough couple of years. She's mostly on her own with my nephew."

"Husband left?"

If only he *would* leave, once and for all. "Something like that."

"That's tough. We've all been there." He huffed a bitter laugh. "Some of us more recently than others."

"Ah," Jesse said. "The fresh start. The move to Toronto."

"Officially I came for the job, but...yeah."

"How long had you been together?"

"Eight years."

Jesse whistled. "Wow. I don't think I've ever even made it eight *months* in a relationship." Not even close to eight months, truth be told, but he didn't want to admit that in front of this guy who so clearly had his shit together.

"Not so impressive, really," Hunter said, "given that I have literally nothing to show for it."

"So you were back for a visit this weekend?"

"Yeah, the dog died. My ex called and said this was it, so I came up to...say goodbye, I guess."

"Man, harsh."

"Yeah, the worst part is that the dog died before I got there."

"Your girlfriend leaves you and your dog dies? It's like a country song—a bad country song."

The doctor didn't laugh, just screwed up his face like he was trying to decide something. Then he said, "It's, uh, not a girl."

"The dog is not a girl?"

"The girlfriend is not a girlfriend. He's a boyfriend. *Ex*-boyfriend."

"Right."

Right.

Jesse had been afraid of that.

This was the part where the rock star would freak out.

Which was fine, because Hunter's dog was dead, his sickest patient was going to keep getting sicker, and his ex, Julian, was still a closet-case bent on sucking all the life out of Hunter.

So a little straight-boy panic induced by accidental proximity to a homo was nothing.

He wasn't into pretending to be anything he wasn't—not anymore, anyway—so the testosterone-oozing musician in the next seat could just feel free to panic.

And he *was* panicking.

But apparently not over the fact that Hunter liked dick.

"Holy shit."

His phone had chimed, and he'd picked it up and was scrolling through what looked like an article illustrated with pictures. Whatever it was, it wasn't good news.

'Twas the season, apparently.

"Holy *shit*," Jesse said again, closing his eyes and letting his chin fall to his chest.

"What's the matter?" Hunter asked, because it seemed rude to check out now.

Jesse opened his eyes and blew out a long, slow breath. "Well, it's nowhere near as bad as your news. That's a good perspective to remember."

"Less-bad bad news. That sounds delightful right about now. Hit me."

He didn't answer, but he handed over his phone.

It was an article on a website called *GossipTO*, headlined **Jesse Jamison making out with mysterious blond—and she isn't Kylie Cameron.**

He read on. Apparently his seatmate was notorious for his stereotypical rock star ways. Before his current girlfriend—this Kylie person—Jesse had enjoyed the groupie lifestyle, if this site was to be believed. Everyone had been shocked when he'd gotten together with Kylie, the story reported. There was also something in there about a trashed hotel room incident.

"I thought you said you weren't a rock star," Hunter said.

"I'm not. Not really."

Hunter chuckled and read part of the article out loud. "'We all know Jesse likes his sex, drugs, and rock and roll, but'—"

Jesse cut him off. "I mean, I have a band. We're doing pretty well in Canada. No one knows our name in the States. Yet. This"—he gestured toward the phone—"is a sensationalistic, B-list Canadian gossip website. But damn, they're out to get me. I can't do anything without them all over my ass. So I enjoy having a little fun from time to time. It's not like I'm breaking any laws." He quirked a grin. "Mostly."

"So they got you making out with this woman who isn't your girlfriend?"

"Yep."

"And your girlfriend is also some kind of celebrity?"

"She's a model."

Hunter couldn't really see anything about the person Jesse was kissing in the blurry shot. Jesse had his back to the camera, and his companion was leaning against a brick wall. She was as tall as Jesse, and models were tall, right? All that was visible of the kiss-ee was shoulder-length, dirty-blond, almost-messy hair—which also seemed kind of model-esque, in that way that models sometimes seemed to strive to look bad in the name of fashion. "So there's no way this could be her?"

"You don't know Kylie Cameron?" Jesse asked.

Hunter searched his mind. "I don't think so?"

"She's Asian. She has long black hair."

"Ah," Hunter said. "I guess you're busted."

"Yeah, and in addition to that not being her, Kylie is like, Canada's sweetheart. She was on *Degrassi* as a kid—before she moved into modeling."

"I'm kind of out of the pop culture loop," said Hunter, though of course he did know the iconic TV show. Everyone who grew up in Canada knew *Degrassi*. Hell, Drake had been on *Degrassi*.

"Yeah, well, everyone loves her. Now I'm the asshole who publicly broke Kylie Cameron's heart."

Hunter squinted at the phone again. If the Kinsey scale was a reliable measure—as a medical doctor, he had his doubts —Hunter was a solid six. Unambiguously gay. And usually he was ruthlessly adept at not developing crushes on straight guys. (Gay guys who pretended to be straight in certain circumstances were another question. Unfortunately.) So the image of Jesse Jamison kissing Ms. Anonymous should have had no effect on him. He should have been immune.

But damn, there was something about that picture. The way Jesse was crowding his not-girlfriend up against the wall. The way he was framing her face with his hands. That was why only her hair was visible—Jesse's hands were clamped possessively on her face.

And if Jesse had this much to lose by being spotted, the fact that this kiss had gone down in public must have meant they'd both been pretty carried away. Hunter shifted in his seat.

"What's her name?" He handed the phone back with an odd reluctance.

"My girlfriend? You mean her real name? It's Kylie—she never used a stage name. And I should probably start calling her my *ex*-girlfriend. 'Cause she is not going to stand for this shit."

"No." Hunter gestured to the phone. "What's the other woman's name?"

Jesse paused before answering. "It doesn't really matter."

"You don't know it!" Damn, this guy *was* a rock star, or at least well on his way to becoming one. Hunter cracked up; he couldn't help it. Jesse certainly looked the part. Choppy dark, messy hair hung around his face. His forearms—he wore a ratty flannel shirt with the sleeves rolled up—were covered with tattoos. He had that kind of sexy-sleazy look.

That was not a look Hunter went for.

Historically.

He liked a more polished look.

Usually.

"Haven't you ever made out with someone whose name you didn't catch?" Jesse asked.

"Not for a really long time." Not since before he'd met Julian. And even before Julian, Hunter had been a serial monogamist. He could count on one hand the number of casual hookups in his past.

Maybe that was what the move to Toronto had been missing so far—some casual sex to break him out of his slump. The prospect was kind of terrifying.

"Well, you should try it," Jesse declared. "Quickest way to get over your loser ex."

"Why do you assume my ex was the loser? Maybe I was the loser."

"Nah."

Hunter wanted to ask how Jesse could possibly know this, but he didn't want to make it seem like he was fishing for compliments.

Jesse's phone buzzed. He picked it up again. "And there it is."

"What?"

Jessie scrolled for a moment, then said, "The breakup text." He sighed resignedly.

"Really?" Hunter was taken aback by the idea of breaking up with someone via text, but he supposed that was part of the jet-set, rock star life his seatmate lived. "Jesus, I'm sorry."

Jesse shrugged. "It's okay. Saves me having to do it. The writing was already on the wall."

"The writing on the wall being something *other than* you making out with someone else against the wall? It seems like your whole problem here is the wall."

All he got in response was a chuckle.

Clearly, Jesse was not the type to invest his heart and soul and the better part of a decade into a relationship.

Hunter should learn from Jesse.

He was downloading Grindr as soon as he got home.

"The more important question is whether my *manager* is going to dump me over this."

"You're more concerned about getting dumped by your manager than your girlfriend?" Hunter asked, though he wasn't sure why—the answer was clear.

"I have a bit of a work-life balance problem?" Jesse shrugged. "And also a manager who basically has me on probation."

"Wow." Who *was* this guy? Hunter had never seen anyone so…unapologetic.

"What are you drinking?" Jesse asked.

"What?" Oh, the service cart was making its way down the aisle.

"I'm guessing whiskey isn't your preferred poison."

When Hunter didn't answer right away, Jesse dropped his magazines into the seat pocket in front of him and said, "Fuck career-ruining photographs." Then he did the same with his phone, holding it between one finger and a thumb like it was contaminated. "Fuck dying kids. Fuck *everyone*. We're single and free. We should toast that shit."

Four hours later, as the conductor announced they were ten minutes from Union Station, Jesse was feeling good.

Eight mini-bottles of red wine could have that effect on a guy.

"We should hide the evidence," Hunter said, slurring a bit and then laughing. He'd only had four mini-bottles. The handsome doctor *was* a bit of a lightweight.

It was adorable.

Jesse had procured most of the aforementioned mini-bottles by sweet-talking a young woman porter after the older man assigned to their car responded to Jesse's request for bottle number four by looking down his nose and saying, "There's only an hour left on your journey, sir."

Hunter reached toward the small garbage bag the train provided, his bottles in hand.

"Hey, no need to 'hide the evidence.'" Jesse grabbed Hunter's arm near the elbow to halt his tidying instinct. Maybe Jesse was an entitled rock star asshole, but he planned to leave a pile of tiny bottles on the seat for the snotty porter to deal with.

Hunter was wearing one of those shirts that looked like flannel, but were actually made of some kind of unbelievably soft mystery material. It was hard to take his hand away. It was hard to do anything but let his hand slide down a forearm that was softer than…all the soft things. A cat? A cloud? A—

—hand.

He'd reached the bare skin of the back of Hunter's hand, and the change in texture was so jarring, he snatched his own hand away as if he'd touched a hot stove.

"No need to hide the evidence, because there was no crime," he said firmly. "These baby boozes were procured with cold, hard cash."

"Cold hard cash and a boatload of charm," Hunter said, and Jesse didn't have an argument for that one. "What about public drunkenness?" Hunter went on. "Isn't that a crime?"

"You might have me there."

Except not. He wasn't nearly drunk enough to plug back into reality. He fished for his phone, dread in his gut. He knew what he would find. Outraged tweets from the public that he had dared to cheat on their beloved Kylie. Incredulous texts from the guys. Anger from his manager, who had read him the riot act about his out-of-control behavior only a month ago.

And there it was.

His second breakup text of the day.

He'd been fired by his manager. Cut loose by the woman who had plucked the band out of the club scene and deftly shepherded them to the next level—they were now routinely selling out midsize venues, and she'd been talking about a major-label deal when they were done with their current indie contract.

It stung like hell. *Way* more than Kylie.

He glanced at Dr. Wyatt the Baby Silver Fox, who was shrugging into his coat.

Since they were approaching the station, Jesse stood and moved into the aisle.

"Well, thanks for the...boozy chat." Hunter stood too, but he lost his footing, and Jesse had to grab him to steady him.

"Whoa," Jesse said, liking the feel of the scratchy wool of Hunter's coat under his fingers. Hunter, with his fuzzy coat and his cottony soft shirt, had Jesse on tactile overload. "Maybe there was too much booze in that chat."

"No." Hunter flashed an impish, satisfied smile. The kind of smile Jesse could imagine coming up in...other contexts. "That was the *perfect balance* of booze and conversation. You made me forget all about my dead dog and my broken heart."

Broken heart. Hunter had been vague about his breakup earlier. It was hard to imagine someone as confident, as obviously accomplished, as *solid* as Hunter getting his heart broken.

It was hard to imagine any man giving him up.

Any man who was in the stage of life and career that promoted being settled and monogamous, that was.

And out.

Which was not Jesse. Not even close.

Which was why he couldn't explain why the next thing he did was dig around in his bag until he found a receipt and a pen, scrawled his email and phone number on it, and said, "Keep in touch."

"Give me one reason I should sign a punk like you?"

Jesse blinked. He was hungover, and his mind was slow. He had gone home last night after that surreal train ride and graduated from mini-bottles of booze to a full-size one. And, in a state of drunken overconfidence-mixed-with-defiance, he'd emailed Matty Alvarado, Canada's most famous artist manager. The guy oversaw a handful of successful musical exports, youngish pop stars mostly, who'd made it big south of the border and beyond. He was known as a rainmaker.

There was no way he'd take on a medium-time rock-and-roll band like Jesse and the Joyride.

Or so Jesse had thought.

But here he was twenty-four hours later, having been summoned to the dude's palatial office, which was decorated with a weird mixture of Catholic paraphernalia and photos of Matty with some of the world's most popular acts.

"You have quite the reputation, you know," Matty went on when Jesse didn't answer fast enough. "The Canadian music scene is small. People talk."

"We've been steadily building momentum for the last couple years." Jesse started in on the speech he'd been rehearsing in his head on the way over. "We've been playing midsize venues. I'm getting better and better as a songwriter. We have one more record left on our contract. After that, a major-label deal is within reach—I know it."

Matty waved a hand dismissively, like all of Jesse's painstaking, incremental work was nothing more than a bit of lint to be brushed off. "There's no shortage of acts in your position. Wannabe rock stars with big dreams are a dime a dozen, so you—"

"We're good," Jesse said, daring to interrupt the famed tastemaker, because why not? This wasn't going well, and he had nothing to lose. "No, we're fucking *great*."

Matty sighed. Drummed his fingers on his huge lacquered desk. "You are," he finally said, as if it pained him to admit it. "But you're also a fucking mess. Look at you—hungover, splashed all over the tabloids every couple of months with some drama or other. That's what I expect from the teenagers I sign, Jesse, not from grown men. What I do is brand people. I *make* them. I can make something from nothing, no problem. But I don't know that I can make something from…a big pile of shit."

Jesse winced.

"Coming back from cheating on Kylie Cameron might be impossible," Matty said.

Might be.

Those two words surged through Jesse. They were a thin edge of crowbar he could use to pry open this door.

Jesse had spent his entire life striving to get where he was. He'd had to beg his parents for piano lessons, for second-hand guitars. Later, when he'd been a bit older, he would have moved into the band room in his high school if his teacher had let him. It had literally been his happy place. Some days, it had felt like his *only* place.

Music was his life. It had been from the start.

And, just as importantly, it was his *living*. He was making a living as a musician. Or he had been, anyway.

All he wanted—the dream he'd had since he'd been old enough to dream—was to be on the cover of *Rolling Stone*.

And he could get there. All the ingredients were in place.

The only thing standing in his way was him.

That's what Matty was saying, and suddenly, Jesse *got* it.

"The way I see it," he started slowly, thinking through his argument with a mind suddenly cleared of cobwebs, "is that the *GossipTO* article was a blessing in disguise."

Matty raised an eyebrow. "That's the first interesting thing you've said since you got here."

"Kylie told me something once. She said that everyone performs who they are to some degree. Despite having gotten her start on a TV show, she had no aspirations to cross back over into acting, but she said she was an actor all the same. 'We all are,' she said. 'All of us whose livelihoods depend on being in the public eye. We perform who we are, consciously or no. The trick to success is to understand this and to learn to exploit it. Learn how to control the performance. Be in control of your own narrative.'"

He had dismissed her approach as too Machiavellian, but he saw now that she'd been right.

"Smart woman." Matty made a "go on" gesture.

"The way I see it, I have two choices. I can live like a rock star—partying, coming in late to recording sessions because I'm hungover, slutting around with anything that moves."

Which was exactly what he'd been doing. He'd been too busy with his degenerate life lately to prioritize what mattered: the music.

"Or…" he continued, trying to formulate his thoughts into a coherent argument. "I can *act* like a rock star."

"What does that mean?"

"I don't know. You tell me. You sign me, and I'll do whatever you tell me to do. But only on the surface. Underneath that, I'm keeping my head down. Cutting way, way back on the booze so I'm clearheaded enough to make kick-ass music and smart business decisions. Keeping my dick in my pants."

Matty was silent a long time, then he said, "Do we need to send you to rehab?"

We. He'd said, *We.* Adrenaline started frothing in Jesse's veins.

"No. Let me give it a shot, and if it doesn't work, I'll go without argument." He was pretty sure now that he'd had his come-to-Jesus moment—maybe all that Catholic stuff on Matty's walls had put the whammy on him—making the necessary lifestyle changes was going to be easy.

"Drugs?"

"Not really. The odd joint to relax after the show if someone offers, but I'm not buying the stuff. And I'll drop that too, if you want."

"No one wants their rock stars to be saints," said Matty. "It's a fine line."

"I get that," said Jesse. That was kind of what he'd been trying to articulate with the whole *live like a rock star versus act like a rock star* thing.

"Fuck me, but I think you do," said Matty. "The question is, are you all talk?"

Jesse smiled, feeling some of his old swagger returning. "There's only one way to find out."

"This is how it's going to work," Matty said. "You and I sign a contract for six months. Consider it a probationary period. A tryout. You know that whole three strikes, you're out thing?"

Jesse nodded and tried not to grin too overtly.

"With you and me, it's one strike. You do the music. I do everything else. You do exactly what I say. I tell you you're going on Howard Stern, you're going on Howard Stern. I say you're going on the Mickey Mouse Club, you're going on the Mickey Mouse Club. I get you a girlfriend, you've got a girl-friend. I tell you to break up with her, you break up with her. I say you're playing a show at the North fucking Pole, you're out shopping for snowsuits. After six months, we regroup. If we both want to continue—and if you've behaved yourself—we sign for real. Got it?"

"Yes." Jesse refrained from babbling about how grateful he was. Matty didn't seem like the kind of guy who appreciated empty words, and Jesse respected that.

"Is there anything else I need to know about? Any other scandals brewing? If I don't know about it, I can't fix it."

Jesse hesitated. As much as he hated to do it, it was probably wise to lay all his cards on the table.

"What?"

"That…person in the photo from *GossipTO*…"

"She going to talk to the press?" Matty did the dismissive waving thing again. "That's no problem. We can spin that to our advantage."

"I don't think so. It's more that she…wasn't a she."

Matty blinked rapidly.

"But I don't think he actually knew who I was," Jesse continued quickly. "We didn't really talk, and he didn't say anything about recognizing me. I met him at—"

"What are you saying, Jesse? You're gay? Because that is not going to work with the brand I'm envisioning for you."

"Not gay. Bisexual. And not even that much." It was true. Jesse thought of himself as mostly straight but…open to other possibilities. But he figured Matty probably didn't care about shades of gray here.

Matty got up and walked around to the front of his desk. Jesse stood, thinking he was being dismissed. *Fuck.* That picture really *had* ruined his life. He'd had the biggest agent in all of Canada *almost* locked down.

"Sit." Matty leaned back against the front of his desk, like he was a school principal.

Jesse sat.

"I don't want to hear another word about this. From this point onward, you are not…*bisexual.*" Matty spat the word like it was a curse. "You are Jesse Jamison, the bad-boy rock star next door. What does that mean? You're a fucking rock star. As I said, no one wants you to be a saint. You're brilliant and prickly and you live large. Or rather, you give the appearance of living large. You do what you need to do to keep yourself clean enough that your head is in the game, but you are not to speak publicly about having a problem with booze or any of that. Jesse Jamison the recovering alcoholic is not what we're going for here. When you appear at high-profile events, you have a fucking craft beer in your hand. You're single now, and we're going to use that. You are going to date casually. You are going to break a heart or two. All that's the rock star part. But you have a soft side. You're a little vulnerable. A sixteen-year-old girl can imagine reforming you. She can imagine you taking her to the fucking prom. Hell, I might make you actually do that. That's the boy-next-door side."

Jesse could see where Matty was going with this. It made sense. Matty's "brand," as much as Jesse hated that word, picked up on Jesse's natural tendencies and…magnified them.

Well, *some* of his natural tendencies.

"But one thing I need to be absolutely clear about is that both the rock star and the boy next door are straight. Those hearts you're breaking are *female* hearts. Those teenagers fantasizing about you are *female* teenagers. If you don't agree one hundred percent with this right now, we're done."

Something pinged inside Jesse's chest, like a pebble being dropped into an empty box. And for some stupid reason, he thought of Dr. Hunter Wyatt, the heartbroken pediatrician.

Then he thought of the cover of *Rolling Stone*. He thought of what he'd been striving for his whole goddamn life.

He stuck his hand out. "It's a deal."

CHAPTER TWO

Two Years Later

Move-ins were the worst.

Hunter loved his kids, but what he loved even more was watching them leave. Saying goodbye meant they were well enough to go home. He took a deep breath outside the door of room 7-102, which would be the home for one Avery Flannigan, age eleven, for the next few months. Avery was a math whiz and an aspiring architect. She could play a pretty mean ukulele cover of any Taylor Swift song.

She also had congenital heart failure.

Hunter had gotten to know Avery when he'd started at the hospital a little over two years ago. She'd been in then to get a new drug regime going. Avery had an indomitable spirit that attracted everyone to her—staff and patients alike. When she'd been well enough, she'd been the one organizing floor talent shows and practical jokes. When she hadn't been, she would still be cracking jokes when he came around, plying him for hospital gossip, even through her exhaustion.

They'd thrown her a party the day she'd left.

But now she was back. He'd always known she would be—more hospitalization had always been inevitable for Avery, as was an eventual transplant—but that didn't make it any easier.

He pushed open the door.

"Hey, Avery, I told you not to show your face here again so soon!" he joked, wagging his finger.

She turned from where she was hanging a poster on the wall of the small room.

"Hi, Dr. W.!" She thought it was hilarious to call him "Dr. W." because, as she'd pointed out, *"Dr. W. contains more syllables than Dr. Wyatt, so it's like the opposite of a nickname."* She taped the final corner of the poster, climbed down from the stool she'd been standing on, and high-fived him. "I couldn't stay away from my favorite doc."

He shared a look with Avery's mom. Her face reflected what was in his heart: fondness for Avery mixed with pain that she was back here so soon.

Avery unfurled another poster. "I'm making the place more homey. Don't tell Marilyn." Marilyn was one of the nurses in the cardiac unit. She ran a tight ship, but she loved the kids as much as anyone, and Avery knew it. Avery enjoyed baiting her, in fact.

"My lips are sealed," he said, walking over to examine her décor. The one she was affixing to the wall was a reproduction of the architectural plans for the Eiffel Tower.

"This is cool." He moved on to examine the next one, which was...

Jesse and the Joyride.

Holy crap.

He tapped the poster and said, "So what's this?"

"Only the best rock band of a generation."

"Wow," he teased. "Pretty high praise. What about One

Direction?" One Direction had been her favorite band last time around.

She made a theatrical gagging noise, and said, "No way. One Direction was a phase. *These guys* are the best. Old-school rock and roll."

Hunter had to tamp down a grin at the notion of an eleven-year-old holding forth about "old-school" rock and roll. Avery sat on the edge of her bed and tilted her head as she examined the poster. He couldn't help but notice how small her frame was—too small for her age, which was a side effect of her condition.

"Also?" She sighed as she gazed at the poster. "Jesse Jamison is sooo hot."

She didn't have to tell him that. He coughed. "Okay, kiddo. I'm not here officially yet. I just dropped in to see how you're getting settled. I'll be back in a couple hours."

Avery sighed again, but it was a completely different sigh than the dreamy one of a moment ago. It was resigned. It contained intelligence that no eleven-year-old should have.

Dear Jesse,

You probably won't remember me, and I'll be surprised if this email address still works, but here I go anyway.

We met on a train from Montreal to Toronto two years ago. I'd recently been dumped, and you got dumped en route. (So maybe you will remember me. That doesn't happen every day—to me, anyway.) Then we got drunk off tiny bottles of wine.

I'm a doctor at Children's Hospital in Toronto. I have an eleven-year-old patient named Avery who has a congenital heart defect. She's in for a surgery that will basically patch things over as best as possible, but she'll eventually need a transplant. Turns out she's a huge fan of you and your band.

Any chance I could convince you to pay a visit? Wouldn't have to be a big deal—I could make sure it was on the down-low and there would be no further obligations. Avery fronts like she's tough —and she is—but meeting you would mean the world to her.

Thanks for considering.

Hunter Wyatt

Jesse looked up from his phone. "What am I doing tomorrow, Amber? We don't have studio time booked until next week, do we?"

The band's assistant looked up from where she was tapping away on an iPad. The band had just come off a session of signing photos for the fan club in a conference room in Matty's offices, and neither Jesse nor Amber had left yet. "Nope, not until next week. Tomorrow you're calling in to Classic Rewind on Sirius at ten in the morning. Then you have a late lunch with Peter."

"Cancel the lunch, will you?"

Amber ceased the tapping—the tapping that made the band's world operate smoothly—and raised her eyebrows. Amber didn't do raised eyebrows normally. Amber was basically unflappable—she was a big part of why the band had been so successful in the past couple of years.

Well, she was a medium-size part of why the band had been so successful. The real reason, the big-kahuna reason, was of course Matty.

After Jesse had sold his soul—willingly—to Matty, eff him if the magical manager hadn't proceeded to get them the major-label deal, line up sponsorship for their next tour, and

conduct a slow-burn PR campaign that seemed to have reposi-
tioned Jesse as the sexy bad-boy—but not too bad—rock star.
"The boy next door with a serious edge," Matty called it.

And, hell, even Amber had been Matty's doing. Jesse had
wondered, when Matty'd hired her, what the hell they needed
a full-time assistant for. Turned out they hadn't known what
they'd been missing. Amber just made everything happen.

And now she was, in her quiet Amber way, shocked that
Jesse was bailing on a lunch with Peter Severson, the band's
A&R rep. They were about to start recording their second
album on AMI. Their first with the label had done really
solidly. They'd toured the US, opening for Green Day, and
had even earned a Grammy nomination for best new artist
last year. A lot was riding on their second major-label
release.

Jesse had spent two years doing whatever Matty told him
to, to the letter. He made nice with prospective producers. He
was charming-with-just-the-right-amount-of-attitude during
interviews. He went to awards shows with ridiculously beautiful starlets, as assigned.

When Peter said, *Lunch*, Jesse said, *When?*

Which was why Amber looked surprised he was canceling.
Keeping the label happy was high on Matty's list of priorities,
and hence, on Jesse's.

But, damn. Could he have one afternoon to do something
off script? Yes, yes, he could.

"Tell Peter I'm sorry, but something came up."

"Okaaay." When he didn't elaborate, Amber regarded him
silently, like she was trying to read his mind.

He should tell her what he was doing tomorrow afternoon.
She'd tell Matty. Matty would be thrilled. *Peter* would be
thrilled. Bad-boy rocker visits sick kids. It fit right in with the
brand. All they would have to do was post one subtle shot to

Instagram, and it would be all over the place. Viral with a capital *V*.

He stared back at Amber and said nothing, until she returned to her typing.

Eff him if he wasn't nervous. As Jesse stood in the lobby the next day and texted Hunter as they'd arranged, his hands shook.

Jesse had played arenas. Smiled at the Grammys as the camera hovered to catch his expression when the band didn't win Best New Artist. Held his own on the *Howard Stern Show*.

There was no reason for him to be nervous about meeting an eleven-year-old girl named Avery.

"Jesse, hi."

He turned toward the voice.

It was possible his nerves were not related to Avery.

Dr. Baby Silver Fox was just as silver and just as foxy as he had been two years ago. And he wore a white coat that made him look much more doctor-y.

Hunter stuck his hand out. "Thank you so much for coming. I never imagined you'd be able to come the very next day."

Jesse let his hand be engulfed by Hunter's—it was as soft as he remembered—and cleared his throat. "No problem. I was happy to be asked. I only hope the real me doesn't let this kid down."

Hunter smiled and squeezed his hand a little tighter before letting it go. "I assure you, that's not possible."

Sometimes Hunter's straight women friends jokingly made reference to their ovaries exploding. That was not generally a sentiment Hunter understood, even beyond the fact that he didn't have ovaries. It was usually a response to the image of a manly man doing something stereotypically not manly, like playing with a baby, snuggling with a puppy, or painting his girlfriend's toenails.

It had never worked on him. He didn't give a shit one way or the other about traditional "masculine" and "feminine" traits. He didn't have a "type" beyond "don't be a slob and have your shit at least moderately together."

Except...

As he poked his head into Avery's room two hours after he'd introduced her to Jesse, he found them sitting side by side on her bed, their heads bent together while Jesse coached Avery on the proper arrangement of her fingers on a guitar... Well, *something* twinged.

It was the juxtaposition that was getting to him. Avery wore a pink sweatshirt and loose scrub-like pants. Jesse, by contrast, was clad in skinny distressed jeans and a leather jacket. A pair of sunglasses was perched on his head, and his hair hung loose to his shoulders. He couldn't look any more like a rock star if he tried.

And it wasn't just the physical contrasts. Hunter had seen Jesse get dumped via text and shake it off. And he'd read about Jesse in the years since that train ride—how could he not? In fact, he'd probably become the band's biggest social media stalker over the age of thirty. The guy didn't just *look* like a rock star; he *was* a rock star. He oozed masculinity and virility as he slouched his way up red carpets with pretty actresses on his arm. He'd had a short flirtation with the famous pop star Emerson Quinn, which had ended with a big blowout in Central Park after Emerson had run into him kissing someone else. Apparently getting caught in public kissing someone he wasn't supposed to be kissing was a pattern for the devil-may-care rocker.

All this to say that Hunter would have assumed Jesse was the type of person who had more to do than fritter away an afternoon in a hospital. Yet here he was, so engrossed in helping a sick kid that he hadn't noticed Hunter's arrival.

Neither of them had.

He cleared his throat, and both heads popped up.

"OMG, Dr. W., Jesse is letting me play his guitar!"

"Yeah, I think it's time this kid graduated from a uke," Jesse said. "She's got talent."

Avery beamed as if she'd been told her heart had been magically repaired.

There was that twinge again.

"That's great, Avery!" Hunter said. "I hate to be the party pooper, but I'm afraid I'm here on official business. You have a consult with the surgeon tomorrow, so I want to check on a few things and get some info. I ran into your mom in the cafeteria, and she'll be here in a few minutes."

Jesse popped up from the bed. "That's my cue."

Hunter hung back, wanting to give the pair some space to say their goodbyes, which were over-the-top effusive from Avery and quieter, though no less heartfelt, from Jesse.

"I'll be right back," he said to Avery as he ushered Jesse out the door.

"I wasn't just saying that to make her feel good," Jesse said once they were in the corridor. "She has some serious raw talent. She should have a guitar."

"Her parents are pretty stretched, both financially and emotionally," Hunter said. "They're not from Toronto. Her dad is back in Owen Sound, working during the week and taking care of her older sister. Her mom's living at the Ronald

McDonald House. I don't think guitars are at the top of the priority list right now."

Jesse nodded. "I'd like to get her one, but I don't want to overstep or make things awkward for her parents. What do you think?"

Hunter grinned. It seemed Avery had snagged herself a rock star fairy godfather. "I think she'd love it."

CHAPTER THREE

Jesse wasn't really into cover songs. He'd never recorded any. He'd tried working a few into the band's live shows over the years—interpretations of songs by his idols, like Lennon and Hendrix and Prince. But it always felt weird, and eventually he'd stopped doing it. He preferred to play his own stuff.

But if he *was* going to play a cover song, never in a million years would it be one of Katy Perry's.

Except…never say never.

"Pick up the pace, girls!" he called as his pupils started to drag. He was playing the bottom strings of his Takamine as a bass, trying to keep Avery, who was lying in bed playing the guitar he'd given her a month ago, and her friend Madison, who was playing a portable keyboard, on beat.

They needed a drummer to really keep them tight. He filed that problem away to solve later as he said, "Okay, here comes the big chord change, Avery. And both of you, keep those vocals energetic! You're supposed to be roaring, right? Remember, you're fierce!"

Which they were, these two sick girls who were facing down their own mortality with courage and good cheer.

They were also slowing down as the song unspooled, a common mistake among beginner musicians.

He started singing along, God help him, to try to speed them up a bit. He pitched his voice to be louder than theirs, so as to force them to match his tempo.

So there he was, belting out a bubblegum-pop teen anthem of female empowerment.

What had *happened* to him?

The thing was, his visits with Avery, which had become a once or twice a week habit over the last two months, fit perfectly into his life. The band was recording the new album, so they were hunkered down in the studio for long stretches. The mixture of creativity and doggedness required to make a record was intense. It sucked the energy out of him. In the old days, he would go out in the evenings and party as hard as he'd worked during the day. He still accompanied the guys, some-times, when they hit the bars, but he always left after one drink. He was sticking to the commitment he'd made to Matty the Rainmaker two years ago and keeping the partying in check.

Coming to visit Avery—and, increasingly, her friends—was the perfect counterpoint to the intensity of recording. It got him out of both the studio and his head and provided some structure in his otherwise formless days. When he had a date with Avery, he had to wrap things up by a certain time. It forced decisions to get made rather than endlessly pushed off. It was like that old adage said: if you want something done, give it to a busy person to do.

The visits were also a stupid amount of fun, even with the Katy Perry.

So, he was freely willing to admit, though his visits prob-ably fell, technically, under the banner of "charity," he got a lot more out of his relationship with Avery than he gave. His visits to the hospital were selfish.

But not just because of Avery.

When they finally lurched to the end of the song, he gave the girls a thumbs-up and glanced at his watch. "Holy shit! It's eight!" Then, belatedly remembering his audience, rephrased. "My goodness! It's eight."

"Nice try," said Avery. "But yeah, you'd better go pry Dr. W.—and by the way, I've decided that *W* stands for 'workaholic'—from his office."

Yes. In addition to singing Katy Perry songs on the reg, Jesse was routinely hanging out with Dr. Hunter Wyatt now too. They had taken to grabbing dinner after Hunter's shift ended on evenings Jesse was around.

It was purely platonic—they were just friends. But it was weird. At his age—twenty-nine—and his level of fame— medium and climbing—a person didn't really make new friends. New faces were either put in front of him by Matty or the label or a publicist for a specific reason. People he met "organically" always turned out to want something from him. Which was fine. There was a certain amount of "You scratch my back, and I'll scratch yours" in this business.

But Hunter was…something else. He wasn't connected to the music industry at all. He didn't want anything from Jesse. He had no image to protect. No secret agenda. Hell, he didn't even know that much about music. They just…clicked.

As friends.

Avery was correct in her assessment of Hunter as a workaholic. Jesse had observed it himself. In fact, that was why they'd gone to dinner the first time. Jesse had popped in to see Avery one evening after dinner and had run into Hunter in the hallway.

"Do you live here?" Jesse had teased. "Because I'm starting to wonder if you're ever *not* here."

"Ha ha," Hunter had said, running his hands through his thick gray hair and trying to stifle a yawn.

Avery, who functioned as the hospital's Gossip Girl, later told him that Hunter was famous for his dedication to his patients. That he worked much longer hours than he was supposed to. She needled him about it, but underneath her ribbing, Jesse could tell, was genuine concern.

So he'd taken up the cause, starting that night, by dragging Hunter out of the hospital to a diner down the street where the good doctor had proceeded to put away meatloaf and mashed potatoes like he hadn't eaten in weeks.

After that, it had become a tradition of sorts. He would stop by Hunter's office on his way out and try to lure him away from the hospital.

And if he timed his visits so they would coincide with the end of Hunter's shifts, well, it was because Hunter needed someone to force him to leave.

But eight thirty might be too late, even for Dr. W-for-workaholic. Jesse had gotten a little too caught up in the Katy Perry fest.

The prospect of missing Hunter was more disappointing than it should have been.

It was just that his once-or-twice-a-week dinners with Hunter functioned kind of like his visits with Avery—they imposed a structure that was good for his creative energy in the studio.

But when he rounded the corner and spied the telltale light on in Hunter's office, he feared the swell of excitement in his chest had nothing to do with his creative energy in the studio.

"Hey." He rapped on the doorframe of Hunter's office. "Time to go, Dr. W."

Hunter looked up, his face painted in warm light by the lamp on his desk—he worked with the florescent overheads off —and smiled.

That smile killed Jesse. It was like each time, Hunter was surprised and then delighted to see him at his door.

"Hey," he rasped, doing his signature move where he raked his fingers through his hair. He wore his hair in sort of a 1950s-style pompadour, but by the end of the day, it tended to lose some of its height and get a little floppy.

Jesse wondered what it looked like first thing in the morning.

"Chop, chop." He tapped the doorframe again with the chunky rings he wore. "All work and no play makes Dr. W. a dull boy."

Hunter got up without a word and started loading his briefcase. A couple of months ago, when they'd started these dinners, he would protest—either that he had too much work, and/or that Jesse had better things to do.

But he'd stopped that. Now he took their dinners for granted. He took Jesse for granted.

It was nice to be taken for granted by someone who didn't want something from him. He couldn't remember the last time that had happened.

"Where to this evening?" Hunter switched out his horn-rimmed glasses for his sunglasses. It was cute the way he always put his sunglasses on inside, like he was pre-arming himself to face the elements.

It also made him look like a freaking model, what with the Ray-Bans and the freakish but undeniably alluring premature gray.

"I'm thinking ramen."

They'd fallen into the habit of Jesse coming up with a new restaurant to try each time, after it had become clear that although Hunter had been in the city for more than two years, he hadn't actually been anywhere.

"Sold." Hunter locked his office. "I think ramen is my desert island food."

As they waited for the elevator, Hunter rolled his shoulders and neck—something in there popped audibly.

Jesse's first impulse was to reach out and rub Hunter's shoulders, but of course he checked it. That was something you did to your significant other, not your new platonic hot doctor friend.

"We walking?" Hunter asked when they stepped onto the street. It was a gorgeous August evening—warm and, since the days were so long this time of year, still sunny.

Jesse put on his own sunglasses and a hat. He hated hats—they made him look like fucking Johnny Depp—but they'd become a necessary evil if he didn't want to be recognized.

Even so, it didn't always work.

"OMG, you're Jesse Jamison!" A woman of about twenty materialized out of nowhere.

Busted. He shot an apologetic glance at Hunter. For some reason, it embarrassed him when fans made a big deal over him in front of Hunter.

"I am indeed," he said, making a point not to smile. There was a sweet spot he could sometimes hit with his demeanor that communicated his desire for privacy without him having to be overtly rude.

It didn't work this time.

"I love you so much!" she squealed, whipping out her phone. "Can I get a selfie?"

"Yep." He grabbed the phone and navigated quickly to the camera app. He was a master at rapid selfie-taking. "Say cheese!" He clicked and handed her the phone. By the time her fingers closed around it, he was already walking away.

There was something utterly surreal about being friends with a famous person.

It wasn't that Hunter didn't think of Jesse as famous, didn't see his star quality. It practically oozed from Jesse's pores. Hunter had seen it two years ago, five seconds after meeting him on the train.

It was just that the image of Jesse and...the *actual* Jesse didn't totally match.

They *kind of* matched, to be fair, if he squinted his eyes. Outwardly, Jesse projected a fearlessness, a devil-may-care attitude, a fierce and sometimes biting wit, and an easy, confident sexuality. Those were all traits he genuinely possessed.

But, like an ill-cut puzzle piece, the image was slightly off, relative to the man.

Because Jesse was *also*, as witnessed by his regular visits with Avery and the other kids, kind, goofy, and, Hunter was beginning to think, sensitive. He wasn't sure if it was a rock star thing, or just a regular straight-boy thing, but Jesse felt more deeply than he was willing to let on.

Jesse ran ahead and held the door of the restaurant for a woman struggling to enter with a baby in a stroller and a toddler in tow. Then he gestured for Hunter to go ahead of him inside, shooting him a big, open smile.

Hunter's belly did a little flip.

No crushes on straight guys.

Still, it was nice to have a friend. A good friend.

Hunter's friends in Montreal had been a mixture of old university pals—he'd gone to McGill—and couples he and

Julian had socialized with. Perhaps it was the move as much as the breakup, but it seemed Julian had gotten custody of the latter group. After a few texts from his Montreal friends, things had dwindled. And here in Toronto, he was…trying. Some of the hospital crowd watched Maple Leafs games together, and though he wasn't particularly a fan, Hunter made himself attend the viewing parties. He was *supposed* to be turning over a new leaf, right?

He was pretty sure though, that if he had a new leaf, its name was Jesse Jamison.

It was weird, and not only because of Jesse's fame. He'd never really had a close friend who was a straight guy. Straight guys usually came mediated by girlfriends who were the initial connection or they came as part of groups.

But Jesse… Jesse was sort of his own category anyway.

"So," the new leaf/own category asked after he'd auto-graphed the hostess's arm in exchange for a secluded table in the back of the restaurant, "how hungry are you? They do a 'giant' size here that is really something to behold."

"Giant. I'm starving. I haven't eaten in…" He was setting himself up to be scolded.

"Since when?" Jesse pressed. "When did you have lunch?" When Hunter grimaced instead of answering, Jesse said, "You didn't have lunch at all, did you?"

"I had eggs for breakfast."

Jesse looked at his watch. "What? Like fourteen hours ago? Damn, I thought doctors were supposed to be smart."

Hunter suppressed a laugh. There was something amus-ingly incongruous in being nagged about nutrition by a rock star. He didn't hate it.

"All right, giant ramen it is." Jesse flagged down the server.

As they ate, they talked mostly about the album Jesse and his band were recording. It was their second major-label release, and Jesse was nervous about it. Hunter didn't see why. The first album—which he had only listened to about a million times—was fantastic. So was the band's earlier, indie stuff. Hunter didn't have a musical bone in his body, but a person had to be brain-dead not to recognize Jesse's talent. Jesse and the Joyride managed to sound new and fresh while also channeling Chuck Berry and Buddy Holly and others from the dawn of rock.

But Hunter supposed creating art was, by definition, scary. Even if your songs weren't overtly autobiographical, they came from you. They exposed you.

That bravery was part of Jesse's magnetism.

"I know you won't believe me, but the album is going to be amazing."

Jesse rolled his eyes and played with his straw wrapper. "You can't know that."

"I can."

"You've only heard snippets."

Hunter shrugged. "Doesn't matter. I know you." It was startling to realize, given his interactions with Jesse had been limited to after-work dinners, but it was true all the same. "Anything you make is going to be good."

Was he imagining it, or was Jesse blushing a little? He didn't have time to consider the matter because his phone dinged. He was on call, so he picked it up.

And put it right down with a snort of derision.

"Julian again?"

If Hunter knew Jesse, it appeared Jesse knew Hunter too. Enough to know that his ex had been texting him. A lot.

He made a vaguely affirmative noise.

"Why don't you block him?"

"It's not that simple."

"Why not? Dude held you hostage for the better part of a

decade, pretending to everyone who mattered that you didn't exist."

"Well, only his family...and his law firm." Hunter's defense sounded weak to his own ears. Yes, they had been out to all their friends, but their friends were a select subset of the world, the people Julian chose to surround himself with.

The people about whom he had no say in the matter? They hadn't known Hunter existed.

The shame of it flooded his stomach. Which, in turn made him mad. First, it wasn't his fault. *He* wasn't the closet case. And, besides that, it had been two freaking years. When was he going to get over it?

He *should* block Julian. Or tell him, once and for all, to knock it off. Nothing his ex said was important. It was all meaningless stuff. The funny observations that had initially endeared him to Hunter. Or shared memories, like this one, which was a picture of random dog hairs Julian had found in the camping equipment that hadn't been used since before the dog died.

Jesse grabbed his phone. Hunter didn't bother objecting. He needed the kick in the ass he knew was coming.

Jesse read the text in a sneering, singsong voice: "'Hey, H, look, I found some of Molly's hair in the sleeping bags. Makes me miss you and your Dustbuster.'" Then he fixed Hunter with an impatient, incredulous look.

"I'm kind of a neat freak," Hunter said weakly.

"I know that. That's not the part I'm objecting to."

Hunter wondered how Jesse could possibly know that about him, since they'd only ever seen each other at the hospital and in restaurants.

Jesse slapped the table. "Look at you, man. You said your-self you came here to start over. But you're working a million hours a week and texting with your ex."

"You know what? You're right." Hunter took his phone back. "You know what I should do?"

"Block your ex?"

"Download Grindr. Or maybe something less hookup focused and more…I don't know, dating focused?"

Jesse raised his eyebrows.

"You know, wash that man right out of my hair? Because let's be real. I can block Julian, but what better way to cut the cord than a new romance? My problem is I'm kind of clueless about this stuff. I met Julian in, like, the actual physical world. But, okay, technology marches on, so I guess it's time to get online."

Jesse shifted in his chair like he was uncomfortable. Maybe they couldn't talk about Hunter's sex life. Maybe this was the limit of Jesse's tolerance for paling around with a homo.

"Are you telling me you haven't…been with anyone since you left Montreal?"

God. It was so embarrassing, especially considering Jesse's renowned womanizing ways. But what could Hunter do but make a vague gesture of assent?

Jesse didn't respond for long enough that Hunter feared he wasn't going to. Finally, he took out his wallet. "Wash that man right out of your hair. Yes. Grindr is ideal for that. Let's go—I'll help you." He threw some bills down on the table and added, "But don't *actually* do anything to your hair. Your hair is perfect."

CHAPTER FOUR

"The place is a bit…unsettled," Hunter said as he unlocked the door to his apartment, which was the third floor of a subdivided old Victorian in Cabbagetown, a vibrant, garden-studded downtown neighborhood.

Jesse snorted. Hunter's definition of *unsettled* would probably change pretty rapidly if he saw Jesse's place.

"I would not call this 'unsettled,'" he said, as Hunter led the way into an immaculate, clean, bright, beautifully decorated living room. The place managed to be classy but not off-putting. It looked like a magazine spread that was actually lived in.

"Well, I've been here two-plus years, and I haven't hung a single piece of art." Hunter waved at walls that were, indeed, blank. "It's lath and plaster, so I can't just stick a nail in it like I would drywall. I keep meaning to get around to hiring someone, but…"

"But you're working a million hours a week at the hospital."

"Something like that. I tried doing it myself. I thought

maybe some of the lighter pieces would be okay on a nail, but the plaster crumbled."

"Yep." Jesse ran his hand over the old walls. They reminded him of the bumpy plaster walls in the piece-of-shit house he grew up in. "You need monkey hooks."

"I need what hooks?"

"Monkey hooks." Jesse set his guitar down. "I'll go get some. There's a hardware store on Parliament. You get started on your Grindr profile."

"You're going to hang my art?"

"I am. You need me to approve your profile—I've appointed myself to that role, by the way—so I might as well make myself useful while you get set up. You have a drill?"

Hunter laughed. "I do."

"Great. I'll be back in fifteen."

When Jesse got back, Hunter had abandoned his phone and was bent over the computer and concentrating so intently, he didn't hear Jesse come in.

"Hey." He laid his hand on Hunter's upper arm. His biceps was...noticeable. The good doctor might be a workaholic, but somehow he was finding time to get to the gym.

Hunter spun on his stool. He looked guilty, and it seemed like he was trying to block the laptop screen with his body.

"Whatcha doing?" Jesse feinted left, which caused Hunter to move left in response, but then Jesse quickly went right and lunged for the computer.

Hunter partially blocked him, but he hadn't been as fast in his correction, and he ended up pushing a shoulder against Jesse's chest, and as Jesse propelled himself toward his prize, the effect was a sort of perpendicular loose hug.

Which Jesse turned into proper, if still perpendicular, hug as he tightened his arms around Hunter so he could move him aside enough to hit the space bar and wake up the computer.

From the looks of things, Hunter had been reading a scientific paper. He was on the website of the *Journal of Pediatrics*.

"Dude! You're *working*!"

Hunter shifted like he was uncomfortable—which he probably was, because Jesse was still hugging him like an idiot.

A fact that Jesse's own body suddenly cottoned on to as it came to life, like the computer coming out of sleep mode. The feeling of Hunter's hard torso against his own...did something to him.

Jesse had kept the promise he'd made to Matty two years ago. Which meant he hadn't had a man in his arms since that ill-fated night caught on film by *GossipTO*.

"Yeah, so..." Hunter pulled back against Jesse's grasp in what was clearly a nonverbal request for him to let go.

Jesse did, with a great deal of reluctance. And, in turn, a great deal of confusion.

"I tried to get up and running on Grindr, but it was so..." Hunter wrinkled his nose and rose from his seat. "Transactional."

"Well, that's the idea behind Grindr, isn't it?" Jesse said. "As I understand it, I mean." Shit. He needed to not sound like an expert on Grindr. And he really wasn't. He'd used the app once years ago, but these days, he only had to lift a finger and women offered themselves to him. And women were "brand-approved" by Matty, so Jesse went with the path of least resistance. It hadn't been a hardship, particularly.

Or so he'd thought.

"I guess," Hunter said. He opened a pantry door, rummaged around, and produced a drill. "This is going to make me sound like a total dork, but I don't think I'm looking for just a hookup. So I texted a younger, single friend in Montreal and asked for advice, and he told me to try Tinder.

It's still casual, but apparently a better avenue for potentially meeting someone to date."

Jesse inspected the drill in order to buy some time to digest this piece of news. *Yep. Drill. Very drill-like.* "So you're looking for what? A boyfriend you don't have enough time to see?"

He wasn't sure why he was being such a dick about this.

"Point taken," Hunter said. "I'm not *opposed* to meaningless hookups, but I guess I want my meaningless hookups to come with the *possibility* of more. I'm not getting any younger."

"You're a romantic," Jesse said. Of course he was. Hunter might be a workaholic, but that was because he genuinely got caught up in the lives of his patients. His big heart was probably also why he couldn't quite cut ties with his ex. He got attached.

"But, for the sake of argument," Hunter went on, "isn't that the point here? Find something to get me away from work? What better way to do that than to get an actual boyfriend?"

"'An actual boyfriend,'" Jesse echoed, unsure why he suddenly felt so weird, like he had one of those monkey hooks lodged in his gut. It was just that imagining Hunter hooking up was one thing. Imagining him with a *boyfriend* was another. If Hunter had a boyfriend, that would almost certainly be the end of his twice-weekly dinners with Jesse.

But what could he do? He had no claim on Hunter. So he picked up his hardware store bag and ordered himself to get his head out of his ass. "Okay. You get to work on Tinder, but tell me where you want stuff hung, first. Then I'll do my thing while you do your thing."

♫♪

An hour later, Hunter not only had a Tinder profile, he had a bunch of matches. He'd right-swiped a handful of people, and damned if most of them hadn't right-swiped him back. He'd even started texting with a couple of them.

Also, and perhaps more exciting, his walls had art.

"Wow," he said, following Jesse around his apartment and taking in his familiar old Montreal art hanging on his Toronto walls. In the bedroom, a beloved painting he'd bought from an up-and-coming artist hung over his bed. It wasn't worth any money, but he adored it. Hadn't realized how much he'd missed seeing it. It was like some forgotten part of himself had been restored.

"Wow," he said again. "I can't believe you did all this."

"Dude. It's not like I, I don't know, *arranged a liver transplant for a kid.*"

Hunter shook his head. Jesse could downplay it, but Hunter was going to remain impressed. That unhung art had been nagging the hell out of him. Had started to seem insurmountable, in fact. Yet Jesse had breezed in and taken care of it all like it was nothing. There was something so…viscerally capable about Jesse. Hunter wasn't downplaying his professional accomplishments, but they were the result of years of training. Jesse, by contrast, just *knew* how to do stuff. He could literally make something—a song, a perfectly hung picture—out of nothing. Hunter was a sucker for that kind of effortless competence.

No crushes on straight guys.

Jesse idly picked up a corner of Hunter's duvet, which was crumpled at the foot of his bed. "I have to say, I would have pegged you as a bed maker."

"I usually am." And of course the one day he hadn't made the bed would also be the first day in years he had someone else in his bedroom. "I had plans to meet for coffee at five this morning with the mother of one of my patients. She starts work at six. I forgot to set my alarm earlier than usual, so I had to bust it out of here."

One corner of Jesse's mouth turned up. Probably because Hunter had launched into a long "the dog ate my homework" style excuse for something as trivial as an unmade bed. Jesse probably slept in a cave strewn with pillows and supermodels. Like a harem.

Yes. He had no trouble imagining Jesse sleeping in a harem.

Which was neither here nor there, on account of the "no crushes on straight guys" thing.

Jesse was still holding the corner of Hunter's duvet, rubbing it back and forth between his fingers.

The way he was paused there, looking at Hunter but not saying anything, it was hard not to spin out fantasies. A disheveled Jesse sprawled in that very bed, his dark scruffiness in marked contrast to Hunter's crisp, white, high-thread-count linens. But also, because Hunter was a dork, Jesse holding one corner of the duvet while he waited for Hunter to come around and take the other so they could make the bed together.

Domestic bliss with the rock star.

Hunter would have been disgusted with himself if he wasn't already laughing inwardly at how ridiculous he was.

He needed to get a boyfriend. Or get laid.

Or maybe both.

A chime issued from Hunter's phone.

"Ha!" he exclaimed. Perfect timing. "Another match!"

Jesse dropped the duvet, and with it, his weird hold over Hunter's imagination. "Is that what that noise is? I've been hearing it almost constantly."

"Yep." Hunter hoofed it to the kitchen, picked up his

phone. Before he investigated the most recent match, he checked his texts. He had some new ones from a guy named Aaron he'd messaged with through the app successfully enough that they'd switched to text. Aaron was a high school biology teacher who liked hiking and baking. Aaron was also adorable.

A ding signaled another incoming text.

"I can see how this could get kind of addicting," Hunter said, surprising himself by how excitedly he clicked over to the photos that another guy—this one was named John—had texted him.

Jesse made an inarticulate noise that was a cross between a grunt and a growl, and Hunter started a little—he hadn't realized Jesse was right behind him.

"Okay, that guy is clearly an axe murderer," he said, leaning over Hunter's shoulder and pointing at the screen.

"John, age fifty, computer programmer into foreign films, is clearly an axe murderer?" Hunter asked incredulously. The picture Jesse was looking at was of a shirtless John standing in a garden in front of a suburban home.

"'Computer programmer' is probably code for 'he lives in his parents' basement in the 'burbs.' Have you checked on Toronto real estate prices lately? That is totally his parents' house."

"I don't know how you get that from this. Or how you get axe—"

"He's also too old for you," Jesse interrupted, still squinting at the picture.

"Well, I'm not going to *marry* him. Who cares if he's a little older?"

"Oh, excuse me," Jesse drawled, his tone suddenly pissy. "I thought you were all heart-eyes-emoji looking for love. If that's the case, John, age fifty, is too old."

"You don't even know how old I am." Hunter sounded as cranky as Jesse. Why were they arguing about this?

"My money's on thirty-four."

That was...exactly right. Hunter laughed, which had the effect of loosening some of the weird tension that had stretched taut between them. "How did you know that?"

"Well, you've been here for a little longer than two years. You said you were in Montreal for ten—you did your med school and residency there. I pegged you as the type who went straight from undergrad to med school, and I did the math."

"Huh," said Hunter. "Gold star for you. People usually think I'm much older than I am on account of the gray hair."

"Nah. Anyone can tell it's way premature."

In Hunter's experience, that wasn't the case. Most people didn't look closely enough. But that Jesse had was...nice.

Hunter let loose a big sigh and set the phone aside on John, age fifty, who, truth be told, probably *was* too old. "I don't know what the hell I'm looking for." He knew only that he needed to shake things up. "I'm sick of the same old, same old." He sat down at the kitchen island.

"Come to the cottage this weekend."

"What?" Hunter blinked, almost startled back to standing by the invitation. Jesse had a cottage in the Prince Edward County region east of Toronto. He and the band spent most summer weekends there. There was a small, makeshift studio on site, and to hear it told, they would noodle around on songs there and then come back to the city to record them properly. "But isn't the cottage kind of a remote studio for you guys? Like a working weekend?"

"Yeah, but you won't be in our way." When Hunter didn't answer right away, Jesse added, "Think about it. What you've said you're looking for with the whole move to Toronto is a new start.

What anyone with half a brain—and by that, I mean Avery and not me—can see is that you're working yourself into the ground. And you just said you're sick of the same old, same old. Come along this weekend. Get out of the city. Out of your head."

It did sound tempting. A lot more appealing than pretending to be interested in the Maple Leafs and being on the emotional roller coaster of Tinder.

"There's no wi-fi," Jesse went on. "And questionable cell reception. Half the time you have to walk out to the main road to get a signal."

"Wow. Total disconnection." Hunter couldn't remember the last time he'd done that. Had he *ever* done that? And he wasn't on call this weekend, so he could actually get away with it.

"Yeah. Everyone kind of putters around doing their own thing—which for the guys mostly means staying up late partying and sleeping in. But you can swim. There's a canoe. You know, the whole cottage deal." The way he was waving his hands animatedly as he spoke, Hunter could tell how much he loved the place. "We do some writing and some studio time as the mood strikes. That's part of why I started dragging the guys up with me. It gets everyone kind of on the edge of boredom. Forces creativity."

Just like he sometimes forgot Jesse was famous, Hunter also sometimes forgot Jesse had an entire life outside of their dinners together and his visits to the hospital. Hunter had never met the other guys in Jesse's band. He'd never met anyone in Jesse's *life*. Jesse existed as a self-contained unit.

He wondered about the others. He'd seen them in the band's videos and sometimes when they were interviewed as a group. Hunter was nothing if not exhaustive about his YouTube stalking, so he knew their names. He knew what they looked like—rock stars. They all had that same tousled, hard, rocker look that Jesse personified.

"Is it going to be weird that I'm..." He made a vague gesture toward himself. He was wearing his standard work uniform. His job didn't require scrubs, and he was old-school —he still believed in presenting oneself smartly and professionally—so he wore a shirt and tie under the white coat he kept in his office. But today's combination of a purple-and-white gingham shirt and a pink-and-navy striped tie, while liable to land him on any list of the city's best-dressed doctors, didn't exactly scream, *Hi, I'm a straight manly man who's good at waterskiing and starting bonfires!*

"That you're what? A doctor? Not at all. You can save Billy from alcohol poisoning."

"No, that I'm..." God. Was he twelve? Hunter was comfortably, firmly out in pretty much all circumstances.

Except, apparently, at Jesse and the Joyride nature weekend.

"A neat freak?" Jesse smirked and raised his eyebrows. "Nah. They won't even notice. You, on the other hand, should probably pack some tranquilizers for yourself because by the end of the weekend... Well, let's just say I have a regular cleaning service."

Jesse was teasing. It felt...good. And Hunter appreciated the hell out of the implied message that his sexuality wasn't going to be a thing.

And in case the implication had been too subtle, Jesse followed it with, "Hey. We're modern men. And it's my cottage. You're my friend. Anyone who has a problem with you can fuck right off."

CHAPTER FIVE

Pull over when you get to Waupoos and text
me. The cottage is only about ten more
minutes from there, but the roads are dark
as hell and the turnoff is hard to see. I'll
walk out to the main road with a flashlight,
and I'll flag you down.

Hunter followed the instructions in Jesse's text, and man, was it ever dark. He and Julian used to camp some, but Julian had been the true outdoorsman, and anyway, it had been years since Hunter'd been out of the city.

Now that he was almost there, he was glad he'd succumbed to Jesse's insistence that he drive out tonight, despite the fact that an unforeseen emergency had kept him at the hospital late. It would have made much more sense to wait till the morning rather than arriving at—he glanced at the dashboard display—2 a.m.

Well, he'd wanted a new leaf, and 2 a.m. in the middle of nowhere with a rock band definitely qualified.

Pulling out from the tiny hamlet of Waupoos, Hunter

headed up the narrow, wooded road toward Jesse's place. Thankfully, the blanket of dark made it so Jesse couldn't see the silly grin Hunter broke into when his headlights lit up the rock star, who was standing by the side of the road with his thumb stuck out, hitchhiker style.

"Hey." Jesse hopped into the car. "Glad you made it."

"I'm sorry I kept you up."

"Nah. I'd be up anyway. The others, uncharacteristically, have gone to sleep—there was a mix-up over who was bringing the beer, so it's a dry night for the guys. But I was on a bit of a tear with a song." He pointed to an almost unnoticeable dirt road protruding from the forest, and Hunter turned onto it. "Everything okay at the hospital?"

Hunter started to say yes, everything was fine. But everything wasn't fine, and he realized with a start how much he missed having someone to talk with about work. He didn't have any doubts about breaking things off with Julian—he couldn't live stuffed in someone else's closet any longer—but he missed that closeness, missed having someone who knew his cast of characters. That was probably why he was having trouble cutting ties once and for all, why he was still responding to Julian's texts.

But actually...it was equally startling to realize that Jesse *did* know his cast of characters. Some of them, at least.

"Well, I'll be a stereotypical doctor and tell you I have good news and I have bad news. The good news is that Avery's post-op infection is clearing up nicely, and I think she'll be able to go home next week."

"Hey! That's great. I gotta say, though, I'm going to miss her."

"I'm under instructions from Madison to tell you that you're not off the hook because Avery's going."

Jesse laughed. "Noted. And I'm happy to stay on the hook." He paused. "Tell me the bad news too."

"I had a teenager unexpectedly go into cardiac arrest this evening." He wished he could say more, tell Jesse about fourteen-year-old James, who was battling a bad lupus flare-up, but patient confidentiality laws prevented him from talking in anything other than generalities.

"Jesus." Jesse shook his head as he gazed out the window into the black night. "Cardiac arrest is not a phrase you should hear applied to teenager. What happened?"

"We stabilized him. But his parents were three hours away. In some ways, that's the worst of it for these kids. Life in the hospital is boring. Most kids have at least one parent who's around the majority of the time. But sometimes they have to go home. They have jobs, other kids." He swallowed, his throat tightening. "And, of course, the scariest thing that's ever happened to this kid has to happen the one weekend his parents have gone home. He fronts like he's too old to be in a children's hospital, but he needed his parents." Thinking of James trying so hard to be brave gutted Hunter.

"So what happened?"

"We called them, and they got right in the car."

"And you stayed with him until they got there."

Hunter had to swallow again. He still didn't trust his voice, so he nodded in response.

It sounded so stupid. It wasn't as if the hospital wasn't full of people who cared about the kids there. Kind, loving nurses who would have been on duty anyway. Did Hunter think he was irreplaceable? That he was the only constant presence in these kids' lives?

"You're a good doctor," Jesse said softly. Then he laid his hand on Hunter's upper arm. "A good man."

Shit, now he *really* had a lump in his throat. He cleared it. "It's just...hard not to seize any opportunity you can to protect them. To make things easier for them. Because so much of the time you don't have those opportunities. So much is out of your control."

"I know."

Something about Jesse's tone drew Hunter's attention. Jesse was staring out the passenger-side window.

"That's why I used to go to Montreal once a month. My sister and my nephew... Well, my sister's ex-husband is a problem. I held on to that gig longer than was rational. I still go, but only a couple times a year. I wish I could get them to move to Toronto."

"Why don't they?"

"My sister has this idea that she shouldn't take her son away from his father." He snorted, and Hunter could practically hear his eyes rolling. "Which is actually *exactly* what she should do."

"Are they in physical danger?" Hunter asked. He couldn't help it. It was the pediatrician in him. He'd been trained to conduct these screenings, to ask these questions.

"I think he might have knocked her around some during their marriage." Jesse gestured to the right. "Turn here." Hunter obeyed, pulling his car into a large gravel clearing. There were already several cars parked. "This is fine," Jesse said, and Hunter killed the engine.

Jesse made no move to get out. "She says he's never laid a hand on Gavin—that's my nephew—and I believe her. It's more...psychological abuse. Her ex is a real dick. It's like he can't accept that she left him. He makes everything difficult—handoffs, any joint decisions like day care and stuff. Won't sign the divorce papers. He's constantly undermining her both with Gavin and with Gavin's teachers. It's hard to explain. It's like..."

"A campaign of terror," Hunter said.

With the dashboard lights out, he couldn't see anything, but he could sense Jesse's surprise in the way Jesse sat up straighter and turned to him. "Exactly."

"Classic abusive behavior. They train you to look for the signs of exactly that in med school, and even more so in peds residency."

"Okay, so I'm not crazy."

"Not at all. It's all about power for these guys."

"Yes!" Then Jesse laughed. "That sounded way too enthusiastic. I'm just glad to have a professional endorsement."

"I think you're right to keep looking after them as much as you can. The more she tries to untangle their lives from each other, the more aggressive he may get."

"I like to think he wouldn't seriously hurt his child or the mother of his child."

Hunter shrugged, though he knew Jesse couldn't see it. He didn't want to alarm his friend unnecessarily, but these things often escalated.

"Come on." Jesse got out of the car.

Hunter followed suit.

"You tired?"

"Not really." He was still buzzing from the adrenaline of the earlier emergency.

"Good. Let's make a fire. That's usually what we do at night, but I didn't want to leave one burning when I left to meet you." Jesse had come around the car and laid a hand on Hunter's upper back to guide him across the dark clearing. He was only doing it, of course, because it was pitch-black and Hunter didn't know the place, but Hunter's breath quickened.

It was possible the buzzing sensation he was experiencing wasn't *entirely* from the events at the hospital.

"This is my favorite place in the world," Jesse said, once

he'd gotten the fire lit—Jesse was effortlessly good at lighting campfires, just like everything else.

"Is this a family place originally?" Hunter asked, watching Jesse tilt his head back to look at the night sky. "You grew up here, right?"

"I grew up in Prince Edward County, yes, but not here." Jesse snorted. "You know how you never heard anything about Prince Edward County before about ten or fifteen years ago?"

It was true. Today, the cottage country east of Toronto was full of wineries and outposts of chic downtown hotels, but Hunter had the sense that was all pretty recent. "Yeah."

"Well, I grew up in a tiny armpit of a town about thirty kilometers from here. There was a lot of poverty in the county back then—still is once you're away from the lake. We lived in a tiny house to match our tiny town, where my father conducted a...what did you call it? Campaign of terror?"

"Ah, so your sister is repeating the past. I hate to say it, but that's not uncommon. Is your father still there?"

"As far as I know. I haven't spoken to him since our mother's funeral six years ago."

"I'm sorry."

"This sounds terrible, and I don't mean this like I didn't love her or I don't miss her, but it was probably for the best. She was never going to leave him. So my sister—Beth—is stronger in that way. I hope." He poked the fire. "Anyway, somehow, despite my shitty origins, Prince Edward County feels like home. So I was happy to be able to buy this place a few years ago. Sounds cheesy, but I'd rather be here than anywhere else. And when I'm here, I'd rather be *here*." He waved his hands to indicate their immediate surroundings. The fire pit was perched a few meters from the edge of a short cliff that abutted the vast blackness of Lake Ontario at night.

They sat in silence for a few minutes. Hunter contemplated the sky. It was ridiculous. The Milky Way was more white than black.

He started thinking about Beth, and about Jesse's mom. He had a good relationship with his own parents. He couldn't imagine having to claw his way out of a cycle of abuse and poverty like that.

"Hey," he said, a thought suddenly forming in his head. "Is 'Repeat' about Beth?"

Jesse didn't answer for a few moments, and Hunter wondered if he'd overstepped. And really, there was no reason to think the song was about Jesse's sister. It wasn't overtly about domestic abuse, merely about a person making the same mistakes, "walking the same plank."

"Yeah," Jesse said quietly, staring at the fire. "It is. But no one knows that." He looked up at Hunter. "Except smart doctors."

"Your secret is safe with me." Hunter was strangely touched that here was this famous, successful musician, surrounded by people, by fans and managers, and he was choosing to let Hunter be the one who knew this about him.

He wanted to ask Jesse about the origins of all his other songs but held his tongue.

Jesse lay down on his back. "My sister and I used to lie on a blanket in the backyard—no fire; my dad wouldn't allow that—and try to spot shooting stars so we could wish on them."

Hunter followed suit, being careful not to lie too close to Jesse. "What did you wish for?"

He regretted the question as soon as it was out. It was too intimate.

But Jesse didn't seem to mind. "I wished I could get away."

"You did." Jesse had gone on to make something of

himself, to will his success into being, and it was damned impressive.

"I did. But Beth didn't. Not really."

"No," Hunter said. "But keep trying."

They lay there in silence for a long time, but it wasn't uncomfortable. Hunter could see why Jesse loved this place. They were surrounded by all the elements—air, fire, earth, and water. It was impossible not to be taken in by it. It was like the universe was reminding him of his rightful place, but instead of being humbling, it was comforting. You could do your best in life—to save your sister from men who would harm her, to prevent children from having heart attacks—but that was all you could do. The universe was, elementally, imperturbable.

"You're freezing."

Hunter hadn't realized it until Jesse said it, but he was. He'd gone home after work and changed into shorts and a T-shirt. It had been hot in the city, even so late at night. But out here, in the middle of the night, by the lake, it was downright cold. He'd put on a light jacket, but that was all he had.

"I probably should have told you to bring warm clothes. Nights get cold out here." Jesse sat up and reached for something outside the circle of light cast by the fire.

Hunter, assuming this marked the end of their fireside chat, sat up too—was starting to stand up, in fact—when Jesse produced a second blanket. Unlike the one they were lying on, it was a Hudson's Bay blanket, made of thick, heavy wool. Jesse unfurled it over his body, lay back down, and held one edge up. "C'mere."

Hunter paused long enough that Jesse let the blanket fall. "Or I can just show you to your room." He started to get up. "I forget that not everyone is as insane as I am about this place."

Hunter made a split-second decision. He knew it was the

wrong one as he was making it. It was not a good idea to snuggle under a blanket with Jesse Jamison.

He knew that.

And yet.

Hunter picked up the edge of the blanket and slid underneath it.

He did prevent himself from physically cuddling up to Jesse.

But only just.

CHAPTER SIX

Jesse had never woken up with a man in his arms.

Over the years, he'd pretty much lived up to his rock star reputation when it came to women. So he'd had plenty of mornings after with the fairer sex. Even in the post-Kylie era, when he'd been keeping a lid on things, relatively speaking, pushing playtime aside in favor of work, he'd enjoyed a fair amount of female attention. It was almost impossible not to. The whole groupie thing was real. He had to actively try *not* to sleep with women.

His liaisons with men, which were now firmly lodged in the past, had always been furtive, though. Spur-of-the-moment. No sleepovers, much less cuddling, had been associated with those encounters.

Not that this was an "encounter."

But whatever it was, it was…unsettling.

He hadn't meant to fall asleep, merely to extend the night a little longer. He'd never told anyone about Beth—what was happening to her or the fact that "Repeat" was about her. The guys didn't even know.

Talking to Hunter had been so easy. It had always been

easy, from that first moment on the train. But add in the dark, and his quiet, encouraging advice about Beth, and it had been…such a huge relief. Like sinking into a warm bath. Which was a ridiculous metaphor considering how cold it was.

Despite his best intentions, he'd conked out. They both had. And it was no doubt the cold that had prompted them to snuggle up together, Hunter burrowed into Jesse's chest.

Hunter started to stir. Jesse tried to untangle himself, but Hunter was draped over his chest, so all he could do was sort of lift his arms up, like he was being robbed while reclined.

But then that seemed absurd, like he was protesting too much, so he settled them back down again. Told himself that they'd fallen asleep outside in the cold. That this was the innocent outcome of logical forces.

So was his morning wood.

Hopefully, one of the benefits of waking up with a man in his arms was that said man would understand the concept of morning wood.

That it wasn't personal.

It was just…biology.

Guys knew that. Right?

"Mmm," Hunter emitted a satisfied-sounding half moan, half sigh as he snuggled closer to Jesse.

Jesse couldn't help it; he pulled him closer. Tighter. There was something delightful about a woman, but this…this chest that was so like his own, this chiseled, stubbly jaw, sliding over his neck, was…also pretty fucking delightful.

"Mmm." There was another one of those moany sighs, and goddamn it, Jesse's morning semi could probably no longer be rationalized away. At least the way Hunter was lying draped over him, there was no contact between his dick and any part of Hunter.

"Oh!"

All at once, Hunter woke up—fully—and as soon as he realized what had happened, he rolled off Jesse.

Jesse felt the loss. It was cold out, but they'd created a pool of warmth between them, and now it was gone—and so suddenly, like someone had plunged his body into the lake next to them.

"I'm sorry!" Hunter said, sitting up and looking, for a moment, adorably bewildered. "I guess we fell asleep." He flashed Jesse a sheepish grin. "I'm a terrible snuggler when I sleep."

"No worries." Jesse sat up too and let the blanket pool in his lap to disguise what was going on there. "I'm the one who's sorry. Some kind of host I am, letting you sleep out here all night."

"Totally worth it," said Hunter, his face tilted upward. The sky was streaked with the pinks and oranges of sunrise. "God, this place is shameless. It's like you think this amount of beauty should be rationed or something, but no. You've got the van Gogh stars *and* the tourism brochure sunrise."

Jesse smiled. That was a good way of putting it. "Well, let's go inside and rustle up some breakfast. Without hangovers, I suspect the guys will be up earlier than usual. And I'll show you your room. In case you go crazy and want, like, an actual bed at any point."

Strangely, Jesse didn't want Hunter to want to sleep anywhere other than his chest.

He didn't say that, of course.

He could never say that.

Two years ago, he'd traded away his right to even think it.

If Hunter had been apprehensive about meeting the members of Jesse's band, he needn't have worried.

In some ways, they lived up to their reputations. After a round of introductions, they were deep into talking about sex. Gay sex, to be specific.

Over pancakes.

"So, like, you have hand signals or something, and then you go at it?"

"Jesus Christ, Billy," Jesse said. "Have some respect."

"It's okay," Hunter said through a chuckle. Billy, the bassist, was both shocking and refreshing in his forthrightness. He'd only known Billy for twenty minutes, but already he could see that he was the type of guy who called it like he saw it.

"I don't know about hand signals," he said. "But there's definitely a pickup culture in some parts of the gay world. It hasn't really been my thing historically."

"But it's easier for a guy to get laid by another guy than by a girl," said Ash, who played a bunch of different instruments ranging from acoustic guitar to sax. Hunter suspected Ash was the "smart" one, relatively speaking anyway. Not that anyone was smarter than Jesse, whose stereotypical rock star looks belied a fierce intelligence. But Ash talked less than the other guys, anyway, seeming to favor listening over speaking.

"I think that's probably true," Hunter said.

"Unless you're Jesse Jamison," said the drummer, Will—not to be confused with Billy. The Joyride's rhythm section was composed of William and William. Billy and Will. It was charming.

Jesse rolled his eyes. "Oh come on, you guys do fine."

"We do *now*," Billy said, stretching like a satisfied cat. "But for a long time there, it was your leavings."

"Still is," Ash said. "Just the leavings are of higher quality now."

"*God*," said Jesse. "Do I need to change the name of the band to Jesse and the Neanderthals?"

Billy ignored him. "So, what about this top and bottom thing? Like, say you have a boyfriend or a husband. Someone is sticking it in all the time and someone is, uh…taking it?"

"Shut *up*, Billy."

"No, it's okay," Hunter said, laughing again. He'd been nervous to meet the band, but he found them, particularly Billy, delightful. If all straight guys were this open to learning about different kinds of people, the world would probably be a much more peaceful place. "Some couples are like that, I think —one person strictly tops and the other bottoms. Some have preferences but sometimes switch. Some don't do anal at all."

"Whaaat?" said Billy. His mouth dropped open. "What's the point of having a dick if you can't, like, stick it somewhere?"

"Time for a tour," Jesse said quickly, standing. He was clearly mortified.

Hunter ignored him. He was enjoying himself.

Billy ignored him too, pressing on with his interrogation. "And what if it's not a relationship? What if it's a one-time thing? How do you decide how it's going to go?"

"Good question," Hunter said. "I had my first 'date'"—he made quotation marks with his fingers—"in a long time the other night, and it was a bit awkward." Well, maybe *awkward* wasn't the right word. The other guy had seemed fine with the clinical negotiation. But to Hunter, it had seemed so…transactional. Which he supposed it was. But still.

"Wait. What?" Jesse said.

Hunter continued to ignore Jesse in favor of talking to the guys. "I think what I learned from that is to be more upfront about it at the beginning." He didn't particularly like that idea, but it was better than interrupting things just as they were heating up to talk about it. "Like, maybe I should put that stuff right in my Tinder profile? I don't know."

"I thought you didn't do meaningless hookups," Jesse said, his voice dripping with such disdain that he finally earned Hunter's undivided attention. "I thought you were into *dating*." The rock star was standing at the kitchen island the rest of them were sitting around, eyebrows raised and hands on his hips. He looked like an overbearing father, which only added to the general sense of amusement Hunter was experiencing this morning.

"I am. I was. I don't know. I matched with this guy. He was nearby. He was…dumb but hot."

"Ha!" said Billy, offering his hand to Hunter to high-five. "You're going to fit right in here."

"You done?" Jesse asked as Hunter slapped Billy's hand.

"Yeah," said Hunter. "Thanks. These were great." Because apparently Mr. Fire Starter and Mr. Art Hanger could make amazing pancakes too.

Jesse topped up both his and Hunter's coffees. "Grab your cup. I'll give you a tour."

It was dawning on Hunter that Jesse was rich.

Which made sense, he supposed. "Rich" often went with "famous."

The "cottage" was on twenty acres of land, much of which was wooded. Hunter had no idea what twenty acres of the Lake Ontario shoreline went for, but it had to have cost a pretty penny. The house itself was large but not ostentatious.

Jesse informed him it had been built in the 1960s and expanded by subsequent owners in the 1980s.

"I should probably renovate, but I don't really give a crap about that *House Beautiful* shit." He glanced at Hunter—they were traipsing across the yard toward some outbuildings. "No offense."

"Why would that offend me?"

"Well, you *do* kind of live in a *House Beautiful* spread."

Hunter wasn't sure if that was a compliment or an insult. "Maybe now that someone hung my art."

"Building this bunkie is really the only thing I've done since I bought the place a couple years ago," Jesse said, stopping in front of a small outbuilding of some sort.

"I'm sorry, *bunkie*?"

Jesse laughed. "Yeah. It's an Ontario cottage word. It's a building where people sleep. Usually it's pretty bare bones—just a bunch of beds, sometimes in actual bunk bed formation. It's for guests. Or you can stick your annoying band members in there. The cottage originally had four bedrooms, but I knocked a wall down between two of them and made a studio—that was the one project I did do in the main house. So I sleep in the house, and the rest of the guys battle it out amongst themselves for the second cottage room—though this time I made them all sleep out here so you could have a proper bedroom in the house."

Hunter was about to reflexively protest that he didn't need the bedroom but thought better of it. Yeah, he was getting along fine with Ash and the two Williams, but that didn't mean they all needed to have a slumber party in the bunkie.

"Don't you have a fifth guy in the band?" Hunter knew Jesse did, thanks to his earlier social media stalking, but he'd only met three of Jesse's bandmates this morning.

"Yeah. Colin, who plays keyboards." Jesse gestured toward

the bunkie. "He's still asleep, otherwise I'd show you the inside. It *is* sort of *House Beautiful* in there, if I do say so myself, at least for a bunkie. Beth picked out the finishes and bedding, so it looks pretty good. She said after I killed myself building it, I couldn't just throw ratty quilts in there."

"Killed yourself building it, meaning you built it *yourself?*"

"Yep."

"You *built* this." Hunter pressed his hand against the wood-frame building. It was a simple, small house-type structure made of a light wood, complete with a mini front porch that was lined with rocking chairs. "Like with your hands."

No, asshole, he built it with his feet. Hunter had to invoke the sentence that had become his mantra of late: *No crushing on straight guys.*

Jesse grinned. "Hey, I was a country kid. A *poor* country kid. We DIY-ed everything out here back in the day."

The tour continued with a visit to the beach. Jesse might have been a poor country kid, but today he had a chunk of lakeshore with all the trimmings—canoes, a jet ski, and a speedboat. All that was missing was…

"Where's the yacht?" Hunter teased.

"Yachts are for pricks." Jesse set his coffee mug on the ground and made a waving gesture like he was physically dismissing the notion of being thought the yacht type.

Or…correction, he wasn't waving. He was crossing his arms over and around to grab the back of his T-shirt in order to take it off.

"Nothing like a morning swim to shake the cobwebs off."

Holy shit, was he going to take his shorts off too?

No. That was…a relief?

Or was it disappointing? It was hard to tell.

When Jesse had disappeared into his room after they woke up fireside, he'd been wearing his usual rock star uniform of faded jeans, a concert T-shirt—last night's had been an old Stones one—a leather jacket, and boots. He'd emerged in flip-flops, another concert T-shirt (Metallica), and shorts Hunter now realized were actually swim trunks.

The transformation had been jarring—and Hunter wasn't just talking about Jesse and his clothes. It was the whole thing. The dark night had become a blue, sunny day. Their cozy little nest by the fire, which had been all Hunter had seen of the place last night, had given way to the big cottage and sprawling grounds. And, of course, the rock star had become...

Well, Hunter's rational brain told him Jesse was getting in the water, and doing that necessitated the removal of some clothes.

Some other part of Hunter's brain was freaking out.

He was covered in tattoos. Of course he was. What had Hunter expected? He'd seen the ones on Jesse's forearms. But his chest was more tattoo than not-tattoo, a swirling mass of words interspersed with images of flowers—roses, mostly. But they were...badass roses, for lack of a better word. They were as much thorn as blossom. Hunter wanted to look more closely, to read all those words inked into Jesse skin. But that would be weird, and anyway, Jesse was striding toward the water.

"You coming?"

"I'm, uh, not dressed for it." Like Jesse, Hunter had changed when they came in from the fire, but he'd put on seersucker shorts and a button-down.

Clearly, he'd packed for brunch in the Hamptons rather than slumming it with a rock band.

"Suit yourself." Jesse waded in up to his waist and then dove under the surface of the water.

The lake in the morning had the cold-shower effect Jesse had been after.

He needed to chill the fuck out.

His mission was helped along by the fact that after he'd submerged himself in the icy water, Hunter turned around and headed back for the cabin, taking his immaculately groomed self and his stories of hookups with "hot but dumb" dudes with him.

But the reprieve was temporary, because a few minutes later he reappeared, and he wasn't wearing a shirt. Just a pair of plaid swim trunks that made him look like he should be starring in a Duran Duran video. He walked down to the thin strip of beach and laid out a towel. His hair was still kind of de-puffed and floppy from last night. Almost as if he could hear Jesse's thoughts, Hunter ran his hands through his hair, which had the effect of flattening it even more. Then he took off his glasses.

Eff him. Jesse liked Hunter's usual pompadour. He liked his glasses. Both suited him immensely.

But he liked even more the sight of Hunter...unraveling himself.

A whoop from the house caught his attention. Billy, Ash, and Will were on their way down from the house. Thank God. Sort of.

Their noise must have roused Colin, because he emerged from the bunkie, and within a minute, everyone had converged on the beach. Jesse swam to shore to introduce Hunter to the last member of his band and to make sure Colin, who was easily the crankiest among them, wasn't going to be a dick.

Which he kind of was, when he started up with, "What happened to 'no guests,' Jesse?"

Jesse had a strict rule about the cottage. It was open to the guys any weekend, but they couldn't bring other people. He didn't want it to be overrun, to become a scene. It was supposed to be a haven. A place where they unplugged, and, if the mood struck, did some work. They'd written some of their best stuff here.

"Yeah!" Billy piped up. "You said no guests. No girlfriends!"

"I said no *girls*," Jesse clarified. "You get an honest-to-goodness girl*friend*, and we'll revisit the issue. I don't want this to become party central. You get enough of that in the city, and on tour."

"Dude." Billy turned to Hunter and rolled his eyes. "He's like our straight-edge camp counselor." Then he swiveled back to face Jesse. "What happened? You used to be fun."

What happened is I grew the fuck up, convinced Matty to take us on, Matty did his stupid "branding" thing, and this band took off as a result. What happened is I decided to take control of my own narrative.

"Billy has a girlfriend," Will tried. "Her name is..." But then he shook his head and chuckled, knowing it was futile.

"Billy has a new 'girlfriend' every other week," Ash said.

"Well," said Billy, "I learned from the best." He waggled his eyebrows at Jesse, who was inexplicably embarrassed. And then mad that he was embarrassed. What did Hunter care who he slept with? Hadn't they all just heard about Hunter's most recent "hot but dumb" conquest?

"Maybe back in the day," said Colin. "But not so much of a player anymore, eh, Jesse?"

"That's kind of true now that I think about it," Billy said, screwing up his face in bewilderment.

Jesse rolled his eyes. "Maybe some of us have learned to be subtle." There was some truth in Colin's observation, though. He wasn't partying nearly as much as he used to. The band didn't know about his deal with Matty, but there was no way for them not to notice he wasn't tomcatting around as much as in the old days. But Jesse's rebuttal was equally true—if he did want some company after a show, he kept it on the down-low. And they weren't sleeping on the bus anymore at most stops, so he could invite the lady in question back to his hotel room and no one would be the wiser. Unless she talked to the tabloids, but that wasn't necessarily a bad thing. As Matty had said, it was a fine line, and the occasional tale of debauchery was good for business. Jesse was trying to act like a rock star, wasn't he? Embody Matty's "bad boy next door brand" that seemed to keep everyone interested in the band.

After that, everyone settled down, even prickly Colin, and they had a good time. The day could actually have been one of those montages you see in movies, because they did pretty much everything that was on offer. They swam and boated. Hunter gave waterskiing a shot, and he was adorably bad at it. Jesse had even handed the boat's steering wheel over to Will and jumped in the water to try to steady Hunter as he attempted to get up and going, but it always ended with the two of them sputtering and laughing as Hunter performed impressively acrobatic tumbles.

On land, they'd hiked and, as the shadows started to lengthen, taught Hunter Billy's ridiculous "croquet with shots" invention.

"I think the rules are changing as we speak." Hunter threw back a shot of vodka after his ball narrowly missed a wicket. "I thought you only drank if you missed two in a row."

"Now you're getting a sense of how it goes, Doc." Jesse clinked his glass against Hunter's before tipping his head back and emptying its contents—he relaxed his no-drinking rule at the cottage. "Billy makes this shit up as he goes along."

"Doc?" Billy's face arranged itself into a caricature of surprise. Billy was prone to overreacting, but when he was drunk? Forget it. "Are you a *doctor*? An *actual doctor*?"

Hunter had barely answered in the affirmative before Billy pulled his pants down.

Jesus Christ. Jesse buried his head in his hands.

"Will you look at this weird bump thing?" He jutted his hip out and pointed at something near the bone of his hip.

Hunter blinked.

"Here we go," said Will.

"Is this a bedbug bite?"

"Pull your pants up, Billy," Jesse said, though he knew it was futile.

"He's obsessed with bedbugs," said Ash to Hunter. "Thinks every bit of dust is one. Sleeps on the bus instead of hotels when we're on the road if he doesn't approve of the hotel's rating on Bedbugs R Us or some shit."

"I'm not *obsessed*," Billy said haughtily. "I had an infestation in my apartment about five years ago, and it was not an experience I would like to repeat."

"Pull your pants up, Billy," Colin growled, echoing Jesse's earlier statement. Colin was usually growling—if he wasn't such a damn good musician, Jesse wouldn't tolerate him—but he rarely agreed with Jesse, so the combination was weird.

"It's okay," said Hunter, whose shock had transformed into bemusement. He bent over, tilted his head, and examined the mark in silence for a few moments. "I'm not a dermatologist, but I feel confident in saying you're in the clear. Bedbug bites usually appear in clusters or lines. I think that's a run-of-the-mill mosquito bite, albeit a big one."

Billy's relief was comically exaggerated, thanks to his inebriation, and it caused the other guys to start mocking him.

"There's lots of research on the psychological impact of bedbugs," Hunter said as Billy (finally!) pulled up his pants. "Everything from sleeplessness to increased anxiety to full-on PTSD has been documented."

"Thank you," Billy said to Hunter, before turning to the guys and sneering at them. "Vindicated by *science*."

"Sorry about Billy's butt," Jesse said to Hunter later, when they were all milling around outside getting dinner organized. The other guys were setting out salads Jesse had picked up from a deli in a nearby town, and Jesse and Hunter were roasting sausages over the fire.

"No problem," Hunter said. "I like Billy. He's very..."

"Insane?" Jesse supplied.

"Authentic," Hunter said. "I like your band."

Jesse was secretly pleased. The guys were complete idiots some of the time—okay, most of the time—but at the core of things they were good people. Even prickly Colin. He was glad Hunter could see that. "Yeah, they aren't the most refined bunch, but what you see is what you get with them."

"That's...a really good quality to have," Hunter said, sounding wistful.

"You're thinking of Julian, aren't you? He really threw you for a loop."

"I think he did. At the time, I'd just had it, you know? He used to have these dinner parties for the partners at his firm—he was a senior associate and was aiming to make partner. He'd invite them and their wives over. I'd clear out. It wasn't anything new. We'd done it a bunch of times over the years. But somehow, that last time, I couldn't take it anymore. Early on, he told me he needed time. To prove himself at work. To become indispensable. He used to apologize profusely. We'd both feel terrible in the days leading up to one of his dinners."

"So what changed?" Jesse asked, trying to pitch the question so his interest seemed milder than it actually was.

"As he was planning the latest dinner, I realized he *didn't* feel terrible anymore. It was just...what we did. Routine. It's not like I *wanted* him to suffer, but then it sort of hit me: I thought, 'My God, if he doesn't even feel bad about this anymore, he's never going to change, is he?'"

"Probably not," Jesse agreed, his heart breaking a little at the idea of someone treating Hunter so shabbily for so long. Surely a lawyer in the modern era could be out without it being a big deal. It wasn't like a lawyer had to live his life in the spotlight, like his success was dependent on projecting a certain image.

Hunter nodded. "And all of a sudden, I wasn't okay with it anymore. It was like a switch flipped inside me. I was done. It's not like I need my boyfriend to be the grand marshal of the Pride parade or anything, but, Jesus Christ. I'm thirty-four years old. I'm not going to pretend anymore. No one— nothing—is worth that."

Jesse could not disagree.

In Hunter's case, anyway.

CHAPTER SEVEN

Hunter was drunk—the inevitable outcome of missing a wicket one too many times at a second round of "croquet with shots."

It was delightful.

He didn't let loose like this very often. He was at that tipping point between loose and sloppy, that sweet spot where everyone was funny and charming. Where *he* was funny and charming.

Well, Jesse Jamison was *extra* funny and charming, because, of course, he was pretty much always funny and charming.

"And *that's* how you do it." Jesse pulled a perfectly golden-brown marshmallow from the fire they'd kept stoked through dinner and into the night.

"*Hrmph.*" Hunter tried not to smile. "I guess that's all right, if for some reason you are unmoved by the thrilling pyrotechnics associated with my flambé approach."

"Yeah," said Billy, the last of the band members still around—the others had decided to go for a moonlit skinny dip, which Hunter gathered was something of a tradition with the group. "And if you don't mind waiting like twenty minutes for it to cook."

Instead of answering, Jesse set about smushing his flawless marshmallow and a generous portion of chocolate between two graham crackers. Then he held it out to Hunter. "Patience is a virtue."

Hunter took the offering and bit down and... "Oh my *God*."

Hunter's previous attempts at s'mores had been delicious, even if they had been made with marshmallows that were raw on the inside and charred to a crisp on the outside. But this one. This one was *transcendent*.

Because, of course, everything Jesse Jamison touched turned perfectly golden.

"Ha!" Jesse stood between Hunter and the fire. He'd thrown a hoodie on at some point after swimming, but he hadn't bothered to zip it up, so a slice of his chest—his tattooed chest—was visible. His hair was as messy as ever—messier. And, backlit as he was by the flames, Hunter couldn't help but think he looked like a god.

Well, come on now, maybe that was going too far.

Demigod.

Hunter sighed. And then he sighed again because that first sigh had made him sound exactly like Avery used to in her One Direction phase.

He was sighing over the quality of his sighs. Nice.

"So, Hunter," said Billy. "This guy you hooked up with—you gonna see him again?"

Hunter eyed Jesse. He was intently roasting another marshmallow, turning it almost imperceptibly slowly. He did not scold Billy for the untoward question, which surprised Hunter, as Jesse seemed to spend a lot of time scolding Billy.

"I don't think so."

"No good?"

Hunter laughed. Man, this guy didn't stop, did he? Normally, Hunter would have his suspicions about an allegedly straight guy asking so many questions, but he was pretty sure Billy the Horndog Goofball was just really interested in sex in all its incarnations. "It was fine."

"'*Fine*'?" Billy echoed. "I thought the guy was hot."

"He was. Superficially. Anyway, I'm glad I got it over with? Ripped the proverbial Band-Aid off." Then, realizing Billy knew nothing about Julian, he added, "A little over two years ago, I got out of a long-term relationship, and until last week, I hadn't...uh...gotten back on the horse yet."

"Duuude. You hadn't had sex in *two years*?" Billy crossed his hands over his crotch like it hurt in solidarity.

"Closer to three," Hunter confessed. "Things were...not great at the end there."

"Holy shit, my friend."

Hunter got a stupid little thrill by being called "my friend" by Billy. Hanging with the band—minus Colin, who seemed to have a stick up his ass at all times—was a lot more fun than he'd expected.

Jesse pulled his latest marshmallow from the fire and started futzing with the graham crackers.

"So, like, I have an idea," Billy said excitedly.

Jesse presented Hunter with another s'more.

"Oh, no." He tried to wave it off. "You have it."

"I made it for you," said Jesse with such an odd earnestness that Hunter could only nod his thanks and accept the gooey offering.

"We should, like, publicize you as our gay friend," Billy said. "Like, on Insta and stuff. Eventually, it will get out that you're, like, one of us. And then you can sit back and let the dick roll in."

Hunter barked a happy laugh. "'Let the dick roll in'?" Billy was a goddamned delight.

"Well, yeah. I was trying to think what the gay version of 'let the pussy roll in' would be." He turned to Jesse. "Do you think we have gay groupies? I don't think we do. But I'm sure we could get some if we tried."

Jesse, who had sat down and had another marshmallow on the go, merely raised his eyebrows. He had gone oddly silent. Not only was he not all over Billy for his presumption, like he'd been earlier in the day, he wasn't talking at all.

"Well, I thank you for the offer, Billy," Hunter said. "I'm touched." He really was. And he actually wouldn't mind hanging out with these guys some more, if not while he waited for "the dick to roll in." "But I kind of have a professional reputation to maintain, and—don't take this the wrong way— I'm not sure being splashed all over Instagram on the prowl with Jesse and the Joyride is a smart move, careerwise."

Billy nodded sagely. "I can see that." Then he stood. "Okay, well, enough chitchat. I'm getting in the lake. Any takers?"

Hunter looked to Jesse. He didn't want to say that he was going to do what Jesse did, but...he was going to do what Jesse did.

"Nope, I'm done swimming," Jesse said.

"Me too," said Hunter.

"Okay, dudes. See ya."

Jesse moved closer to Hunter to allow Billy to escape around him—he'd been blocking the main path that led to the fire pit.

"Finally." Jesse sighed. "Sorry about all that."

"He speaks!" Hunter teased. "I thought maybe the fire had hypnotized you."

Jesse smirked. "Pro tip: the fastest way to get Billy to go

away is to stop talking to him. Also, I sort of gave up trying to protect you from him by about the time croquet with shots started. Billy's an acquired taste. I figure you've either acquired him by now, or you're never going to."

"I think I've acquired him."

Jesse liked that answer, judging by the unguarded smile that blossomed as he pulled yet another exquisitely bronzed marshmallow out of the fire. "Are you ready for another one?"

"No!" said Hunter, holding his stomach.

"Okay, I'm done too, so I'll torch this, then." Jesse moved the poker back to the fire.

"Wait!" Something in Hunter rebelled at wasting such a meticulously cooked marshmallow. "Give me the marshmallow without the other stuff."

Jesse pivoted, and the poker came out of the fire, the marshmallow pointing at Hunter. He started to grab it, but Jesse suddenly pulled it back.

"Careful!" Jesse said. "You'll burn yourself." He retracted the poker and started to remove the marshmallow from it.

"And you won't?"

"I'm an expert at this," Jesse said, and Hunter would have thought he was joking, but his face betrayed no hint of amusement. And, of course, he *was* an expert at marshmallow-toasting, along with about a million other things, so why wouldn't he be an expert on removing molten marshmallows from sticks?

"Here," Jesse extended his hand. The marshmallow rested between his thumb and first two fingers. But then the marshmallow stared to sag, and Jesse said, "Whoa!" and rotated his hand to try to save it.

Hunter didn't even think about it until Jesse's fingers were in his mouth. His aim as he lunged—his imperative—had been to save that perfect marshmallow. The idea of all Jesse's work landing unceremoniously in the dirt had seemed unacceptably tragic at that moment.

But then, of course, Jesse's fingers were in his mouth.

And maybe it was the booze, but they might as well have been on his dick.

They might as well have been everywhere on his body, actually, all at once. Everything in him jumped to attention, even as his brain started to panic. What the hell was the matter with him? He'd just sucked Jesse Jamison's *fingers* into his *mouth*.

But, damn, his Tinder date from the other night had wrapped his mouth around Hunter's cock and hadn't been able to summon the kind of reaction Jesse had with a couple of fingers in Hunter's mouth.

A couple of fingers that were not moving. They remained in his mouth, and Jesse's eyes sparked.

Maybe. Or it might have been the reflection of the fire.

It was probably the fire.

The booze had made Hunter slow. He didn't understand why Jesse hadn't pulled his hand away.

Probably because Hunter hadn't actually eaten the marshmallow, which, of course, had been the whole point.

So, as awkwardness started to creep in, he did. Tried to dislodge it without too much...sucking. He had to resort to sort of scraping his teeth along Jesse's fingers, which judging by the way Jesse's nostrils flared—like he was about to lash out in anger, almost—hadn't been any more welcome than sucking would have been.

He pulled his mouth off as quickly as possible, ordering himself not to look at the shiny, marshmallow-coated fingers he'd left behind. "Sorry," he tried to say, but since his mouth was full of oozing marshmallow, it came out as an inarticulate mumble. He hammed it up a bit, chewing exaggeratedly, but Jesse didn't even crack a smile.

Still, he forced himself to play it cool, to not look away. To look away would signal that he was embarrassed, that he was imbuing what had happened with more meaning than it deserved. "I didn't want all your hard work to go to waste there," he said when he had finally swallowed the damned marshmallow.

Jesse didn't move. Not only had he not moved back to the spot he'd been occupying before Billy left, he hadn't lowered his hand. Which left them face to face, staring at each other, Jesse's hand floating in the air near Hunter's lips. Jesse's mouth was closed, but his jaw moved slightly, like he was grinding his teeth, and he was still doing that flaring thing with his nostrils. He looked like he was at war with himself.

God damn, Hunter hoped he hadn't ruined everything. With a start that cut through his tipsy sluggishness, he realized Jesse Jamison was, functionally, his best friend.

And now, his functional best friend was, rightly, pissed off, and—

No. Wait.

Now his functional best friend was…about to kiss him?

While he was performing his mental self-flagellation, Jesse's hand, which had been hovering so close to Hunter's cheek, made contact with it.

It was like a brand. A brand that sucked the air out of his lungs. He was breathing heavily—short, sharp exhales through his mouth—as he watched Jesse's face get closer and closer, the flames from the fire painting its sharp planes with a shifting light that was both eerie and beautiful.

And if Jesse had been at war with himself, suddenly, it was over. The victorious side emerged in the form of a smile—a small, knowing one he flashed for only a second before he placed his mouth over Hunter's.

The kiss was loose, a little bit sloppy, and insanely hot.

Maybe it was the fact that they were both buzzed. Or maybe it was more of Jesse's inherent ability to know exactly what was called for in any given situation, but Hunter had never had a first kiss like this. There was no lead-up. No orderly progression from "now we are kissing tentatively with closed mouths" to "now someone is making an incursion" to "okay, now we're all in."

No. Jesse just lowered his already open mouth over Hunter's, like this was something they did all the time, and let their tongues sink into each other's mouths.

Jesse groaned.

No wait, that noise, that moan of relief, had been *Hunter*. It was like his body, his entire being, was setting down a huge burden, falling onto the warmest, fluffiest bed after days of toil.

It was followed by a matching groan he was pretty sure was Jesse; though, honestly, he was no longer certain about the boundary between them. And, as their tongues licked deep into each other's mouth, he didn't really care.

But then, another hand. Two hands on his head. Anchoring it. Tipping it back, holding it in place so Jesse's desired angle could be achieved. And once it had been, the hands started working back along his skull, into his hair, pressing hard against his scalp.

Jesse was *kissing* him.

Jesse Jamison. Rock star. Famous person. Functional best friend.

A straight man.

Or at least a man everyone—Hunter included—assumed was straight.

Hunter had no idea what was going on with Jesse, but he'd be damned before he'd let himself be a piece on the side or an "experiment" for a straight rock star. No freaking way was he doing that again.

Hunter's next groan was one of defeat, frustration, and, truth be told, a little bit of anger as he pressed his palms against Jesse's gorgeous chest—his hands making contact with the bare skin he'd been admiring all day, touching it for the first and last time—and shoved. Hard.

Then he flinched in pain, because Jesse's marshmallow-coated hand, which had been buried in Hunter's hair, came out so fast and decisively that it took a chunk of his hair with it as Jesse was propelled backward.

"Shit," Hunter said. Both because having his hair ripped out had hurt, but also because he was afraid Jesse was going to stumble into the fire. So, even though he'd just pushed Jesse away—and rather forcefully—he now lunged for him, aiming to save him from being burned.

But Jesse held his hands up in a "don't touch me" gesture as he righted himself. Then he stepped away, so there was a good three feet between them. He muttered something unintelligible and tilted his head up to look at the sky.

"I'm sorry," they said in unison, which had the effect of diffusing a little bit of the tension swirling around them. Because, really, as annoyed as he was at Jesse, Hunter had to shoulder his share of the blame.

"I don't know why I did that," said Jesse. "*God*. I'm so sorry."

"It's okay. I started it by, uh, licking your fingers."

"I held my fingers out to be licked," Jesse countered, holding up the fingers in question, which still had several strands of Hunter's hair adhered to them.

Hunter started to laugh. He couldn't help it. The sight of his hair stuck to Jesse's fingers was objectively funny.

To his relief, Jesse joined in. But as the laughter died down, he figured he should probably make one thing clear, as awkward as it was going to be.

"Jesse, I…" Damn. Hunter had no idea how to say this. *How do you tell your rock star functional best friend that you can't be his boy toy, if in fact he wants a boy toy, be it you or someone else, which you aren't presuming he does?* "Jesse, are you…?"

"No," Jesse said decisively. "I literally have no idea why I did that."

"Good," said Hunter. "Because whatever my future holds…" Aww, damn. Why was this so hard? Jesse was looking at him with utter seriousness, paying so much attention it was like Hunter was about to reveal the secret to cold fusion. "I can't live my life in the shadows anymore," he finished.

"I know." Jesse turned to stare at the fire. "I know you can't."

Well, that was a relief.

It was also a huge bummer because that kiss? Hunter was never going to forget that kiss. In fact, it was probably going to be the last thing he thought about before he did the proverbial shuffling off of this mortal coil.

Jesse, still staring at the fire, blew out a breath. "Can we chalk this evening up to too much booze and…"

"Too much booze, definitely," said Hunter. "Sober croquet only from now on." He paused, trying to stop himself from asking his next question, but he couldn't help it. He had to know. "What else were you going to say? Too much booze and what?"

"Well, we're friends, right?" Jesse glanced over and Hunter nodded. "So, like, forget that you're gay and I'm…not. I don't think I've ever had a friend…God." His eyes went back to the flames, and he picked up his discarded marshmallow stick and started scratching the dirt with it. "This sounds so stupid. Hello, am I eight years old? But fuck it. What I was going to say was, I've never had as close a friend before. I mean, there's the band, but that's different." Then he dropped the stick and looked at Hunter once again. This time, he kept looking. "When you're a famous person, you don't really meet people who actually appreciate you for you, who have no secret agenda. So having someone like you around? It's new to me, and apparently I don't know how to behave as a result. But I'd hate to have messed things up between us, because you…you get me."

Hunter grinned. His face heated, and it wasn't from the fire. He felt like he'd been picked to be on the cool jock's team in gym class. He knew what Jesse meant. He and Jesse had sort of been friends at first sight, platonically falling for each other that day on the train and then effortlessly picking up their friendship again two years later. Normally, Hunter would be highly suspicious of a self-proclaimed straight guy who planted one on him and then insisted he was still one hundred percent straight, but they had a weird sort of chemistry that was hard to know what to do with given that they didn't play for the same team. But all that stuff aside, Jesse was right. They got each other. "Yeah. I, uh, feel the same way."

"So." Jesse stood and zipped up his hoodie. "We cool?"

"Yeah," said Hunter, a strange mixture of relief and disappointment swirling through him. "We're cool."

CHAPTER EIGHT

The funny thing was, they *were* cool. In a million years, Jesse wouldn't have thought his little backpedalling campfire speech would have worked so well, but after the cottage weekend, things went back to normal—on the surface, anyway. As the months slipped by, the band moved from recording to post-production and started gearing up for a big tour, and Jesse continued his hospital visits. Somehow, he'd gotten roped into judging an informal talent show the kids had decided to mount. Avery came back to visit and to help organize it. Every time he saw her, he said a prayer of thanks that she had remained well. All of the kids, actually, wormed their way into his thoughts more and more.

Jesse had never thought of himself as a kid person. He wasn't patient or wise. He lacked the qualities required for good parenting. His sister had those qualities. Hunter had them too. They were often on display in his interactions with the kids.

But none of the kids seemed to care about Jesse's short-comings. They just hung out, usually in a conference room the hospital set aside to give them some room to spread out and play. Sometimes he and Madison and some of her friends played formally, a band working on mastering a song of the kids' choosing. Sometimes he jammed, taking requests. Sometimes they goofed around taking selfies and talking about life in and out of the hospital.

Sometimes they talked about death.

Because sometimes one of the kids would be too sick to come by.

And sometimes—twice, to be exact—kids Jesse had known died.

They died. *Children died.*

He wasn't an idiot. He knew that people died every day, children included. But all the same, it seemed unbelievable. They lived in a prosperous, learned society. How could this happen? He wanted to go up to the roof of the hospital and shout that very question, so loud everyone in the city had to pay attention. *How can we let this happen?*

Which was why, despite his original intention to go incognito—the kids had respected his request not to post about his visits on social media—he found himself agreeing to the hospital CEO's request to record an ad for their new fundraising campaign.

All those suits had to do was ask him to do something, and he sighed, thought of Avery and Madison and the rest of them, and capitulated.

Matty was all for it. He was thrilled, in fact, when he learned of Jesse's long-standing involvement at the hospital and started pressing Jesse to take selfies on his visits, a request that Jesse mostly ignored, even though ignoring Matty was not usually something he did.

So Jesse was at the hospital a lot more.

He was seeing a lot more of Hunter.

And, yeah, on the surface things were the same as they'd

always been. They went to dinner. Sometimes they got takeout and took it to Hunter's apartment or to Jesse's house. When he could get away from the hospital—Dr. Baby Silver Fox said he was working on it, but to Jesse, he seemed like as much of a workaholic as ever—Hunter came to the cottage. He'd even started hanging with Jesse and the guys in the city occasionally.

Which was normal. They were buddies. Friends. Best friends, basically. As Jesse had so schmaltzily proclaimed that night at the cottage, they "got" each other.

So everything was fine. The same.

On the surface.

"Hey," said Hunter, looking up from his desk and flashing a smile the same way he always did as Jesse rapped on the doorframe the same way he always did.

Except…nothing was the same.

That kiss had happened seven months ago—not that he was counting—but it had changed everything.

For example, he couldn't look at Hunter's lips anymore, forming that innocent, one-syllable *hey* without remembering how soft they'd been under his. Without imagining how they would feel roaming all over his body.

It had been a very long seven months.

Hunter looked at his watch. "You're early."

"I'm not early. It's seven thirty. You were off at seven." Then he added his usual adage: "All work and no play makes Dr. W. a dull boy."

Which was hilarious because Hunter Wyatt was many things, but dull was *decidedly* not one of them. His stupid golden eyes positively glittered, for fuck's sake, as he started shutting down his computer.

"I have an idea for the Junos," he said, grinning, and even his teeth gleamed.

"Yeah?" Jesse said warily. He was going to the Juno Awards next week, though not because the band was up for any awards. They didn't have any eligible music this year, but they were going to debut the first single from the new record in advance of a North American tour that would start in a couple of weeks.

Jesse was also going to present an award, and Hunter had been trying to talk him out of his customary red-carpet attire, which was basically a slightly less messy version of his standard outfit. He was planning on wearing nicer, darker jeans than usual; a plain black T-shirt; and his leather jacket.

Hunter picked up his work bag and a garment bag. "You can't wear that jacket to the Junos."

"It's not the Grammys," Jesse said. The Canadian music industry awards show had nowhere near the profile of its American counterpart. Nobody outside of Canada paid attention to the Junos, except to the extent that they sometimes imported a big-name American star to host.

"That's not the point." Hunter locked his office door and nodded for Jesse to precede him down the hallway. "It's an honor to be asked to present. And anyway, I happen to know you wore that jacket to the Grammys that time you were up for Best New Artist."

Jesse flushed with pleasure over the idea that Hunter knew what he'd worn to an awards ceremony that had occurred before they'd become friends.

He fucking *flushed with pleasure*. Another example of how things had changed beneath the surface. He performed a shrug meant to convey unconcern. "I'm a rock star. People expect me to look a certain way."

People expect me to act a certain way.

And playing that role had brought him success beyond his

wildest dreams. As Matty was forever reminding him when he jokingly called him his "star pupil."

They exited the hospital, and Jesse scanned the street. A group of twentysomethings were headed toward them, but he didn't think they'd seen him yet. It would only be a matter of time, though.

Hunter reacted seemingly automatically, gently pushing Jesse back under the protective awning of the side door they'd used to exit the hospital. "Wait here." Then he hailed a cab, and, once the car was stopped, he opened the back door and held out his hand, gesturing for Jesse to precede him into the back seat.

It was...really nice. To be taken care of like that. To have someone who wasn't on his payroll instinctively anticipate his needs. To be protected.

Hunter gave the cabbie Jesse's address.

"My place?" he asked.

"We'll order food," Hunter said. "Humor me."

"Go get your nicest jeans and nicest black shirt." Hunter, reclined on Jesse's bed, pointed at Jesse's closet.

Jesse shot Hunter a skeptical look but moved to follow his orders.

Hunter had probably overstepped.

Hell, there was no "probably" about it. As Hunter waited for Jesse to reemerge, he started to backpedal.

"You know what? This was a bad idea. You have your thing, and it's obviously working for you." It was. It totally was. Jesse exuded sex appeal and easy confidence. "Why mess with success?"

"Nah, we're here," Jesse called. "Might as well hear your

big idea. As long as it doesn't involve a tie. I'm allergic to ties." He came out of the closet shirtless. Shirtless! Once again, what the *hell* had Hunter been thinking?

Jesse walked over to Hunter and flicked his tie. "You're always well put together, Doc, so hit me." He gestured at himself. "These are the nicest jeans I have. Will they do?"

Hunter, resigned to his fate, tore his gaze from Jesse's chest and studied the dark jeans that were, indeed, much nicer than Jesse's usual ripped, grungy pairs. "They're perfect."

"And I have this or this." He held up two T-shirts in turn.

Hunter took them both. "I think this one," he said. It was an Armani made out of a stretchy fabric, and it looked like it had never been worn.

"Yeah, I think that was left over from some photo shoot or other." Jesse grabbed it from Hunter and lifted his arms to put it on, which had the effect of displaying his whole torso. As he stretched, his muscles rippled, and Hunter had to restrain himself not only from asking about the tattoos, which was bad enough, but from outright touching them. His fingers itched.

"All right," he said once Jesse was decently clothed again. "Now don't freak out when you see this." He unzipped the garment bag to reveal a royal-blue velvet blazer. "Jimi Hendrix wore velvet jackets all the time."

The jacket suited Jesse perfectly. It was formal, but paired with jeans, the overall effect would be totally badass. He didn't expect Jesse to agree, though, not at first, anyway. He braced himself for derision, or at least incredulity.

But Jesse tilted his head, regarding the garment, and said, "Huh."

"No tie," Hunter said, seizing the opening. "You wear it over the T-shirt and jeans. And check this out." He flipped open one side of the blazer. It was lined with a silk fabric printed with tiny guitars.

"Holy shit." Jesse came forward to feel the blazer. "Where did you find this?"

"Oh, you know." Hunter shrugged. "I'm connected." The truth was when he'd been hanging with the band and listening to the other guys talk about their Juno wardrobes— the others weren't as resistant to cleaning up as Jesse was— he'd immediately pictured Jesse in a royal-blue blazer. And when he'd found this particular one on a vintage website? Forget it.

"Try it?" He held it up for Jesse, who nodded and shrugged into it, murmuring his thanks.

Hunter looked around for a mirror, but there wasn't one.

"Sorry, no mirror here," Jesse said, reading his mind. Of course, Jesse wasn't the kind of guy who needed a mirror. He just rolled out of bed looking like his usual irresistible self. "How do I look?" He spun around.

"Amazing," Hunter said, and it was the truth. "Like yourself, but with a little edge of glamor. But not like you're trying too hard." He hesitated before adding, "And that blue really makes your eyes pop." When Jesse didn't say anything, just stood there looking at Hunter with an inscrutable expression, he said, "Check yourself out in the bathroom."

"Nah, I don't need to. I'm gonna take your word for it."

"Really?"

"Yeah, who needs a mirror when I've got you, Doc? Me with an edge of glamor? I'll take it." He wiggled his arms a little. "This is actually surprisingly comfortable."

The doorbell rang, which was for the best because Hunter had no idea how he was going peel his eyes away from Jesse Jamison, shimmying in his new blue jacket, otherwise.

"That was fast," Jesse said. Hunter had ordered pizza when they'd first arrived.

"I'll get it while you change." Hunter turned for the stairs.

He dug out his wallet while he swung open the door to reveal a woman and a little boy.

"Oh," he said, "hi."

The woman's eyes darted around. She was wary, confused. Her eyes were a telltale blue-green.

He knew those eyes. This was—

"Beth?" Jesse jogged down the last few stairs. "Beth! Gavin!" The delight in his voice was palpable, but it quickly turned to concern. "What's wrong? Why do I suspect you're not just paying me a surprise visit?"

She burst into tears.

"Bethie." Jesse pulled her in over the doorstep and gathered her in a hug. He turned an apprehensive gaze to his nephew, who remained on the porch.

Hunter, galvanized, leaned over. "Hey, Gavin, my name is Hunter. You wanna come in?"

The boy was skeptical. He looked so vulnerable, weighed down by a backpack that was almost as big as he was. Hunter's heart twisted.

"It's okay, Gavin," Jesse said, letting go of his sister. "Hunter's my friend."

The boy must have decided that was enough of an endorsement, because he stepped over the threshold.

"He canceled my cell service," Beth said. "He somehow got my credit card canceled too, so I couldn't get another phone. I tried to call from a pay phone, but I know you don't pick up unknown numbers."

Jesse inhaled sharply and led Beth into the living room, his eyes scanning her body. "I do now. What happened? What did he do?"

Beth glanced at Gavin.

"Gavin," said Hunter. "You know your Uncle Jesse has a sweet tooth, right? What do you say we go into the kitchen and see if we can find any ice cream? We have pizza coming soon, but I think it would be funny to start with dessert, don't you?"

The boy smiled. It looked strange on his face, which had been so serious and pinched until then.

Jesse shot Hunter a grateful look and mouthed, *Thank you*, as Hunter led Gavin out of the room.

Uncle Jesse had lived up to his reputation, and ten minutes later, Hunter and Gavin were tucking into bowls of mint chocolate chip with Hershey's syrup when Jesse popped his head into the kitchen.

"Hunter, any chance you can stay here with Gavin for an hour or two?"

"Of course."

Beth came in too, and Jesse introduced them.

"Sorry for the dramatic entrance," she said.

Hunter waved away the apology. "Hey, no problem."

"We'll be right back," Jesse said to Beth, then he towed Hunter out of the kitchen.

"He took Gavin from school on a day that wasn't his. She went to pick Gavin up, and panicked when he wasn't there. Turned out her ex was watching her from his car the whole time. Thought it was hilarious. Then he canceled all her accounts—they were joint, and she hadn't taken him off any of them."

"Jesus," said Hunter.

"I want her to talk to a lawyer—a different lawyer than the asshole who isn't getting shit done in Montreal—and she's agreed. Her ex still won't sign the divorce papers. And they've been operating on this informal custody agreement, but it's time to get the courts involved. I texted Matty, and he's getting someone lined up to meet this evening."

"Good."

"But I don't think Gavin should be there for the lawyer stuff. Are you sure you're okay with watching him?"

"Of course. If Beth is cool with it."

"I told her you were a pediatrician. That's like babysitting gold."

"Take as much time as you need. Gavin and I have ice cream, pizza's on the way, and I assume your giant-ass TV comes with a kids' channel or twenty."

"Thank you," said Jesse urgently, his voice going scratchy. Then he said it again, more softly, as he laid his hand on Hunter's arm. "Thank you. I don't know what I did to deserve you."

Jesse's surge of emotion was contagious. "I…" Hunter didn't finish verbalizing the thought that had bubbled up. He said, merely, "Good luck." But the thought was still there, simmering under his skin.

I would do anything for you.

CHAPTER NINE

"He's finally asleep," said Beth a week later, tiptoeing down the stairs to join Jesse and Hunter, who were sacked out on Jesse's couch. Jesse was surfing the web on an iPad and Hunter was reading a medical journal.

"Nice job." Jesse raised his hand for his sister to high-five.

Gavin had been having trouble sleeping. He didn't want to be left alone, and Jesse couldn't blame him. The whole fake kidnapping, power-tripping stunt his dad had pulled had no doubt freaked him out.

Jesse scooted closer to Hunter to make room for his sister on the sofa. "Let's watch a movie."

It was strange having so many people in his house. Jesse lived in a small house tucked up against one of the city's ravines. It was a pretty secluded place, by design. He wasn't a condo person, so as soon as he could afford it, he'd settled in this ravine-adjacent neighborhood that housed Toronto's wealthiest citizens. His neighbors were CEOs, pro athletes, and the denizens of Toronto old-money society—people who understood the importance of privacy. Most of them had mansions; he had an incongruous little 1920s Tudor, but it suited him fine. It did the trick for when he couldn't be at the cottage.

He had his sister and Gavin in the guest bedroom, and Hunter was coming over most nights after work to help out. He'd made himself indispensable when it came to Gavin, logging major hours with the kid while Jesse accompanied his sister to meetings with her new lawyers, who were doing their best to untangle Beth from her husband as rapidly and decisively as possible.

"Shouldn't you be getting ready for the Junos?" Beth asked as Jesse pulled up Netflix.

"The Junos are tomorrow."

"Right. So, shouldn't you be, like, getting your nails done and your aura cleansed?"

His sister couldn't keep a straight face while she razzed him. He liked it. Historically, she'd always made fun of his fame. This week, though, she'd been dead serious about everything. Joking had disappeared from her repertoire, which was understandable given the situation. It was nice to see some of her old humor coming back, even if it was at his expense.

"The Junos will be lucky if he takes a shower," Hunter said.

"Hey!" Jesse said, affecting outrage. "I plan on showering." He smirked. "I might even wash my hair."

"Your starlet du jour will thank you," Beth said. "Who is your starlet du jour, anyway?" she asked, glancing between Jesse and Hunter.

"If you mean who is my date for the show, it's Penny Marks."

"I have no idea who that is."

"Up-and-comer on the label," Jesse said. "Her debut album came out earlier this year. Matty thinks we have synergy." Whatever that meant.

Beth picked up her phone and, after a few moments of

tapping, made a theatrical gagging noise. "What is she? Seventeen?"

"She's nineteen," Jesse said defensively. He knew because he'd asked Matty the same question.

"Why do you let them do this to you, Jesse?"

"They're not *doing* anything to me." Jesse had to tamp down a flare of irritation. "I'm single; she's single. I'm a snarly rocker; she's a little pop princess. People will get a charge out of the idea of us together. Everyone will sell some records. It'll be fine."

Beth curled her lip. "I think you should take someone you actually know."

"You want to go?" he asked, startled. "I will totally throw Penny Marks over for you." It had never occurred to him to ask Beth to accompany him to anything like this, asshole that he was, but maybe she would get a kick out of getting all dressed up and doing the red-carpet thing. Forget her troubles for a while.

"Somehow, I think being seen on national TV isn't going to be the best thing for me and Gavin right now, given that we're, I don't know, kinda hiding out from my evil soon-to-be-ex-husband?"

"Right." Okay, now he really *was* an asshole. How could he not have thought of that?

"Take Hunter," she said with what seemed to Jesse like oddly exaggerated casualness.

"What?" he said, as did Hunter.

"Yeah, you guys are besties, yes? You'll have more fun with him than with that teenager."

Jesse couldn't argue with her. On either front.

But he couldn't do it.

It was one thing for him to be photographed with Hunter in daily life. It didn't happen a lot—he was pretty good at keeping his shit locked down—but it had happened a few times. The captions always said, *Jesse Jamison and pal*, or *Jesse Jamison, band members, and an unknown friend*. But that wasn't how red-carpet events worked. People would find out Hunter's name. They'd do some digging, and they'd find out that he was "Openly gay pediatrician Hunter Wyatt."

They'd start losing their shit over his gray hair and gold eyes and perfectly tailored suit.

"No, no," said Hunter in response to Beth, but he hadn't demurred right away. There had been a few beats of silence while they'd both watched Jesse.

Fuck.

Did Hunter want to come to the awards show? Because it couldn't happen. Jesse had no problem being friends with Hunter. Hell, he needed Hunter, basically. Wasn't sure how he had functioned without him for so long.

He just…couldn't show up at something as high-profile as the Juno Awards with him. Matty would blow his top.

And more importantly, Matty was right. Jesse hated that they lived in the kind of world where his success as a musician was dependent on his "image," but it was what it was.

That didn't mean he wanted to spell it all out for Beth and Hunter, though.

They were both looking at him. Waiting for him to say something.

"I'm not sure that's the best idea."

"Why?" Beth asked.

Jesus. Was she going to make him say it?

"Don't worry about it," Hunter said, and shame, heavy and ugly, uncurled in Jesse's stomach, because Hunter knew what he wasn't saying. He knew why Jesse couldn't take him.

They all knew.

Well, that had been weird. It wasn't like Hunter *wanted* to go to the Junos with Jesse. Per se. It had never even crossed his mind as a possibility.

But did he want *Jesse* to want him to go to the Junos?

He wasn't sure.

He certainly didn't want Jesse to actively *not* want him to go to the Junos.

Gah. He was making his own head spin.

He and Jesse didn't have a public friendship. He had always assumed that was because Jesse was famous, because Jesse wanted to keep his personal life out of the spotlight as much as possible. In fact, he had always admired the way Jesse did exactly that, using the media selectively and for his own ends when he needed to but keeping a low profile the rest of the time. Jesse always maintained that famous people who complained they were constantly stalked by the paparazzi were, to a large extent, bringing it on themselves. *"Don't eat at the Ivy in LA if you don't want the press all over you,"* he'd say. *"You figure out which places to avoid at which times, and that's half the battle. It's not that hard to control the narrative."*

It had never occurred to Hunter that maybe he was being kept away from Jesse's public persona because he was gay.

No. He had to be wrong about that—he was getting unnecessarily paranoid. Jesse wasn't like that.

"Well, okay." Beth rolled her eyes. "If you insist on attending with Miss Jailbait, that's actually good for me because…" She turned to Hunter. "You and I can hole up here and watch it?"

Her eyes were hopeful. Hunter felt a rush of affection for his friend's sister. She'd been through so much, and she hadn't let it cow her. He'd enjoyed getting to know her over the past week. She was charming, like her brother, and brave as hell. And like Hunter a couple years ago, she was new to the city. She didn't have any friends.

"I'd love to. We can shout rude things at TV Jesse." He looked at his watch. It was still early, but he suddenly felt the need to get home, to be back on his own turf. "For tonight, though, I'm gonna head out."

"No movie?" Jesse asked, and Hunter couldn't read his tone. Had no idea if that little inflection in his delivery was disappointment or relief.

"Early committee meeting in the morning," he said, and it was the truth. "I'm on the annual hospital gala planning committee, God help me."

"Hospital gala?" Beth asked. "What does that mean? A ball with everyone wearing fancy scrubs?"

Hunter smiled as he shook his head. "The charitable foundation attached to the hospital runs it. All the wealthy donors and society people come out. There's usually some top-draw emcee, a silent auction, and—wait for it—a bachelor and bachelorette auction. Which I thought I was avoiding this year by being on the planning committee, but no."

"You mean you stand up there and the audience bids on you?" Beth asked incredulously.

"That is exactly what I mean. Unfortunately."

Beth cracked up. "Awww, you see that stuff on, like, Lifetime movies, but I had no idea it was a real thing!"

"It is. Alas. This will be my third year. The last two were so horrible I told them I'd do anything but that this year. So I got put on the planning committee. But then somehow I'm *also* on the auction block. They already printed the programs, and it's too late to make a change."

"So who has, uh, won you?" Jesse asked. "In past years."

Hunter sent his mind down bad-memory lane. "The first

year, it was this twenty-two-year-old trust fund woman. Her parents are big donors to the hospital. She insisted we go to Eigensinn Farm for our date." He looked at Beth. "That's this really chichi farm-to-table place two hours north of the city. So we had this endless drive there and back. She spent the whole time talking incessantly about how 'passionate' she was about children's health but being all grossly flirty about it. She also pretty much live tweeted the date. We had to take a bunch of selfies. It was strange."

"Did she know you were gay?" Jesse sounded annoyed.

"She did. It was right there in the program, and the emcee made this bizarre big deal about it during the auction." That had actually been the worst part—worse than the date, which was saying something. It had been exceedingly uncomfortable, being showcased like that, almost like he was a mascot or something. *Look! We have a gay doctor!* "They kept calling me 'the hospital's own Anderson Cooper.' Because, you know, gay, premature-gray hair. They thought it was hilarious."

"And what about last year?" Jesse asked.

Hunter huffed a bitter laugh. "Still with the Anderson Cooper thing. The emcee was all wink-wink, nudge-nudge about my sexuality. And get this: Last year, the winning bidder was the first woman's *mother.*"

"Ahhh!" Beth made a face. "That is so *weird!*"

"Right?" Hunter smiled despite the unpleasant memory. It was absurd enough that part of his brain could, objectively, recognize the humor in the situation. "And *she* spent the whole time talking about this charity she's launching to donate dog and cat food to areas of the world stricken by famine, because if people are starving, mustn't their pets be too? Then she tried to make this convoluted case I still don't understand about how there was some kind of cosmic affinity between 'the gays' and the poor famine victims because we were all 'so oppressed,' and I was like, 'Lady, I make a hundred and eighty grand a year, I'm white, I live in Canada—get a new stump speech.'"

"Fuck *off*. You're kidding." Jesse's vehement outburst drew both Hunter's and Beth's attention.

"Yes. She asked me to be on the board of directors. I told her I wasn't an animal person. She told me she'd bid on me again this year and work on me some more."

"Like hell," Jesse said.

Hunter wanted to ask Jesse what he was going to do about it, but that was mean. They both knew Jesse had no jurisdiction over the matter.

Jesse was going to the Junos with a teenager.

"Hang on a sec," Jesse said as Hunter stood and grabbed his bag and discarded tie—he'd come right from work.

Hunter didn't want to *hang on a sec*. He wanted to go home. But he waited, his hand on the door.

"I'll be right back. Don't go." Jesse jogged up the stairs.

Hunter glanced at Beth, who was still on the couch. He was embarrassed. She'd seen Jesse reject him, basically, possibly because of his sexuality. And now he was paused here like a trained puppy, waiting for his master's okay to start moving.

He should just leave. Preserve some shred of dignity.

"We need to talk about snacks," Beth said.

"Snacks?" he echoed dumbly.

"For tomorrow?"

"Ah! Right!" It was the perfect thing to say. It put him immediately at ease. "Tell me what you want, and I'll make it happen."

"I think fancy snacks are in order," she said. "Fancy snacks and maybe one item that's throwable. Like, we can throw Cheetos at the TV while we eat caviar?"

"That sounds perfect," he said, and it did.

Jesse was listening at the top of the stairs. Hunter could

sense him hovering there before he appeared. "This is the new album," he said, jogging down once the snacks had been planned. He held out a memory stick. "If you leak any of it, I'll murder you. And I would miss you if I had to murder you, so don't do it."

Hunter didn't know what to say. He'd heard snippets of it at the cottage, as the guys worked, but the album wasn't coming out for two more weeks. It was a strict secret. Last he'd heard, the only copy was kept under lock and key at the label.

He opened his mouth to object, but Jesse said, "I'd like you to have an early copy." He continued to hold out the memory stick.

Was it a consolation prize? Probably. *I can't be seen with you in public, but here's a treat to make you feel special.*

"Please," Jesse said, and his tone was imbued with such sincerity that Hunter extended his hand.

Once the transfer was made, Jesse smiled. "Go home. Get some sleep."

Yeah, right. As if that was going to happen now. He would go home, but he would not sleep, at least not for a good long while. No, Hunter would spend the rest of the evening listening to the new Jesse and the Joyride album on repeat, and when he finally succumbed and fell asleep, it would be with his best friend's voice in his ear.

CHAPTER TEN

The Junos were a drag.

These things always were, but they were an *extra* drag this year.

Partly because of the teenager. Beth had been right that coming with Penny was a mistake.

She wasn't uninteresting or vapid or any of the things Beth had seemed to be implying. But she was young and guileless and had no sense of musical history. Jesse ended up feeling like he was babysitting rather than going on a date.

But it shouldn't have mattered. This wasn't a real date; it was a work date. This whole evening was work. Get in front of the cameras, debut the new single, get people talking, whether it was about his music or the pretty girl on his arm.

That was the game, and you had to play the game.

So what was the problem?

The problem was Penny Marks was not Dr. Hunter Wyatt.

It had never occurred to him to take Hunter to something like the Junos, but once Beth had suggested it, he couldn't get it out of his mind.

What would Hunter wear to an event like this? Probably

something classic like a tux or a black suit, impeccably tailored. Hunter managed to look at ease in ties, unlike Jesse, who always felt like they were strangling him. But whatever Hunter wore, it would come with a hint of quirk, like a crazy pocket square.

He had never seen Hunter in black. At work, he wore his white doctor's coat over a shirt and tie. His silver hair would probably look amazing against a black tuxedo.

Jesse made his way over to Matty at the label's after-party. "I'm going to jet."

"You just got here."

He'd shown his face. That was what mattered. "I have a killer headache."

"What about Penny?"

"She's fine." Jesse nodded in her direction. She was in the center of a group of people, laughing and talking. "I'll offer to drop her at home if she's ready to leave."

They both knew she wasn't. She was new to this scene, and she was soaking it all in. Rightly so.

Matty frowned. Jesse usually worked hard to make sure Matty never frowned. "I really think it would be good if the two of you left together. I was going to say later, but an early departure, if it's noticed, could be good too."

Hunter knew what Matty was implying. He'd tip off some publication or other about the fact that Jesse Jamison and Penny Marks couldn't keep their hands off each other at the AMI Junos after-party and had left together at an exceedingly early hour.

There was a moment where Jesse teetered at the edge, caught between doing what he wanted and doing what Matty wanted. But then he got angry at himself. Could he not leave one party early one time? He'd manufactured the headache, but suddenly, he did sort of ache. In a generalized way, like his body was too heavy to keep dragging around.

"I can't deal with this now, Matty. Set something up with her for next week if you like, before we leave on tour." He glanced around. Ash and Rob were huddled in a corner. "Or get one of the other guys to do your brand management. They'd probably be into it."

"It's your band, Jesse. You *are* the brand."

He pressed his fingers against his temples. "Well, the brand is leaving."

Now, while there was a chance Hunter was still at his house.

Matty's face changed from annoyed to concerned, and Jesse had a momentary twinge of guilt for having manipulated the man who had done so much for him. "Jesus, Jesse, I thought you were bullshitting about the headache. You need a doctor?"

Yes. I need a doctor. Just not one I can have.

Finally dismissed with a promise to text Matty in the morning with an update on the state of his head, he grabbed an Uber, and in fifteen minutes he found himself standing outside his own front door, unaccountably nervous.

He stood out there for an embarrassingly long time. He wasn't sure what his problem was. This was what he'd wanted, right? To get home. The lights were off in the living room, but there was that flickering that TVs made in the dark, signalling someone was still up.

It might be Beth on her own. The broadcast had finished ninety minutes ago. Hunter could well have left by now.

A twig snapped somewhere, startling him. He looked around. The last thing he needed was for a fan to have followed him home. Nothing seemed out of place, though, and he was alone. It must have been a racoon—the neighborhood was full of them, and he swore they'd evolved opposable thumbs.

He unlocked the door and once it was pushed open a crack, he heard a rumble of laughter.

Masculine laughter.

The fact that Hunter was still there made him sag in what felt like relief. They hadn't spoken since last night. He wondered what Hunter thought about the new album.

No, he didn't *wonder*. *Wonder* implied idle curiosity.

Not knowing what Hunter thought about the new album was *killing* him.

Especially "When You're Mine." Hunter had somehow magically intuited that "Repeat" was about Beth, and part of Jesse feared he would also divine the truth about "When You're Mine." But that was impossible. The song was written in second person and contained no incriminating pronouns. Anyway, there was no big "truth" to discover. It was just a song. A thought experiment. He wrote songs like that all the time, songs the press insisted were autobiographical when they weren't.

"Hey," he called as he stepped into the entryway and disarmed the alarm. "Party still going?" He stuck his head around to peer into the living room as he took off his shoes.

His sister flipped on a light, and Hunter shot Jesse a smile. They were both happy to see him. Relief flooded his chest.

"Nice job, bro," Beth said. "I didn't even throw anything at the TV. That jacket looked *amazing* on camera, by the way. And the performance was great."

"The whole album is great," Hunter said, his golden-brown eyes sparking with warmth.

The two of them were cozied up on the sofa, under a giant afghan. Jesse wanted to get in there with them. But that was ridiculous.

Instead, he scanned the remains of their feast. "Are those…
lobster tails?"

"Yep!" said Beth. "I told Hunter I wanted fancy snacks,
and boy did he ever take me seriously. We had lobster, caviar,
and the most amazing cheese and charcuterie plate. He even
got fancy-ass hot dogs for Gavin."

"Want some bubbly?" Hunter held up a bottle of Veuve,
and Jesse's heart squeezed to see Hunter taking care of his
sister like this, treating her so well after she'd had such a hard
run. It was so like him. He wasn't sure he deserved to have
Hunter in his life, but Beth did. He had to think of some way
to smooth over—

His thoughts were interrupted by a pounding on the door
—a pounding loud enough it made him jump.

"Jesse!"

It had been a while, but he knew that voice.

Beth's eyes widened in fear. "Russell," she whispered.

Jesse *hated* that look in his sister's eyes. It made him want
to fucking punch her asshole of a husband.

"Beth!" came the voice, and the pounding grew more
insistent.

"How does he know where you live?" Beth whispered,
standing with her elbows bent like she was ready to fight—or
to protect herself from attack.

It was a good question. Beth's soon-to-be-ex-husband had
never been to this house—had never been to Toronto in the
time he'd been with Beth, as far as Jesse knew. And Jesse was
unlisted.

"He must have followed you from the awards." Hunter's
voice was low.

"Go upstairs," Jesse whispered urgently. "I'll take care
of this."

"Jesse, open up, or I'll break this goddamned door down!"

"*Go*," he said, talking to Beth but looking at Hunter and hitching his head toward the stairs. "Get Gavin and hide in the closet in my bedroom."

Hunter jumped into action, taking Beth's hand and leading her up the stairs, meeting Jesse's gaze with a look of concern.

Jesse debated adding that they should call the cops. Beth had a restraining order against Russell now, but in theory, Russell didn't know Beth was here, and Jesse thought keeping it that way was probably their smartest, and safest, move.

"Hang on!" Jesse called, and, when his people were out of sight, he waited another few seconds, ignoring the increasingly aggressive pounding before going to the door and opening it.

"What the hell?" he said, feigning confusion even though it seemed impossible that his unease wasn't visible on his face.

"Where's Beth?" Russell tried to step inside, but Jesse spread his legs and blocked the doorway.

"How the hell should I know?"

"Because she's here." He got past Jesse then, goddamn it, and pushed into the living room. "I know she's here." He reeked of alcohol.

This was bad. *Fuck.* Jesse should have blocked him more aggressively. He scanned the room, praying there was nothing incriminating laying around, like one of Gavin's toys. His heart was beating out of his chest, but he had to play this right. Strike the right balance between annoyed but mystified. "Look, you asshole, Beth's not here."

"Then where is she?" he yelled, and Jesse added to his list of fears that Gavin would hear his dad's angry voice and start crying, thereby giving them away.

He forced himself to breathe and affect a casually sneering tone. "Even if I knew, I wouldn't tell you."

Russell lurched farther into the room. He was clearly

drunk and a bit unsteady on his feet. Jesse pondered whether he could take him. The booze would make him slower, but probably also angrier.

"There's someone else here," Russell declared. "The house wasn't empty when you came home."

"Listen to yourself, man," said Jesse, trying another tactic. "*Look* at yourself. She's divorcing you. The only question left is how difficult you're going to make it. How much you're going to get to see your kid. How much self-respect you're going to hang on to."

"She is not divorcing me!" Russell roared, and Jesse regretted his decision not to tell Hunter to call the police. He could only pray they were hearing this from upstairs and coming to that conclusion on their own.

The volume of that last declaration must have startled even Russell himself, because he went silent then, staring at Jesse and breathing heavily.

Jesse was paralyzed. What the fuck was he going to do?

"There is someone else in this house," said Russell, recovering himself and replacing heat with ice as he nodded at the remains of Hunter and Beth's feast and the TV, which was still on. "You're hiding her somewhere in this house."

He made a move toward the stairs, and Jesse pivoted to block his access. But what could he really do when it came down to it? If he tried to take Russell and failed, where would that leave his people upstairs?

Fuck. *Fuck.* Jesse felt a hint of the terror that Beth must have around this criminal. Terror and powerlessness.

"Are you coming up or do I have to come down there and move you along?" It was Hunter, calling from upstairs, but in a weird, fakey-sounding voice. Jesse was confused, but that was better than the panic that had been threatening. "Anyway, we left the champagne down there, so I'm coming down."

And then Hunter appeared, walking slowly down the stairs...with no shirt on?

"Oh, hello," said Hunter mildly, letting his eyes roam up and down Russell's body.

Russell's mouth fell open as he gawped at Hunter.

Jesse took a deep breath. Hunter's appearance had let much of the air out of the confrontation, had given Jesse a moment to collect himself, to think.

"Jesse." Hunter raised his eyebrows like he was not impressed. "Are you going to introduce me to your...friend?"

"Nope." Jesse instinctively moved to stand in front of Hunter, who was perched on the bottom step. He was pretty sure Russell was only gunning for Beth, but he'd be damned if Russell laid a finger on Hunter.

"Holy shit." Russell barked a sloppy, drunken laugh. "Holy *shit*."

Hunter rested a hand lightly on Jesse's shoulder. "Well, in that case, perhaps it's time for—"

"You to leave," Jesse broke in, glaring at Russell. Hunter's hand on his shoulder was an anchor. Hunter—brilliant, sweet Hunter—had saved them. Had shifted the situation enough that they had the upper hand. "Get out of my house before I call the cops."

"I always knew there was something off about you," Russell said, almost thoughtfully.

"Get the fuck out of here!" Jesse roared, and, miraculously, Russell did, without even another word about Beth.

Jesse started shaking then, like a stupid frightened animal. What were they going to do? What was *he* going to do? He was supposed to leave on tour next week. He couldn't abandon the whole thing and leave the band, not to mention the hundreds of people who worked for them, in the lurch. But he also couldn't leave his sister here, an open target.

"Jesse," Hunter whispered, and he took his hand off Jesse's shoulder.

That was the opposite of what he was supposed to do. Jesse needed that hand back. He needed *more* than that hand. So he turned in place and wrapped his arms around Hunter, buried his head in Hunter's chest. They were normally the same height, but since Hunter was standing on the bottom step, Jesse's head notched perfectly under his chin.

Hunter hesitated for a moment, but then his arms banded around Jesse.

"Thank you," Jesse whispered.

"I'm sorry if I made more trouble for you. I couldn't think what else to do, and it seemed like this might get rid of him. He was on that tear about you hiding someone. I know you don't want people to think you're—"

"No," Jesse interrupted, shaking his head against Hunter's chest, his evening stubble grazing Hunter's smooth skin. The difference in textures where their bodies touched made him shiver. "That was brilliant. That was perfect."

Hunter squeezed him tighter, and it felt so *good*. Jesse wanted to stand there forever, safe in Hunter's arms. Screw the tour, screw the label, screw his image, screw everything.

But he couldn't have that. For a million reasons, not least of which was Hunter himself, who was now patting his back awkwardly, like the hug had gone on too long.

Jesse cleared his throat and pulled away.

Back to reality. He had a week to figure out how the hell he could go on tour and also keep his sister safe. They needed to get all the lawyers together on Monday. They needed—

"I think your sister and Gavin should move into my apartment while you're gone."

"What?"

"While you're gone, we'll swap." Hunter gestured around

the living room. "I'll move in here, keep an eye on the place. Beth and Gavin can move to my place. Her husband has seen me, but he has no idea who I am, and my address is unlisted. Plus, my place is on the top floor—much safer than being on ground level like this. We'll trick it out with a top-of-the-line alarm system. She was looking into enrolling him in a school downtown anyway—my place is much closer."

"You would do that?" Jesse asked, even though he knew the answer was yes. Because Hunter was a good man. Kindness came naturally to him.

"Of course." Hunter flashed Jesse a big, guileless smile that nearly took Jesse's breath away. "Now let's go talk to Beth. She's freaking out. And we have a ton of stuff to get done before we send you away on tour."

CHAPTER ELEVEN

There was a rap on Hunter's office door, and he looked up, grinning.

But of course it wasn't Jesse. Jesse was on tour, had been for two months.

The grin was Hunter's Pavlovian response. His body had been conditioned to respond to a knock on his door in a certain way: his mouth to smile, his stomach to flutter with excitement. Which was stupid. Was he thirty-four or fourteen?

"Dr. Wyatt, do you have a moment?"

It was Andrea Bingham, the president of the hospital's charitable foundation. Her presence probably meant she was going to ask him to do something he'd rather not.

But maybe it wouldn't kill him to agree to whatever she was going to suggest. Hunter had been hanging out a fair bit with Beth and Gavin, and he and Jesse had taken to texting at night. Hunter was losing sleep—literally—because he was staying up to chat with Jesse after his shows, which, depending on which time zone the band was in, could be quite late. So, yeah, it was probably a good idea to devote some mental energy to something that *wasn't* Jesse for one moment of the day.

"For you? Of course. Hit me."

"What do you think about asking Jesse Jamison to emcee the gala next month?" Andrea asked.

Hunter laughed. Threw back his head and let it rip.

It didn't matter that Jesse was currently in Houston. There was no escaping him. The rock star from the train had infected every nook and cranny of his life.

"No?" Andrea frowned. "And here I thought it was such a good idea, if a long shot. Those PSAs he did were so well received. And I looked at their touring schedule, and they don't have a show on the tenth."

"I thought you had Darren Singleton on board." Darren Singleton was a Toronto Raptors player. Not a superstar, but a longtime player who was quite involved with the hospital foundation.

"I did. I do." She made a sheepish face.

"But you're thinking of firing him for Jesse."

"I wouldn't call it *firing*, per se." When Hunter raised his eyebrows, she said, "The band's new album is so popular." It was true. It had debuted at number fifteen on the charts and had spent the month since climbing. It was currently sitting at number two.

Not that Hunter was obsessed with checking or anything.

"Do you think there's any chance he'll do it?" Andrea asked.

Hunter chuckled. "Yep."

"And will you ask him for me?"

The chuckle became a resigned sigh. "Yep."

Jesse got out of the shower and tried to pretend for five seconds that he wasn't going to check his phone before he was even dry.

He lasted three.

It was probably too early. They usually didn't start texting until midnight his time. Depending on the show, and the venue, he wasn't always back to his hotel room before then. But tonight had gone like clockwork, and they were just staying a few blocks from the arena, so it was only eleven.

His pulse skittered when he saw a text from Hunter had indeed arrived while he was in the shower.

```
Good show?
```

He dried his hands and picked up his phone and replied.

```
Jesse: Yeah. The new amp was fine. No
glitches. Everything went smoothly. Defi-
nitely best show so far. Something in the
air in Dallas, I guess.

Hunter: You're in Houston.
```

Jesse laughed. That about summed up touring.

```
Jesse: Right.
```

When he was younger and striving, and they'd go on little regional tours, crammed into their vans and doing their own roadie-ing, he would sometimes get confused over what day it was, where exactly in the world they were. But he'd blamed that on the partying. There was booze at every stop. There were girls at every stop. It all blended together, like one long bender.

He wasn't sure what his excuse was this time.

```
Hunter: Avoid the bowls of white powder.
It's bad for memory. Doctor's orders.
```

He laughed again. This tour, *this* was his constant. No matter where he was, no matter how the show had gone, he could rely on a text from Hunter to make him smile.

"Jesse, dude! Get dressed!"

It was Billy, who'd pushed his way into Jesse's room—along with two women wearing Jesse and the Joyride T-shirts and extremely short cutoff shorts.

Jesse tightened the towel around his waist. "Jesus, Billy. Have you heard of texting?"

"Dude. I did. You ignored me."

Jesse looked down at his phone, backed out of his stream with Hunter, and sure enough, there was one from Billy a few minutes ago—he wasn't sure how he'd missed it—exhorting him to get ready because the rest of the guys were setting up shop in the hotel bar.

In the meantime, another text arrived.

```
Hunter: I have something kind of weird to
ask you.
```

Billy tapped the doorframe the way Jesse used to when he'd pick up Hunter at his office. "You promised to come out with us tonight, old man."

He had. Had even kind of been looking forward to it. The show had gone extremely well, and he was still buzzing a bit on the triumph. Plus, he'd learned that making an appearance every few nights at whatever the guys had going went a long way toward keeping morale up—and morale was important for maintaining the momentum needed to power their three-month excursion. He was keeping his promises to Matty, but on the road, he needed to make sure everyone was happy.

"Hey!" Billy said as a song snippet Jesse had set as Hunter's custom tone signaled another incoming text. He plucked the phone out of Jesse's grasp. "Dude! Is that Hunter? I have to ask him something!"

Jesse lunged for the phone, but Billy held it out of reach. And before Jesse could stop him, Billy initiated a FaceTime.

Cutting his losses, Jesse turned around, looking for some clothing.

"Doc!" Billy exclaimed when Hunter picked up. "I need you to look at something for me."

"Keep your pants on, Billy!" Jesse shouted.

"Is this a bedbug bite?" Billy extended his neck and aimed the phone at a spot near his collarbone. "Hang on. Let me move into better light."

"Billy!" Jesse tried to stop Billy from pivoting his body because that was going to put Billy's entourage as well Jesse's towel-clad self in the picture Hunter was seeing.

"Oh, hey!" said Billy, apparently surprised by the appearance of others behind him. "Doc, meet, uh..." He turned and squinted at one of the women.

"Kelly," she supplied.

"Kelly!" Billy echoed. "And...Kelly's friend."

Now he was zooming the phone over the women.

Jesse contemplated hiding in the bathroom, but there was no point. Billy would just hunt him down and it would *look* like he was hiding, which was somehow worse than not hiding to begin with.

And in reality, he wasn't doing anything wrong. It wasn't

like Hunter expected an accounting of who was in his hotel room in what sort of attire—or lack thereof.

So when the phone scanned over him, and Billy said, "And you know this asshole, of course," Jesse gave a little wave.

And tried not to audibly inhale at the sight of Hunter clad in a tight, gray tank top.

"Did you know that Jesse has that Bon Jovi song 'Bad Medicine' as your custom ringtone?" Billy asked.

"Really?" Hunter chuckled.

Fucking hell. Jesse wanted to die. It had seemed like a funny diversion, but Jesus Christ, assigning your friends custom ringtones? Not exactly on-brand. What had he been *thinking*?

"So." Billy craned his neck again and turned the phone back on himself. "Is this a bedbug bite?"

There was a moment of silence, and then Hunter's voice from the phone. "I'm pretty sure that's a hickey, Billy."

Jesse barked a laugh.

"Oh, *riiight.* You're totally right. I forgot about that." He made a face at Kelly that was half apology, half leer, and Jesse braced himself for a remark about being in need of one on the other side so he could have a matching set or some shit, but for once, Billy spared them.

"Okay, thanks, Doc." He swiveled the phone to Jesse, who'd been rummaging through his bag looking for clothing. "Say goodbye to Jesse, because he's coming out with us tonight."

"Wait!" Jesse straightened and tried to look dignified—as dignified as a person could look wearing only a towel in a hotel room full of groupies.

"Uh, okay, have fun, you guys. I'll talk to you later, Jesse."

"No." Jesse grabbed the phone from Billy. "I'm not going."

"What?" Billy managed to sound butt-hurt, like he was five and Jesse had stolen his favorite toy. "You promised."

"Tomorrow," said Jesse, holding up a finger to Hunter to try to forestall him from hanging up. "I'm tired. I'm going order up some food and then go to bed."

Suddenly, "Kelly's friend," who had heretofore remained silent, said, "Oh, come on—pretty please!" with what he suspected she thought was a sexy, pleading voice.

"Nope." Seriously. Behind curtain number one was the usual bar scene, populated by the guys and Kelly and her friends. There would be fawning. There would be flirting. There would be as much action as Jesse could want.

Behind curtain number two was Hunter. Who would have been enough on his own, honestly. But Hunter with "something weird" to ask him?

No contest.

"Out," he said, raising his voice and opening the door. He tried not to laugh at the parade of forlorn faces that filed past, Kelly's friend again aiming for sexy, this time of the pouty variety, and Billy looking like a forlorn puppy.

He bolted the door behind them, sighed audibly in relief, and brought the phone back up to face level.

"Sorry about that. Billy and his groupies invaded my room a minute ago," Jesse said, but then immediately felt weird about it, because, again, it wasn't like he owed Hunter an explanation of what he'd just seen.

"Seriously, don't let me keep you," Hunter said. "You've worked hard—sounds like it was an amazing show. Go have fun."

Jesse tried not to stare at him too intensely. He was lying in bed—the bed in Jesse's guest room, because he was staying at Jesse's place while Beth and Gavin occupied his—bathed in the golden glow of the bedside lamp. He looked like the subject of a Renaissance painting. Like he only had to reach his hand up and God himself would come down and high-five him.

They had been texting pretty much daily since the band had departed, initially under the auspices of Jesse asking after Beth's well-being. But that had morphed into chatting—about the ins and outs of the tour and the ins and outs of the hospital.

But it had all been over text. They hadn't *seen* each other until now.

In fact, Jesse had never seen Hunter in pajamas before, assuming that was what that tank top was. He wondered what Hunter slept in on the bottom. His money was on classic pajama bottoms, plaid, cotton.

Which should not have been particularly sexy.

And yet.

He could imagine Hunter padding around his dark house, Hunter's work spread out on the kitchen island.

Hunter wasn't wearing his glasses, and his hair was down, for lack of a better word. Instead of being slicked back into his daytime pompadour, it hung loose, like he'd just washed it or brushed it or something. As at the cottage, there was a casualness about him that wasn't part of his public persona. An informality that felt, suddenly, extremely intimate.

"You're not keeping me," Jesse finally said. "You're saving me. I'm not in the mood for the party scene tonight." He lay down on the hotel bed and rolled over onto his side, angling the phone against a pillow so he didn't have to hold it. "What's up? You wanted to ask me something?"

"Yeah. Andrea Bingham from the hospital foundation asked me to ask you if you'll emcee the hospital gala on June tenth. Apparently you don't have a show that night."

Jesse blinked. It was a perfectly reasonable request. Not to be overly self-impressed, but if he were Andrea Bingham, he'd be asking him too.

So why was he disappointed that *that* had been Hunter's big question?

"Don't feel any pressure," Hunter said quickly, making a dismissive gesture with one hand. "I said I would ask you, but I didn't promise you'd do it."

"Oh, I'll do it." Of course he would. He couldn't say no to that hospital anymore. He was in deep. In fact, he was already talking to his money people about making a big donation.

"Really?" Hunter looked surprised but pleased.

It occurred to Jesse he would probably get to see Hunter in a tux. "Do I have to wear a tie?"

"Normally, I would say yes, but I'm pretty sure they'll take you in any format."

"Can Avery come?"

"I don't see why not, if they're up to making the drive in. She's doing really well."

"Actually, I think you should get Avery and her friends who've been practicing that terrible Katy Perry song to perform. There is no way the rich and famous of Toronto can see that and not be inspired to open their wallets."

"That's a brilliant idea," Hunter said. "Andrea will love it. Will you accompany them?"

Jesse laughed. "Sure. Let me have Amber look into flights and touch base with Andrea about the details."

"This is looking like it's going to be the best gala yet," said Hunter with what seemed like real happiness.

A thought occurred to Jesse. "And will my duties include auctioning you to the highest bidder in the bachelor auction?" He wasn't sure how he felt about that aspect of things.

Hunter quirked a resigned smile. "They will indeed.'"

Hunter was glad Jesse was away on tour. At least that was the party line.

Things between them had gotten too...fraught. He pinned it on that kiss at the cottage so many months ago. Even though it had initially seemed like they'd gone back to normal afterward, Hunter was starting to wonder if they actually had. Because going back over it, it was kind of like there were two phases of his relationship with Jesse. Pre-kiss and post-kiss. Pre-kiss, they'd seen each other a couple of times a week for dinner. Then his straight friend had planted one on him, and all of a sudden they were all up in each other's spaces? Their lives had become totally enmeshed. They hung out all the time. They told each other shit. Like the stupid bachelor auction—Jesse knew how freaked out Hunter was by it. And Hunter was in deep with Beth and Gavin. Not to mention examining Jesse's bandmates for phantom bedbug bites.

He was living in Jesse's *house*, for God's sake.

It was like they were a couple without...the benefits that came with being a couple.

So, yeah, a little break should have been just what this doctor ordered. Without Jesse around, sucking up all the available air simply by being himself, Hunter was free to do his own thing.

Which was what?

That was his problem.

Because it seemed like, "his thing," was a combination of falling back into the trap of working insane hours and obsessively checking his phone for texts from Jesse.

"Hey." Charlotte, a psychiatric nurse who was a regular at the Maple Leafs TV nights, caught up to him as he left the cafeteria.

"What's up?" He liked Charlotte. He didn't have a ton of interaction with her at work, but from what he could tell, she was a great nurse—she was whip-smart and just the right blend of tough and kind.

"Have you met the new night nurse in psych? His name's Faheem?"

"I don't think so."

"Well, I'm aware this is going to make me sound like I'm in junior high, but he likes you."

He choked on the coffee he was sipping. "What?"

"Yeah, he's hard-core crushing on you." She smirked. "I'm not supposed to tell you."

Hunter blinked, struggling to assimilate this astonishing news.

"He's adorable. He's young—twenty-three or something. He must have graduated, like, yesterday, but he's super competent. The kids all love him."

A twenty-three-year-old had a crush on him? Still stunned, Hunter opened his mouth to say something, but…what?

It didn't matter because Charlotte wasn't done.

"I don't think it's a match, though."

"Then why are you telling me all this?" he asked.

"Because I can't stand it anymore. You gotta either reject the boy or go out with the boy. He needs to stop talking about the idea of you two together. *Everyone* needs to stop talking about the idea of you two together."

"Why don't you think it's a match?" he asked, aware he was now the one who sounded like he was in junior high.

"You know how straight people always try to match up all the gay people they know? Like, 'Oh, look, you're both gay—go off and have babies'? I think that might be what's going on here."

Hunter laughed. "I *do* know." Wait. What was she saying? "Do *you* know? Like, from experience?"

"I do." She raised her eyebrows and smiled.

Well. If gaydar was a thing, Hunter had never had it. But still, he'd had a colleague all this time who wasn't straight, and he'd had no idea?

"Okay, so this kid— What's his name? Faheem? Why is he not my prince charming? What's wrong with him?"

"Nothing's wrong with him. Like I said, he's adorable. I just think if you're in the market, which, for the record, I'm not presuming you are, you need someone who's going to be more the yin to your yang, you know?"

He raised his eyebrows, encouraging her to elaborate.

"Not someone who's going to take you to the bar across the street and talk your ear off about new techniques in SSRI dosing," she clarified.

"How do you know all this?"

She shrugged. "I'm a student of the human condition."

"Okay." He smiled despite himself. "What *do* I need, then?" Hell, she was a psych nurse. Maybe he could get some real insight here.

"You need someone who's going to force you out of your comfort zone."

Right.

And, naturally, a text from Jesse arrived at that very moment. He could tell because he'd set up one of the new songs—"When You're Mine," his favorite—as Jesse's custom ringtone. If Jesse could have a silly custom ringtone for Hunter, then he'd figured he could do the same for Jesse. He'd been careful, though, to choose an innocuous snippet of verse rather than the chorus. He didn't need anyone thinking he was associating the phrase *you're mine* with Jesse.

Charlotte was still talking. "Basically, you need someone

who's going to force you to loosen up a bit. Shake you out of your usual patterns." She winked. "That's my professional opinion, anyway."

Hunter had been reflexively going for his phone. But he stopped. Pulled his hand out of his pocket.

"You have my number, right?" he asked. "From those group texts about Maple Leafs night?"

Charlotte nodded.

"Give it to this Faheem kid. Tell him to use it."

Jesse checked his phone. He was in Atlanta. It was one in the morning.

His last text, sent thirty minutes ago, was still marked *Delivered*.

Not *Read*. Just *Delivered*.

He stared at the single-word text.

`FaceTime?`

After that night Billy had made Hunter examine him remotely, Jesse and Hunter had kept up with the FaceTiming, rather than texting. One of them would usually shoot the other a text to confirm availability, and within minutes they'd be gabbing about that night's set list, what was up at the hospital, how Beth and Gavin were doing, and so on.

Then the delivery status on his text turned to *Read*.

Finally. He grinned and smoothed his hair as he lay back on his bed and muted the TV.

But nothing happened.

Nothing happened for a good ten minutes.

Then he got those dots, the floaty things that indicated the other person was typing.

Hunter: Can't right now. I'm out. Maybe in like an hour if you're still up?

Jesse blinked. Sat up. Refrained from typing any of the questions swirling between his brain and his fingertips:

You're out at one in the morning?

Where are you?

Who are you with?

What could he do, though? Hunter was a grown man. And, objectively, Jesse knew it was good for him to get out. When Hunter was out, he wasn't working. Going out was good for him.

In theory.

He checked the Maple Leafs website. No game tonight.

Damn.

He had no other leads. No idea what Hunter could possibly be doing or with whom.

But, again, what could he do? Certainly not ask about it.

Anyway, the gala was the day after tomorrow. He would see Hunter in person soon. So what did it matter whether he saw him on a tiny screen right now?

He went to bed.

And woke an hour later to the sound of "Bad Medicine," his embarrassing ringtone for Hunter.

He fumbled to turn on the light and answer the FaceTime.

"Hey," he said, then cleared his throat because he sounded like a frog.

"I woke you. I'm sorry. Go back to bed."

"No. It's okay. I'm up." He ran his fingers through his hair. He'd fallen asleep with it wet, so it probably looked ridiculous. "You're out late for a school night."

Hunter didn't answer right away. His face formed itself into something halfway between a grimace and a smile. "I was on a date, actually."

"Well." A strange buzzing started up in Jesse's arms and hands. "Good for you." Shit—that had come out sounding all snippy. He tried again. "How was it?"

Hunter shrugged. "Okay. All the pieces were there."

"'All the pieces'? What does that mean?"

"Well, the Tinder thing didn't really work out, right? This was the reverse. Someone from the real world. A guy I work with—Faheem. He's a new nurse at the hospital. He's smart, good-looking, in the market for a relationship."

"And those are 'the pieces'?" Damn. It was harder than it should have been to keep that snide tone from creeping back into his voice.

Hunter didn't take offense, though. "Well, what else is there, really?" He laughed bitterly and rolled his eyes. "Though I guess after Julian, I should add: *not a closet case*. But that wasn't a problem here. This kid is literally on the steering committee for Pride Week, and he's founded a support group for gay Muslim youth."

"'Kid'?"

"Twenty-three."

"Way too young for you."

"Maybe." Hunter shrugged. "Anyway, it doesn't matter because, though all the pieces were there, there wasn't a spark. I guess sometimes all the pieces don't add up into the whole you're looking for. I'm going to have to text him tomorrow that I won't be seeing him again. Better to nip it in the bud now, because we have to work together. Our jobs don't really overlap, but still."

Thank God.

But Hunter looked so sad, dejected even.

So Jesse said, "I'm sorry," because that was what he was supposed to say. "Is this guy going to be at the gala?" He didn't know what answer he was hoping for.

"I don't know. We didn't talk about it." Hunter let loose a big sigh, like he was bearing the weight of the world, and Jesse's heart twisted a little. "I just..."

"What?" He hated seeing Hunter like this, all beaten down. It didn't suit him.

"I've been acting like I needed to change things up after Julian, after Montreal. And, yeah, I don't want a closet case for a boyfriend—absolutely not. But I guess I'm realizing that I *do* want a boyfriend. I'm *good* at couplehood. I give good backrubs. I make good pancakes. It's been three years, and..."

Jesse closed his eyes. Hearing the longing in Hunter's voice was hard enough without the accompanying visual. But with his eyes closed, he pictured a Saturday morning featuring those pancakes and backrubs, which wasn't any better.

"Which I guess means I'm going to have to start dating in earnest," Hunter said.

Jesse forced himself to open his eyes.

"Which is, in turn, depressing." Hunter rolled his eyes. "Because how often do you find someone who has all the right pieces but also gives you...that feeling?"

"Not that often," Jesse ventured. He'd never... Well, shit. He had to abort that thought because it wasn't really true, was it?

"I just want someone awesome to love me—publicly." Hunter snorted, sounding like he was disgusted with himself. "Is that too much to ask?"

"No," Jesse said softly. He swallowed against a lump that had suddenly materialized in his throat. "No. That's not too much to ask."

CHAPTER TWELVE

Jesse was excited as the taxi dropped him off at the gala. Stupidly excited. Even though he was wearing a goddamn bow tie.

He was going to see Avery. Accompany her and some of the other kids as part of the performance. Hopefully sneak in a quick visit with Beth and Gavin tomorrow morning, before he had to fly back to rejoin the tour.

And he was going to see Hunter.

Jesse had never before come back from a tour and felt so much like he was...coming *home*. Which sounded like a sentiment that belonged on a Hallmark card, but there it was.

The gala was being held in an old brick quarry at the bottom of one of Toronto's ravines. It had been restored and transformed into a stunning event venue surrounded by reclaimed wetlands and trails.

He was early, as instructed. He checked his watch. Actually, he was earlier than instructed. Probably on account of the whole "stupidly excited" thing.

The venue was a cavernous converted industrial space covered by a soaring roof that must have been forty feet high, but aside from the roof, the space was open to the outdoors. Everything was draped with some kind of flowy white material, and workers were busy hanging up strings of lights that would look amazing when it got dark.

"Jesse!"

Andrea Bingham approached and kissed him on the cheek. "You look wonderful!"

She said it with such over-the-top enthusiasm he suspected Hunter had prepped her to expect him to arrive in his usual slovenly state.

"You have everything you need? I have an extra set of cue cards."

"I brought mine." Jesse patted his breast pocket, which held the cards Andrea had couriered to him on the road. They contained his canned opening and closing remarks, and he'd added his own speech to the middle, as instructed.

"Okay, great. We're going to do a sound check in about fifteen minutes, but we won't need you before that. Why don't you have a stroll around the grounds? They're really something. And it looks like it's going to rain, so this might be your only chance."

"Is, ah, Dr. Wyatt here yet, do you know?" There was probably no reason for Hunter to be here this early, but maybe he'd been tasked with a job because he was on the planning committee.

"I saw him somewhere around here," said Andrea, looking around, and Jesse's stomach did a stupid little dance.

"It's okay. I'll find him."

He headed out to the back of the property, which was studded with a series of ponds that could be traversed via a network of boardwalks.

And there Hunter was, leaning on a railing overlooking the

farthest section of the ponds, his back to Jesse. He was leaning so his entire head was obscured, and he was wearing a tux rather than his usual work dress clothes. So technically, Jesse shouldn't have been able to recognize him from this far away. He should merely have looked like a generic man in a penguin suit.

But Jesse knew the curve of that spine. The angle created by that arm resting on the railing.

He knew.

He forced himself to walk slowly, to keep up a steady rhythm with the clicking of his shoes on the wooden planks. There were frogs croaking. Or crickets? Despite all his time at the cottage, he wasn't good at this nature shit, but something natural was making noise in a regular pattern. So his footsteps were in symphony with those creatures.

There was also his heart, which was not keeping time as neatly.

He was close enough now.

"Dr. W.," he called when he was about twenty feet away, using Avery's name for Hunter.

Hunter turned.

Jesse's gaze locked onto those beautiful shimmery eyes, which were…crying?

They were. Or they had been. Hunter tried to hide it—he swiped a hand over his face and then he managed a weak smile. "Hey."

"What's wrong?" Jesse tried to tamp down a spike of adrenaline. Something was wrong with Hunter, and Jesse's body automatically surged into fight mode.

"Nothing. I got some bad news today, but it's okay. Hey, it's good to see you in the flesh. How was your flight?"

Jesse wasn't having it. "Tell me what's happened." That had come out too strong. He gentled his voice. "Please."

Hunter turned back to the pond, but he answered. "Lost a kid today. Unexpectedly."

"Oh." Jesse felt it like a spear, an icy blade slicing through his insides.

"I wish I could tell you about him—he was such a great kid—but privacy rules..." He stopped talking and shook his head at the pond.

Jesse hated not being able to see Hunter's face. Hunter sounded more in control of his voice than he had earlier, but Jesse needed to see his friend's eyes. He moved closer. Came to stand next to Hunter at the railing. He wanted to lift his hand, to let it float down onto Hunter's shoulder, but he held back.

"I should be used to this by now."

There was derision in Hunter's tone. Self-disgust. Something inside Jesse snapped at hearing it, because that could not be allowed to stand.

"*No*," he said, and the force of it drew Hunter's attention. His eyes were dry but troubled. "*Not* getting used to kids dying is what makes you such a great doctor. You get used to that shit, you're not the same person anymore."

Hunter closed his eyes, made fists, and pressed them against his temples. "And now I've got to stand up in that fucking bachelor auction and smile and be a good sport while everyone titters over the gay doctor with the weird gray hair." The fists came around and dug into his eyeballs. "Fuck."

Jesse was startled. Hunter didn't swear much—not like this anyway. Not beyond a good-naturedly frustrated "damn it." Jesse was the one who needed a swear jar.

"Hey." Jesse gave in to his previous impulse to lay a hand on Hunter's shoulder. It was like petting a brick wall. He was holding himself so tight—his shoulders were scrunched up near his ears and his upper arms were jammed into his sides like he was bracing himself for some sort of impact. "Hey,

hey," he said again, using both hands on Hunter's shoulders this time to force him to turn so they were facing each other.

Jesse did what came naturally—he wrapped his arms around his friend. Hunter's own arms were still bent at the elbow and pressed against his torso, so Jesse encircled all of Hunter in a great big hug.

And he kept holding on, silently, waiting. For what? He had no idea. Maybe for some of Hunter's pain to leach out of his body and into Jesse's. He would gladly take it.

It wasn't just the kid who had died today. Hunter had been upset last night too, about his less-than-inspiring date and everything it signified. And he still had that stupid auction to get through this evening. It was a perfect storm of awfulness, and Jesse wished more than anything that he had the power to do something about it.

But maybe, miraculously, he did. After a few moments of standing there feeling like he was hugging a marble statue, Jesse felt Hunter's body started to relax. It began with a sigh. Then his shoulders lowered. Jesse stood unmoving, bolstering him, until Hunter's hands came away from his face and his forearms pressed against Jesse's chest. Jesse stepped back then, enough to allow Hunter's arms to come all the way down, but the minute they did, he gathered him right back close.

He didn't want to let go yet.

Maybe something about the surge of emotion he'd just witnessed was contagious, because when Hunter's arms snaked around his waist, returning the embrace, Jesse was hit with a wave of something he couldn't name. Some of it was sympathy, sure, but some of it, he thought, was relief. Selfish relief that he had the power to calm Hunter. That Hunter granted him that power. Whatever it was, it lodged high and sharp in his chest, harder and more solid than Hunter's body against his own.

Finally, Hunter pulled away and looked at him for a few moments, not speaking. Something happened to his face as he did so, though. It...settled. His eyes warmed. "You got your hair cut," he said quietly, one corner of his mouth turning up.

Jesse smiled. "I did." He'd had several inches chopped off, leaving it about chin length, and had washed and tamed what was left so it was tidy. He was never going to be mistaken for a banker, but this was as clean-cut as he'd been in a decade. "I figured I was already wearing a tie, so..."

"Thank you for doing this."

Jesse wasn't sure if Hunter meant emceeing the gala or... what had just happened between them. "No problem," he said, because it would apply to either.

"There was a turtle down here." Hunter turned back to the pond. "A big one."

Jesse leaned over to look, but there was only dark, murky, lily pad–studded water.

"Jesse?"

He straightened quickly, like he'd been caught doing something much less benign than looking for a turtle.

It was Andrea Bingham.

"We're ready for you for the sound check. And the kids are here." She paused and looked between the two men. "Whenever you're ready."

"Right," he said. "Yes."

He wanted to tell her to wait a minute. He wanted to tell Hunter to bail on the auction. To do what he needed to do to protect himself.

He wanted to fix everything for Hunter. To stand next to him and hug him until all the shit went away.

But then he thought back to their phone call last night, to Hunter's simple, sad declaration about wanting someone to love him publicly.

He pasted on a smile and aimed it at Andrea. "I'm ready now."

The gala went as expected. There was a certain predictability to these things. First, cocktails, which involved being shepherded around and introduced to donors. Which in turn meant having to explain a hundred times what a hospitalist was. Which was fine, if tiresome. Hunter reminded himself these people's generosity paid for a lot of what happened at the hospital—and for the research that would someday help kids in ways medicine currently couldn't.

After cocktails, they were invited to take their seats, the salad course was served, and then the speeches started.

The chairwoman of the hospital foundation board started. Then the CEO of the hospital itself. Followed by the hospital's vice president of research.

Because he was on the planning committee, Hunter knew each speaker had been allotted five minutes. None could manage anything close to it. Even though they all gave a speech that was simultaneously the same as they—or their counterparts—had given last year *and* basically the same as each other's, they couldn't help themselves.

Hunter sighed and stabbed his lukewarm chicken breast.

Forty-three minutes later, they were back to the chair of the board. She had a very exciting surprise for them. A special guest who had taken a break in his busy touring schedule and flown here to join them tonight.

Hunter could practically see everyone yawning, even as a weird fluttering feeling overtook him. He suppressed a grin.

"Ladies and gentleman, please welcome Jesse Jamison."

A current of electricity arced through the crowd.

Jesse had definitely cleaned himself up. Put on the dreaded tie and the expected costume. Cut and tamed his hair. He could play the role. But none of those trappings had the power to mask his swagger. His essential Jesse-ness. The thing that made him a star.

As he walked out to the podium, grinning knowingly, the crowd went crazy. The scions of Toronto industry, the ladies who lunched, the movers and shakers—they all whooped and hollered like teenagers at a Jesse and the Joyride show.

After several unsuccessful attempts to calm the besotted crowd, he just started talking.

"I came to the hospital initially for the wrong reasons."

That did it. No one wanted to miss what Jesse Jamison was going to say, especially when he opened with a provocative line like that. The room quieted instantly.

Once he had their attention, he started again. "I came to the hospital initially for the wrong reasons. I was 'doing a good deed,'" he said, making air quotes with his fingers. "Visiting a sick kid who was a fan. You'll meet her later." He paused and grinned. "Actually, maybe you should meet her sooner." He stared into the crowd for a long moment. Hunter knew he had his speech on cue cards, but he didn't seem to be using them.

"I was going to talk about how I figured out pretty quickly that my involvement in the hospital wasn't charitable. That I was gaining more than I was giving as I met the most incredible people. Nurses." Jesse's eyes scanned the crowd. "Doctors." His gaze stopped—for a mere heartbeat, but it was enough—on Hunter. "And of course kids." He paused, like he was trying to decide something.

"But you know all that. You've heard enough variations on that already tonight." He smiled at the crowd. "I'm not much of a speaker. I've always been better with music than talking. So I think maybe I'll get straight to the point." He glanced at the wings and nodded. "Without further ado, ladies and gentlemen, please welcome a band made up of current and former patients. They're calling themselves— No, we're calling *ourselves* Avery and the Abscess."

Hunter jumped to his feet along with everyone else at the sight of three girls making their way onto the stage to join Jesse. A curtain that had been behind Jesse rose to reveal a keyboard and drum set. Avery carried her guitar, and someone in the wings handed Jesse his.

Jesse nodded encouragingly at the drummer, and she banged her sticks together and counted them in. "One, two, three, four."

The band launched into the Katy Perry song they'd been practicing for so long. It was much improved from its early incarnations, but it was still a bunch of kids plodding through it. It didn't matter. What they lacked in technical skill, they made up for with enthusiasm. And you had to be dead not to be swept away by the message of female empowerment, of fighting and enduring, being sung by these girls who had endured so much.

When they were done, everyone leaped to their feet, hollering and clapping. Hunter, who was seated at the same table as Andrea, caught her eye. She smiled at him triumphantly. Yep, thanks to Jesse, tonight a lot of people were going to be opening their wallets wider than they ever had before.

Jesse had done it again.

CHAPTER THIRTEEN

Jesse had never had this much fun in a tie. Admittedly, the bar was low, considering how many times in his life he'd worn a tie, much less a bow tie, but still. After the first part of the program ended, and they paused for dinner, he asked if he could sit with Avery and some of the other kids and their families. He was supposed to sit at a table with the hospital bigwigs, but because he was Jesse Jamison, everyone scrambled to accommodate him.

He'd met Avery's mother, of course, several times. But to see everyone in a party setting was surprisingly buoying. Away from the machines and gowns and institutional green walls, the kids were giddy.

Usually when he was at a fancy event like this, the only questions he got asked were what kind of clothing he was wearing or who he was dating.

This was real talk. They talked about music. They talked about the kids' favorite doctors—and their least favorite. They talked about missing school.

They talked about death, and whether to be afraid of it.

It all sort of blew Jesse's mind. It was a living example of what he'd so inexpertly said earlier about getting so much more than he gave with this "charitable" endeavor.

Then Andrea tapped him on the shoulder and cued him that it was time to start the auction.

Damn it. That fucking auction.

But what could he do? He followed Andrea to the stage.

"Everyone's all lined up over there." She pointed at a clump of people milling in a makeshift holding pen to one side of the stage and handed him a program. "Go in the order on the program, as we discussed. Read each person's bio, then open the bidding. I'll be over on the other side of the stage herding them on and off."

"Right." He eyed the program. First up was Juan Ramirez, pediatric anesthesiologist.

Dr. Ramirez was a handsome guy. Jesse worked the crowd, and after a round of spirited bidding, Dr. Ramirez "went" for fifteen hundred dollars to an embarrassed but smiling young woman.

"Winners will collect their dates after the entire auction is over," Jesse read, trying to settle the crowd. "Next up, we have the emergency medicine specialist Dr. Ramona Pope," he said, reading from the program as he'd been instructed to. "Dr. Pope has spent nearly a decade working in critical and acute care settings."

There were three more paragraphs after that, and they looked just as boring. "Okay, let's translate that for those of us who haven't been to a hundred years of medical school. I think that means Dr. Pope is like Doug Ross from *ER*. Remember that show?" Everyone laughed. "What's the funniest emergency you ever had to deal with, Dr. Pope? Kids get weird stuff stuck up their noses, right?"

Dr. Pope was a good sport. She smiled mischievously and

said, "Not to mention other places. But I'd say the weirdest thing I've seen in a nose is a Barbie arm."

The crowd cracked up, and Jesse said, "What do you like to do when you're not, you know, saving defenseless children?"

"Kayak," she said. "Also, I hate cooking, so if someone wants to cook me dinner as part of this date, I'd be super into that."

"All right!" he said, and he started the bidding, auctioning off the charming Dr. Pope for two grand.

And on it went. He kept off script, ad-libbing, joking, and drawing the person on the auction block into bantering with him. The crowd was loving it, and Andrea was smiling and giving him a thumbs-up, so he even had official approval for his deviation from the plan.

He tried not to glance at Hunter waiting off to the side as he went. This didn't seem so bad. For the most part, everyone —auctionees and audience—was taking it in the lighthearted spirit in which it was intended. He had one surgical nurse who was extremely nervous. He couldn't get her to loosen up, and the proceedings became a bit awkward.

But Hunter wasn't interpersonally awkward. Not at all. He had a sense of humor.

But what the hell was Jesse going to say about Hunter?

Hi, here's my best friend. Yes, he is exceedingly attractive, isn't he? Be nice to him—he's had a rough day.

Or: *Here's my best friend. He's looking for love for real, so if the ladies in the crowd will kindly back off...*

Maybe: *This is Hunter. He has a really big heart. Deserve it.*

The question was, was there anyone here who did? He scanned the crowd, unsettled. Then he went through the motions with bachelorette number seven, neonatal ICU nurse Kristi Farmer.

"And next up…" He cleared his throat. "Hospitalist Dr. Hunter Wyatt."

Hunter walked out, smiling self-consciously and waving at the applauding crowd.

Jesse still had no freaking idea what to say. He glanced at the program. As with the other listings, it was several long, boring paragraphs about Hunter's educational background and job duties. With the others, he had suspected the bios didn't do justice to the actual people in front of him. And he'd been right, hadn't he, as evidenced by the fact that they'd learned Dr. Pope liked to kayak but not cook and Nurse Farmer had seen the musical *Hamilton* nine times?

He'd suspected there was more to the others than was written on the piece of paper he held.

With Hunter, he *knew*.

He knew if you wanted Hunter to stop working, you had to physically drag him from his office. He knew Hunter was adorably clueless when it came to handyman stuff. He knew Hunter's patience was so boundless he would examine every stray mark that appeared on Billy's body at any time of the day or night and do it with a smile on his face.

He knew what Hunter's mouth tasted like.

Well, shit.

Everyone was looking at him expectantly.

"So, Dr. Wyatt," he said, "I have to start with the obvious question: what the hell is a hospitalist?"

It broke the ice. Everyone, including Hunter, laughed. He seemed to relax a little as he answered too.

"I'm getting tired of the usual questions, here, and Dr. Wyatt's an old pal of mine," Jesse said, to disguise the fact that his brain was actually completely devoid of questions to ask Hunter. "So let's play a lightning round. Favorite food?"

"Ramen."

"Lark or night owl?"

"Night owl." Jesse should hope so, otherwise all their midnight FaceTimes were going totally against Hunter's natural tendencies.

"Middle name?"

"Edward." Ha. Jesse had known that, but it always sounded so incongruous.

"What would you be if not a doctor?" That would stump him. Hunter couldn't imagine being anything other than a doctor.

"Uh...nurse?"

Jesse cracked up. That was such a "Hunter" answer. "Okay. Cake or pie?"

"Cake."

"Invisibility or superstrength?" Jesse knew the answer already. There wasn't much they hadn't talked about during their late-night tête-à-têtes.

"Superstrength."

Okay, how about one he didn't know? "Boxers or briefs?"

"Boxer briefs."

Damn. He could imagine it. He could imagine it very well. He cleared his throat. "Katy Perry or Jesse and the Joyride?"

"Jesse and the Joyride, of course." Hunter's face lit up with a great big, guileless smile that cut off Jesse's train of thought. Sucked all the intelligence—such as it was—out of Jesse's brain.

Should he ask anything else? He'd been thinking of trying to work in a nod to the fact that Hunter was gay, to signal as much to the audience. But they'd probably read the program, and to hear Hunter tell it, everyone knew anyway.

Nah. Better to get this over with. Even though Hunter

didn't want to be here, Jesse was pretty sure he wasn't having a terrible time so far. That smile suggested as much, right?

"Okay, so let's open the bid—"

"Four thousand dollars!" a woman of about sixty dressed in a sparkly sequined gown shouted. There was a murmur in the crowd. The highest price so far had been four thousand, so to start with that figure suggested the bidder meant business.

Was this the mother from the creepy mother-daughter team? The pet-food-charity woman who'd won Hunter last year and threatened to come after him this time? He glanced at Hunter, whose face had gone totally blank, like his smile of a moment ago had been a mask that had slid off.

It was the same woman. Jesse could tell.

He looked back over the crowd, trying to will someone else into bidding.

"Forty-five hundred," came a voice. He followed it to see a handsome man in a black suit and skinny tie. A *young* man. A man who looked to be of Middle Eastern descent.

Faheem the nurse.

It had to be, given the way the kid was grinning at Hunter and the way Hunter's eyes had briefly widened in alarm before shuttering again.

Damn it.

The crowd, though, was loving it. They hooted when Faheem stepped forward, though Jesse couldn't say whether it was approval or something more like glee with a slight edge of jeering to it. Jesse could sort of see what Hunter meant about feeling like the gay mascot of the event.

"Five thousand," said Lady Sequins.

"Fifty-five hundred," Faheem shot back.

How the hell did a nurse have fifty-five hundred dollars to spend on someone who had already told him he wasn't interested? Also, what kind of a jerk did that? The kid probably thought he was making some sort of grand romantic gesture.

"Six thousand," Lady Sequins called out, sending a withering look at her rival.

Jesse glanced at Hunter. He was watching the proceedings with his lips pressed firmly together in what was probably supposed to be a smile but was actually more like a grimace.

No.

Jesse set the program down on the podium and walked over to Andrea, not looking at Hunter as he passed.

This was not happening.

Not on his watch.

♪♫

Where was Jesse going?

As Jesse made his way over to Andrea, said something in her ear, and then strode off the stage, Hunter had to physically prevent himself from following.

He had arrived at the gala unsure how he was going to get through the auction. Then Jesse had come, and he'd changed his mind to thinking he could bear it as long as Jesse was emceeing.

Seeing Jesse had made all the difference. Not like he had magically waved away the shitty events of the day, but there was something about his presence, his solidity, that steadied Hunter.

And he wasn't just talking metaphorically. That embrace, back there at the pond, had literally given him something—someone—to lean on for a few minutes, and it had felt so good. Knowing someone had his back, unconditionally. That was the best part of couplehood.

He assumed. He'd never really had that with Julian, not

really. How could you have someone's back if you were only selectively acknowledging your partnership with that person? Strangely, he had more of it in his friendship with Jesse than he'd had in his whole relationship with Julian.

After Jesse worked his magic, Hunter had actually started to have fun, which was not a sentiment he had ever expected to associate with this evening. Jesse was, as usual, charming and disarming, totally at ease, even in this environment that wasn't his usual scene.

But then, as things had started getting weird—Faheem and Sandra Worthington the Dog Food Philanthropist both bidding on him—Jesse disappeared? He'd just left?

"Sorry about that." Andrea stepped up to the podium. "Jesse needed to take a break." She smiled a little too widely, obviously uncomfortable with this turn of events. "Shall we continue? Let's see. I believe the bidding on Dr. Wyatt left off at six thousand dollars?" She gestured to Mrs. Worthington.

"Six thousand five hundred," said Faheem, and who the hell did this guy think he was? Did he think he would somehow win Hunter's affection with this creepy behavior? When Hunter had texted him that he didn't think a romantic thing between them was in the cards, Faheem had seemed to take it in stride. But apparently that was only because he'd been retreating to hatch this stalktastic plan. Honestly, he'd rather have Mrs. Worthington.

Which it seemed like he was going to, because she called out seven thousand dollars, and surely that would be the end?

He looked back at Faheem and *fuck off*—the little shit was opening his mouth.

But the voice that rang out over the space came from someone else.

"Twenty thousand dollars."

Jesse.

Standing at the back of the room.

Holy shit.

Everyone gasped. Hunter would have too if he'd had any air left in his body. What the hell was Jesse doing?

Well, he *knew* what Jesse was doing. Jesse understood how not-pleased Hunter was going to be with either of his potential suitors, and he was…intervening.

"Twenty-five thousand," called Mrs. Worthington, her brow furrowing.

Hunter, along with everyone else, looked at Faheem.

He sat down, defeated.

Hunter smiled. He couldn't help it.

"Thirty thousand." Jesse walked forward, his eyes on Hunter.

Mrs. Worthington pressed her lips into a thin line. But then she opened her mouth and said, "Forty thousand."

Okay, this had gone on long enough. Sure, the guy was rich, but there were good deeds and there were good deeds. Hunter could survive another night with the Dog Lady. He shook his head slightly at Jesse, who was still staring intently at him.

"Two hundred thousand dollars," Jesse said calmly.

There was a brief but large uptick in the noise level in the room, then everyone went quiet.

Or maybe it was the blood rushing in Hunter's head causing temporary deafness.

Jesse continued to stare at Hunter, so intently it was almost like he was angry. But that made no sense, because Hunter wasn't making any of this happen. He was just standing there existing.

"How exciting," said Andrea, finally breaking the stunned silence. "We have two hundred thousand dollars on the table for Dr. Wyatt. Are there any other bids?" She looked at Mrs.

Worthington. So did Hunter. So did everyone else. Except Jesse, who kept his laser-like focus on Hunter.

Mrs. Worthington took a step back, and Hunter rejoiced silently.

"No? Two hundred thousand going once. Two hundred thousand going twice... And we have a winner." She grinned. "Well, that was a bit of a thrill."

The room burst into applause, which seemed to startle Jesse from the trance he'd been in. He smiled and jogged back up to the front to join Andrea at the podium.

He winked at the audience. "Dr. Wyatt's an old friend, and I've been meaning to make a donation to the hospital, so I thought I'd drive his price up a little." He looked down at the podium. "Okay, where are we?" He clapped his hands once. "Yes, our tenth and final bachelor is Mr. Ted Jackson, a surgical nurse."

Well, shit.

When Jesse went back to the podium to finish his damned job—there was still one more bachelor to be auctioned off— he was a bit off-kilter.

He'd lost his mind a little, there. The world had shrunk to him and his mission. His imperative.

He felt like he'd come off a bender, except it hadn't been booze fueling his obsessive singlemindedness just then.

It had been Hunter.

The idea of that woman getting her hands on him again, abusing his good will...or, worse, Faheem. Who might *literally* get his hands on Hunter.

No.

He couldn't regret it. Would do it all again. He *had* been

planning to make a big donation to the hospital anyway. Maybe not to the tune of two hundred grand, but whatever.

So, onward.

He bantered with Ted—and felt bad when Ted only fetched three grand. In addition to making a fool of himself bidding on Hunter, Jesse had totally upstaged Ted.

But there. Ted was dispatched and the auction was finally over. What was supposed to happen now? He glanced down at the stack of cue cards he'd abandoned for the auction. Right. There were a couple red ones with his closing remarks on them. Time to go back on script.

The first one had a list of people they wanted him to thank. He ran through them, added his own, and flipped to the last card.

"'This concludes the formal portion of our evening,'" he read. "'We'll start the dancing with our traditional dance of the bachelors and bachelorettes with their successful bidders.'"

Wait. *What?*

Andrea had the bachelors and bachelorettes filing back onto the stage.

He had to force the last sentence out. "'So, winning bidders, please come forward to collect your prizes. Dance, make plans for your date, and have fun.'"

Right. He'd forgotten about that part. He'd been so focused on getting Hunter out of the clutches of Faheem the Creeper and Weird Dog Lady that he hadn't thought through the logical consequences of actually winning.

The DJ started playing. Jesse took several moments longer than required to tidy his cue cards on the podium, trying to think how to handle this.

When he looked up, Hunter was ambling over, his eyes twinkling. Gone was his discomfort from the auction, as well as his pain from earlier in the evening.

There. That alone was worth two hundred grand.

"You. Are. Insane."

Jesse couldn't really argue with that assessment, so he smirked. "I didn't like your prospects."

Hunter shook his head in disbelief. "Let's hit the bar. I, for one, could use a drink."

"What about the dance?" All around them, the winning bidders were collecting their "prizes" and leading them out onto the dance floor.

Hunter's smile dimmed. "Oh, you don't have to dance with me."

You don't have to dance with me.

When Jesse didn't reply right away, Hunter said, "Come on. You did me a solid—a very expensive solid—but you didn't sign up for the dancing-and-dating part."

He started to walk away. Jesse thought about that time he couldn't take Hunter to the Junos.

No, that time he *wouldn't* take Hunter to the Junos.

He thought about that fucker Julian, and all the quiet, unseen damage he'd done to Hunter.

Fuck all that shit.

He jogged to catch up with Hunter, grabbed his arm, and started towing him toward the dance floor.

He would have paid another two hundred grand for the look on Hunter's face—it was surprise, yes, but also pure, unadulterated happiness.

But just for a moment. He shuttered it quickly—it was replaced by a smile tinged with sadness—and reverted to protesting. "Jesse, quit it. You're off the hook."

"What if I don't want to be off the hook?"

Hunter planted his feet and halted their progress, but he didn't pull his arm from Jesse's grip.

"Hey," Jesse tried. "I paid two hundred grand for this

package. It was supposed to include a dance, and I'm damn well getting a dance."

"But you can't," Hunter said, lowering his voice and stepping closer. "People are going to think…"

"People are going to think what? That some deluded rock star did something crazy and now he's dancing with his friend? Big deal."

It *was* kind of a big deal, but Jesse wasn't about to back down now. It was all in how he approached it. How he carried himself. Anyway, it wasn't like they were in public-public. He'd charmed the hell out of this crowd. They weren't going to rush to misinterpret an innocent dance between friends. He'd *told* the crowd that Hunter was an old pal and that he'd been looking for an opportunity to donate to the hospital.

So he kept Hunter's hand and started backing him toward the dance floor. Hunter came reluctantly. "Unless *you* don't want to dance with *me*," he teased. "Afraid I'm going to mar your upstanding reputation, Dr. W.?"

Hunter shook his head and laughed, and more importantly, he kept coming.

"Come on," Jesse exhorted. They were almost there. "The song's half over."

They were playing Louis Armstrong's "What a Wonderful World," which was the perfect song for a bunch of people dancing semiawkwardly with strangers. It wasn't too mushy or too slow, so you could kind of do a shuffle that wasn't a fast dance but wasn't a slow dance either. You could be in each other's arms but not have to be pasted together. It was a song that invited joyous silliness.

So as Jesse led them onto the parquet floor, he traded Hunter's elbow for Hunter's hand, extended his arm, and then reeled Hunter in with an overexaggerated flourish. The joking theatricality kept things light.

They both grinned.

Then Jesse pulled Hunter close to him, reflexively lifting his left hand, which was holding Hunter's right, into the air.

Wait. Was that wrong? That was how he would dance with a woman.

He'd never danced with a man before.

But Hunter didn't seem to mind. In fact, Jesse could feel his body relaxing, like it had outside earlier, by the pond. Hunter laid his other hand on Jesse's shoulder.

"There now," said Jesse, who had no idea where to put *his* other hand—it was hanging awkwardly by his side. "That wasn't so bad was it?"

If Jesse were dancing with a woman, that other hand would have come to rest somewhere on her back. Maybe on her mid-back, under her shoulder blades, if it was a formal thing, if they didn't know each other well. Probably lower if they did.

He wanted to put his hand on Hunter's back.

No, it was stronger than that. It was like Jesse's hand had its own consciousness. It was simultaneously more intelligent and more primal, and it wanted to be on Hunter's back. *Needed* to be on Hunter's back.

The hand floated up, but Jesse forced it to stop short, to land on Hunter's elbow. It was a more casual placement. It went with the whole "We're swaying goofily to this silly song but we're not *really* dancing" vibe.

It was a cop-out.

His hand didn't want to be there, resting on a pointy elbow. It wanted the wide surface area of Hunter's lower back. It wanted room to splay its fingers.

It wanted territory to mark.

Jesse shifted his weight a little, suddenly too hot and hit with an intense infusion of the tie-as-noose sensation.

But Hunter didn't seem to notice anything amiss. "You are…"

"What?"

"You are amazing," Hunter whispered.

Every part of Jesse felt those three words. They were sharp and stinging and…perfect. He had to look away.

The song was ending. Too soon. They'd only just got themselves situated.

Jesse's hand still wasn't where it was supposed to be.

They stood there, swaying until the last strains of the song faded.

And were instantly replaced by the opening notes of "When You're Mine."

Hunter's song.

Holy shit.

But they couldn't know. It was clearly a nod to Jesse's presence as emcee, and the song happened to be the third single from their record, the one that was currently climbing the charts.

Before he could overthink it, Jesse pulled Hunter in. All the way in—into a proper slow dance stance, lining them up from thigh to shoulder and letting that hand slide around and press against Hunter's back. How could he hear Hunter's song and have Hunter in his arms and not?

He realized too late that he was popping a semi.

Had he been too busy anthropomorphizing his hand to pay attention to his dick?

Hunter's eyes went wide.

This was Jesse's cue to back off, his opening to apologize. To step away.

Instead, he leaned over and said, "Do you have shit you still have to do for this shindig? Or can we get out of here?"

It was possible that his dick had taken over for his hand in the driver's seat.

But that didn't seem quite right either, because although he was attracted to Hunter—he had always been attracted to Hunter, if he was being honest with himself—that wasn't his driving force right now. No, he just wanted more time together. He wanted...

"My date. I want my date now."

"Now?" Hunter echoed, looking dazed.

"Yes." Jesse had to fly out to who-the-fuck-knew-where tomorrow to resume the tour, and then it would be another month before it was over. "So are you done here? Do you have official duties to perform still?"

Hunter shook his head.

Jesse enjoyed having struck Dr. Hunter Wyatt dumb.

"C'mon, then." He stepped farther away from Hunter, and all his parts—in symphony—protested. He hitched his head toward the entrance, and once he'd made sure Hunter was following, he used one hand to loosen his tie and the other to order an Uber.

"Where are we going?"

"I have no idea." Where did you go on a date that cost you two hundred grand? But then, he knew. "Ramen?" He'd barely touched his dinner—he'd needed to stay on his toes with the hosting duties and had been chatting with the kids and their families during the brief break in the program—and he was suddenly starving.

"Yeah," said Hunter, and goddamn it, he was gazing at Jesse with something that looked a lot like admiration, or no, something...deeper than that? Something more serious. "Ramen is...perfect."

CHAPTER FOURTEEN

Twenty minutes later, they were ensconced in a little hole-in-the-wall ramen shop near Jesse's house, sitting side by side at the end of the counter, slurping spicy, salty broth in their tuxedos.

Hunter had always admired Jesse's competence, but tonight was almost too much to bear. The way he'd worked that crowd with his unique brand of humor mixed with authenticity. Jesse saw something he wanted, and he went after it, whether that something was an album he envisioned being recorded a certain way or a fundraising goal on behalf of the hospital.

Or Hunter.

To be the object of that intense focus during the auction, where Jesse had thrown out bids like he was using Monopoly money, was something Hunter would never forget.

This was the part where Hunter should remind himself of the rule: *no crushes on straight guys.*

Especially not straight guys who also happened to be his best friend.

But damn.

Could he, for one night, just...let it go?

Pretend the gorgeous, tuxedoed, brilliant man next to him was his? Even if it was only for one date?

One two-hundred-thousand-dollar date.

The money made it so surreal he kind of thought maybe he *could* let himself have that fantasy for one night.

And, honestly, he was pretty sure whatever suspension of reality was happening, it wasn't just him. He hadn't imagined that boner during the dance.

Not that anything would happen beyond the little fantasy he was going to allow to play out in his head. Because whatever was going on with Jesse, whatever had caused that boner when they'd been dancing—whatever had caused that kiss all those months ago—it clearly wasn't something he was willing to acknowledge, even to himself.

Still, it was nice to think, for one fleeting second, that whatever the weird unnameable connection Hunter sensed between them was, Jesse felt it too.

And, if he was being totally honest with himself, even if Jesse was in fact as straight as he claimed, it was super flattering to be the one man in the world who'd tested the boundaries of that straightness.

He glanced at Jesse, who was already looking at him, but Jesse averted his gaze, trying and failing to stifle a smile.

Hunter looked away too, suddenly extremely interested in his almost-empty bowl.

God. It felt like they were on a first date. But not a Faheem-style first date. A *promising* first date. The air was charged, liquid, like an invisible river was flowing between them, its currents swirling around them, softening the edges of everything so the lines between categories, between black and white, between friends and…something else were blurring a little bit.

"You done?" Jesse's voice was husky.

"Yeah."

Jesse reached for his wallet. Hunter did likewise—they usually split the bill when they ate out—but Jesse shook his head.

"You just spent two hundred grand!" Hunter protested, taking out his card. Jesse batted his hand away, caught the waiter's eye, and laid a wad of cash on the table.

Jesse was on his feet then, making an *after you* gesture.

There was a murmur from a group farther down the counter. Hunter had grown familiar with that kind of murmur. Someone had recognized Jesse.

Jesse repeated his oddly chivalrous gesture—he clearly wanted Hunter to precede him out of the restaurant, but then he added a *hurry up* flourish to it, and as someone said, "Is that Jesse Jamison?" Hunter got his ass in gear.

He didn't want to be reminded of who Jesse was. What Jesse was. He didn't want reality right now.

Neither, apparently, did Jesse, because as he held the door for Hunter, he pressed his hand into Hunter's back, applying enough pressure to make his point.

Hunter hoofed it out into the—

"Rain?"

It was pouring.

"Shit." Jesse looked at the sky and then over his shoulder, as if he were expecting pursuers.

Hunter pulled him back under the awning. "Stay here." He moved into his usual protective mode, stepping to the curb and looking both ways. He needed to get Jesse into a cab, but the street was deserted. The heavy rain had sent anyone with a brain scurrying indoors.

Suddenly Jesse was behind him, pressing on his back again.

Hunter turned. A pair of teenaged girls pushed through the door of the restaurant, Jesse clearly in their sights.

Jesse leaned over and whispered in Hunter's ear, "I'll buy you a new tux." Then he grabbed Hunter's hand, and they ran.

"Ahhh!" Hunter shouted, a cross between delight and dismay as they stepped off the curb and into a street awash in ankle-deep water the storm sewers couldn't swallow fast enough.

Jesse whooped, no dismay in his tone, just delight.

They ran. They ran and ran, laughing and panting and holding hands.

The rain soaked through the light wool of Hunter's suit. It squished in his shoes as he tried and failed to leap over puddles. It ran in rivulets down his face. It plastered his hair to his head.

It all should have been uncomfortable.

Instead, on this magically reversed night when the laws of nature—and relationships—seemed to be suspended, it felt like the rain was powering them. Imbuing them with the stamina to keep running indefinitely.

They had long since escaped the girls, but they just kept running along empty, slick streets.

And then, out of nowhere, a flash of lightning lit up the world with a blinding, eerie light. A deafening crack of thunder threatened to rip the sky in half.

In that instant, it seemed like anything was possible. Like the rules hadn't merely been suspended; they'd been transformed. Like *Jesse and Hunter* had been transformed, made into something new and unnameable, like Frankenstein's monster brought to life with a jolt of supernatural electricity.

Jesse must have felt it too, because he stopped running and, panting and grinning like his face was going to crack, repeated the same gesture he'd used to get Hunter onto the dance floor earlier, extending his arm fully, like they were a ballroom dancing pair, then reeling him in. On the dance floor at the gala, the gesture had been formal, graceful, a parody of courtliness. This time it was abrupt, inexpert. Jesse's back hit the brick wall of a building as Hunter hurtled toward him, unable to gain purchase on the slippery pavement to slow himself down.

"Ooof," Jesse huffed, grinning as their torsos collided.

The impact knocked the wind out of Hunter. He panted, trying to get a decent breath in as he grinned stupidly back at Jesse.

The sky ignited again.

Lit up his best friend, the man who meant more to him than anyone.

Lit up Hunter too, somewhere deep inside him, under his skin, which started to prickle, like there was a layer of buzzing, gentle electricity just beneath it, animating him.

Which perhaps explained why, once their chests collided, he hadn't put his hands out to stop his continued forward motion.

Why he'd let their noses collide too.

That saying: *his heart was in his throat*? It wasn't enough. Hunter felt his pulse *everywhere*—in his throat, in his chest, in his temples, under every inch of skin, inside his very brain, beating a kettledrum. If he stood there any longer, he feared it might beat itself outside of his skin. That his body would turn itself inside out. That all the soft, damageable stuff on the inside would be exposed to the storm—and to the man at the eye of it.

He rested his hands lightly on Jesse's throat. There, too, was a drum. Together, they made an entire percussion section.

Jesse hissed at the contact, which made Hunter realize his hands were freezing. Jesse's neck was hot. He started to pull his hands away, but Jesse grabbed them, covered them with his own, slid all four hands down until they were resting at the center of this chest—over his heart, the source of the drumming.

The source of so much else: amazing music, incredible acts of kindness.

Another flash of lightning and crack of thunder.

And people. People right *there*.

The drumming kicked up a notch thanks to the added infusion of panic.

Had they recognized Jesse? No, they were merely regular passersby, talking and laughing under umbrellas.

But their presence galvanized Jesse. He let go of Hunter, stepped away from the wall, and started jogging again. "We'll never find a cab," he said over his shoulder.

Hunter followed. What else could he do? The world was drenched. It was upside-down. And anyway, in the regular world, he would follow Jesse Jamison just about anywhere. In this one, there were no qualifications, no "just abouts."

"Don't talk," Jesse murmured as Hunter caught up with him, so they were running side by side. "Don't talk."

Hunter was down with that plan. Jesse didn't even know how down with it he was, on this through-the-looking-glass night. So he grinned, stuck his steamed-up glasses in his pocket, shook his drenched head like a dog, and kept running.

They quickly covered the half block remaining on the major road they'd been on and turned the corner to the smaller street that would take them to Jesse's house. It seemed impossible that the giddy momentum that had powered them out of the restaurant, down the street, and into each other's arms would continue, but it didn't falter.

A few minutes later, they ran up Jesse's front walk, the right-angle turn in dress shoes on wet pavement making them both start to lose their footing.

"Ahhh!" Jesse half laughed, half shouted as he pivoted and tried to stabilize Hunter, but they were both still moving forward in space, the force of their running too powerful to allow them to come to an orderly halt.

Hunter tried to stop sliding forward, but the flagstone of the walk might as well have been ice. Pitching forward, he crashed into Jesse's chest, knocking him onto his ass about halfway up the short flight of stairs to the porch.

"Ooof," Jesse grunted at the same time Hunter tried to apologize.

There was no room for him to get the words out, though, around Jesse's tongue.

Upside-down. Through the looking glass.

Jesse's tongue was in Hunter's mouth. His arms were banded around Hunter's torso, pulling him in tight, like he was afraid Hunter would float away otherwise, when in fact Hunter was made heavy by his soaking clothes and the weight of his want. His cock was hard and so was Jesse's, and they were pressed against each other and it was *astonishing*.

It wasn't like last time, which was funny, because last time, Hunter had been surprised by how not-proper, how not-polite Jesse's kiss had seemed.

He hadn't known. He hadn't known what it was like to be *devoured* by Jesse Jamison.

There were lips and teeth and tongue everywhere, a dirty, reckless kiss like it was the last night of the world. Like apocalyptic rains had arrived to sweep them away, and they were going to go down fighting.

Jesse worked Hunter's mouth endlessly, sweeping his tongue deep inside again and again. At some point, he must have become satisfied that Hunter wasn't going to bolt, because his arms left Hunter. Hunter felt the loss. It was like being un-hugged. Being granted a freedom he didn't want. Freedom would allow space for second thoughts. It would end this kiss, which, at all costs, must not end. A moan of protest ripped from his chest, surprising him with both its volume and its neediness.

But it was okay, because it turned out the hands were merely moving. They came to rest on the sides of Hunter's face, and an image slammed into his brain, arising through the fog of lust like a TV turned from static to a perfect high-definition image.

"That picture," he mumbled, pulling away enough that he could speak but still touching Jesse's face with his mouth, letting his lips move against Jesse's skin as they formed the words. "That picture from that gossip website."

"Don't talk." Jesse's hands slid back down to where they'd been before, but they hugged Hunter tighter this time.

He didn't want to, understood how talking too much might puncture the fragile casing of this upside-down night. But he had to know. There was one question he needed answered before he could be silent.

"That person you were kissing." He dragged his mouth along Jesse's throat as he talked, relishing the way Jesse writhed beneath him like he simultaneously couldn't stand it and wanted more. Hunter bared his teeth and let them graze against Jesse's stubble, let the scraping sound of bone on flesh roar in his ears. "That picture you showed me on the train."

"Shut up," Jesse growled, hitching one leg around Hunter's waist as his restless, indecisive hands made their way back to Hunter's head and tilted it up, putting them nose to nose for a moment before he plunged his tongue back into Hunter's mouth.

Or tried to. Hunter was stronger than Jesse, when it came down to it. "I will," he said, pulling against Jesse's grip with his upper body at the same time he ground their hips together, a carnal guarantee to back up his vow. "I will shut up, but I have to know one thing first. That person you were kissing in that picture. That wasn't a woman, was it?"

The question stopped Jesse. His entire body halted, like in the games of freeze tag he and Beth and the neighborhood kids used to play.

Well, that wasn't entirely true.

There was still the relentless pounding of his heart, the battle drum that had been the visceral soundtrack to this night.

This could go so many ways.

The answer to Hunter's question could kick off a discussion that never ended. That derailed everything happening here. A discussion he wasn't ready to have right now.

A discussion that could ruin his career.

But a lie wasn't possible. Not to Hunter. Not now.

So he told the truth, as succinctly as he could. "No. It wasn't a woman."

Hunter immediately lowered his mouth back to Jesse's, so the answer must have been enough. Enough to keep this going, anyway.

And, what, Jesse asked himself with his final grasp on rationality, was *this*?

Hunter's hands came to Jesse's face in an echo of their previous position. They were cold, objectively, but he felt them like brands. Like tomorrow he would have a mark on him. Hunter's mark.

But they weren't painful brands. They were like putting the last piece of a jigsaw puzzle in, like wiping a foggy mirror. They were a *relief*. Such a tremendous fucking relief.

He would do anything to get more of that relief. To keep it flowing. Which was why he'd told Hunter to shut up earlier. Why he'd tried to *make* him shut up.

Another flash of lightning—this one at the same time as the clap of thunder. The storm wasn't close anymore; it was upon them.

Hell, maybe it was *in* them.

"Inside," he growled, pressing against the weight of Hunter along his body. As soon as they were upright, he tugged Hunter up the steps to the porch, then let himself be pressed against his own front door from behind. Let his hair be lifted off his neck as he struggled with his key. Shuddered when a hot mouth came down on his wet neck.

When he finally managed to open the door, they stumbled inside, clumsy as their combined weight suddenly had nothing bracing it.

Jesse turned the tables, shoving Hunter against the inside of the door, but not before he slid his hands inside Hunter's sodden suit coat and pushed it down his arms.

Hunter repeated the action with Jesse.

Like a chess game, it was Jesse's move. Hunter was wearing a vest rather than a cummerbund, and Jesse snarled his frustration even as he set to work on the buttons.

Hunter let his head loll back against the door. It might

have been a gesture of solidarity, an expression of his own frustration. It might have been an exhortation.

Jesse chose to take it as the latter, and put his mouth on Hunter's throat, alternately abrading and soothing it with teeth and lips as he worked on the buttons. Hunter smelled spicy, like cloves.

When Hunter was free of the vest, there was, of course, the shirt. The fucking shirt.

Jesse *hated* suits.

Hunter shocked him then by reaching up, undoing his own tie—Jesse had long since stashed his own in his pocket—and sliding a hand in above the top button of his shirt and yanking.

Jesse gasped as the top two buttons popped off. One of them pinged against the wall. The image of Hunter, of proper, dapper Hunter, who had remained flawlessly attired all evening, literally ripping his own clothes off... *Fuck.*

Jesse finished the job for him, ripping open the shirt and sending the rest of the buttons flying. Then he repeated his earlier gesture, sliding the shirt off Hunter's arms to join the jacket on the floor.

He'd seen Hunter's chest before, of course, every time they'd been at the cottage as well as that time Hunter had saved them from Russell by pretending to be getting into it with Jesse. But he'd never seen it heaving like this. Jesse reached around Hunter and flipped on the entryway light because, suddenly, he needed to see. Needed to fill the space with light.

Yes. He'd never seen that chest accompanied by the hunger in those eyes. Flashing like the fucking pot of gold at the end of the rainbow.

Hunter lunged at Jesse, and time was looping in on itself, because once again, they were stumbling forward together.

Once again, they were stymied by a flight of stairs, this time the one to Jesse's second floor. Once again, Jesse was on his back, sprawled out over the stairs. He tilted his head up, lifting his face for more kisses. Without the rain cramping their style, Jesse was pretty sure he could kiss Hunter forever.

But then the time loop got unstuck and lurched forward: Hunter undid Jesse's pants, shoved them down along with his boxers.

There was a momentary pause as they stared at each other, panting. Less than a second. Long enough for Hunter to let loose a predatory growl.

Jesse closed his eyes against the golden, glowing beauty in front of him. He needed a break, just a tiny one.

"Is this okay?" Hunter whispered. Jesse nodded, knowing what Hunter was asking even with his eyes closed.

They flew open when Hunter took Jesse's cock into his mouth.

"Oh my God," Jesse bit out, his hands flying up into the air like he was in a gospel choir, as an electric sensation shot through him. His whole body was a live wire, conducting a current that came from Hunter.

He left his hands up there, reaching for the heavens, not knowing what to do with them.

He wanted to bring them down on Hunter's head. To anchor it while he thrust into Hunter's mouth.

But he couldn't do that. This wasn't some slutty hookup, some guy he would never see again and could use accordingly.

This was his best friend.

No. He couldn't think that way. If he thought too much about that, he would stop. And he couldn't stop. He needed this. This relief.

So he let his hands settle lightly in Hunter's hair, his

strangely beautiful gray hair. He didn't press against Hunter's head like he wanted to, though. He held himself back.

Hunter moaned and took Jesse in deeper, almost to the root—almost as if Jesse *had* exerted pressure on his head. Did he *want* Jesse to?

Fuck. He didn't know how to do this. How to read signs. How to take what he wanted without taking too much.

How to give something back.

He let the pads of his fingers press against Hunter's scalp, let them massage it a little. He was rewarded with another moan. Another deep stroke that felt so fucking amazing his vision blurred.

Hunter rearranged his body to free his hands. He'd been kneeling a few steps below Jesse, using his hands on the step below Jesse to brace himself, but now he settled his hands on the fronts of Jesse's thighs, even as he kept working Jesse's cock with his mouth.

Jesse's quads flexed of their own volition, almost like they were straining up to meet Hunter's touch. Pressure gathered at the base of his spine.

Hunter kept sucking, humming his desire as he bobbed up and down on Jesse's dick—his dick that had never been harder. It was different with a guy. It just was.

Or maybe it was different with *Hunter*.

Jesse let his head fall back on the step behind him. It was the same impulse as before, the sense that if he didn't take a small break from watching, he might die. Or cry. Or something.

And, as before, his moment of visual inattention was rewarded. Or maybe punished? He had no idea—maybe it was both at the same time.

Hunter's hands slid around the sides of Jesse's hips. Tapped them. They wanted Jesse's ass, access to which was obscured by the step he was sitting on.

He lifted his hips obediently. Right now, in this crazy moment, Hunter fucking *owned* him.

Hunter levered his hands between Jesse and the step he was sitting on, grabbed an ass cheek with each hand and, manually thrusting Jesse's pelvis forward, pulled Jesse even deeper into his mouth. He'd made a vice, trapping Jesse between his face and his hands, and Jesse hadn't known. He'd had no idea that—

"Oh fuck," Jesse bit out, taking the gesture as permission to thrust a little, and— "Oh my God, oh fuck, Hunter."

Then, God help him, a finger started circling his hole. He had to bite back a scream. He didn't know whether to continue bucking forward into Hunter's mouth or back onto Hunter's finger. The urges were equally strong.

The finger didn't breach him, just stroked along the edges. "Holy fuck."

He wanted more. He wanted— Too late. He was coming, a pleasure so intense it was almost painful washing over him.

He would have pulled out if he'd had any warning, but the orgasm—both its arrival and its force—shocked him. He still tried to, but Hunter held on as best he could. The result was that Hunter partially swallowed, but the rest ended up on his face.

Jesus Christ. Jesse never would have done that on purpose. Wouldn't have dreamed of such presumption, but the sight of Hunter, the fucking sight of him, face flushed, lips swollen, gold eyes incandescent, with Jesse's come on his face...Jesse's throat tightened. That sense he'd had before that he might cry returned.

But there was a stronger pull at work, something that underlaid the urge to cry, and he needed to focus on that. Not only because he didn't want to cry, but because this was Hunter, who deserved everything. Jesse couldn't manage everything, not even close, but he could do *this*.

"Get up," he said gruffly.

Too gruffly, maybe, because those beautiful eyes, which had been burning with desire, suddenly widened in shock and...hurt?

He softened his tone and tried again. "Get up." A slow smile spread across his face. "And take your pants off." He pushed gently against Hunter's shoulders as he spoke. "We're going upstairs."

With Hunter off him enough that he could stand, he hiked his pants up, turned, and started up the stairs, trusting Hunter would follow.

Please let Hunter follow. Please don't let reality come crashing in yet.

He wanted to return the favor. *Needed* to return the favor. Even though he had no fucking idea what he was doing.

"Why am I taking my pants off while you appear to be putting yours back on?"

Jesse cracked up. "It's merely a temporary measure. I can't walk with them halfway down my legs."

Thank God his explanation worked. Reality was not yet going to intrude: Hunter was taking his pants off, and, for now at least, all was right with the world.

Hunter couldn't get over Jesse's cock.

It was big and pink and uncut and...glorious.

He was fixated.

Generally, just as Hunter didn't really have a type, he didn't care that much about the particulars of dicks. Cut, uncut, large, not-so-large, whatever. He liked them all. He wasn't picky.

Or at least he'd thought he wasn't.

But, God, once he'd clapped eyes on Jesse's, which seemed so…perfectly Jesse—which was dumb, but it was how he felt —he'd needed it in his mouth. He'd needed it as deeply in his mouth—his throat—as was physically possible.

The ridiculous thing was he hadn't even been thinking that much about Jesse.

Well, that wasn't true. He'd been surrounded by Jesse. His smell, mixed with the smell of the rain they'd brought in with them from outside. The still-astonishing vision of him walking forward at the gala, forcefully bidding on Hunter at the action. Hunter even heard little snippets of Jesse's music, for God's sake, a tape playing on a loop in his head.

His senses were *infused* with Jesse.

So it wasn't correct to say he hadn't been thinking about Jesse. It was more that he hadn't been thinking about Jesse's *pleasure*.

Selfish fool that he was, he'd only been thinking of his own.

About getting more of that Jesse-ness that was all around him.

And since he couldn't climb inside Jesse, that had apparently translated into trying to swallow his dick.

"Ha!" The syllable exploded out of him, half amusement, half genuine joy.

"Are you coming, you nutbar?"

Jesse was already at the top of the stairs. Maybe even in his bedroom. Hunter could hear him but no longer see him, and that was, suddenly and decidedly, unacceptable.

Kicking off the second leg of his pants, Hunter hightailed it up the stairs. Probably to his doom, but the prospect of doom wasn't as strong as the still-ubiquitous sense of Jesse-ness that permeated the space around him. Permeated *him*.

He could not let that fade.

He took a deep breath at the doorway to Jesse's room, steeling himself on the threshold, though for what, he wasn't sure. Rejection? The best sex of his life? Either seemed equally likely.

What he saw made him laugh again. "You *did* take your pants back off." *And the fact that you did so is unexpectedly, utterly delightful.*

"Of course I did." Jesse heaved himself backward onto his bed. "Though I don't need them off for what's going to happen next." He beckoned Hunter, and *God*, lounging there with his muscles and his tattoos and his long hair, he should have been a painting.

"What's going to happen next?" Hunter's dick led the way as he obeyed Jesse's summons.

When he reached the bed, Jesse rose onto his knees, walked on them to the edge, grabbed Hunter, and fell back, pulling Hunter down on top of him. Then he flipped them, using the weight of his body to pin Hunter to the bed.

"What's happening next is I am going to attempt to blow you." Jesse moved down Hunter's torso as he spoke.

"'Attempt'?" Hunter chuckled and reached down to tuck a loose strand of Jesse's hair behind his ear. Jesse made it sound like it was an exam rather than a blowjob.

"Well, I'm *going* to blow you. I just might not be any good at it. I've never done it before."

What? "Hang on a sec. I thought—"

Jesse stuck out his tongue and licked from the base of Hunter's dick to the tip in one long, firm, wet stroke.

Oh my God. "Jesse, you don't have to—"

The tongue started at the tip this time, swirling around the head. Then it zoomed all the way back down and kept going. "I want to," Jesse whispered, just before he started lapping at Hunter's balls.

"Ahhh," Hunter moaned, trying again to find words that would make sense of the situation. It was harder this time— what he wanted to say had receded from his reach. "Jesse."

"How about you stop talking, Doc?" Jesse said, right before he took Hunter's cock into his mouth.

It worked. There were no more words. Speech was no longer possible.

Jesse Jamison was sucking his dick.

His beautiful, talented friend. The man among men.

Hunter lay back on the bed, propping himself up on his elbows so he could see, and surrendered.

Jesse wasn't taking Hunter very deeply. Was holding on to the base of Hunter's cock with a fist and moving his mouth up and down a few inches. But his mouth was hot, and, as he applied suction, so deliciously, perfectly tight.

His hair had fallen over his face, though, making a curtain that separated him from Hunter.

"Move your hair," Hunter said, the command coming out gruffer than he'd intended.

Jesse paused, mouth near the head of Hunter's dick, and Hunter entertained a momentary, panicked thought that he might stop. That couldn't happen.

"I want to see you," he explained, allowing himself to thrust his hips forward slightly, enough to communicate that he didn't want them to break contact. It was why he had tucked the hair behind Jesse's ear earlier. "If you're going to do this, I want to see you." *I want to memorize you.*

Jesse used his free hand to pull his hair back. He looked up at Hunter, a question in his eyes, even as he kept sucking.

"Yes." Hunter stroked one of Jesse's hollowed-out cheeks. "Exactly like that."

"Mmm." The smile in Jesse's eyes as he hummed around Hunter's dick just about did him in. Hunter bore down, trying to slow the oncoming train.

This is Jesse, his mind kept chanting. *Jesse. Jesse is sucking you off.*

And now he could see it all perfectly.

And Jesse could see him. They maintained eye contact as Jesse kept working Hunter's dick, his cheeks hollow and his eyes wide, and—

"Oh God! I'm not going to last," Hunter bit out, shoving Jesse off him. Jesse didn't need a mouthful of come his first time.

His orgasm shot through him. Jesse replaced his mouth with his hand and jacked Hunter as he shouted and came, his hips jerking manically as light exploded all around him like the lightning outside.

It took a while to come back to himself, but once he did, he found his voice. His words. His question. It was right there on his lips, demanding to be asked.

"You've never done that before? I thought the guy in the picture…"

But the picture had been of a kiss. Shit. He had sort of assumed, once things had…started happening between them, that Jesse had some experience with guys that he'd been keeping secret. And, damn, he would have done things differently before, on the stairs, if he'd known. Been gentler. "You've never been with a guy before?"

"I've been with a few guys." Jesse heaved himself up and turned over onto his back, lying next to Hunter so they were both looking up at the ceiling. "Years ago. When the opportunity presented itself. It's just that it's always been my dick in their mouth and never vice versa."

Hunter barked a laugh. Of course it had. Jesse the rock star was nothing if not consistent. When the world was salivating over your dick, there was no need to return the favor, right?

He wanted to ask a million more questions, starting with *Who were those guys? Did anything happen besides blowjobs?* And, most importantly, *What the hell?*

Why hadn't Jesse ever told Hunter any of this?

Also: *What's going to happen now?*

With that last question, fear started to curl around the edges of his mind.

He moved onto his side, propping his head on his hand.

Jesse turned his head, made quick eye contact, and then looked back at the ceiling. "Don't ask me the questions."

Hunter decided to play dumb, decided to pretend Jesse couldn't read his mind. "What questions?"

"The millions of questions swirling around your head right now."

Damn. How did he *do* that?

"I know you deserve answers, but can we just...not? Not right now? Can I just have my date night and..." He trailed off, rolling his eyes in self-disgust.

"I was only going to ask about your tattoos," Hunter lied.

That drew Jesse's attention, and his head swiveled over once more. "What about them?"

"Can I look at them?" Hunter could see Jesse starting to protest. "*Really* look at them," he added, because he knew Jesse was going to say that Hunter had already seen them.

Jesse seemed startled, but he nodded.

Hunter sat up. He needed answers to the real questions, but for now, he'd surf right over those waves of panic and do what he'd wanted to do since that first day at the lake. He kneeled over Jesse's chest.

There was so much to see. Jesse's chest and arms were covered with a swirling mixture of words and foliage and flowers.

He let his hand trail over one shoulder, leaning closer to read some words there. "These are song lyrics?"

"Yes," Jesse said, his voice solemn, low. He stared at Hunter, saying nothing more as Hunter used his hands to guide his gaze, sweeping methodically over Jesse's skin so he wouldn't miss anything.

He recognized snippets from Jesse's songs as well as some unfamiliar phrases.

"You don't have any tattoos, do you?" Jesse asked.

"No."

Jesse nodded as if that was the answer he'd expected. "It offends your sense of order."

That was…exactly right. Hunter had never thought about it like that, but it was true. Covering his body with ink was so far from being something Hunter could imagine doing. It was part of why he was compelled by Jesse's tapestry.

"What's this?" Hunter moved down to the top of Jesse's rib cage, just below his pecs, tracing the word *Imagine*.

"John Lennon," Jesse said.

"Ah."

Jesse shifted then, like he wanted to wiggle free.

Hunter wasn't done—he wasn't remotely done—but what could he do? He could hardly pin Jesse here, hold him against his will.

Jesse rolled over. "I've got a new one."

Hunter let his gaze fall to the lone tattoo on Jesse's back. More words, tattooed over his shoulder blade: *I'll set down my burden.* They were flanked by an old-fashioned curtain, the red velvet kind seen in old-school theaters.

Hunter gasped. "'I'll set down my burden and draw back the curtain,'" he said, recognizing the graphical representation of a line from "When You're Mine." He traced the image with his fingertips.

"Yes," Jesse said quietly.

Hunter loved "When You're Mine," and it was a bit of a shock to realize Jesse had tattooed it on himself. It must be hugely significant for Jesse too, to have earned a permanent place on his body.

The song was about unrequited love. It started out mournful and slow, the narrator singing about wanting someone he couldn't have, but then it became more up-tempo as the narrator imagined an alternative world where his love was returned, gradually building momentum until a triumphant bridge. But then it ended with a final verse, apart from the others, where the singer remembered that it was all just a fantasy. It was a great song, so infectious but then so unexpectedly gutting at the end.

Hunter lowered his hands. He wasn't going to press for answers to his questions this evening, but he was going to seize the opportunity to touch Jesse, knowing it might be his last. "This is my favorite song from the new album. My favorite of all your songs, actually."

Jesse shivered under his hand and, looking over his shoulder, found Hunter's gaze. "Is it?"

"Yes. It's like…a happy song and a sad song rolled into one." That sounded dumb, didn't it?

Jesse nodded, though, like he wasn't surprised by Hunter's interpretation. "We're going to start filming a video for it as soon as we come off the tour."

Something about Jesse's tone seemed off, like he disapproved of this turn of events.

"But you don't want to?"

"I do. I just don't like the concept the director is pitching."

"Which is?"

"Your basic thwarted love narrative. I play my guitar by a rainy window and look plaintive."

"That doesn't sound so bad. It basically *is* a thwarted love narrative, no?"

Jesse, who'd been craning his neck to look at Hunter, sighed and stopped craning, which left him gazing to the side of the room. "They want Kylie to play the love interest. Matty approached her without asking me. She's agreed."

Hunter lifted his hands from Jesse's back. Kylie was a reminder that they didn't belong there.

"It will stir up rumors of a reconciliation," Jesse said, his voice flat, like he was reciting lines in a play he didn't particularly want to be in. "Draw lots of media attention to the video that it wouldn't otherwise get." He scoffed. "Or so they say."

Hunter couldn't argue with the theory. Sticking Kylie Cameron in a Jesse and the Joyride video would have the tabloids frothing at the mouth. "Who are *they*?"

"Matty. Peter, our A&R rep at the label. The guys. Everyone. But mostly Matty, the brains of the operation."

Hunter didn't generally have any problem with being naked. He wasn't modest that way. But, suddenly, he needed clothes. He slid off the bed and moved to the door, intending to head to the guest room, where he'd been staying while Jesse was away, to find his pajamas.

"This is the part where I'm supposed to say I'm sorry, right?" Jesse said.

Hunter turned, his hand still on the doorknob. Jesse had

flipped over and was lounging back against the headboard, seemingly unselfconscious about his nudity.

Hunter sighed. "No, *I'm* sorry. If I'd known that you hadn't…"

He didn't know how to finish the sentence. He could hardly say, *If I'd known that your experience with guys was limited to a few illicit liaisons, I wouldn't have swallowed your dick and almost stuck my finger in your ass.* God. A few hours ago, he'd been operating under the assumption that Jesse was straight. Then that assumption had been upended—dramatically and suddenly. But only temporarily, it seemed, because then Jesse had said he'd only fooled around with guys when the *"opportunity presented itself."*

God. His mind was spinning.

"Well, I'm *not* sorry."

Hunter gasped. He actually gasped. The sentence had been delivered with such vehemence, such feeling, it took his breath away.

He met Jesse's eyes. They glittered. Burned. Like they were daring him to object.

"The only thing I'm sorry about," Jesse continued, "is that my plane leaves in six hours."

Right. Jesse, regardless of his degree of queerness, was leaving. Going back to his real life.

The upside-down world righted itself. The drumbeat soundtrack that had been powering this extraordinary night went silent.

Jesse was going to Pittsburgh. It would be an international flight. He would need to get to the airport a couple of hours ahead of time. And the band did their sound checks at two in the afternoon, so he'd have to go right there from the plane. Tomorrow was going to be a long day for him. "You should sleep for a couple hours."

"Yes." Jesse lifted his arms up, like kids did when they wanted to be hugged.

What?

Hunter's confusion must have been written on his face, because, still keeping his arms aloft, Jesse said, "Come here." Then he waggled his fingers. "Sleep with me."

Hunter was gobsmacked.

He couldn't just...do that. Not without getting his questions answered. Not without knowing what it all meant.

Could he?

Hunter's recent Tinder hookup had not included a sleepover. The last time he'd slept—slept as in *slept*—with someone had been Julian.

No. Wait. That wasn't right.

The last time he'd slept with someone had been Jesse. By the fire at the cottage.

He wondered what it would be like to wake up in Jesse's arms in a fluffy warm bed instead of on the lumpy cold ground. He wondered what it would be like to sleep skin to skin.

No, that wasn't right, either. He didn't *wonder*. There was no idle conjecture going on here. He yearned to know. Burned to know.

"Get in the bed, Hunter."

He got in the bed.

Then: a lovely, slow sinking sensation. The cessation of effort, of surrendering his weary body to a soft bed.

Or to a hard chest.

Jesse had maneuvered them so he was spooning Hunter. His hands came to Hunter's neck, and he pressed against the taut muscles there. Just like at the pond, but this time they were horizontal and naked.

Hunter's eyes slipped closed in ecstasy as the massage continued.

"You've had such a long day," Jesse whispered.

Hunter wanted to argue that if that was true for him, it was doubly true for Jesse, who'd performed last night and then flown in to do the gala.

But the softening that was occurring in his neck muscles seemed to have infected his jaw. All that came out when he tried to speak was an inarticulate, "Mmmph." He tried again, "Jesse, I—"

"Shhh. I know everything's weird," Jesse whispered in his ear, stopping the massage and pulling Hunter's back flush to his chest. "We'll talk in the morning. Sleep now."

CHAPTER FIFTEEN

They did not talk in the morning.

Because Jesse was a fucking coward.

He always had been. What was that line from Beth's new therapist she was forever quoting? *"You can't change people."*

Which was why he left the note.

Jesse told himself he couldn't bear to wake Hunter. It was a convincing enough lie to propel him out of bed and out of the house. Hunter had been so beautiful when he was asleep. Well, he was always beautiful, but that morning, there had been such an exquisite vulnerability about him. He looked so young, even with the gray hair. Jesse hated to think of the world weighing heavily on his friend—of entitled socialites and dying kids and all that bullshit.

He wanted to protect Hunter from all of it. The idea that he might have succeeded, at least last night, made Jesse feel like that asshole Leonardo DiCaprio on the *Titanic*: "I'm the king of the world." He wasn't sure which had been the better feeling: the moment Hunter had wrapped his lips around Jesse's dick or the moment Hunter had come into his arms and lay back against his chest, trusting Jesse enough to lay down his burdens, set aside his unanswered questions, and sleep.

But, later, on the plane, Jesse forced himself to be objective about the situation. Between dying kids and entitled socialites, Hunter had indeed had a hell of a day yesterday.

Probably, though, all that paled in comparison to asshole rock stars wreaking havoc in his life and then not even sticking around long enough to answer a few totally fucking reasonable questions. Jesse hadn't even been able to face his sister after such a shitty move—he'd begged off seeing her and Gavin.

It was just that as he'd lain there this morning, awake before Hunter, he'd started to think of Matty. Matty the rainmaker, who'd done exactly what he promised: done his stupid "branding," cleaned up the mess Jesse had made, and transformed the band into a powerhouse.

Delivered Jesse's heart's desire.

He sighed as the plane touched down in Pittsburgh. There was going to have to be a reckoning with Hunter. He understood that—he wasn't *that* much of a dick. All he'd done, he could see now, was postpone it.

But first, he had a sound check.

Good. Sound check would be a kick in the ass. A good way to steel himself. A reminder of his first principle, which was increasingly painful but no less true for it.

He would do anything to protect the music.

Three days had passed since Jesse left, and Hunter couldn't get one phrase out of his mind: *pity fuck*.

Two little words. Eight letters.

They should not have had such power.

But there they were, floating just below Hunter's

consciousness pretty much all the time. At the most inappropriate times, actually.

"What's the matter with you, Dr. W.?"

"What?" *Crap*. Avery. "Sorry. I was daydreaming for a minute there."

Day-nightmaring was maybe a better word for it. Glazing everything he thought had happened two nights ago with a thin wash of his new favorite phrase: *Pity fuck*.

Avery had come to town for a checkup with her cardiologist, and she and her mom had popped into his office to say hi—and to share the happy news that her latest test results were all good. It was looking like they wouldn't need to get her on the transplant list for a few more years.

He held himself back from ruffling her hair. She was twelve now—not a little kid anymore. This must be a taste of how parents felt. One day you had a little kid. Then you blinked.

"Avery, will you invite me to your wedding?" he asked impulsively.

Her brow furrowed. It was the wrong question. He'd meant it only as a wish, a prayer. A promise that he would see her survive. That he would be able to mark a big, adult milestone with her, like a wedding. But it had been a poor example. He shouldn't make bullshit hetero-normative assumptions about how anyone's life was going to play out, much less a pediatric patient's.

"Or to your college graduation," he said. That made more sense.

"We'll invite you to *everything*," Lisa, Avery's mom, said, her voice quiet but resolute. She was leaning against the doorframe of Hunter's office, like Jesse used to do.

"How come you're not married?" Avery asked with her

signature forthrightness, swiveling the guest chair she was seated on back and forth.

Good question. Julian had talked about it sometimes, but Hunter had always brushed it off. Maybe some part of him had known from the start that the lie they were living wasn't going to sit right with him indefinitely. That it would eat away at him until there was more gangrene than healthy tissue left. But he couldn't deny it was something he secretly wanted, someday. What could he say? He went in for all the heteronormative romantic crap he'd just been reminding himself not to project onto Avery.

"It's harder for me," he said slowly, trying to think how to answer her question. They'd never talked about it, but Avery and her family knew he was gay. It wasn't a secret. It had been right there in the program at the gala they'd all attended.

"Gay marriage was legalized in Ontario in 2003," she said, and her inflection suggested 2003 was so far in the past, it might as well have been 1903. But, he supposed, 2003 was more than a lifetime ago for her.

He shared an amused smile with her mom. "It's not that. It's more the odds. Only a small proportion of the population is gay. So finding a match sometimes seems like finding a needle in a haystack."

Avery nodded, like she understood. But then she made a full rotation in her chair and said, "I miss Jesse. Don't you?"

Hunter tried to conceal his surprise at being thrown that curveball.

"I do," he said, because it was the right thing to say in the circumstances but also because it was true.

Missed him so much he almost felt sick.

Pity fuck.

When he looked back on the extraordinary events of the other night, he no longer knew how to interpret them. Not that he ever had—Jesse had promised they'd talk the next morning, but then Hunter had awoken to that bullshit note.

Couldn't bear to wake you. Talk soon. —J.

Jesse bidding on him at the auction had seemed, as it was unfolding, a gesture that was both grand and kind. Befitting of Jesse. Of the larger-than-life rock star, who was, at his core, and no matter how much he tried to project otherwise with his manager's "bad-boy" label, a really nice guy.

Rationally, Hunter understood Jesse had done it because he'd felt bad. He hadn't wanted Hunter stuck with Faheem or with Mrs. Worthington. Hunter had, at the time, interpreted it more as a friend doing a friend a solid. A really big, really expensive solid, but that was Jesse for you.

But maybe it had just been pity.

Maybe it had *all* been pity, the auction and everything that had happened afterward.

But then…that was ridiculous. People didn't have sex with their best friends out of pity. Did they?

It had been real in the moment. He'd seen the effect he'd had on Jesse.

Maybe… Shit. After all, they hadn't spoken.

On the other hand, it had only been three days. They had gone three days without talking during the tour.

Not very often, though, and never without a few texts.

He was going crazy. Gaslighting himself.

"Did you know he invited me to a show? He said I could come to any of them."

Damn it, what was the matter with him? He was at *work*, for God's sake. Talking to a former patient. Time to shake off the existential crisis and do his damn job.

"That sounds like him," he said, schooling his voice to neutrality.

"My mom said I could go if you signed off," she said, grinning goofily.

"That's why we're here, really," said Lisa. "The cardiologist said it was okay if we took precautions, but I'm not sure about her getting on a plane. I know enough time has passed, and she has to live her life, but I worry so much about infection. And we…well, we trust you more than anyone."

Hunter's chest warmed at the praise. "What about going to see them in Buffalo? Then you could drive. I think they have a show there soon?"

They had a show there five days from now. He knew because he knew everything about the current Jesse and the Joyride tour.

"That's a great idea," said Lisa. "I think we could all use some fun." But then she quickly followed that with, "Oh, but I don't want to presume that he'll give us four tickets."

"I'm sure he will," said Hunter.

Avery clapped her hands in glee. "Will you ask him?"

Hunter was tempted to tell Avery to ask him herself. She had his number. But he was the adult here. Was he going to let his own neuroses get in the way of doing his job? Of making one of his all-time favorite patients happy?

"Sure," he said, trying to infuse the word with enthusiasm he did not feel.

Funny that his first contact with Hunter, after their initial meeting on the train, had also been on Avery's behalf. Of course, it was different now, because of everything that had happened. Because…

Pity fuck.

♫

Jesse stared at his phone. Like maybe he could press Send with the power of his mind.

His finger certainly wasn't cooperating. It was shaking like a goddamned leaf.

It was just a stupid, inconsequential text.

```
How's Avery? How's everything? Show was shit
tonight.
```

But he was too much of a fucking coward to send it. Maybe he should take a shower. He'd retreated to his room after the aforementioned shit-tastic show—both Cleveland and wherever the fuck they were now (Indianapolis? Minneapolis?) had not been shows for the record books—and composed The Text That Could Not Be Sent before doing anything else, including changing out of his sweaty stage clothes.

Fine. Shower. Maybe the hot water would clear his head.

He stripped and sighed. The problem was not the text. The problem was—

Hunter's custom ringtone rang through the silent, dark hotel room. Jesse pivoted and tripped over his guitar as he lunged for the phone on the nightstand.

"Fuck!" he shouted as his toe caught on the corner of the metal bedframe. Pain lanced through him. He ignored it. All that mattered was he get to the phone.

If Jesse had thought his hands were shaking like a leaf before, now his petal-fragile fingers were being battered by a hurricane.

```
Hunter: Avery wants to come to your Buffalo
show.
```

That was it?

But what the fuck did he expect? He was the jerk who'd left the breezy note. He was the asshole seemingly bent on glossing over everything that had happened between them. And now he was gonna get pouty when he was getting what he wanted?

```
Jesse: Of course. I'd love to have her. Is
she up to it?
```

```
Hunter: Yes. We had her in for her one-year-
postsurgery checkup, and her cardiologist is
really pleased with how she's doing.
```

Jesse pumped his fist like he'd just gotten a Grammy nomination.

```
Jesse: Awesome. I'll have Amber get in touch
with her tomorrow to work out details. Tell
her—and I'll tell Amber—that if she can be
here early enough for the sound check, we'd
love to have her at that too.
```

There was no immediate reply.

Fuck. It was up to him. He'd signaled the way things were going to be with that stupid note, and Hunter had taken the cue. If Jesse wanted…something else, if he wanted his friend back even, it was up to him.

The fingers-as-leaves-in-a-storm metaphor was still apt as he painstakingly typed.

```
Jesse: Will you come too?
```

```
Hunter: Do you want me to?

Jesse: Yes.
```

The floaty bubble things that indicated Hunter was typing a reply appeared. Then they disappeared. Then reappeared.

Jesus Christ. He felt like he was in a game show where he had chosen curtain one over curtain two, and he was waiting to see what his future would be. Only instead of *nothing* versus *a new car*, it was, *nothing* versus...*everything*.

Fuck that shit. He wasn't waiting for the bubbles. He banged out a reply, his hands steady this time.

```
Jesse: Look, I know we need to talk. I know
I made everything weird. Come to the show.
We'll talk. The next day is an off day. I
was going to head back to Toronto, but we
can discover the deindustrialized wonders of
Buffalo instead, maybe?
```

He had no fucking idea what he was going to say during this "talk," but he'd figure that out. Or, more likely, he wouldn't, and he'd make a hash of things again. Regardless, he needed Hunter with him. He knew that now with certainty. Something about having him right on the other end of the phone crystalized how much he missed Hunter, regardless of what had happened between them in the past or would happen between them in the future.

There was no answer to his text, though.

"Damn it!" He pounded the mattress.

All right, then. One more try.

```
Jesse: I miss you.
```

It was the unvarnished truth.

After that, the answer came right away.

Hunter: OK.

His second fist-pumping victory in the space of five minutes.

Hunter: How was the show tonight?

Relief surged through him. He had Hunter back. In some format, anyway.

Jesse: It was shit.

As he typed, he slumped back against the headboard, limp with relief and... Noticed his toe was bleeding like crazy? What the hell?

Hunter: Why? What happened?

Damned if he was going to leave Hunter hanging with no reply, no matter if he was bleeding out the Red Sea here.

Jesse: Hang on a sec. I'm bleeding. BRB.

He got up and hobbled to the bathroom for towels.

The sound of Hunter's ringtone echoed through the room. Several times.

"Damn it!" Grabbing a couple of towels, he hopped back to the bed and picked up the phone.

There was a string of texts from Hunter.

What?

Like actually bleeding?

What happened?

And now there was an incoming FaceTime.

The mini medical emergency was a blessing, really, because he didn't have time to freak the fuck out before he picked up.

"What happened? Are you okay?"

And there was Hunter, concern unfurling across his beautiful face. Jesse couldn't stop looking at the phone. Hunter was wearing a tank top and he was in Jesse's living room, but he was standing, as if the news of Jesse's injury had brought him to his feet.

"Yeah, I'm fine. I stubbed my toe on the bed frame a bit ago, and I didn't notice I'd actually cut it."

Because I was too busy falling over myself to get to the phone. To get to you.

"It's actually pretty impressive looking in here," he said, surveying the previously white sheets on which he'd unknowingly been resting his bleeding foot. "Very Bates Motel. It's good. I haven't destroyed a hotel room on this tour yet. I'm falling down on the job. Matty's going to be on my case for not being 'bad' enough to maintain my rep."

"Let me see your toe."

"It's fine."

"Let me see it." Hunter scowled and a certain pissy bossiness had crept into his tone.

"I'm not Billy. I don't need a video exam."

"Show me your goddamned toe, Jesse."

"Okay, sheesh. Hang on." He set the phone down temporarily, hoisted his leg onto the bed and gingerly removed the towels he'd been using to staunch the blood. There was a deep cut there, but it was clean, and it seemed to be done bleeding. He turned on the bedside lamp, aimed the phone at his foot, and reversed the camera.

"You're going to need a stitch or two in that."

Jesse made a dismissive noise. He didn't have time for stitches.

"Turn me around," Hunter said, still with the bossy voice. "Look at me."

Jesse reversed the phone and got himself situated against the headboard, belatedly realizing he was still naked—he'd come bolting out of the shower when Hunter had originally texted, and he hadn't yet gotten dressed. He pulled the covers up over himself.

Hunter cleared his throat. "The bed frame was metal?"

"Yup."

"When was your last tetanus shot?"

Hunter was in efficient-doctor mode. It was pretty cute. "I have no idea."

"Ask for a booster when you get your stitches."

Jesse didn't say anything, but Hunter must have—correctly—interpreted his silence as lack of enthusiasm for this plan. It was just that he hated doing stuff like finding a doctor on the road. It fucked with their finely honed routine.

"Listen to me," Hunter said, slipping into full-on Lecturing Doctor mode. "That's a deep cut. It could get infected. And if you don't get it stitched, it will heal funny, and then you'll have an ugly toe. Do you want an ugly toe?"

Jesse chuckled. "Point taken, Doc. I'll have Amber take me tomorrow."

"Promise?"

"Promise."

Silence settled then, but, miraculously, it wasn't an

awkward one. It felt like they were back to normal. Was that possible? Probably not. Not in any real way. It couldn't be that easy. But it was nice to pretend for a while.

"Why was the show shit?"

Oh, right. Jesse had forgotten about that. The foul mood he was in earlier had slipped away, bled out of him with his actual blood, maybe.

"The video projection was messed up, so we had one screen blank a bunch of the time." But that wasn't his real issue. He was pissed about that yes, but ultimately the problem had been him. "But the bigger deal was I missed a bunch of cues. Last night too."

"What happened?" Hunter asked.

"I don't know."

He did, though. He knew exactly what had happened that had thrown him so utterly off his game.

You did. You happened.

CHAPTER SIXTEEN

It had been five days since Hunter had examined Jesse's toe over FaceTime.

In the meantime, they had talked five times: every night around midnight. Just like old times.

Only not.

They talked about everything. How the shows went—they were getting better. Hospital life and politics—they were the same.

Well, not actually *everything*.

As Hunter pulled into the parking ramp of the Buffalo Marriott, part of him was afraid they were never going to address the elephant in the room—the "elephant," of course, being the most spectacular sex of his life.

Not to mention the sleeping afterward.

Oh, the sleeping. Wrapped up tight in Jesse's arms, his chest rising and falling against Hunter's back, making him believe for those few moments before sleep took him that everything might be okay.

If the night of the gala had been Upside-Down World, and life before the gala had been whatever the opposite of that was

—Right-Side-Up World, regular life—Hunter was currently in limbo. Stuck in a purgatory of uncertainty. He felt like he was on a seesaw that had frozen, perfectly and perpetually balanced on its fulcrum. He needed something to happen. Someone needed to kick that seesaw and get it moving again. He almost didn't care what the result of this day was as long as there *was* a result.

Actually, that wasn't entirely true. Part of him feared he would accept whatever ambiguously defined scraps Jesse offered him. Anything to keep him around.

No. He wasn't doing that again.

Hunter was going to kick the damned seesaw. He wasn't leaving Buffalo without getting some goddamned clarity about what he and Jesse were to each other.

When he reached the lobby, he pulled out his phone to text Jesse.

I'm here.

Avery and her parents and sister had driven down earlier in the day and attended the sound check—Jesse had sent pictures of Avery palling around with the band onstage. They'd invited Hunter to drive with them, but he'd had a couple of afternoon commitments at the hospital he couldn't reschedule, so he'd set out later in a rented car.

Besides, Avery and family were driving back to Toronto tonight after the show.

Hunter needed his own car.

Maybe.

He didn't even know if Jesse was still in the hotel. The border crossing had been backed up, and Hunter was later than he'd planned. It was already seven, and he knew the band generally aimed to be at the venue about the time the opening band started, if not earlier, so it was very likely they were already gone.

He jumped when Jesse's text arrived, even though he'd been staring at his phone.

`Tenth floor. 1007.`

The elevator disgorged him into an empty, softly lit hallway. He had no idea what to expect. He knew that while the other four guys doubled up and roomed together on the road, Jesse always got his own room. "It's *my* band," he would say. But Hunter got the impression the guys sort of free-floated among their rooms and those of the crew. So they might well be together now. He might be walking into the midst of the band and hangers-on in their preshow mode. He might have to examine Billy's butt. He was prepared for a crowd.

Or maybe Jesse would be alone. It was unlikely they would launch right into The Talk before the show. Hunter wasn't enough of a dick to force a discussion an hour before Jesse had to perform in front of tens of thousands of people, but, hey, if Jesse wanted to talk, Hunter was prepared to talk.

He was not prepared for the door of room 1007 to open and for a leather-clad arm to snake out, grab him by the shirt, and yank him inside.

He was not prepared to be shoved up against the door and kissed.

"I thought you'd never get here." Jesse took his mouth off Hunter's only long enough to mutter those words, and then it was back, hungry and insistent, licking the seam of Hunter's lips until they slid open. As Jesse's tongue made its rough intrusion into Hunter's mouth, Hunter moaned, thinking suddenly of Jesse's dick doing the same thing. Jesse fucking his mouth.

This was a bad idea.

This was the opposite of seesaw kicking.

Even as the rest of his body roared to life, Hunter lifted his arms, intending to push Jesse away, but when his hands hit that leather jacket, when they felt the solid mass of chest underneath it, the intended shove turned into something else.

His stupid hands grabbed the jacket like they wanted to ensure its owner wouldn't flee. Which was probably redundant, given that Jesse and Hunter had their tongues in each other's mouths.

Jesse was still holding on to Hunter's shirt with one hand too. So there they were with fistfuls of each other's clothes, making out like the world was ending.

It felt like flying.

A loud knock on the door behind his back brought them crashing down to earth.

"Jesse!"

Hunter leaped away from the door like it was made of glass and whoever was on the other side could see what they were doing. Jesse didn't let go of him, though. When Hunter moved, Jesse adjusted, pivoting with him and lowering his forehead to Hunter's.

"Jesse, are you in there?" It was a feminine voice. "We have to go!"

"Yes! Give me two seconds." Jesse sighed and finally let go of Hunter—but slowly, like his hands didn't want to.

"That's Amber," he said to Hunter, glancing at his watch with one hand and using the other to pinch the bridge of his nose. His voice had come out all scratchy. He cleared his throat before saying more. "The others are already at the arena. I told her I'd be late, but she freaks out if we're not there by seven thirty. I guess she decided to stay and play babysitter."

It was probably a good thing. Hunter wasn't sure that that incendiary kiss would ever have ended otherwise. And the more they kissed, the harder the postshow seesaw tipping was going to be.

Jesse made his way over to his bed, grabbed a knapsack, and was back at the door before Hunter could catch his breath. His eyes raked over Hunter.

Hunter forced himself to meet Jesse's eyes, though it was oddly difficult. They hadn't made eye contact yet, not really—the instant lip contact had precluded it.

"You okay?" Jesse asked. "For now?"

Hunter nodded.

Jesse flashed a small, wicked smile and opened the door to reveal a petite brunette dressed in jeans and a crisp white blouse holding a clipboard. "Jesse, I'm not sure what you were waiting for that was so important that I couldn't..." She trailed off, her eyes sliding over Hunter.

"Amber, this is Hunter. Hunter, Amber."

"Oh!" Amber was surprised, but quickly covered it, extending a hand to shake Hunter's. "Right. I've heard so much about you."

"You too," said Hunter. "Nice to finally meet the boss around here."

Amber grinned and gestured for them both to come into the hallway. "I like him," she said to Jesse, who just smirked.

Amber produced a lanyard with a badge hanging from it and handed it to Hunter. "This is an all-access pass. It will get you in anywhere. Do you want a ticket, or do you want to watch the show from the wings?"

"Oh, I want a ticket." Hunter might have no freaking idea what was going on between him and Jesse, but he wanted to see the full show. He'd watched enough live footage of Jesse's shows on YouTube, seeing him prowl around the stage, flirt with the audience, transport them to another world with his talent.

No matter what else happened, there was no way he was missing that.

♫

Jesse was glad Hunter had chosen to watch the show from the audience.

It was funny to think Hunter had never seen him live. But, then, when would he have? Their current tour hadn't hit Toronto yet—the Canadian leg of the tour came after the US. And Jesse and Hunter had only known each other a year. Not long enough for him to have been around for previous tours.

It just *felt* like they'd known each other forever.

Egomaniac that he was, he was determined to put on an amazing show. Blow Hunter's mind.

He did kind of wish, though, that Hunter had elected to sit with Avery and her family in the luxury box Amber had arranged. But no. Hunter had opted for the second of two seating options Amber had offered: the front-row seat.

Which meant Jesse could see him.

Like, constantly.

All he had to do was look over there.

Which he was trying not to do more than, oh, twenty times a minute.

He was hyperaware of Hunter. It was incredible to see him smiling and singing along, gazing up at the stage. Shit, it was almost as good as when he was gazing up at Jesse with his lips around…

Fuck. Jesse was the one on stage, but he felt like Hunter was the one sucking up all the energy in the vast space.

He had to stop this.

He moved over to the other side during a long interlude when he didn't have to sing. He didn't usually do that during this song, so he was probably throwing the guys for a loop, but whatever. It was his band; he could do what he liked.

There. That was better.

Arenas, he had learned, weren't like smaller venues. You had to be "big" in an arena. Make the kid in the nosebleed section feel like you were singing to him. There was a certain energy that flowed between the performer and the audience that you learned to cultivate. It was like a dance. A two-and-a-half-hour love affair. The quality of the music mattered, yes, but the overall success of a show depended more on the way that group energy flowed.

And that was only going to happen if he paid attention to the audience. To the *entire* audience. Not just one member.

He mostly managed. Until the encore. The first song of the encore set was "When You're Mine." Their big hit off the current album.

Hunter's song.

He tried not to look at him. But then, as they were playing, he started thinking about the storyboards for the video. The plan was to cut between him gazing out the window at a rainstorm, flash to "happier days" with him and Kylie dancing and kissing in the rain, and, of course, the requisite "concert" shots, which were, in this case, the band playing on the roof of the building Jesse had been brooding in earlier. Then, in the end, it would start to rain on the band, and Kylie would emerge onto the roof and they'd kiss in the rain some more.

It would be visually striking and dramatic. The director had a great portfolio. There was no doubt Kylie's presence would set tongues wagging in a way that would get people talking.

It was a good concept.

It was also total bullshit.

It made him so fucking angry.

So angry he started to lose his place in the song.

So he gave in. Capitulated. Looked at the person who should have been, but never would be, in the video.

The only person in the audience.

It calmed him right down, to see Hunter's rapt face. There was a crescendo in the song where the lights turned out to the audience. Jesse usually took the opportunity to scan the entire arena, to marvel at the fact that *they were here*. That he'd really made it. That he was a fucking rock-and-roll star.

But today he just looked at Hunter. Let himself look and look and look.

Let a big, goofy, guileless grin spread over his face.

Hunter smiled back.

With a burst of energy, he played the shit out of the rest of the song.

♫

"Jesse!"

Jesse emerged from his dressing room. Usually he waited until he got back to the hotel to shower. Generally, there was a crowd assembled backstage, and depending on his mood, he might stick around for a bit and hang out, but he preferred showering in the privacy of his hotel room. But tonight, given the presence of the visitors from Toronto, he'd decided to wash his stinky body on site.

Which was good, because the first thing he saw when he stepped out into the crowded green room was Avery running toward him.

The sight of her, out in the world and smiling like crazy,

just about made his heart burst like he was in a fucking Disney movie.

So, he went with the Disney theme. Instead of hugging her, he picked her up and twirled her around. He wouldn't have been surprised to see a parade of singing woodland creatures make their way backstage.

"You were so great! And I can't believe you dedicated a song to me! This is the greatest day of my life! I posted on Insta, and I have, like, a billion comments already!"

Next up were Avery's parents and sister, less over the top than Avery but all smiling. They'd been chatting with the rest of the band, whom he'd ordered to be on their best behavior. The guys actually seemed to be complying. Billy even had all his clothes on and had—so far—not acquired any female admirers, though the room was filled with a lot of women Jesse recognized as groupies. And Cranky Colin was autographing a poster for Avery and chatting like he wasn't the band's own Ebenezer Scrooge. It *was* a fucking Disney movie.

Of course, there was also Hunter.

They hadn't spoken directly. The crowd was big and everyone was kind of focused on Avery, but Jesse was aware of Hunter's every move. Saw when he made his way to the catering spread Amber had ordered up—they didn't usually eat on site after a show, so this was all for Avery's benefit.

Even though everyone, Jesse included, was having a good time, the minutes passed slowly. He wished he could bail. Grab Hunter and hightail it out of here.

Well, not literally *grab* him.

Even though that was *exactly* what he wanted to do.

He felt someone watching him and turned, dragging his gaze away from where Hunter was locked in conversation with Billy and Will.

It was Colin. Standing next to him—where had he come from?—and silently watching him.

"What?"

"Nothing," Colin said, but his brow was furrowed ever so slightly, like he was trying to puzzle something out.

"*What?*"

"*Nothing.*"

Fine. Something was up with the keyboardist, but it was impossible to get anywhere with Colin when he was determined not to talk. Time for a new topic. "Thanks for being nice to Avery."

Colin smirked. "I'm not a *total* dick, you know."

"Could have fooled me."

"Hey," came a voice from over his shoulder.

It was Hunter's voice, so of course he whirled. Hunter was the Pied Piper, and he was the fucking rat. A perfect analogy.

"You were great." Hunter glanced at Colin and expanded his comment. "You guys were great. You've really got the touch for live shows."

Heat crept up Jesse's neck. "Thanks."

He was about to say more, something self-effacing, because he was uncomfortable as hell with the praise, when a woman sidled up between Colin and him. She was wearing a backstage pass around her neck, which meant someone had authorized her. She had platinum hair and big blue eyes—and she was wearing a T-shirt with a picture of his face stretched tight over her boobs. She was objectively gorgeous. And she didn't have a press pass. Which meant she was probably your garden-variety groupie, if better looking than most. He sighed, wondering which crew member she'd sweet-talked into giving her the pass.

"I *had* to come over and introduce myself."

Here they went.

"I'm from Toronto too—I drove over for this show, and I'm seeing you the day after tomorrow in Boston. I'm like, your biggest admirer. I have a scrapbook of you." She laughed good-naturedly and rolled her eyes at herself. "It's like I'm thirteen or something."

"That's great," he said, trying to infuse his voice with at least a little bit of genuine enthusiasm. "Thanks."

She seemed to take his not-rudeness as an invitation—she stepped closer and laid her hand on his forearm. "My name's Jessica," she said, grinning and looking like she'd told a hilarious joke and was waiting for her audience to get it.

"Uh, nice to meet you, Jessica." He stuck out his hand, but only so he could shake his arm out from under her touch. "I'm—"

"I know! Jesse. Jesse and Jessica!" She lowered her voice and put her hand back on his arm. "And I am *not* thirteen."

"Right." This was the part where he was supposed to say something flirty, something about how it was meant to be. He knew how to do that. He knew how to play the game.

He did not know how to get rid of Jessica without being a total dick.

Hunter broke through the uncomfortable silence that followed. "I'm pretty beat, so I think I'm going to head back to my room and crash."

What? "Your room? Did you get one at the Marriott?"

Shit. Now he'd let on to Jessica that the band was at the Marriott. Not that it was a state secret—any groupie worth her salt would have that info. But still. His mind had gone soft.

Jesse hadn't thought about where Hunter would stay. Which was kind of dick-ish, given that he'd invited Hunter to the show. He should have had Amber make arrangements for him.

Also: *what?* That was it? Hunter was done for the night?

He tried to wiggle his arm out of Jessica's grip without being too overt about it.

"Yep. Amber arranged one. I checked in after we…after you headed over to the arena."

Why did that…hurt so much? Fuck it. He went ahead and shook Jessica's hand off.

What had he thought? That Hunter was going to spend the night cuddled up in Jesse's room?

Yes. That was pretty much what he'd thought. Well, no, what he'd *hoped*.

"Hang on a sec." He turned to Jessica. "I'm sorry. Could you excuse us for a moment?"

She blinked.

Please let her have some pride. It could go either way here. He'd seen women take rejection gracefully, and he'd seen them get nasty.

"Sure," she said, and Jesse blew a breath of relief. He looked around and caught Amber's eye. He waved to her and pointed at Jessica. "See that woman over there?"

Jessica nodded.

"Tell her I asked her to set you up with some great seats and passes for the Boston show."

Jessica smiled a little sadly and made her goodbyes.

When she was gone, he turned back to Hunter. "Okay, so we're sampling all this rustbelt metropolis has to offer tomorrow, right?"

Hunter didn't answer right away, but Colin made a strange snorting noise.

Jesse hadn't even realized Colin was still lurking. Why hadn't he left? Once upon a time, he would have pounced on Jessica once it became clear Jesse was taking a pass.

"You're not coming back to Toronto with us?" Colin asked Jesse. The band was driving back first thing in the morning for a twenty-four hour hiatus. But Jesse didn't see why Colin cared one way or the other. Why he was still staring at Jesse with a weird, uncharacteristic intensity.

Jesse turned his attention to Hunter, who still hasn't answered about tomorrow. Jesse had sort of assumed, when Hunter had agreed to come to the show, that he'd agreed to everything Jesse had suggested in that text, including the tour of Buffalo the next day. But he hadn't really thought it through, had he? Hadn't even considered whether Hunter might want a hotel room of his own.

He had taken everything for granted.

Suddenly, Hunter's answer took on huge symbolic significance.

Was he going to get up tomorrow and go home, or was he going to spend the day with Jesse?

Was he staying, or was he going?

The suspense was fucking killing him. Turning his whole body into a rubber band stretched almost to the limit.

"There's a surrealism exhibition on at the art gallery," Hunter finally said, and Jesse could have melted into the floor right then and there. His insides had liquefied with relief. Hunter smiled a little bit. It was a reluctant smile, though. The kind adults gave kids who had done something stupid but loveable.

"Surrealism," said Colin flatly. "Sounds about right."

Jesse gave Colin his full attention. What was up his butt?

But he only smirked and sauntered away. Finally.

Which left Hunter and Jesse alone. Alone-but-not. Alone in a crowd.

Don't leave.

Take me with you.

Come to my room.

"So I guess I'll see you tomorrow?" Hunter asked, clearly trying to excuse himself.

Jesse started to protest, when Avery came bounding up, followed by her family.

"Jesse, my parents say we have to leave." She rolled her eyes, like the two of them were in on the secret of just how oppressive parents were. Then she lowered her voice. "Can you pleeease say something to them so we can stay?"

Jesse noticed Avery's mom looking intently at Hunter as if trying to telegraph him a message. Hunter made eye contact with Avery's mom. He must have gotten it, because he said, "Sorry, kid, but your doctor says you should go too. It's been a long day, and it's really late. I'm dead on my feet myself."

Hunter hugged Avery and said goodbye to her family. Then Jesse was pulled into the same routine, but they were more extensive farewells as everyone expressed their appreciation for having been invited and given the VIP treatment.

While Jesse was hugging Avery, Hunter said, "I'll see you tomorrow, Jesse." Then walked away, presumably back to his hotel room.

Yeah, that was not happening.

CHAPTER SEVENTEEN

Tomorrow my ass. What room are you in?

Hunter had just gotten out of the shower and changed into his pajamas when Jesse's text came.

He'd been expecting it. He was, after all, kicking the seesaw.

He picked up the phone to reply, impressed that his hands weren't betraying the quaking in his heart.

If he'd been worried Jesse would put the whammy on him, that he would somehow emerge from this weekend without any more clarity than he'd had at the outset, *Jessica* had put that concern to rest. Because having witnessed that little show, Hunter wasn't leaving without resolving things.

He shouldn't be so sneery. Jessica had been acting rationally. Who in their right mind *wouldn't* want to get into Jesse Jamison's pants? And she was a useful reminder that he and Jesse didn't exist in a vacuum.

It so often felt that way. Idiot that he was, he had somehow convinced himself earlier that he was alone in the audience. That there was a bubble around him and Jesse, and that everyone else—the rest of the band, the rest of the audience—existed outside it, their voices dampened and their impact muted.

But that was incorrect. There had been tens of thousands of people at that show, many of them women, many of them screaming.

And Jesse fed off it. It was part of his magic. That swaggering, flirtatious appeal.

That *heterosexual* appeal.

Or so everyone thought.

But Hunter had data that suggested otherwise. And that was really why he was here, wasn't it? To force a reckoning regarding that...data.

There was a loud rapping on the door.

Hunter took his shirt off before moving to open it. Because, hell, if he was going to force a reckoning, he might as well use all the leverage he had.

And there Jesse was.

God. The way he leaned against the door, like he couldn't be bothered to stand up straight. Like he expected the world to just...prop him up.

And he was sucking on a lollipop.

Damn, take James Dean, swap out the cigarette for a sucker, and there you had it.

"Hi," Jesse said around the lollipop, not even trying to hide how hard he was checking out Hunter's bare chest.

Hunter swung the door open and stepped back, wordlessly inviting Mr. Sex on a Stick inside, feeling as though he might as well be Little Red Riding Hood rolling out the welcome mat for the big bad wolf.

"What's with the lollipop?"

"I mainline them on tour. They soothe my throat."

Hunter was a bit annoyed he hadn't known this. But then

annoyed at himself for being annoyed. Who cared what weird stuff Jesse ate on tour?

He did, though. He cared.

"It's the only picky thing on my rider. Classic Dum Dums suckers. Red ones only. I make those mofos pick out all the other colors, like I'm Mariah fucking Carey." Jesse grinned.

"You're lucky your teeth haven't rotted," Hunter said, because yes, playing the role of the humorless doctor was exactly what was needed right now.

Jesse pulled the sucker out again and grinned an exaggerated, toothy grin, as if to demonstrate superior oral hygiene. "Want one?" Then he reached into his pocket and produced a handful of the small suckers, which he proceeded to dump on the table.

"You are incorrigible," Hunter said, unable to stop himself from smiling. He went over and examined the pile. They were all variations on "red"—he saw strawberry, cherry, and as he sorted through them, fruit punch. Also…a condom?

A spike of adrenaline shot up Hunter's spine. He stopped sorting and looked up.

Jesse either hadn't noticed Hunter noticing the condom or else he had and was unbothered. He gazed evenly at Hunter, then popped the sucker out again—*Jesus*—took a step closer—close enough that he was officially in Hunter's space—held out the sugary orb, and said, "Or maybe just a taste of this one?"

Hunter started to shake his head. He'd been eyeing the glistening lollipop, so he didn't notice Jesse's lips until they were right there.

He'd thought Jesse was offering him a taste of the actual sucker, but of course he wasn't.

He was offering him a taste of his lips.

The maddening thing was that although there was a layer of sickly sweet, artificial strawberry on those lips, underneath it he could still taste Jesse. He couldn't even put it into words, but the taste of Jesse, the flavor of his Jesse-ness, was familiar.

That startled the hell out of him.

He was letting himself grow familiar with the taste of a man he couldn't have. Not on any terms he could live with, anyway.

No. Not again. Anger, sudden and sharp, arrived inside him.

He pushed Jesse away. Laid a hand right in the center of his chest and moved him back.

"I can't do this."

"Do what?" Jesse said, popping the sucker back into his mouth. *Damn* him. He was going to dissemble *now*?

He knew perfectly well what Hunter meant. Fine. If he was going to be like that, Hunter would play his stupid game.

"What's the condom for, Jesse?" When he didn't answer, Hunter puffed up his chest and took a page from the Jesse Jamison handbook, stepping into the rock star's personal space. "Was it for Jessica?"

"No," Jesse shot back immediately.

"So what was it for, then?" Hunter didn't usually get angry like this. Belligerence wasn't part of his repertoire. But, damn, it felt kind of good. "Was it for us?"

Jesse dropped his eyes to the floor. Quickly, just for a second before they were back on Hunter's, looking as widely innocent as they had before. But Hunter hadn't missed the unsettled moment.

He took another step closer, determined to goad the truth out of Jesse. "Was it for me?" Now their chests were almost touching. "Or for you?" Hunter's nipples pebbled, and it wasn't because he was cold. But he didn't care. Suddenly, in this context, obvious evidence of his arousal didn't feel like weakness. It felt like power.

So he shifted his hips, angling his lower body so his now-erect dick pressed against Jesse's thigh. "Are you a top or a bottom, Jesse?" When his only answer was a quick, sharp inhale, he pressed on. "Were you thinking I'd fuck you or you'd fuck me?"

Because I was thinking the latter.

He forced the thought away. He needed to stand his ground here.

Jesse took the sucker out of his mouth, closed his eyes, and lowered his chin to his chest. Then, he looked back up, eyes filmed with liquid and, to Hunter's utter astonishment, said, "I don't know. I don't know what I am. I just know that I...that you..."

A single tear escaped from the corner of Jesse's eye.

Jesus Christ, he'd made his best friend cry. What kind of a monster was he?

"Jesse," he said, gentling his voice and reaching out to swipe the tear with his thumb. He left the hand on Jesse's cheek. "I'm sorry."

This was the moment. They were perfectly balanced, a plank lying straight across the fulcrum. As easy as it would be to let that hand move downward, to let his mouth come down on Jesse's, to give and seek comfort and pleasure, he couldn't do it. If this was going to work in any way Hunter could live with, he needed Jesse to choose him. To choose him publicly.

He took his hand away. It was an un-claiming. An un-branding.

It hurt as much as searing iron on tender skin, though.

He said it as clearly and kindly as he could. "I can't be the rock star's piece on the side, Jesse."

Jesse winced and turned away. Walked over to Hunter's minifridge and retrieved a little bottle of whiskey. Twisted off the cap and drank it in a few swallows as he made his way to Hunter's window.

Gazed out at the nighttime view of the river.

"I was thinking about something on my way over here." His voice was low, so low Hunter had to keep perfectly still to hear him. He didn't dare breathe for fear of missing something. "I'm always saying—out loud and to myself—some variation on 'It's my band, I can do what I want.' For example, I had Amber move our usual meet and greets around to free me up to spend time with Avery this evening. I decide the set lists. If I want some weird piece of equipment all of a sudden, everyone jumps to get it for me." He'd gotten a bit louder as he picked up speed. Hunter still didn't move, though. Hardly breathed. "Or the goddamned lollipops." He gestured at the candy on the desk even as he continued to look out the window.

Hunter smiled. "No green lollipops for the rock star."

Jesse huffed a laugh that was tinged with self-disgust. "But it all means nothing if I can't have what I really want. Sometimes, I almost feel like I would trade all of it—just throw it all away—if I could have what I really want."

Hunter sucked in a sharp breath. "And what do you really want?"

"But other times, I think, no. I'm not brave enough," Jesse said, not answering Hunter's question. "Most of the time, actually, if I'm being honest."

Hunter asked it again. "What do you really want?"

Jesse turned to look at Hunter. "You. I want you."

Oh my God. A tiny splinter of hope worked its way under Hunter's skin. But once again, he had to be crystal clear about his terms. "I want you too, Jesse, more than you know. But I can't live in the shadows again. I can't—"

"I know." The interruption had been sharp, aggressive

even. Jesse gave a soft smile and repeated it, this time more gently. "I know."

Did he, though? Hunter needed to make absolutely sure. "I've told you casual hookups aren't what I'm looking for. I've told you I'm never going to be in the closet again, not for anyone. I need to know that you're putting those pieces together correctly, Jesse."

"I am." The answer came quickly, and then he swallowed and added, "I get it."

Hunter had to stifle a gasp. He had imagined this going a lot of different ways. A fight. An outright rejection. He had been concerned about the fate of their friendship. But underneath all that there had been hope. Irrational, tender, fragile hope that was now, suddenly, exposed to the sun after so long underground.

Jesse extended his hand, and Hunter walked over and took it.

"It doesn't mean I'm not scared as hell about the consequences," Jesse said quietly. "About Matty."

"I know." Hunter squeezed Jesse's hand. "You're also brave as hell. Smart as hell." There was no one more capable than Jesse. When Jesse put his mind to something, he made it happen. Hunter had seen it dozens of times.

And now, it seemed what Jesse had put his mind to was *Hunter*.

"Ha!" He barked a laugh, unable to keep the astonished joy contained.

Jesse blinked rapidly and started to pull his hand away, uncertainty creeping into his face. Shit, Jesse probably didn't know how to interpret Hunter's laughter. Hunter held on to him, prevented him from taking his hand back.

"I need you to understand, though," Jesse said, "that I'm

not going to go on *Ellen* tomorrow and burst out of a rainbow cake."

Hunter laughed again. He couldn't help it. The image was so not Jesse.

"I would never do to you what that fucker Julian did. But if we're..." He looked at the floor, and was he *blushing*? "If we're going to do this, I'm going to have to have a plan. It's going to have to come out—no pun intended—in a way I can live with, in a way that makes me feel like I'm doing everything I can to protect all the hard work that's gotten me to this point."

"I get it." He did. Jesse was taking a big step here. "What do you always say? Control the narrative?"

"Exactly. I thought that when we got back to Toronto, I'd hire a PR person. But I don't want you to think that it's because of you, that being with you requires spin. That's not it."

"I would never think that. I think it's smart to have a strategy in place. If you can find someone to advise who—"

"Who isn't Matty." Jesse ran the fingers of his free hand through his hair, agitated. "I need to find someone not in Matty's circle."

"Is Matty really going to care that much?" Hunter had never met Matty. The guy seemed to have a lot of sway over Jesse, but still, he was just a man, capable of making mistakes, of harboring unreasonable prejudices.

Jesse shuddered. He actually shuddered. Wow. He was really shaken—which was fair. Coming out was hard enough for a private citizen. "Do you think, maybe..."

"What?" *Anything*, Hunter wanted to say. *You name it, I'll make it happen.*

"Do you think maybe we can talk about the rest of this later?"

Hunter smiled. That was an easy request to fulfill.

He already had one of Jesse's hands. He took the other, took both of his best friend's hands between his, and tugged. Pulled him away from the window like he was leading a spooked horse away from a cliff. As they passed the desk, he let go with one hand to snag the condom from the pile of suckers.

Jesse's eyes widened.

Hunter led him to the bed. He scooted back onto it and sat cross-legged, nodding at the space in front of him to indicate he wanted Jesse to go there. Jesse smiled self-consciously as he settled himself, mirroring Hunter's pose. It was like now that he'd declared himself, all his signature swagger had drained out of him. It was oddly touching to see the usually confident rock star so vulnerable. To know Hunter was the only person who had ever seen this particular version of Jesse.

To know he knew how to fix it. How to get the swagger back. All it would take was a combination of humor and dirty talk.

He threw the condom down on the bed between them.

"The way it was playing out in my head—and, Jesse, it played out in my head *a lot*—you were fucking me."

Jesse's eyes widened, and he was *definitely* blushing this time. Damn. Hunter was a little drunk on this power.

"But I'm flexible," he went on, smiling. "I'll take you however I can get you." *As long as it's not in the shadows.* He placed his hands on Jesse's knees. Leaned his weight into them. Thought back to Jesse pressing him against the door and working his mouth possessively. "But I kind of have a feeling you might be imagining things the way I'm imagining them."

"You're not wrong," Jesse whispered. "I just… I've never done that."

Hunter pressed a quick, hard kiss to Jesse's mouth. He was

so…sweet right now, Hunter couldn't help himself. "It's so good. You're going to love it."

"You've, ah, topped?"

"I've been known to. I prefer bottoming, but like I said, I'm flexible. And it's all pretty damn great with…" He didn't know if he should go that far.

"With what?" Jesse was looking at him so intensely, Hunter's face heated.

"With the right person." He laughed at himself. "Hell, it's good enough with the wrong person, but it can be pretty spectacular with…someone you like. With someone you trust."

With someone you love.

Hunter had made Jesse feel all kinds of shit he'd never felt before, so it made a certain kind of sense that he was nervous as hell over what was about to happen.

He usually had the upper hand in a sexual encounter, partly because he was a little bossy in bed by nature, but partly because it came with the territory of being a famous person. People deferred to you enough that habits formed.

It wasn't just the physical stuff that had him apprehensive; it was everything he'd said to Hunter about their relationship, about…making it public. There was going to be fallout. He knew that. But faced with the choice of losing Hunter or having him… Well, there had been no choice.

So he'd think about the fallout—and a plan to deal with it —later. Concentrate on one anxious-making thing at a time. For now, he was gratefully setting aside the damn narrative he was always working so hard to control according to Matty's specs.

"We don't have to do anything, you know," Hunter said gently.

Jesse forced his swirling mind to focus on his…boyfriend? Partner? Those words seemed weird. But there was absolutely no doubt in his mind that Hunter was his person. His kind, generous, funny, gorgeous person.

They were facing each other, each sitting cross-legged. It kind of reminded him of the last scene of *Sixteen Candles*, where Molly Ringwald and whatever that guy's name was sat like that on a table.

"Did you ever see that movie *Sixteen Candles*? My mom was obsessed with it."

Hunter quirked a smiled. "Yes."

"At the end, they sat like this, facing each other. He leaned over and kissed her, like you just did me."

The smile grew. "Yes, and they had a birthday cake between them."

They both looked down at the condom.

Then, on cue, they both cracked up.

"What do you think they did after she blew out the candles?" Hunter asked.

"Weren't her parents out of town? Honestly, I think they probably had sex."

"I don't know." Hunter shifted so he was lying back on the bed, his upper body bolstered by the headboard. "Maybe they just watched a movie and cuddled." He grabbed the remote from the bedside table, tossed it at Jesse, and held out his arms.

He was communicating, this time with actions rather than words, that nothing physical had to happen between them. He was creating a safe space for Jesse. He wasn't sure anyone had ever done that for him before. Tears prickled behind his eyeballs.

He didn't pick up the remote, but he did fall into Hunter's arms.

They banded around him, strong and sure.

That was all it took for his nervousness to evaporate. Hunter was still shirtless, and Jesse turned his head and buried his nose in Hunter's neck. Savored the faint clove smell of his aftershave for a moment before pressing his lips to the pulse visible there.

Hunter grunted, and Jesse, who was half draped over him, felt Hunter's cock stiffening. As if embarrassed, Hunter tried to shift his lower body out from under Jesse, but Jesse wasn't having it. In fact, he slid his other hand under the waistband of Hunter's pajama bottoms and stroked, relishing the growly groan that resulted.

His own cock was mirroring Hunter's, and suddenly, he needed out of his tight jeans. He pulled away and stripped off all his clothes.

"You don't have to prove anything—to me or to yourself—you know," Hunter said, watching him intently from his repose. He had a dark-red blotch on his neck where Jesse's mouth had been. The sight of it—of his mark on Hunter—sent a bolt of possessive lust though Jesse. "There's no hurry," Hunter added.

"While I appreciate your concern, there is in fact a big fucking hurry."

Hunter raised his eyebrows.

"If I don't get my hands on you right now, I'm going to lose my goddamned mind." When Hunter didn't do anything but grin, Jesse snarled, "Take off your pants."

Hunter's eyes widened.

He also took off his pants.

Good. As interesting as all this newness was, Jesse liked being in charge, because it was familiar, but also for its own sake.

They were both naked now, staring at each other, Jesse standing and Hunter half reclined on the bed. Jesse was greedy, drunk on the idea that this expanse of skin, this man, was his. There were so many possibilities.

A world opened before him.

Hunter sat up, inserting himself into the pause created by Jesse's inability to decide what part of his lover to grab first, and licked the tip of Jesse's already leaking cock.

The gesture crystalized his path. "No way." He pushed Hunter onto his back. If Hunter did that, Jesse wasn't going to last, and he wanted to…do what Hunter had suggested earlier. He laughed at himself. Since when had he become all squeamish about sex? He couldn't even think the words? No.

"I want to fuck you," he said. The declaration echoing through the space between them ratcheted his need up a few thousand points.

It seemed the same was true for Hunter, because he moaned and closed his eyes, like the world was too much to look at just then.

Jesse prowled forward and climbed onto Hunter. With a woman, he would be careful not to rest all his weight on her, but Hunter was big and solid and could hold him.

So he laid himself out on Hunter and kissed him. Let the deep, drugging sensation of Hunter's mouth working his, of Hunter's tongue sweeping through his mouth, diffuse through his veins. Let himself be heavy. Surrender.

After a few minutes—hours? He didn't know—of deep kissing, Hunter's moans were becoming more urgent, more needy. Jesse shifted partly off Hunter and let his hand drift down to grab Hunter's cock even as they continued their joint assault on each other's mouths. He used the moisture he found at the tip to stroke Hunter a few times, and from there, it seemed the most natural thing in the world to slide his hand around and trace the edge of Hunter's ass.

Hunter broke their kiss, panting. "There's lube in there." He nodded at the bedside table, on which rested a small toiletries bag.

Lube. Right. He should have thought of that. He retrieved it, coated his fingers, and returned to tracing the edge of that sensitive opening, carefully assessing Hunter's face for clues.

He saw desire. Lust. And, as Jesse worked a finger in, Hunter's eyes slipped shut on a moan.

He was so beautiful as he gave himself up to pleasure, and it was *Jesse's* doing. How utterly shocking—and wonderful.

It almost hurt to watch. Jesse hadn't realized he'd stopped moving his hand until Hunter opened his eyes. A furrow appeared between his brow, and he whispered, "Please."

Jesse started moving again, watching Hunter like a hawk as he carefully slid the finger deeper inside him, loving the feeling of resistance, and then relaxation, he encountered.

"More," Hunter said, his voice low and desperate, and Jesse moved to oblige, gradually adding a second finger.

"Stretch me a bit," Hunter commanded. Then he added a rasped, "Please, Jesse."

Jesse moaned. The interplay at work here, him with his fingers in Hunter's ass, Hunter simultaneously bossy and begging, it was…beyond words.

A wave of lust tore through Jesse, and he widened his fingers a little, which summoned a string of barely intelligible curses from Hunter that finally resolved themselves into one recognizable word: "Condom."

He needed both hands to retrieve it, so he pulled his fingers out of Hunter, relishing the forlorn whimper that resulted. Fuck, it made him want to beat his chest like Tarzan. Hands made clumsy by lust, it took him a few tries to tear open the condom package. Hunter's hands appeared, taking control.

"Oh my God," Jesse said as Hunter jacked him a few times before rolling the condom on. His eyes slipped closed in bliss and then flew open at the sensation of Hunter taking his hand and pouring slick liquid into it.

When he spread his thighs in clear invitation, Jesse said it again, louder, "Oh my God."

If his hands had been clumsy before, now he was a janky, ill-programmed robot who could barely control his renegade limbs. But he managed to massage some more lube into and around Hunter's hole and to coat his own dick with the remainder.

He grabbed the base of his cock and positioned the head near Hunter's entrance.

But then a hand reached up, cradled his cheek.

He'd been singularly focused on the obscenely gorgeous sight of Hunter's body, of him lying there with his legs splayed. He raised his gaze to meet Hunter's.

"Are you sure this is okay?" Hunter asked with so much kindness, so much concern, it took Jesse's breath away. "This doesn't have to happen now. There's plenty of time." He smiled. "We have nothing but time."

There were those tears threatening again. The answer to Hunter's question was yes, he was okay with this. He was more than okay with this, but to be asked…well, it did something to him. Jesse had always thought of consent as something the person doing the fucking should get from the person being fucked. It was a dick-centric view of things, he supposed. But to be asked? For Hunter to not assume that because he was topping, that he was automatically raring to go? It was so… chivalrous. And, really, who was fucking whom here? He realized it wasn't about which dick went where, even though they'd used that verbal shorthand before, in their standoff. They were fucking each other. It was so much more complicated than his past experiences, but also...so much *less* complicated.

"Sweetheart," said Hunter, and the endearment was another lance to Jesse's chest. He was being dismantled, one loving word at a time.

Hunter started to sit up, and Jesse realized he was interpreting Jesse's lack of an answer as the absence of consent. Which was a decidedly incorrect interpretation.

Enough weepy existential revelation. Time for fucking.

He pressed Hunter back down on the bed, clamped his hands down on Hunter's hips, and tried for his best leer. "I am very okay with this. And there is not plenty of time. There is only *now*."

But wait. He should make sure that feeling was mutual, and he probably shouldn't be pinning Hunter down while he did so. He broke contact, sat back on his haunches, and said, "Are *you* okay with this?"

Hunter's answer was to grab Jesse's hands and put them back where they'd been, and to let his legs fall open again. Then he crooked a finger in a "come here" gesture until Jesse got close enough for him to reach his head and pull him down for another one of those greedy kisses.

As Jesse started to breach Hunter, though, Hunter pushed him away. "I need to see you."

That was what he'd said months before, after the gala, when Jesse had been blowing him. Jesse smiled as he complied, boosting himself up on an elbow, shaking his hair out of his face.

He liked the idea that Hunter wanted to watch him. He liked the nonanonymity of it. Like he specifically was the only one who could do this job—fucking Hunter—the right way.

And he did. Pushed gently past the initial resistance and—
"Oh fuck."

He hadn't known. He'd had *no* idea.

He tried to move slowly, sinking into Hunter's body inch by excruciating inch, until he was buried to the hilt. Hunter's jaw had fallen open, and he was blinking rapidly.

"Okay?" Jesse prayed the answer was yes. Because this? He *needed* this. This pressure, this tightness, this feeling of being totally engulfed—this was what had been missing his whole goddamn life.

"Yes," Hunter breathed. "Yes. Move."

Jesse moved, pleasure shooting down his spine, everything in his body turning inward, pressure building in his dick and his balls.

"Harder." Hunter shifted his position a bit under Jesse, like he was trying to find a different angle.

It was almost too much. He took one of Hunter's hands, interlaced their fingers, and pressed their joined hands down on the bed. His other hand reset itself on Hunter's hip. "Ready?" he breathed.

When Hunter nodded, Jesse let himself go. Pounded into Hunter over and over again, the resulting slap of flesh on flesh exhorting him to find even more strength, to set an even more punishing pace.

"Oh!" Hunter cried out, his eyes widening. "There!"

Jesse tried to keep doing exactly what he was doing. His eyes wanted to roll back into his head, but he made himself keep looking at Hunter, both because he knew it was important to Hunter and because, egomaniac that he was, he loved seeing the effect he was having on him.

"Please don't stop," Hunter whimpered, using his free hand to stroke his own dick. The sight of Hunter jacking himself, Jesse's dick buried in his ass, almost undid him.

"Please don't stop," Hunter said again. It became a mantra he repeated over and over, the words melding together.

Jesse wanted to roar at the rightness of this—no, he *was* roaring. The gap between his thoughts and the expression of them had narrowed so much, it had disappeared. That was what Hunter did to him. "I'll never stop," he growled, his mouth expelling dirty thoughts the instant they arose. "I'll fuck you as long and as hard as you want, baby. I'll never stop."

As soon as the last sentence was out, Hunter shouted and started to come. Great big spurts, wave after wave, and it was the most beautiful thing Jesse had ever seen. He tried to keep going. Forever, he'd said, and he'd meant it. But it was only a couple of more wild thrusts before he was coming too, his body convulsing with the strength of the most powerful orgasm he'd ever had.

After it was done, they stayed where they were, staring at each other, panting.

Holy fuck.

Jesse didn't know what to do. What to say. Whether to laugh or cry.

After a few moments, Hunter laughed. A breathy, shaky, disbelieving, joyous laugh.

It unfroze Jesse. He grinned, carefully pulled out, and dealt with the condom. "Be right back," he said, and he jogged into the bathroom to clean himself up. He grabbed a clean towel, dampened a washcloth, and headed back to bed to take care of Hunter.

CHAPTER EIGHTEEN

Hunter woke up, and everything was different. It wasn't like in novels where the protagonist wakes up and needs a moment to remember everything had changed. He *knew* immediately that everything had changed. There was a tattooed arm over his chest, and his ass ached. His body was heavy with the delicious sensation of having been well and thoroughly used.

He'd gone all the way through the looking glass and back. And brought Jesse with him. Or kicked Jesse off the seesaw. Or something. He laughed at himself. His stupid metaphors were falling apart. But that was okay, because he didn't need them anymore.

He shifted and stretched the parts of his body that weren't pinned down by a slumbering Jesse. He was sore and stiff and *alive*. The only thing better than the dirty, loving, crazy-making fucking he'd had last night was the notion that he'd get to spend the day goofing off with the dirty, loving, crazy-making man who'd delivered it.

An all-day date with the rock star in Buffalo.

In public.

This was what people had been talking about all the time

when they'd told him to stop being such a workaholic. This feeling of wanting time with someone, wanting to gather great big handfuls of it and hoard it.

He got it now.

"I get it now," he whispered, because thinking it in his head wasn't enough.

"You get what?" came a muffled voice from behind him.

"Ahh!" Hunter laughed. "You faker!" Jesse had been so motionless, his breath so even, his arm so heavy, Hunter had assumed he was still asleep.

All at once, Jesse came to life. Rearing up, he was briefly backlit by the stream of sunshine slanting in from the half-open curtains. Then, laughing, he pinned Hunter to the bed and started pressing kisses to Hunter's neck, speaking between them. "I was just." Kiss. "Laying there." Kiss. "Sort of." Kiss. "Taking everything in."

Then he flopped back on the bed, sprawling over the tangled sheets, looking every inch the self-satisfied libertine.

Hunter had wondered what this morning would be like. He wouldn't have been surprised if, after all that had transpired, Jesse would be a little embarrassed. Hell, Hunter almost was. Their coming together had been so intense, so exquisitely intimate, he felt a little exposed.

But no, Jesse was still himself. Still the sanguine, cocksure rock star.

"I gotta take a leak." Jesse swung his legs over the edge of the bed. "And drink about a million cups of coffee." It was true—they hadn't gotten much sleep last night.

Hunter openly ogled Jesse's fine ass as he walked to the bathroom, calling after him, "What are we going to do today?"

"I vote for more fucking," came the answer from the bathroom.

Hunter laughed. "And after that?"

He heard Jesse finish up and flush. Then his head popped into view briefly, just long enough for an arm to snake out and snag the coffeepot. "Um, I'm going to go with more fucking?"

A tiny fear started to niggle at the edge of Hunter's mind. A day in bed had undeniable appeal, but was Jesse suggesting that because he wanted to hide out?

That he wanted to hide *Hunter*? That wasn't what he'd said last night. Hunter understood Jesse needed time to work on a strategy for coming out. He wasn't planning to be all over Jesse in public or anything, but he'd assumed they'd still be able to spend the day together.

"But," Jesse said, coming back into view and flipping on the little coffee maker, "if my dude wants to see surreal art or some shit, that's fine by me."

My dude.

That was such a Jesse way of saying it. Hunter grinned like a teenager as all his fears flittered away.

"I don't think the two are mutually exclusive," he said, laughing as Jesse mimed putting his mouth directly under the stream of coffee that had started from the coffee maker.

"I think they probably frown on fucking at the art museum."

Hunter threw a pillow at Jesse, who deftly ducked out of the way. "I meant, like, one at a time. In different locations."

When the coffee finished brewing, Jesse poured a cup. Then he lined up the edges of a bunch of powdered creamer packages and ripped them open. Jesse took his coffee black. Which meant Jesse was making the first coffee for Hunter.

It was just a small, probably meaningless, gesture, but Hunter's throat tightened all the same.

After Jesse finished doctoring the coffee, he delivered it to Hunter in bed. Hunter had to swallow hard. When was the last time someone had taken care of him like this?

"One at time, you say?" Jesse pretended to think about it as he returned to the coffeepot. "I can be down with that plan as long as the fucking comes first." He waggled his eyebrows suggestively. "And also maybe third."

Bang, bang, bang.

A pounding at the door. No, a battering—it sounded like a band of marauders was trying to get in.

"Shit!" Jesse had dropped his coffee and was shaking his hand as if he'd burned it.

"Jesse!" came a voice from the door. "Jesse, you asshole! Are you in there?"

Colin? Was that Colin? What would he be doing here?

The pounding continued. The door shook on its hinges.

"Colin!" A second voice, one Hunter recognized as Amber's, confirmed the identity of the first. "There's nothing to be done at this point! Leave them alone!"

Jesse was frozen with his burned hand extended in front of him.

"Fuck that! Jesse, if you're not in there, I'm going to find you at the fucking surrealism thing."

Hunter was frozen too, waiting for Jesse to do something. Say something. Hope mixed with dread in his gut. Clearly there was some sort of emergency. Would Jesse cop to being here? His mind started flipping through excuses. It was a quarter after nine. It wouldn't be that weird for Jesse to be in Hunter's room at that hour. But they were naked. They would need time to—

No. He wasn't doing that anymore.

Jesse making a PR plan to come out to the world was one thing, but hiding from his band was another. Jesse understood the difference. *Right?* Hunter's stomach clenched.

One more bang on the door, a single, short pummel, like a fist giving it a final shot.

"Hold your goddamned horses, Colin!" Jesse shouted, and relief slammed into Hunter. That Jesse wasn't going to hide, to dissemble... Hunter felt like his heart was going to crack open, but only because it wasn't big enough for the surge of emotion inside it. He sagged against the headboard, but only for a moment, because when he saw Jesse was hurrying to dress, he followed suit. Whatever it was, they would face it together.

With a glance over his shoulder, probably to check that Hunter was decent—which he was, but all he'd had on hand to scramble into was a hotel robe—Jesse yanked open the door.

"What?"

Colin marched into the room, angry and entitled.

Amber followed. "I'm sorry." She looked devastated.

"What the fuck is going on?" Jesse demanded, stepping between Colin and Hunter, and Hunter was grateful for it, because Colin was staring at him with undisguised hatred.

But then, over the course of a few breaths, all the rage bled out of him. As he took stock of the situation—Hunter in a robe, only one of the two beds slept in—he just...deflated.

"Check your phone, man," Colin finally said, shaking his head at Jesse. He said it again as he turned. "Check your phone. Google yourself."

Colin left, but Amber remained, unmoving. Looking stunned. "I'm sorry. I shouldn't have told him which room you were in."

"What the hell was that about?" Jesse asked.

"It's probably best for you to check your phone," she said softly. A little sadly. She squeezed his forearm. "Matty has been calling, but you take your time. I'll be here when you need me."

And then they were alone again.

But not like before.

All the joy from earlier, all the teasing happiness, had whished out of the room. Colin's invasion had punctured the balloon.

Wordlessly, Jesse reached for his back pocket and pulled out his phone.

"It's dead," he said, and his voice was too.

Hunter's own phone was charging on the nightstand. He disengaged it and nodded toward the cord, feeling a little like he was handing Jesse a gun with which to shoot him.

But no. He was being melodramatic. Obviously, something dire had happened, but it was better to know than not. He sat on the bed to wait.

It was taking a while for Jesse's phone to come to life. When Jesse, seated on the unused bed across from Hunter, glanced up, Hunter attempted a smile, even though his stomach was churning.

Jesse returned it. Well, his face did. It wasn't a real smile. It wasn't coming from inside him.

That was when Hunter really began to panic.

Jesse started scrolling through texts. His face went white.

"What is it? Is it Beth? Has Russell done something?" The chasm of dread snaking through his gut widened into a pit.

It couldn't be that, though. That wouldn't have brought Colin pounding the door off its hinges.

Jesse laughed, but there was no delight in it. There was only disbelief. Bitterness. Regret.

"In a manner of speaking, yes, Russell has done something."

He handed the phone to Hunter, rose, and walked over to the window.

Time folded in on itself then, because Hunter was looking

at a post on *GossipTO*. The three-word headline took his breath away.

Jesse Jamison Gay?

He read on, ignoring notifications of several incoming texts.

We couldn't figure it out. Our sources had dried up. There's been nothing on Toronto-based bad-boy rocker Jesse Jamison of Jesse and the Joyride for months. Years, really, now that we think about it. No pretty groupies ready to kiss and tell. No leaks from his crew telling tales of bender-fueled mischief. Where have the trashed hotel rooms been? Where have the broken hearts been?

Where has the infamous Jesse we all know and love been?

It turns out he's been in the arms—and bed?—of one Dr. Hunter Wyatt, Toronto-based doctor and a stone-cold silver fox if we do say so ourselves.

Allow us to present the evidence. After all, a picture is worth a thousand words. Or a thousand dropped jaws.

Hunter's jaw dropped too. They had pictures of him and Jesse from the gala. There was one of them dancing, toward the end, when Jesse had suddenly drawn him close. And another, a really grainy one, like someone had taken it with a telephoto lens, of them at the pond, Jesse hugging Hunter. From that photo alone, it wasn't clear it was them. Just like that initial shot Jesse had shown him on the train, he thought bitterly. But together with the dancing shot, it could be pieced together, based on their clothing and Hunter's hair color.

It took his breath away, the way they had intruded on

those moments, those beautiful, private moments and twisted them into something salacious, something to mock.

He went back to the article, his skin prickling all over.

GossipTO has also been in touch with one Mr. Russell McDaniel, Jesse's brother-in-law, who reports that on an impromptu visit to Jesse's house, he caught the pair looking very cozy, if you know what we mean.

What followed was a bullshit interview with Beth's asshole ex, and then the article breezily wrapped up.

Jesse! You sly dog. You've managed to shock us, and that's saying something.

Another text arrived. He could see from the preview that it was from Matty, Jesse's manager.

He looked up. Jesse was still at the window, his back turned, still as a statue.

It was a gross invasion of privacy, but Hunter didn't care. He tapped the message and was flipped into Jesse's texts. To a huge string from Matty. He backed up and started reading from the first one, time-stamped at ten past two in the morning.

Call me. Important.

Check your voice mail.

Goddamn it. CALL ME.

I fucking told you to stay out of trouble. I

told you to stay on brand.

That one had a link to the *GossipTO* story. After that, he kept going.

It's all over the place. Everyone's asking
for statements. People. USA Today. Fucking
Rolling Stone, Jesse. Call me, you asshole.

I have a crisis communications firm engaged.
Standing by for whenever you decide to grace
us with your attention. If, you know, you
care at all about not ruining your career.
About not ruining all of our careers.

Then, the one that had just arrived.

I'm sorry I flipped out on you. Please call
me. We can fix this.

"*We can fix this.*" Hunter had a pretty good idea how Matty would propose to "fix this." They would trot out evidence to discredit Russell—that wouldn't be hard. They'd get someone who was at the gala to explain what had happened there. Likely someone from the hospital's PR team, who would testify to Hunter and Jesse's longstanding platonic friendship and come out with Jesse's previously unpublicized donation. There probably wasn't such an easy way to explain away the hug by the pond, but he was sure the Jesse Jamison machine would come up with something. The fucking *crisis communication* team, because God knew, falling for a man was nothing if not a crisis.

Fuck that. He tossed the phone onto the bed as a tide of

anger rose through his body.

He didn't know to whom it should be directed, though. None of this was Jesse's fault, and being angry at "the world" wasn't helpful.

And what Jesse needed right now was help. He was probably scared. He'd admitted as much last night. Okay, they could handle this. They just needed to come up with a plan. They needed to find that PR person who was not in Matty's orbit, as Jesse had said last night.

Hunter forced down his anger and spoke to Jesse's back. "So…you're gay? Or bi?" They hadn't actually had a conversation about the details last night, because honestly, Hunter didn't give a crap what Jesse's labels were. He'd needed only to be sure that this thing between them was real. Was going to be acknowledged. But now the shit was hitting the fan, and they needed to establish some facts so they could decide how to proceed.

Jesse answered but didn't turn. "Bi."

"Does anyone else know?"

Jesse turned. Scoffed. "They do now."

"I meant, does anyone close to you know. Beth?" He'd been thinking about whether they could pull together a support team of sorts.

"No. She'll be as surprised as everyone else." Then he softened and sank into a chair near the window.

"It's going to be okay."

"But is it? My whole career is built on this image of me," he said slowly, his eyes slipping shut, like looking at Hunter was too much to bear.

"I know." Hunter did. He understood. For Jesse, coming out was going to be a lot harder than it was for most people.

Jesse opened his eyes. They were different. Shuttered. Dimmer.

Hunter had shoved his anger away a minute ago, but it had left behind an empty space, one that was now filling with unease.

"You remember that photo?" Jesse shifted his gaze to the ceiling. "The one I showed you on the train?"

"Yes." Of course he did. That photo had dogged him.

"That's what I used to do. Pick up the occasional guy. Not even that. Just…not resist when the occasional guy hit on me. But I sort of had these…rules about…what could happen."

"You'd let them suck your dick, but not the reverse. Not anything else." Classic closeted behavior.

"Yeah, because somehow, in my mind, if I stuck to that rule, I wasn't…gay, or bi, or whatever. I was just…an opportunist."

"Okay." Hunter waited for Jesse to voice some sort of plan. Some intention. He hadn't operated by that irrational "rule" last night, after all. He had looked into Hunter's eyes, said, *"I get it,"* vowed to come out, and then fucked him.

Jesse did not articulate any sort of plan, though. Instead, he kept talking to the ceiling, telling Hunter stuff he already knew. "After that shot came out, I got crucified in the press for cheating on Kylie."

God. If Jesse would just *look* at him, it would feel like he was helping Jesse make a plan instead of listening to Jesse recite a speech. Hunter tried to prevent the unease swirling around in his chest from mixing with Jesse's weird detachment and alchemizing into panic.

"Our manager at the time dumped us," Jesse went on. "Said it was the final straw. The guys were livid. It was a big fucking mess. I'd ruined everything. But then, somehow, I convinced Matty to take us on. He was way out of our league at the time. It felt like…a reprieve. So I cleaned up my act. No more pot. No more partying. No more…"

"No more guys," Hunter finished for him, no longer able to hold back the panic and struggling against gray spots in his vision, because this *was* beginning to sound like a speech. A very particular kind of speech.

Jesse nodded. "I told him the truth about the picture. He told me—and he was right—that the world wasn't ready for Jesse Jamison with a dude. Made it a condition of signing us."

How do you know he was right? Hunter wanted to shout, but he refused to come off as desperate. If Julian had taught him anything, it was that he was only ever going to let himself be with someone who wanted him. Who *chose* him.

"Matty *made* us," Jesse went on. "We were doing this bullshit regional touring, selling maybe a hundred thousand copies of a record. Then Matty comes on board with his 'rebranding,' and suddenly we're headlining arenas in the States and our records are going gold."

Hunter wanted to object, to say that *Jesse* had made *himself.* Because to think that it wouldn't have happened without Matty? That was ridiculous. But Hunter saying it wouldn't make Jesse believe it.

Jesse kept talking. "And I thought, well, I like women too, so there's no problem here. It wasn't like I was looking for anything serious. I wasn't expecting..."

"You weren't expecting what?" Hunter whispered, a single ember of hope left glowing in his chest.

"You. I wasn't expecting you."

Jesse finally made eye contact with Hunter, and Hunter knew it was over. The ember went black. Acid flooded Hunter's mouth, pungent and sick-making.

It was happening *again.*

It was as bad as Julian. Worse.

"What about last night?" he said, trying to make himself sound angry instead of hurt.

"I thought I could do it. I was going to…come out on my terms," Jesse began, but then he fell silent.

"And what were those terms?" Hunter asked, his voice, thankfully, under control. "What was that going to look like?" He could see now he should have asked this question last night. Shouldn't have given in when Jesse had said he didn't want to talk anymore. Shouldn't have been so trusting.

"I don't know." Jesse's voice was heavy with emotion.

Hunter moved to his suitcase and began methodically pulling out clean clothes. It was all he could think to do.

"You have to understand—"

"I do understand," Hunter said. The disdain in his voice shocked him, but it also gave him something to hang on to. Anger was a scaffolding, a structure that would get him through the next few minutes with his dignity intact.

"This isn't just about me." A pleading note had crept into Jesse's voice. "There's the whole band, the crew."

It is *about you*, Hunter wanted to argue. Jesse was always coming out with that, "It's *my* band," line, but apparently that was only true when it was convenient.

They stared at each other for several excruciating moments. Finally, Jesse broke the standoff, returning his attention to the ceiling. He sat for a long time like that. Then he said, "I gotta go. I gotta talk to Matty." He got up, grabbed his jacket, and without looking at Hunter, said, "I'll call you."

And left Hunter alone in a hotel room with a pile of lollipops and a broken coffee mug. A broken heart too.

No. That wasn't right. Hunter's heart had already cracked last night—that time because it hadn't been big enough to contain all the happiness inside it. Now that the happiness was gone, he was left with an empty shell—two pieces of something that used to be a heart.

CHAPTER NINETEEN

"Are you sure it's not better for Jesse to address the controversy head-on?" Matty said, drumming his fingers on the table in the conference room at the label where they were all meeting to discuss the fallout resulting from the fact that Jesse had fallen for the wrong person.

"Absolutely not," said the crisis communications woman—Nicole? Nancy? He couldn't remember, but she was made for the job. Equal parts soothing and firm, she'd outlined a strategy that involved them saying nothing official but planting a reporter who would ask a rehearsed question that Jesse would then answer seemingly off the cuff. "It's vastly preferable that he not protest too much."

"I'm inclined to agree," said Peter, their rep from the label.

"This is an opportunity, really," said Nicole/Nancy. She wasn't sitting at the head of the table—that was always Matty's spot—but Jesse had to admire her low-key confidence. "We can use Jesse's image as the swaggering, devil-may-care rock star to shrug this off. He's so attractive, everyone with a pulse wants him. If we play this right, it's not just damage control. We can end up bolstering the brand."

The brand.

Nicole/Nancy's plan was that they would play on his reputation as a womanizer. He was a hypersexual, devil-may-care playboy who, though he was straight, had embarked on a little gay experimentation à la David Bowie, because why not? The world was big and full of beautiful people.

The interesting thing was no one had asked him what he wanted. Which was fair, he supposed. He'd always done what they told him. Lived up to his bargain with Matty. Because up until now, he had been content to implement Matty's version of how the Jesse Jamison narrative should be controlled.

He had gone on public dates with women they chose for him. And, hell, not so long ago, there *had* been groupies talking to gossip rags about being with him. He did used to be a slut. The perfect bad-boy rock star next door.

He *was* the brand—he'd given them no reason to believe otherwise.

Which was why the rest of the band wasn't here. He'd asked about it, and Matty had told him they'd be briefed on the plan later.

Nicole/Nancy said, "So if we're all agreed, this is what's going to happen: After tomorrow night's show in Boston, Jesse and the band will leave the venue on foot. There will no doubt be a crowd of genuine reporters assembled, but we'll have our guy there too." She slid a piece of paper across the table to him. "He'll be wearing a purple shirt—you won't be able to miss him. Everyone will be shouting questions at you. You stop, smile, and say that you're feeling generous and will take one question. Chose our guy. He'll ask you directly if you're gay. Then you say that." She pointed to the paper. "Memorize it. Practice it. If it doesn't sound natural, it won't work."

Jesse looked down at the paper.

"Then you push onward, acting like everything is normal.

Like you find the whole thing amusing. Ignore any other questions. You walk a block or so, laughing with the guys, and we'll have a car there. Get in it, and you're done."

The room went silent. Everyone looked at him. Finally.

"I want to talk to Hunter," Jesse said.

Matty reared back like Jesse had struck him.

"I want to talk to him first."

"Jesus Christ, Jesse, you're not telling me that this is *actually* a thing? That you're going to make it a thing?"

"If that's the case, we need to regroup," Nicole/Nancy said calmly.

Jesse stood. "I'm not saying we need to regroup. I'm just saying I need a fucking hour to have a conversation."

Matty was about to erupt again, but Ms. Calm in the Storm spoke first. "Fair enough." She shot a quelling look at Matty. "Everyone needs to be on board for this to work. Let's all reconvene here in two hours."

I need to talk to you.

The text came while Hunter was on his way to his place. Beth's place. To evict her, basically. He felt bad about it, but he would give her a lot of notice. She was already looking at apartments, anyway, since she and Gavin really needed two bedrooms. He could move into a hotel in the meantime.

But the text. *I need to talk to you.* He had to pull over to gather himself.

It was probably not going to be good news. If a conversation was going to end with, *I love you enough to risk everything*, it generally didn't begin with the lukewarm, *I need to talk to you.* But what could he do? Jesse had said, this morning, that he'd be in touch, and here he was. And Hunter's stupid, stupid heart. It held out hope.

Hunter: OK.

Jesse: Are you back in town? Can you come here?

Yes, you asshole, he wanted to type. *Even though you fucking abandoned me in Buffalo this morning, I'm not still sitting in that hotel room pining after you.*

Hunter: Where's here?

Jesse: The label — Queen West, north side, just west of Spadina.

Hunter: OK.

Jesse: I'll send a car for you.

Hunter: I'm actually still in the rental. I have it until tomorrow. I can drive.

Jesse: No, I'll send a car. Where are you?

He was willing to talk to Jesse. He was willing to get his hopes up one more time. But only if there was a chance, however slight, that they wouldn't be trampled on again. Pride was a funny thing. It was possible it was leading him to be oversensitive, but he had to check.

Hunter: What kind of car? A black one with
tinted windows? One that will drive in some
sort of secret back entrance?

Jesse: Don't be like that.

Hunter: Don't be like what?

Jesse: Can you just do this one thing
for me?

Hunter: What thing?

When he didn't get an answer, he typed another text.

Hunter: Hide? I think the word you're
looking for is "hide." And no. No, I
will not.

Fuck. That. That was not happening. Never again. And
fuck *Jesse*. Jesse *knew* that.

So much for hope.

He threw the phone on the passenger seat. Then picked it
up again immediately to finish this shit.

Hunter: I'll have my stuff out of your house
by the end of today.

Then he got out of the car and walked up the porch to his
place to go evict his ex–best friend's sister from his apartment.

The next evening, he was glad he had. Because when he
saw a clip of Jesse, strolling along the street with the guys after

a show, what he saw made him thank his lucky stars he'd ended things on his own terms.

Jesse didn't even seem bothered by the phalanx of reporters hanging on him. "Okay, dudes, one question!" he laughingly said, calling on a reporter whose name and outlet Hunter didn't catch.

"I'm just going to go ahead and ask the big question," the guy said. "Are you gay?"

Jesse grinned. "Nah, man. But everyone's allowed an experiment or two, right?" Then he winked. He fucking winked.

And then, laughing, the band made its way out of the picture, cheerily ignoring everyone shouting after them.

An *experiment*.

The dried-out halves of Hunter's broken heart splintered into a million fragments.

CHAPTER TWENTY

After Jesse looked at the stupid purple-shirted fake reporter and told the biggest lie of his life, there were only two weeks left of the tour.

They had been the longest two weeks of his life.

On paper, everything was fine. Everything was more than fine, because eff him, but the "controversy" regarding his sexuality had caused a spike in sales. Matty was crowing about how the crisis communication people had been right—what had looked like a potential disaster had actually turned into an opportunity.

"But no more," he'd laughingly told Jesse. *"I'm not as young as I used to be. My heart can't take it."*

Jesse's heart couldn't take it, either.

Of course, he'd tried to contact Hunter. But his texts were going unread, and Hunter had an autoreply on his email saying he was "away from email for the foreseeable future." What the fuck did that mean?

But could he really blame Hunter for cutting him off? He'd known Hunter's deal from the beginning, was aware of how much Julian had hurt him with his failure to acknowl-edge their relationship.

And, really, a man like Hunter shouldn't have to hide. It felt like a crime against nature.

So, yeah, Hunter had his bottom line, and ultimately, Jesse had his. They'd come to an impasse.

That was the rational interpretation.

The real interpretation, *the truth*, was that his heart was broken, and he was pissed. He knew he was supposed to be angry at himself. And he was. If any crimes against nature had been committed, he was the guilty party.

He'd had a glimpse of…everything. Of how life could be. And then he'd traded it away.

But he was also angry at…fucking everyone else. At the whole world.

Stepping outside the terminal at the airport, he spied his sister's car. They'd flown in from their last tour stop, and she'd insisted on picking him up.

It was just as well. He was spoiling for a fight, and she would give him one. She'd been riding his ass since she found out what had happened with him and Hunter—from Hunter, he assumed, since he hadn't told her about any of it.

"Why does Hunter's email autoreply say he's away for the foreseeable future?" he said, after he'd thrown his bags in her trunk and climbed in the passenger side.

"Hello to you too," she said, her tone clipped.

The back seat was empty. "Where's Gavin?" He'd been looking forward to seeing his nephew. It was the one bright spot in the shit storm his life had become.

"Babysitter," she said curtly as she pulled away from the curb.

"Is that safe?"

"It's one of the teachers from his after-school program."

"Not at my house, I hope." Not that he didn't want his family at his house, but he didn't trust Russell. Somehow, the legal A-Team that Matty had assembled for Beth had resulted in Russell finally signing divorce papers and a court awarding temporary full custody—pending a trial that was scheduled for next week—to Beth. But just because Russell had signed his name and suddenly expressed a desire to play fair didn't mean the motherfucker wouldn't turn on them.

"No. At my place. Hunter's place. Which is back to being my place."

He whipped his gaze to her. She remained impassive, calmly checking her mirrors as she merged onto the highway as if she hadn't just detonated a grenade in his lap. "I thought you were moving." That was the last he'd heard from Beth. Hunter had asked her to start looking for a new place, and of course she'd agreed.

"We were going to. Hunter was going to take his place back. But then he...didn't need it. We're formally subletting it for the next nine months."

"Where is Hunter?" He had tried to keep his voice controlled. He had not succeeded.

She pressed her lips together. He waited her out until she finally spat, "Don't you think you've given up the right to know the answer to that question?"

"Yes!" he shouted. "Yes, I bloody well have! But I don't fucking care, Beth!" Why wouldn't she answer the goddamned question? "Where is Hunter?"

She flinched. Physically cringed away from him.

"I'm sorry," he said quickly. What a dick he was. Of all the people to subject to an unhinged roar. "I just... Please. Please tell me where he is."

"He's in Syria."

What. The. Fuck.

"I'm sorry, *Syria*?" Like, probably the most dangerous place in the world right now, Syria?

"Yeah, with Doctors Without Borders."

"Jesus, Beth, why didn't you tell me?"

"He asked me not to!" It was her turn to get loud. "And it's none of your damn business anymore! The only reason I *am* telling you is because you can't go chasing after him there."

He put his head in his hands. He was going to throw up.

"He said he'd come to Toronto to start over, to do things differently. Said he thought for a minute there he'd succeeded because he'd found—" Her voice hitched and she cleared her throat before continuing. "Said he'd found the love of his life here. But in the end, it was no different than Montreal. So he needed to go somewhere else. To do something radically different. Something that mattered. He had a friend running a field operation there who pulled some strings and got him deployed really quickly."

Jesse rolled down the window and retched.

It must have awakened her maternal instincts because she said, "Oh, sweetie. I'm sorry."

"Is he coming back?" His voice sounded small, defeated. Scared.

He *was* scared. He was so fucking scared. Jesus Christ, people were *leaving* Syria by the thousands. Risking everything to escape the violence there. And Hunter had walked directly into it?

"I don't know. He said he'd be in touch toward the end of his placement and we'd talk about the lease. I'm paying the landlord directly now, so I don't even know how to get ahold of him. He…" She took one hand off the steering wheel and grabbed one of his. "He wanted it that way."

"What do I do, Beth? What do I do?"

"What can you do? Say your prayers."

CHAPTER TWENTY-ONE

In the next month, Jesse learned a lot about Syria.

Civil war, local politics, munitions—he was an expert at all of it now.

The problem was, he had no idea where in the country Hunter was. He thought about asking someone at the hospital. Andrea Bingham, maybe. But in the end, he decided he couldn't be that much of a dick. Beth had been right. He'd given up his right to know what was going on with Hunter.

Officially.

But like hell was that going to stop him from poring over maps and setting up macabre google alerts: *Syria + airstrikes*, for example.

He even got wi-fi at the cottage, because God forbid he be unable to ingest the news every moment of the day.

The band was taking a break before work started on the next album. The tour had been followed by filming the stupid Kylie video, and everyone was exhausted. Jesse had been holed up at the cottage for a month, and he'd created an obsessive routine of sorts centered on repeatedly checking various outlets for any news out of Syria. Coffee, news, more coffee, news, breakfast, news, a punishing swim, news, lunch, news, dinner, campfire-and-brood, news, bed. Rinse and repeat. He hadn't been able to write. He wasn't even trying, really. Couldn't rouse himself to care that they would need a pool of potential songs ready to go when they started recording the next album in a few months.

The only deviation from his routine so far was when Beth and Gavin had spent a week. The divorce had been finalized, and Russell, given his past threats of violence, had been granted only supervised monthly visits with Gavin. As much as he hated to see Beth having to haul Gavin back and forth to Montreal once a month—as much as he hated her having any contact at all with that asshole—it seemed like a decent outcome. The court had also okayed Beth staying in Toronto permanently, the judge ruling that the Toronto-based family support system would benefit Gavin.

"Family support system" being Jesse. Ha. Poor Beth. Hunter had been the real support system. In addition to giving them his apartment, it sounded like he'd really stepped up while Jesse was on tour, helping them with court dates and generally being the great guy he was. Beth wasn't saying it in so many words, but he got the sense that she and Hunter had become genuine friends. So in pushing Hunter away, not only had Jesse lost him, his sister and Gavin had too.

The sound of a car crunching over the gravel out front plucked Jesse from his reverie. He closed the book he was reading—*Syria: A Recent History*—and prepared for the onslaught.

It was the guys, arriving for the weekend. He hadn't seen them for a while. He should be looking forward to their visit.

He sighed. Except for Beth's visit, he'd been alone for a month, and honestly, he wanted it to stay that way.

"Dude! The final cut of the video is done!" Billy cavorted

his way inside, his sprawling enthusiasm feeling as out of place in Jesse's life as a lion in a library. "It looks amazing!"

Jesse opened his computer. "Okay. Let me download it. Did they email it?"

"You got wi-fi?" Colin asked. The others looked at Jesse in bewilderment.

"I did." The notion of the cottage as a creative haven had gone right out the window as soon as the whole Syria obsession had begun.

"Well, we didn't know that, so we have it on a memory stick," Will said.

Jesse took the thumb drive, stuck it in his computer, and they all huddled around to watch.

It was great. He'd known it would be. With the combination of song, director, concept, and Kylie, there was no way it couldn't be.

It was also all wrong.

"What's the matter?" Ash asked when it was done. "You don't like it?"

They were all looking at him expectantly.

"It's…fine," Jesse said. It was. It would achieve its aim. It would sell records, and it would keep the buzz around the band going.

"It's not *fine*," Billy declared. "It's fucking amazing. It's the best video we've ever done."

"What's wrong with the video, Jesse?" Colin's tone bordered on aggressive.

"Nothing." Jesse wanted this conversation to be over. "The video is great." He scanned the bags they'd brought. "Did you guys bring any booze?" His month of solitude had been dry, except for a bottle of wine he'd shared with Beth, and he could do with a drink right about now. He could do with many, many drinks.

"You wanna have lunch first?" Billy asked. "We brought pizzas from town."

"No," Jesse said. "No, I do not."

♫

That night after dinner, the guys went for a moonlight swim, and Jesse settled in by the fire for his nightly torture session. He would stare at the fire and replay the night he'd kissed Hunter here. That buoyant feeling that anything was possible. The joy of having his favorite person visit his favorite place.

The wonderful shock of Hunter's lips. The life-changing shock of *him*.

And then his mind would move on from the fire. To the gala and the explosion of exhilaration he'd unleashed in himself as he'd bid on Hunter. To that charged embrace outside the ramen restaurant. To running in the rain. To the incredible, utter rightness of being allowed inside Hunter's body.

He knew it wasn't healthy, to obsess like this. And yet, he did it every night. Exactly the same.

Except tonight was a little different. Tonight, Jesse was drunk, so he was extra maudlin. He actually felt like he might cry.

Well, that would be a new addition to the routine.

"Hey."

It was Colin, wrapped in a towel, shivering. He came to stand by the fire. "It's a cold night."

Jesse hadn't noticed. He didn't notice shit like that anymore. Hot, cold, day, night: it was all the same. "You got any pot?" he asked, suddenly feeling like maybe a few tokes would deliver the oblivion his day of drinking had not.

"No. And if I did, I wouldn't give you any."

"Well, thank you very much for that."

"What's up your ass lately?" Colin pulled up a camp chair and settled in.

Now he was supposed to have a big heart-to-heart with Cranky Colin? No, thanks.

"You don't do drugs anymore." Colin's brow furrowed as he took in the half-empty whiskey bottle resting on the picnic table next to Jesse.

Jesse rolled his eyes.

"You did something a couple years ago, when we signed with Matty. You don't talk about it, but you cleaned up your act. You started making us come up here to write."

Jesse didn't confirm, but he didn't deny.

"We got *better* after that," Colin said. "That's when everything started to happen—after you made all those changes. And now you're going to become a pothead?"

"Jesus Christ, Colin," Jesse snapped. "I just asked you if you had a joint."

"Why are you reading books about Syria?"

"Why do you think?" he shot back, growing increasingly pissed. He almost regretted telling the guys about Hunter's deployment, but they needed some explanation for why he suddenly wasn't around. They'd all accepted it without comment—except Colin. Not that he was commenting, but he was…needling. Colin and Amber were the ones who had seen him with Hunter that morning. Amber had tried to talk to him, right around the time Ms. Crisis Communications had him rehearsing his fake Q&A. He had brushed Amber off. Colin, though, seemed unable to let the matter rest.

"You know I'm only a dick because I care about this band," Colin, apparently tonight's king of non sequiturs, said.

That took some of the piss out of Jesse, because it was true.

Colin took the music more seriously than the others. He sighed. "I know."

"But I think maybe I made a mistake. I think maybe we both made a mistake."

"What the hell does that mean?"

"It means some things are more important than success. Than money. Than fame."

"Will you quit speaking in riddles?" Jesse said. "If you have something to say, just fucking say it."

"Do you love him?"

And there it was. The real question. He considered not answering. He considered a lot of things actually: punching Colin, getting up and going inside, running into the lake. But he was so tired. So scared for Hunter. So he told the truth. "Yeah."

Colin nodded. "And that's what's wrong with the video, right?"

Jesse stared at the fire unblinkingly, letting the smoke burn his eyes. "That song is about him."

"All right," Colin said, pulling his chair closer to Jesse's. "So what are we going to do about it, then?"

CHAPTER TWENTY-TWO

"Thank you all for coming," Jesse said to the group assembled in the same boardroom they'd met in a little over a month ago. It was strange to be at the head of the table, to be the one running the meeting.

Matty was going to lose his mind. The label might drop them.

This might be the end of Jesse and the Joyride.

He took a deep breath and looked at the guys. They were all looking back at him encouragingly. God, he was a lucky motherfucker. Hell, if he'd known how supportive they would be, maybe he would have come out of the fucking closet months ago.

He had to correct his earlier fatalistic thought. No matter what happened, this wasn't going to be the end of Jesse and the Joyride. They'd assured him as much, that night when Colin had hauled them all out of the lake and they'd stood around the fire dripping and shivering while Jesse told them he was in love with Hunter. Colin, to Jesse's shock, had then announced they were trashing the video for "When You're Mine" and starting over.

"Dude," Billy had said. "So you like dick. Big deal. I wish I liked dick. I feel like it would be so much easier to get laid."

And then they'd stayed up all night, hatching their plan.

"You all know Ian Logan," Jesse said. Ian had directed the original "When You're Mine" video, so the suits all nodded. Smiled at him. Turned out Ian had been totally on board with their new plan, excited about the buzz the new video would no doubt create. He had been happy to huddle with Jesse and the guys to work out a new strategy.

A strategy they were now going to blindside the team with.

"There's no easy way to say this," he said, trying not to fidget, "so I'm just going to say it." He straightened his spine. "We're going to do some reshoots for 'When You're Mine.'"

"That's it?" Matty said. "Jesus, you scared me with this big formal meeting. You know we always want to hear your feedback on videos and stuff."

Ha. They had no idea.

And, *fuck*, he was scared.

He looked at Colin, who nodded down at the pictures lying upside down on the table in front of Jesse.

"All right," Jesse said. "I don't want Kylie in the video. I've talked to her. Explained it all. She understands." And, amazingly, she had. Add another name to the list of people who had been nothing but supportive of Jesse's news.

Matty sighed. "Jesse, I've told you the strategy behind using Kylie."

"The rest is good," said Jesse, talking over his manager. "The rest is great. The concept remains unaltered. We just want to replace Kylie with someone else."

Matty started to object, but Peter from the label waved his hand. "Let's hear him out. Who do you want?"

Here it was. Jesse lifted the top picture. "I want this guy."

There was stunned silence from the men around the table and a gasp—a happy one, Jesse thought—from Amber.

"The song is about someone very specific," Colin said calmly. "It's important the video reflect that."

"What the fuck, Jesse?" Matty's quiet tone was at odds with his harsh words. It would almost have been easier if he'd yelled. Jesse had been prepared for that. He had not been prepared for quiet, contained rage. He...didn't know what to do with that.

"Jesse likes dick now," Billy said.

Jesse had never been happier to have Billy on his team.

"I'm pretty sure Jesse has always liked dick," said Will contemplatively.

Will too. All of them. Their unwavering show of support, delivered with their own personal flourishes, was exactly the bolstering he needed here.

Matty looked like his head was going to explode. "We've talked about this. We talked about this on *day one*, for Christ's sake."

"I'm bisexual, Matty, and I'm done hiding."

"You can't just put your boyfriend in the video," Matty shot back.

"It's not him," said Jesse. "It's a model who looks a little like him." They'd all decided it was best to evoke Hunter in the video, but not cast a carbon copy of him. The latter seemed a little too creepy, given that Hunter basically didn't want anything to do with him. "Anyway, he's not my boyfriend. He took off because I was too chickenshit to call him that."

It felt good to say those words out loud, as painful as they were.

"Regardless, it's not about him. It's about me. About standing up and saying, 'This is who I am.'"

Did a small part of him hope that somehow, irrationally, Hunter would see the video and come home to him?

Hell, yes.

But that wasn't the point.

Billy turned to Matty and made a surprisingly—for Billy —smart argument. "You were willing to put his actual ex-girlfriend in the video. So who cares about a dude that sort of looks like a guy he likes?"

Hope started to swirl in Jesse's chest. As the guys had been reminding him, they didn't need the label to make the video. They didn't need Matty. They had cash, and they had a director. They could reshoot the whole thing and put it on YouTube themselves if they wanted to. But it would be so much easier not to get dropped by the label.

Peter turned to Jesse. "Look. You gotta do what you gotta do. I'm, uh, all for that. I'm going to level with you. We've been dedicated to Jesse and the Joyride. We've done good things together, I think."

Jesse nodded his agreement.

"But this business is ultimately about money. I can't promise anything, but I think the label will be fine with this direction as long as the next album does as well as the last. Deliver the goods, and I don't care who you sleep with, is what I'm saying." He raised his eyebrows. "Hell, seeing the numbers after last month's so-called crisis, I'm not convinced this won't *boost* sales."

"Thank you," Jesse breathed, his legs going so weak with relief he had to sit. He surveyed the table. Peter was packing up to go—onto his next meeting no doubt—and the guys and Amber were smiling at him.

Which left Matty.

"I need...time to absorb this, Jesse."

"That's fine." Jesse didn't need Matty to run out and join PFLAG. "But you should know that—"

"No." It was Billy, standing as he spoke. "You're either with us, or you're not."

Jesse blinked. They hadn't talked about this, about what would happen if the label was on board but Matty wasn't.

"That's right." Will popped up next to Billy, the Williams of the rhythm section providing a united front that took Jesse's breath away. "It's not that complicated. And, frankly, you'd be an idiot to let Jesse Jamison go. He's made you a shitload of money. But if you don't want us, we'll have no trouble finding someone who does."

Then it was Colin's turn. "Anyway, it's not like anything is going to change. We'll make this video, everyone will freak out, but then we'll still be making the same music. He's still Jesse."

And finally, Ash: "And we're still the Joyride."

Amber stood too, tears running down her cheeks. She didn't say anything, but her message came across just the same.

"Thanks, guys," Jesse croaked, swallowing the lump in his throat. "Why don't you give me a call next week, Matty?"

And then he stood up too, grinned at his ragtag little army, and walked out of the conference room.

He had shit to get done.

Time to face the music.

CHAPTER TWENTY-THREE

Three Months Later

Hunter wasn't expecting to come home early.

Even so, that didn't explain why, when he stepped into a taxi at the airport and the driver said, "Where to?" he had no earthly idea what to say.

He'd had plenty of time to think about it, first in Germany, where they'd sent the team when they evacuated the hospital in Syria, then on the long flight home.

So why hadn't he? Why was he back on Canadian soil with no plan and nowhere to go? Maybe he should have asked them to reassign him.

He was so tired, though.

It wasn't just the long flight. It was…existential tiredness.

He'd left Toronto wanting a change, and he'd gotten one. Life in northern Syria had forced all the Jesse-related drama out of his mind. The past several months had been about pure survival—that of the people he'd treated and, during the airstrikes that had prompted the evacuation, his own.

At one point, he'd wished he could click his heels like

Dorothy and be home. But what had he really meant by that? Where was home?

He could call Beth. He could show up at his apartment, and she would no doubt make room for him. He wasn't sure why he hadn't called her already. *Hey, I'm coming home early, and I'll need my place back.* How hard was that?

Too hard, apparently, for his tired brain.

He could go to a hotel for a few nights. That might be the best thing. He was having trouble wrapping his mind around the fact that he was back. That it was autumn in Toronto. That regular life here had been cheerily unfolding as it always did. Maybe a few days in a hotel, a big downtown one where he could get a room high above the city, would function as a decompression chamber of sorts. Like one of those air locks on spaceships that astronauts go through to transition between outer space and the controlled environment inside.

He pulled out his phone—a brand-new, unfamiliar one, as he'd lost his in the evacuation—to book something, and opened his mouth to tell the cabbie to take him downtown.

What came out instead was Jesse's address.

Jesse would rather be at the cottage, but, all things considered, a party at his house in the city wasn't a bad way to pass an autumn evening.

All the guys were here. A bunch of staff from the tour. Amber. Beth. Kylie. A couple of his neighbors, even. It was a motley crew.

But it was his. And they were here to celebrate the fact that the video for "When You're Mine" would drop tomorrow night.

Avery had sent her good wishes too. He'd emailed her the

video and sworn her to secrecy. She'd responded with a string of emojis and slang he was pretty sure was an enthusiastic endorsement of the idea of him and Hunter together.

His motley crew did not contain Matty. Jesse still felt the sting of that blow, but they had moved ahead and signed with a new manager. And it felt like a coup that they'd snagged Tony Spencer, who was megastar Emerson Quinn's manager.

Emerson, with whom Jesse had had a little flirtation a few years ago, was another person who'd offered her support when he'd come out to her. He'd reached out to her because he'd read in the industry trades that she'd recently made a management switch, dumping her established management company in favor of Tony. So far, Tony seemed good. They'd taken a bit of a risk on him, given that their sound was quite different from Emerson's, and Colin had freaked the hell out over the prospect of having an "American bubblegum-pop Svengali" overseeing their careers, but the guy really seemed to get them.

And more importantly, when he'd given Tony a variation on the directive Matty had given him, Tony hadn't blinked.

"You do the business stuff, and I do the music stuff," he'd said. Then he'd added, *"I also do the personal stuff."*

So on paper, things were looking up. It felt good to be actively taking charge of his future. To be the one giving the orders instead of the one taking them.

It was starting to feel like a moot point, though. All of it— the management change, the video, the coming out. Because he was pretty sure he was never going to actually be with another man again.

Or a woman, for that matter.

No one measured up.

He had tried to move on. He wasn't obsessively checking the news anymore. His heart didn't feel like it was going to shatter every time he went to the hospital, where he was still visiting kids. But it felt like he was only going through the motions of having a life without Hunter in it. Without him around, even just in his capacity as best friend, the world was...less. Less interesting, less bright, less imbued with possibility. The idea of falling in love again, with anyone? Impossible. The idea of going back to his old womanizing ways—even if now they were officially "personizing" ways—seemed so far off as to be laughable.

But, regardless, onward he went down the path he had committed to.

Because even if he never saw Hunter again, the only thing Jesse could think to do was to make himself into the kind of person who might be worthy of a man like Hunter.

Maybe in the process he'd also become a worthy man, full stop.

"Is this a bedbug bite, do you think?"

Billy was showing Beth his elbow.

Jesse laughed. He *did* have his army of weirdos. That wasn't nothing.

It was getting dark, and the party was ramping up. It was a video-release party, so they should probably watch the video? Except for a couple of his neighbors, everyone in the room had seen it, but what the hell. He moved through the room toward the TV, picking up empty beer bottles, moving one of his guitars, which had migrated to the center of the room, into a safe corner.

He was about to start fiddling with the TV to get it to mirror his phone so he could play the video, when the doorbell rang.

He reversed direction and threaded his way through the crowd, trying to think who it might be. Maybe Avery and her family had shown up to surprise him? He had invited them, but Avery's mom had nixed the idea, as it was a school night.

He kind of hoped it wasn't Avery, frankly. There was nothing untoward about the party, but it was getting loud, and the booze was flowing. Gavin was with a babysitter, and that was for the best.

He stooped to pick up another stray half-drunk beer bottle from the floor in the entryway, and swung the door open as he stood back up.

The bottle slipped right out of his hands and shattered on the wood floor.

He didn't recognize the sound that came out of him then. It wasn't a sob, not really—that word was too anemic.

It was the sound of reprieve, of deliverance. Of his worst fear—Hunter being killed in Syria—the fear that had dogged him so intensely for so many weeks, just...evaporating.

Hunter looked terrible. His face was ashen, and there were circles under his eyes.

"I was in Syria." Hunter's eyes were wary, like he was unsure of his welcome. "With Doctors Without Borders."

Jesse was frozen, the beer he was standing in seeping into his socks and his breath coming out in short, desperate pants. He felt like he was floating outside his body, but somehow he managed to force himself to nod. He tried to say, *I know*, but he couldn't get any sound to come out.

"There were airstrikes," Hunter went on, probably to fill the silence that had been created by Jesse's inability to speak or move. "They pulled us out. I'm not supposed to be back yet." His sentences were short and clipped. He broke eye contact and ran his hands through his hair. "I didn't know where to go," he said to the pavement, his voice small in a way Jesse never wanted to hear again.

It unstuck Jesse. He reached out and pulled Hunter over the threshold and into his arms.

"You come here. That's where you come. You come here."

This was what Hunter had been looking for, without realizing it, what he'd been casting around for restlessly, unable to settle on any particular course of action.

Home.

Jesse's arms.

They banded around him—hard and strong and steady, like they were gathering all the disparate pieces of him that had started to float away. He knew he could never have Jesse, not the way he wanted. But this Jesse—any Jesse—was better than nothing. He'd missed his best friend so damn much.

"Come inside," Jesse said gruffly, after they'd stood, embracing silently for several long moments.

Hunter hadn't been able to hear anything but the harsh rush of his own breath, but once he stepped over the threshold, the rest of the world made itself known. That had always been the problem with Jesse and him, hadn't it? The rest of the world.

"You have people here." God, he was so tired. He couldn't deal with people. He started to pull himself away from Jesse, but Jesse held on.

"Go upstairs." He pressed his hand against the small of Hunter's back and propelled him toward the stairs. "I'll get rid of them."

Get rid of them? "You don't have to do that, I'll…"

But he was gone. A couple seconds later, Jesse shouted, "Party's over!" Then he clapped his hands. "Everybody out."

There was an explosion of confusion. Incredulous voices. A lot of indignant exclaiming about a video. Hunter went halfway up the stairs so as to be out of sight. He knew he'd have to face real life soon, but he…couldn't deal with humanity right now.

Jesse kept shouting, not angrily, but resolutely. "Sorry, guys, I love you, but get the fuck out."

Hunter sat down on a step as he realized the old attraction was right there. It hadn't gone away. There was Jesse, doing his competent, bend-the-world-to-his-will thing, like nothing had changed. And the fact that he was doing it on Hunter's behalf only made it worse.

Well. He had no choice here. He was going to have to find a way to carry on this friendship, hiding the fact that he was secretly in love with his best friend. Because he might have no idea what the hell he was doing, but this homecoming had crystalized one thing in his mind: he couldn't live without Jesse.

As for how to actually find a way to carry on without getting his heart rebroken day after day, he'd figure it out later. Jesse would let him crash here tonight, and Hunter would get his shit together tomorrow. He was so tired. He just wanted to retreat to Jesse's guest room and become unconscious.

He watched as Jesse stood at the door while everyone left, deflecting both indignant complaints (Billy) and concerned inquiries (Beth). No one noticed him, perched as he was halfway up the dark stairway.

Jesse held Amber back, though, and spoke into her ear for a long time. She visibly started at one point, but then her shock was replaced by a wide smile. He kept talking, and she kept nodding.

When he was done whispering in her ear, she threw her arms around him and hugged him.

Was it Hunter's imagination, or did she spot him as she did so? Her face didn't change much, but there was something there. Recognition. The tiniest whisper of a knowing smile.

"I'll talk to Tony tonight," she said. "We'll make it happen. I'll text you when I know something."

"I think Will was headed out of town," Jesse said.

"Not anymore he's not." Amber blew Jesse a kiss as she slipped out the door.

Jesse turned. The light was on in the entryway, so he was fully illuminated in all his Jesse Jamison glory. His hair was a little shorter than it had been when Hunter had left, but everything else was the same. The frayed jeans, the faded, vintage Iron Maiden T-shirt.

Hunter's stomach flopped like it was a sentient creature. He had no earthly idea what Jesse was going to say to him. Would he be angry that Hunter had left so suddenly? Angry that Hunter was even here?

"Come into the kitchen," Jesse said. "I'm going to make you something to eat."

"You don't have to do that. If I can just crash here tonight, tomorrow I'll figure out—"

"When was the last time you ate?"

Hunter had to think about that. "I, ah, had some pretzels on the plane."

"The plane from where?"

"Germany. They took us there to debrief after the evacuation."

Jesse turned and disappeared from view. "Come into the kitchen," he called as he retreated. "I'm going to make you something to eat."

Hunter got up. When had he ever been able to resist Jesse?

He followed Jesse to the kitchen and sat at the marble-topped island he knew so well from his time here.

The kitchen was littered with party debris, but Jesse moved through it with cool efficiency. He produced a loaf of bread, a stack of that processed cheese that came in individual packages —Hunter hated that cheese—and plopped some butter in a frying pan.

"Want a drink?"

A drink. Hunter hadn't had a drink since he'd left Toronto four months ago. He surveyed the empty beer bottles everywhere. "Do you have any wine?"

Wordlessly, Jesse opened a cabinet. Hunter couldn't look away from the long lines of his body as he reached for a wineglass on an upper shelf. His T-shirt rode up, and his jeans were loose enough that they hung low, exposing the top of one hip bone.

Something stirred inside Hunter, started pricking through the blanket of fatigue he'd been carrying around.

That strip of exposed skin disappeared as Jesse moved to the refrigerator and extracted a bottle of wine. He pivoted and placed the glass in front of Hunter, like he was a bartender. Filled it with pale-yellow liquid.

Jesse stood and stared at Hunter. He seemed to be waiting for him to take a drink.

The wine was tart and cold when it hit his tongue.

Sauvignon blanc, his brain said, and he realized there was a whole history inside his head, a normal life he had lived that had contained things like sauvignon blanc instead of the wounds of war.

They had made him see a shrink before he'd left Germany. She'd screened him for PTSD and all that and pronounced him basically fine. Told him it was normal to feel sad, overwhelmed, restless, guilty that he had escaped Syria when so many could not. He felt all those things. He'd been having nightmares, which she'd said was also normal. The shrink had told him things would probably get measurably better when he got home. As he took another sip of wine and the cool liquid paradoxically spread heat in his belly, he had the first glimmering that perhaps she had been right.

Jesse was making a grilled cheese sandwich. The stove was

situated so Jesse's back was to Hunter as he worked. It occurred to Hunter that he'd never really seen Jesse cook, other than pancakes at the cottage. Jesse dined out. He ordered takeout.

Jesse plated the sandwich and slid it across the island to him, then leaned back against the counter and stared at him.

Hunter knew he wasn't getting out of this without eating the sandwich, so he lifted it to his lips and took a bite.

"Oh my God," he said through that first gooey, buttery mouthful. It was so good. Crispy and oozy and hot, and suddenly he was famished. Suddenly he loved processed cheese.

He wolfed it down in a few bites.

Jesse smirked. "You want another one?"

Hunter shook his head. Probably now was when Jesse would unleash a million questions at him. Get angry, even, for leaving without telling him. That he hadn't so far had Hunter on edge.

"What do you want?" Jesse asked.

A good question. He had no idea. But for tonight… "I was hoping I could crash in your guest room."

Jesse nodded and pushed off the counter. Topped up Hunter's wineglass, picked it up, and hitched his head toward the stairs.

Jesse's guest room, which had been Hunter's for several months before he'd left town, was achingly familiar. It was small and cozy, filled entirely by a desk and a double bed. Hunter had brought his own bedding over when he'd vacated his apartment for Beth on the eve of the band's tour, and it was still here. He must have forgotten it in a haze of heartbreak when he'd cleared his stuff out that day. There they were: his duvet, the perfectly calibrated pillows he favored. He was surprised Jesse had kept them around.

Jesse set Hunter's wine down on the nightstand. "You need anything? Something to sleep in? Toothbrush?"

Hunter shook his head. He'd left all his stuff in Syria in the chaos, and what he'd accumulated in Germany and wanted to keep, he'd shipped to himself at the hospital. There was a small toiletries bag in his backpack. He had no immediate needs. No material ones anyway.

I need you to stay here with me.

But he wasn't allowed to need that, so he settled for being grateful there wasn't going to be an interrogation this evening and that he could lie on a familiar bed and try to sleep.

"Okay, then." For a moment Hunter thought Jesse's eyes had filled with tears, but it must have been a trick of the light. He rapped his chunky rings against the doorframe, just like he used to do at Hunter's hospital office, and the sound sliced through Hunter, both painful and welcome. "Good night."

CHAPTER TWENTY-FOUR

When Jesse awoke to shouting, his first thought was that he didn't remember arming the alarm system last night. Which was weird, because he'd been diligent about security since Russell's surprise visit last winter.

But then he remembered why he'd forgotten.

Hunter.

Hunter, who was currently crying out as if in pain in the guest room.

Jesse flew out of bed like it was on fire and tore down the hall.

Hunter was having a nightmare, thrashing around in the bed. He wasn't shouting anymore, just mumbling. Nothing Jesse could make out, but it was definitely distressed mumbling.

"Hunter," he said, trying to pitch his voice loud enough to cut through slumber but not loud enough to frighten. "Hunter." He sat on the edge of the bed and laid a hand on Hunter's shoulder.

Hunter woke with a start. Shot up to a sitting position, his eyes wild, darting around the dark room. Violently shoved Jesse's hand away.

"It's okay." Jesse put his hands up in the air even though that was the opposite of what he wanted to do. "It's me. It's Jesse. You're at my house. You're having a nightmare."

Hunter's body relaxed a little, but he started shaking, like he was freezing.

Fuck this not-touching thing. If Hunter really didn't want him to, he wouldn't, but he had to try again. Moving slowly so Hunter could clearly see what he was doing and had the opportunity to object, he let his hand float back down and land on Hunter's upper arm.

This time, Hunter clasped his own hand over Jesse's, as if he wanted to make sure it stayed there.

Jesse opened his mouth to comfort, to reassure, but no words came. Instead, he pulled Hunter into his arms. Hugged him tightly, as if physical pressure could somehow ease the shaking.

And eff him if it didn't eventually work. As they sat there, Hunter's breathing slowed. His body quieted.

It might have been ten minutes later, it might have been an hour, when Hunter started to extricate himself. Jesse's instinctual reaction was to tighten his grip, but he forced himself to go limp. He wanted to howl at the wrongness of letting go, but for now at least, he had to mind the boundaries. After tomorrow night, things might be different.

But then, a miracle: Hunter hadn't let go, not entirely. He'd just pulled away enough to shift his body. He wanted to lie down. He wanted...Jesse to lie down with him?

"Stay?" Hunter whispered, the syllable tentative on his lips, almost embarrassed, like he didn't think he should be asking but couldn't help himself.

A surge of...something moved through Jesse's chest. Something he couldn't name. He lay back, taking Hunter with him, keeping Hunter in his arms. Then, once they were situated, he used his foot to draw the comforter, which was scrunched down at the bottom of the bed, up enough that he could use one hand to grab it and cover them.

"I've got you," he whispered into Hunter's hair. "I've got you." He was supposed to be comforting Hunter, not vice versa, but a profound settling happened inside him, a surrender of effort and a laying down of worries.

They didn't speak after that. Just lay there holding each other in a bed that was too small for two grown men. It wasn't sexual, not exactly. It had that potential—when Hunter was around, that potential was always there, simmering under the surface of whatever else was happening—but there was another, bigger sensation cresting inside him.

It was whatever that surging feeling in his chest had been before.

He knew what it was.

Tomorrow, he would name it.

When Hunter awoke, he felt…peaceful?

He hadn't felt this way for a long time.

Peace was quickly replaced by embarrassment, though, as he remembered waking from the nightmare he'd been having off and on since the evacuation. But then, Jesse, with his warmth and silent surety, an unexpected anchor in the storm.

As sheepish as he felt at having exposed himself so utterly, he couldn't quite make himself regret it, because after Jesse had gotten into bed with him, Hunter had *slept*. He hadn't done that for months. The psychologist had said the nightmares would fade with time.

Apparently they also faded with *Jesse*.

He picked up his phone from the nightstand to check the time. It was *noon*.

"Ha!" He was giddy, awake, and, he realized with astonishment, content.

Also hungry. Ravenously, distractingly hungry.

He threw on his clothes from yesterday—he'd have to either buy some new stuff or take a cab to his storage locker. He peeked around Jesse's bedroom door, which was ajar. It was empty.

Downstairs, the place was still a mess, post-party, but the kitchen had been tidied.

There was a note on the counter.

Sleeping Beauty,

We have a show tonight, if you can believe it. We're doing one of those pop-up surprise shows. It's at Massey Hall at eight. Will you please come? If you can't manage it, I understand, but...

There was a bunch of stuff crossed out then. Hunter held the note up to the light, intensely curious to read what Jesse had written, then deemed not right, but he couldn't make anything out.

It would mean a lot to me if you came. Amber is arranging a ticket for you. I don't have your number (I think you changed it?), but if you text it to me, I'll pass it on to her, and she'll be in touch with details.

Regardless, make yourself at home, crash here for as long as you need. I got a few staples, and there's breakfast in the fridge. Don't run off. Talk tonight.

J.

Hunter blinked, trying to process all this information. If he'd been asked yesterday if he wanted to go to a rock concert, the answer would most decidedly have been no. He felt much better today, but even so, the idea of a crowd of people shouting, of loud music blasting from speakers, was not appealing.

But then he imagined Jesse at the front of that crowd.

"It would mean a lot to me if you came."

Also: *"Talk tonight."* Yes, they did need to talk. To clear the air once and for all between them, so they could move on. Yesterday had settled one question for him. He was incapable of not having Jesse in his life, so if Jesse would still have him as a friend, which seemed likely, Hunter would have to get on with the business of sublimating his feelings. It wasn't ideal, but it was...life.

So, all right. He was going to a rock concert tonight.

He picked up his phone.

It's Hunter. Of course I'll come tonight. And...sorry about last night.

The reply came immediately.

Good morning! Don't be sorry. I'm not. Well, I am sorry I abandoned you. We have tons to do to get ready for this show tonight.

Then another one.

Did you eat breakfast? You should eat. I got stuff for you to eat.

Hunter smiled.

Hunter: Cool your jets. I'm about to.

Jesse must have gone out this morning because the fridge contained fancy deli breakfast sandwiches, and there was a box of assorted pastries on the counter. He took a bit of everything, along with a giant cup of coffee, to Jesse's breakfast nook. It was cool but sunny outside, and the light streaming in from the skylight above energized him.

Once full, he contemplated the rest of the day. He should probably get in touch with Beth and figure out the living situation. Contact the HR office at the hospital and make a plan to return to work.

Instead, he started cleaning up the remnants of last night's party. He wasn't even sure why. Jesse would object if he knew. But there was something about cleaning up the concrete mess in front of him that was immensely satisfying. To do something specific and finite and to see a pleasing result. Everything else could wait.

It took him a couple of hours. He probably left the house cleaner than it had been to start with, and that made him smile.

Then he went out to lunch, to the ramen place, in fact. He bought a newspaper to read while he ate.

Bought some clothes to wear to the concert.

Went back to Jesse's and took a nap.

It was all very surreal. But it all felt good, felt *normal.*

When he was about to head underground to get on the subway, he fired off a text to Jesse for no reason other than that he wanted to.

Hunter: Break a leg tonight.

Jesse: You're coming, right?

Hunter: Yep. See you soon.

Then he composed one more message. As lovely as the day had been, inhabiting Jesse's empty house, going to the ramen shop, getting his land legs back, he knew this break from real life couldn't go on forever. They had to have the talk. Kick the seesaw again—but he was feeling less aggressively metaphorical about things now.

Hunter: I'm hoping we can talk after
the show?

Jesse: Yes. Absolutely.

All right, then. Amazingly, less than twenty-four hours after his plane had touched down, he was off to a Jesse and the Joyride show.

CHAPTER TWENTY-FIVE

And what a show it was. It was unusual these days for Jesse and the guys to play such a small venue. As great as Jesse was at playing to large arenas, he was born to play a place like this. The nineteenth-century theater held a few thousand people, Hunter guessed, and was known for its intimacy. The small stage was close to the audience, and the balconies—Hunter was seated front row center in the first one—jutted way out over the main level, creating a cocoon effect.

Jesse was killing it. *"Well, hello,"* he'd drawled after they'd ambled on stage. *"Fancy meeting you here."* The crowd had gone wild, and the band had launched right into the opening song, a rip-roaring number that was one of their biggest hits. When it was over, he shrugged and said, *"Sometimes you just feel like putting on a show."*

And so it went. They were in top form musically, and Jesse was in the zone, doing his bantering-rock-star thing.

It was good for Hunter's soul, as stupid as that sounded. He couldn't be here and not smile. Not sing along. Hunter wasn't a music person, or at least he hadn't been before Jesse, but he felt every note slide through his bloodstream, better than any drug.

"This is the best I've ever seen them!" the woman next to him exclaimed to her friend, and Hunter had to agree.

He didn't want it to end. And for a while, it felt like it wouldn't. The band never seemed to tire. They didn't take an intermission, just kept rocking.

But then it did end. The final notes of the last song faded, and the band came together at the front of the stage to bow. Hunter joined the audience on its feet, cheering and clapping. The applause continued even after the band left the stage.

"They'll do an encore," said the same women next to him. "They haven't played 'When You're Mine' yet."

And as if she'd willed it to happen, Jesse appeared on stage again, but he was alone. He smiled and waited, and when the crowd didn't quiet, he made shushing motions with his hands. "We have a little surprise for you tonight," he said when he could finally be heard. "Sit down and be good, or you don't get it." He flashed a signature Jesse Jamison flirty smirk and the audience shut up—mostly. There was a catcall or two from people who just couldn't resist.

"The video for 'When You're Mine' releases tonight at midnight, but we're going to show it to you all here first." He gestured at a pair of video screens flanking the stage. They'd been blank for the duration of the concert, and Hunter had assumed they were superfluous, infrastructure left over from something else that they hadn't been able to get rid of due to the impromptu nature of the show. "And then we'll come back and play you a couple more songs before we say goodbye," Jesse finished. "Sound good?"

The crowd went wild.

Hunter did not go wild.

If memory served, this was the video that Jesse had told

him about, the one he wasn't excited about. The one with Kylie Cameron in it.

All the fizzy joy that had been frothing through his thirsty body evaporated.

But it was a good reminder. He'd been living in this weird little bubble today, but bubbles were ephemeral by nature. He was resigned to salvaging his friendship with Jesse, and that meant he had to accept Jesse—all of him, including his limitations.

The video started with a shot of a funky, brick, warehouse-type building in the rain. The camera moved up and through a window. Inside an open loft-like structure a few floors up was Jesse, staring forlornly out the window.

The crowd got louder when he appeared. He did look broody and irresistible, singing and gazing out at the rain. It went on for most of the first verse, then there was a cut to a crowded restaurant. This scene was brighter, and as Jesse's character walked into the shot, he was happy, smiling, walking toward someone off camera. This would be the flash to happier times, with Kylie.

Except, the camera widened and it wasn't Kylie Jesse was walking toward with a grin.

It was a guy with a gray pompadour and black glasses.

The bottom dropped out from the balcony. Hunter was falling. Falling.

But then he forced himself to stop. To pay attention.

Oh my God. It was the ramen shop. The Jesse character slid into a table next to…the Hunter character? It wasn't a replica of him or anything, just an actor about his age with gray hair. But there wasn't any other interpretation, was there?

If he'd been unsure, the next scene sealed it. The action moved to a formal evening. People dressed up and dancing.

Tuxedoed Jesse leading the Hunter stand-in onto a crowded dance floor and taking him into his arms.

Hunter took long deep breaths. If he hyperventilated, he would miss something, and that was unacceptable.

After a little bit more of the "happy" montage, the action cut back to Sad Jesse in the building. Then it moved up to a rooftop. Another day, because it wasn't raining anymore. The rest of the band was there, playing the song. Then Jesse emerged from a door, walked over, and picked up a microphone and started singing along, coming in at exactly the right time. But he was still Sad Jesse, pensive and restrained. This coincided with the part of the song where things got quiet and subdued.

Then there was a great big streak of lightning as the rain started, and the Hunter character burst through the door.

Jesse's face changed, even as the rain picked up, transformed itself from resigned and morose to…overjoyed. Even more amazing than the video itself was that the song was different. They'd recorded a different ending. Instead of ending on the sad note, the song swelled again as Jesse dropped the mic and ran to the Hunter actor and kissed him. A great big Hollywood kiss with the cameras revolving around them and the storm raging overhead. It went on and on as the smiling band played and the rain fell.

With perfect music video coordination, the kiss ended just in time for Jesse to retrieve his mic and sing the last lines of the song. The final shot of the video was him looking directly into the camera, breaking the fourth wall with his signature Jesse smirk, as if to say, *This is me, and I dare you to object.*

Holy shit.

The lights went out. It was utterly silent in the theater.

Then, after a painfully long second, the crowd lost its

collective mind. Rose to its feet and screamed and whooped and whistled and clapped.

Hunter's mind was stumbling. Moving slowly to try to process what had just happened. *"This video is releasing tonight at midnight,"* Jesse had said. A video wasn't made overnight. He had been planning this. Was going to release this video even though he'd thought Hunter was gone.

Hunter jumped when the lights came back on onstage. The band filed out and took up their instruments. They were, to a man, smiling.

Jesse came last. Calmly put on his guitar, but then slid it around so it was hanging off his back, and approached the mic.

Smirked. "So, in case you didn't get that, that was kind of a personal song for me. A love song. Because you see, what happened was..." He lifted a hand to his forehead, shielding his eyes from the bright stage lights. "Can we have some house lights, please?"

The theater went from darkness to light, a reverse dimming. Jesse scanned the crowd. He must have known where Hunter was sitting because it only took a few seconds for his gaze to land on its target.

"What happened was, I fell in love with my best friend." He grinned, an *aww shucks* grin like he was a teenager at a school dance, and Hunter's eyes started leaking.

"His name is Hunter," Jesse went on, "and this song's for him."

He swiveled his guitar into place, turned, and nodded at Will, who banged his drumsticks together to count them in, and the band played Hunter's song.

"How do you feel?" someone asked Jesse as the band spilled offstage. He wasn't sure from whom the question had come, but everyone looked to him for the answer.

"Like I should have done this years ago."

It was the truth. He wondered now what he had been so afraid of.

It was like he'd been running a marathon, out of breath and exhausted, struggling forward at any cost, and he'd suddenly…stopped running.

There would probably be blowback tomorrow, but right now, he was undaunted by that prospect. The disapproval of the wider world, or the internet, felt like a bug on his clothes he could easily brush off.

But he couldn't let himself rest fully, couldn't enjoy his victory, until he knew if his Hail Mary pass had been successful. He'd been so focused on pulling off the insane stunt of an impromptu concert, working furiously all day alongside Amber and Tony, who'd flown in from LA to secure the venue, get all their shit there, and release ticket info, that he hadn't thought about what would happen…after.

He tried to socialize, to pay attention to the people surrounding him, to be gracious in the face of their good wishes, but he kept scanning the crowd, looking for that familiar flash of gray.

After fifteen minutes, he started to panic. The show had been last-minute, and they didn't have the usual meet-and-greet obligations, so the backstage crowd wasn't very big—just the band and crew and a few friends.

He caught Amber's eye. She'd been unsettled too, perusing the crowd. When her gaze met his, her brow knit in concern. Shit. If Amber was giving up…

But then something happened. Her face changed so quickly, it would have been comical in other circumstances.

The furrowed eyebrows sprang in the other direction, climbing her forehead as her mouth fell open. She came running over.

"Oh my God, Jesse! I gave him a ticket, but I forgot to give him a backstage pass!"

Something exploded inside Jesse then, something insistent and delirious that was too big for his body to contain. He whipped his gaze to the door. Instead of one of their usual security guards, a beefy stranger stood in front of it.

"Hank and his crew are on tour with Bieber!" Amber said, reading his mind. "These rent-a-cops don't know Hunter."

He was already at the door. "You see a guy with gray hair here?"

"Sure did," the guard said. "Persistent little fucker kept trying to get in. Finally had him removed."

"Where? Which way?"

He pointed. "Out the backstage door."

Jesse went barrelling down the hallway, his heart pounding in time with his feet. The door was manned by another big dude. He must have sensed the urgency, because he stepped out of the way in a maneuver that was half solicitous door-man, half taking cover.

Jesse flung the door open so violently it banged against the exterior wall of the building.

And there he was. Leaning against the bricks all tousled and gorgeous. He'd been typing on his phone, but he looked up when the door opened, his eyes wide.

The security guy came to stand next to Jesse on the threshold. "Threw this guy out a few minutes ago. He's insisting it's a free country and he's allowed to loiter in the laneway if he wants."

"It's okay." Jesse eyes latched on to Hunter. "He's with me."

Hunter had pushed off the wall but hadn't otherwise moved. He seemed stunned. They stared at each other.

"You are, aren't you?" Jesse asked, suddenly entertaining the stomach-dropping possibility that his big declaration had been too little, too late.

The question seemed to unstick Hunter. A slow smile blossomed. "Yeah. Yeah, I am."

And Hunter's smile, in turn, unstuck Jesse. He'd intended to have Hunter come inside, but that would have required more talking, and right now his priority was to get his hands on Hunter.

They crashed into each other in a tangle of arms and laugher and relief.

Their lips found each other. And it was different, this kiss. Like always, Hunter lit Jesse up, a thousand firecrackers exploding inside him. But knowing the beautiful man in his arms was *his*—for real this time—made everything bigger. Hotter. More.

He needed more leverage, so he planted his hands on Hunter's hips and walked him backward, never letting up on the kiss. When Hunter's back hit the brick wall opposite the theater, Jesse let his hands float up to Hunter's face, tilting it back so as to deepen the angle of this kiss he never wanted to end. Their bodies lined up perfectly. He ground his hips against Hunter's, relishing the low moan that ripped from Hunter's throat.

Hunter tore his mouth away and panted, "This is just like that picture."

"What picture?" Jesse moved his mouth to Hunter's neck and nuzzled. If Hunter wanted to talk, Jesse was willing to listen, but he still needed his mouth on some part of Hunter's body.

"That picture from that gossip website." He whimpered a

little, and Jesse loved it. Loved that he had the power to summon those sounds from Hunter.

"The one you showed me on the train," Hunter added, breathless.

Jesse's response was to grunt and move back to Hunter's mouth, to sweep his tongue deep inside, working it over mercilessly.

It *was* like that picture on the train in that they were making out against a brick wall, but in every way that mattered, this was different.

This time, he wasn't hiding.

Hunter pushed against Jesse's chest. He seemed to be trying to talk again, damn him. "What?"

Hunter nodded at something behind Jesse. "We're, ah, not alone anymore."

Jesse looked over his shoulder. A small crowd had formed. The guys and Amber were watching from inside the still-open backstage door, grins on their faces—even Colin's. The laneway itself had filled with a dozen or so people he didn't know. They were watching, rapt. Some of them held their phones aloft, taking pictures or filming, no doubt.

He turned back to Hunter. "Well, we'd better give them a good show, then."

And Jesse bent down to keep kissing his man.

EPILOGUE

One Year Later

> ### *Jesse Jamison stepping out on his silver fox boyfriend?*
>
> *Thanks to a tip from a reader in London, we can confirm that Jesse Jamison, whose band is touring Europe, was seen in the company of this unknown blond beauty. The leggy lady and Joyride front man were seen, heads together, smiling and laughing, in Bond Street.*

Jesse rolled his eyes and stuffed his phone into his pocket without finishing the article. Fucking gossip rag was going to dog him the rest of his natural life. He returned his attention to the people emerging from the customs hall in the international arrivals section of Heathrow's terminal two.

The band was on tour with a new album, and the European leg had been tough. Six endless weeks since he'd been home. The North American leg hadn't been so punishing. They'd scheduled it with breaks every two or three days so they could return to Toronto, but of course that wasn't possible overseas. Nightly FaceTimes with Hunter—which were frequently nightly SexyTimes—were not enough. Not remotely. His hands itched. He had to get them on his man. Now. Hunter was joining them for the last two weeks of the tour. And then they'd go home together. A frisson of excitement ran through him, and a dirty slide show started in his head.

He was lurking in a corner where he could see everything but still be somewhat sheltered from the crowds—he'd be damned if he missed Hunter's arrival because he was signing autographs. Since he was semihiding, he saw Hunter before Hunter saw him. Hunter emerged, and Jesse's breath caught. That silver hair, those fitted jeans and slightly dressy button-down, and, when Hunter finally spotted him, that incandescent smile.

It was always like this, every time he clapped eyes on Hunter after they'd been apart. He was suffused with a mixture of love and gratitude and disbelief.

Also lust. There was definitely some lust in that mix.

He started forward. Hunter was holding a magazine in his hands. He shook it at Jesse as he approached. The latest issue of *Rolling Stone*. The one Jesse was on the cover of.

Jesse grinned. He couldn't not. It had been his heart's ambition for so long, so it was a sweet victory. An ironic one too, because they'd wanted to talk to him on the one-year anniversary of his very public coming-out.

It was also a *smaller* victory than it would have been for his former self. It wasn't that he didn't appreciate it, just that there was so much more important stuff in his life now.

Like the guy holding the magazine.

So he waved it away in favor of enveloping Hunter in a hug. He wanted to fucking pick him up and twirl him around like they were in a sappy movie, but he settled for a long, hard embrace. Followed by a long, hard kiss.

"I hear you're cheating on me with a mysterious blond woman," Hunter teased as Jesse picked up his bag, slung an arm over his shoulder, and started propelling him toward the exit.

Hunter was kidding—they were solid and they both knew it—but Jesse rolled his eyes and leaned down to whisper in Hunter's ear. "I have a six-week case of blue balls that says otherwise."

"I'd like to see that." Hunter laughed. "Purely as a medical curiosity, you understand."

"Oh, you will." Jesse wagged his eyebrows as he held open a taxi door for Hunter. "You will."

There was nothing like having an international rock superstar for a boyfriend to cure a man's workaholic ways, Hunter reflected as said international rock superstar boyfriend tried to steer them through the lobby of the Four Seasons London.

In the last year, Hunter had taken all of his vacation days, flying to join Jesse for little stretches of his tour. And when Jesse was home, Hunter was out of work the moment his shift was over. And not always to spend time with Jesse, even, but because Gavin had a school performance, or Beth was making dinner for them. And when Jesse was away, he made himself go to the Maple Leafs viewing parties. Worked with the Canadian organization he'd helped found to bring war orphans from Syria and elsewhere over for treatment. Just generally tried to have a life. He didn't want to be one of those guys whose entire life was his boyfriend.

He laughed at himself as he watched Jesse deftly deflect fans as they aimed for a bank of elevators. Who was he kidding? Still, it was important to make an effort, so: Go Leafs!

There was a bit of a crowd assembling. Jesse took Hunter's hand. He was always doing that, like he was afraid they might be separated.

Hunter fucking loved it.

This was what had been missing in his life. He didn't need grand public declarations—though that night in Toronto had been magical—but to be claimed by small gestures like this one, on an ongoing basis, made his heart ache with joy.

With the help of a bellman who kept other people out, they managed to get into an elevator alone.

Jesse dropped Hunter's hand like a hot potato, dropped his bag like another one, then grabbed his ass and kissed him.

Hunter had developed a pretty serious case blue balls himself on the endless taxi ride to the hotel. So while he opened his mouth to Jesse's plundering tongue, he yanked Jesse's T-shirt up and ran his hands over his back, needing to touch bare skin.

Too soon, the elevator dinged, and the door opened to their floor. Jesse grunted his displeasure, but picked up the bag and retook Hunter's hand. Speed-walked them down the hallway.

The other elevator dinged behind them.

"Hey! Doc!"

It was the band. Hunter stopped. Jesse rolled his eyes and made a vague noise of frustration.

"Hi, guys," Hunter said. He was glad to see them—they'd become close over the last year, and he'd missed them too.

As everyone exchanged greetings, Billy rolled up the cuff of his pants. "Doc, can you look at—"

"Later." Jesse planted a hand on Hunter's lower back and pushed.

Laughing, Hunter let himself be propelled to a door a little farther down the hallway. As Jesse clicked the door open, Hunter called over his shoulder, "I'm sure it's fine, Billy, but I'll look at it later to make— *Oof!*"

Jesse shoved him into the room, bolted the door, and pulled his T-shirt over his head as he turned. Then he toed off his shoes and reached for Hunter's shirt.

"I should fucking rip this off you," Jesse growled. "That'll teach you to wear a goddamned button-down shirt when you're coming to see me."

"You love my button-down shirts," Hunter teased, starting on the buttons from the bottom since Jesse was working his way down from the top.

"Only because I love everything about you." Jesse lowered his head and took one of Hunter's nipples in his mouth. "I might love you *more* in a T-shirt, though."

Hunter moaned at the sharp lance of need that sliced through him when Jesse's lips made contact with his body, and then again in protest when Jesse pulled away.

Jesse started unbuttoning his own jeans. "Get naked," he ordered.

Hunter started to obey, but he only had his pants shoved down to his upper thighs when Jesse, who'd had a head start, fell to his knees and took Hunter's dick out.

"Ahhh," Jesse sighed, nuzzling it with his face for a few seconds before swallowing it.

"Oh my God!" Hunter bit out. He started to lose his footing—Jesse literally made him weak in the knees—but Jesse steadied him with a palm to each ass cheek.

This was where he belonged: caught between Jesse's mouth and hands, trapped. His heart swelled as pressure built in his lower back. "You're going to make me come way too fast."

Jesse popped right off. "Not yet. I need to be inside you." He looked up at Hunter, his pale eyes glittering. "Okay?"

"Yes," said Hunter, this time giving in to the weak-kneed thing and falling back on the bed.

This was big. They'd both had STI testing done when they first—finally—got back together and had them repeated recently. The results of the latest round had come in last week, and they were both clear. Which meant—

"I'm going to fuck you bareback," Jesse said, lubing up his dick. "I'm going to come inside you."

Hunter moaned, his cock leaking at the bold declaration.

Jesse finished stripping off Hunter's pants, and then he was everywhere, kissing him frantically on the mouth, spreading lube around Hunter's hole, his fingers massaging, preparing the sensitive opening.

"Do it," Hunter exhorted, bearing down against Jesse's fingers as the burning gave way to pleasure. "Do it now."

Jesse reared up, sat back on his knees, took his dick in hand, and slid in. "Oh, *fuck*, you feel amazing," he said, blinking rapidly and pausing once he was buried in Hunter to the hilt.

Jesse was always doing this thing where he stopped when he was fully sheathed in Hunter and gazed at him in wonder. He'd done it the first time, and he continued to. It was like he couldn't believe his good fortune, like he had to stop and take everything in. Hunter appreciated it, but it also drove him bananas.

"Move," he gasped, afraid he would come right then and there, before getting to experience any friction.

Jesse did, pulling almost all the way out and then sliding back in.

"Harder," Hunter said. "More."

"Bossy," said Jesse, but he grabbed Hunter's ass, tilted it up a bit, and started thrusting.

"Oh fuck, just like that." Hunter tried to keep his eyes focused—his vision was going blurry from the onslaught of pleasure as Jesse grazed his prostrate with every stroke. He didn't want to miss anything. Wanted to memorize the sight of his beloved, brow furrowed as he worked, long dark hair tousled, gaze never leaving Hunter's.

"You," Jesse said when he was at the bottom of the next stroke, buried fully in Hunter. Then he pulled out, saying, "Are," at the bottom of the next stroke. It was like he wanted to punctuate the importance of what he was saying, to fuck the words into Hunter. With the next stroke, he reached down and jacked Hunter's cock as he bit out, "Mine."

"Yes," Hunter said, both because he agreed with the statement, but also because it was the only word he could summon—it seemed like the only word in the world just then—as they came together.

Jesse collapsed on Hunter's chest, and Hunter held him, stroking his hair as they came back to earth. Eventually Jesse rolled off him, reached for the bedside Kleenex box.

"You hungry?" he asked as he cleaned Hunter up. "When did you last eat? Let's order room service."

Hunter smiled at the sudden—yet predictable—change in topic. There was no use arguing, he'd learned, and truthfully, he loved it when Jesse fussed over him. And he *was* starving.

When the knock signaling the arrival of their food came, Hunter's stomach growled audibly. A waiter pushed a trolley in, set up a table, uncovered their meals, and opened a…bottle of champagne?

Hunter shot Jesse a questioning look. He'd been in the bathroom when Jesse had placed the order. Jesse shrugged.

Hunter walked the waiter to the door, tipped him, and locked it after him.

"Oh!" He jumped when he turned, because Jesse was right there—he'd expected him to already be seated at the table across the room.

"I did see a mystery blond woman in Bond Street," he said quickly, his eyes darting around like he was nervous.

"What?" Jesse had pledged to be faithful to Hunter while on tour, and Hunter had never doubted Jesse's loyalty. But maybe he should have? He was confused more than truly worried, though. "What are you talking about?"

"I was in a store when that shot was taken. They must have taken it through the window. I was in Harry Winston. The mysterious blond woman worked there. She helped me pick this out."

Jesse dropped to his knees.

No, he dropped to *one* knee.

"Holy *shit*." In a million years, he had not seen this coming.

Jesse quirked a smile that was half-amused, half-nervous. "That wasn't really the answer I was hoping for."

Hunter opened his mouth to say yes. Just because he hadn't seen it coming didn't mean he hadn't secretly fantasized about this.

Jesse cut him off, though. "But that's okay, because I haven't asked properly yet. I thought about doing a big public thing at a show, or writing a song or something. But then I thought, no. I want it to be just us. You standing there and me saying, you are the most unexpected thing that has ever happened to me. You exploded my whole life. My heart. I love you so much, it's *astonishing*. And I know we haven't talked about it, and maybe you think getting married is straight-people bullshit, but I don't care. You can say no then. But I can't not ask." He took a deep breath and blew it out slowly as he opened the small velvet box he'd been holding. Inside was a slim platinum wedding band. Simple and shiny and perfect. Hunter had to bite his lip to keep from crying.

"So," Jesse continued, "Dr. Hunter Wyatt, will you marry me?"

"Yes." It was still the only word in the world when it came to Jesse.

And then they were hugging and laughing and maybe crying a little too. When things started getting heated, Jesse pushed him away. "You know Billy is going to burst in here any moment asking you to look at his butt, so you'd better eat." He led Hunter to the table and poured the champagne. "You're going to need your strength—we both are—because this time, I think maybe they really are bedbug bites."

ACKNOWLEDGMENTS

This book was originally published by Riptide Publishing, and I'd like to thank everyone there for helping bring it to life— and for reverting the rights to me when I asked. Sarah Lyons, Chris Muldoon, and Alex Whitehall edited, and L.C. Chase designed and did the cover.

My agent, Courtney Miller-Callihan, for working on this book—twice.

My friends Audra North and Sandra Owens provided extremely helpful feedback on early drafts.

Medical romance writer extraordinaire Amy Ruttan helped me with some of the hospital stuff.

Elle Keck and Sarah McDonald schooled me on the world of dating apps and their accompanying notification sounds.

A.J. Cousins and Rose Lerner answered lots of questions about the logistics of publishing a reverted book in a time when I needed advice that was both reliable and timely.

CONNECT WITH ME

Connect with me

Sign up for my newsletter at jennyholiday.com/newsletter. I send newsletters when I have a new release or a sale, and I sometimes include giveaways and access to freebies only for subscribers. Or you can find me on Twitter at @jennyholi or Instagram at @holymolyjennyholi. (I'm technically on Facebook, but I'm rarely actually there.) Visit my website at jennyholiday.com.

Reviews really help authors, not only because they help us find new readers but because more reviews means more favorable treatment by retailers' algorithms. If you're moved to leave an honest review of this book or any of my others on the retailer's site where you bought it, I'd be most grateful.

ABOUT THE AUTHOR

Jenny Holiday started writing at age nine when her awesome fourth grade teacher gave her a notebook and told her to start writing some stories. That first batch featured mass murderers on the loose, alien invasions, and hauntings. (Looking back, she's amazed no one sent her to a kid-shrink.) She's been writing ever since. After a detour to get a PhD in geography, she worked as a professional writer for many years. Later, her tastes having evolved from alien invasions to happily-ever-afters, she tried her hand at romance. Today she is a USA Today bestselling author of all sorts of romance novels: contemporary and historical, straight and gay. She lives in London, Ontario.

www.jennyholiday.com
jenny@jennyholiday.com
Twitter: @jennyholi
Instagram: @holymolyjennyholi
Newsletter: jennyholiday.com/newsletter

BOOKS BY JENNY HOLIDAY

AN EXCERPT FROM FAMOUS

Available everywhere ebooks are sold, and in paperback from Amazon. Read on for an excerpt.

Everyone knows her face. He knows her heart.

Emerson Quinn is famous. Girls want to be her. Boys want to date her. Each record outsells the last. All that remains is to continue transitioning her brand from its teenage fan base to a more mature, diverse audience. So she's under strict orders to play nice with her army of assigned co-songwriters and to knock off the serial dating that keeps landing her in the tabloids. If she follows instructions, she can look forward to an indefinite run at the top of the celebrity ecosystem. There's only one problem with this plan: Emerson is miserable.

So she runs away, impulsively fleeing her L.A. life and heading for a small Iowa college town where a guy she once knew lives. He's the only person in the world she can think of who might be enough of a nerd to not know about Emerson Quinn the brand. Who might be willing to provide a haven where she can lay low and write her new album by herself, on her own terms.

Art history professor Evan Winslow knows a thing or two about leaving your past behind. He's worked hard to establish himself far from the spotlight of his infamous father. He's up for tenure soon, which will mean job security for life. All he has to do to lock down his hard-won, blessedly quiet existence is keep his head down. Too bad the most famous pop star in the world—who also happens to be his long-lost muse—has just shown up on his doorstep.

CHAPTER ONE

Seven years ago.

Sometimes a wedding was not just a wedding.

This one, in which Evan Winslow's friend Tyrone pledged his eternal devotion to his girlfriend Vicky, was, in fact, a test. It looked like a normal wedding, with white funereal-looking flowers and ill-fitting tuxedos, but it was *also* Evan's Hail Mary pass: one last attempt to hold on to his life in Miami, to his nascent career, to his entire freaking life.

His final experiment to measure how extensive—how *permanent*—the damage inflicted by his father on the Winslow family's reputation was going to be.

Evan had laid low for the past two weeks, hoping the whole "out of sight/out of mind" adage would prove true, and now it was final exam time.

This test had one question: Could Evan attend his friend Tyrone's wedding and not be recognized, not upstage the proceedings with his mere presence?

The answer was no. Fail. Flunk.

Which meant this was it. Today was the end of life as he knew it, which sounded melodramatic but was no less true for it. Because if Evan knew one thing with certainty, down to the dusty corners of his soul, it was that he could not live with the fame—the *infamy*—his father's crimes had brought down on his head. He had already been coming around to accepting the idea that his painting career was done before it had even really started—thanks to the crimes of Evan Winslow Sr., Evan Winslow Jr. was destined to be persona non grata in the art world—but now he'd brought the goddamned paparazzi to his best friend's wedding.

He'd tried to hedge against that prospect, and he initially thought he'd succeeded. He'd spent the night at his brother's place. Evan's brother wasn't in the art world—the family business—having opted instead for life as an overgrown trust-fund baby. So he wasn't getting as much media attention as Evan. Evan had called a cab to his brother's house, timing things so as to arrive at the church just before the ceremony started.

But he'd miscalculated, emerging from the taxi as a limo pulled up and disgorged the bride and her attendants.

He'd held out a shred of hope that the flashbulbs that started going off were actually for the bride. But how many brides hired half a dozen photographers with zoom lenses to photograph their nuptials?

How many wedding photographers yelled things like "Were you in on it too?" and "Will you attend the sentencing hearing?"

So he'd hustled inside ahead of the bridal party and tried to make himself inconspicuous.

Which, of course, had set off a series of whispers among the guests. People talking behind wedding programs, some openly pointing at him. The bride's mother glaring, no doubt because he had upstaged her daughter before she'd even made an appearance.

It didn't even matter that everyone recognized him, really. The fact that he had failed his test was regrettable but not elementally important. Because even if the infamy died down, could he live with the lie? With the notion that everything he had—his luxe condo; his painting ability, honed over years of lessons from the world's greatest artists; his expensive grad school—was all built on lies and paid for with stolen money?

The answer to that question was also no.

So it was time to go. To start over somewhere else. Pack his shit up, transfer to another college to finish his degree—say goodbye to his entire life.

He had no earthly idea how to do that, but that was a problem to be solved tomorrow, on day one of his new life. Right now, the last day in his old life, he had a wedding to attend.

Thankfully, the music changed at that moment, signaling the start of the ceremony. Everyone turned, and he breathed a sigh of relief. For a few moments anyway, there were people in the room who would attract more attention than he would.

He almost laughed as the first bridesmaid appeared. The dress was ridiculous. She looked like a short, puffy, pink mummy. Evan didn't know fabrics, but he suspected that the multi-layered, shiny dress she was wearing had not been constructed from any fiber or dye that occurred naturally in this world.

And there was another one, and another. They kept coming, parading down the aisle in ascending order of height, like caricatures of bridesmaids rather than actual bridesmaids, with their identical upswept hairdos and identical pink heels.

His wrist twitched. They would make a great painting, all of them lined up like nesting dolls.

No, correction: as the final bridesmaid appeared at the top of the aisle, Evan had to revise his previous thought. They would make a great painting, but *she* would make a spectacular painting. He would title it *Bridesmaid Number Seven*.

Tall and thin with long limbs, she was the sort of person people might describe as gangly. It was like someone had taken a regular, average woman and stretched her out like taffy. But she was too graceful to be rightfully called gangly. She had an ease about her, which was rather remarkable, given the packaging and spackling she'd been subjected to.

Evan noticed those sorts of details when a painting was emerging. It was like his brain clicked into some other mode as it swept over a scene, processing, neutrally assessing everything with equal attention, waiting for the jolting spike of feeling that signified the correct take on a subject.

He was a beat behind everyone else standing for the bride because he was still looking at the last bridesmaid. She and her colleagues arrayed themselves at the front of the church and turned to watch the bride process. Her face had interesting angles: sharp cheekbones and slightly unruly brows arching high over eyes that should have been too close-set to be called pretty.

Where would he put her? In a forest, maybe? In her ridiculous pink dress in a forest, Titania styled by Barbie? No. That wasn't quite right.

As the bride passed his pew, he forced his gaze from her tallest attendant and considered his friend Tyrone's soon-to-be-wife with more attention than he had ever found it necessary to bestow on her before. Vicky had the same facial structure as the bridesmaid, but less of it. The cheekbones were there, just not as prominent. The two women had to be related. Sisters, maybe?

As Vicky's father kissed her and sat down, the bridesmaids

turned their backs to the congregation, presenting the assembly with a row of identical bows on their backsides, each one a little higher than the one next to it thanks to the arrangement of attendants from shortest to tallest.

He was still thinking about her face, though.

He would start with Yellow Ochre and add tiny amounts of Cadmium Red Light to start with, and then he'd layer in the planes of those gorgeous cheekbones.

It was with a jolt, a great wrenching, invisible blow, that he realized: *no*.

Not that those were the wrong colors, but that he wasn't going to paint her.

He wasn't going to paint anything.

After today, he didn't paint anymore.

"Is that cute guy in the corner the son of the infamous art criminal?" Emmy whispered to her cousin Vicky. Now that dinner and the first dance were over, she'd finally gotten a minute alone with the bride so she could ask about the handsome man sitting alone at a table in the back of the ballroom. She figured he must be "the one" since she'd seen him intently speed walking past a clump of photographers on his way into the church.

He'd been staring at her much of the evening.

It started when she was walking back up the aisle after the ceremony on the arm of her assigned groomsman. The intensity of his gaze had drawn her attention, but he'd looked away when she caught him staring.

And she'd *kept* catching him. His appraisal had continued throughout the toasts and as she'd tried to make conversation with the rest of the wedding party over dinner. She'd glance over at him only to find him already looking at her—enough times that he'd started grinning sheepishly, like he knew he'd been busted.

But of course if she kept catching him, it meant *she* was staring at *him* as much as he was staring at her.

It was just so hard *not* to look at him. He was tall and broad-shouldered under his impeccably tailored suit, and when he smiled as she'd catch him looking, he did it with his whole face.

"Don't look!" Emmy shriek-whispered as Vicky turned to peek over her shoulder.

"I can't tell you who he is if I can't see him," Vicky declared, not even trying to make her surveillance subtle. "Oh! Yep, that's Evan Winslow!"

"His dad even made the papers in Minnesota," Emmy said. The story of the jet-setting art dealer's fall from grace had all the makings of a Greek tragedy, and it was playing out in the tabloids. It was a true-crime story that had the nation fascinated, except instead of dead bodies there were Ponzi schemes and counterfeit art.

"Yep," said Vicky. "The trial was huge. They were one of the richest families in Miami. It's been all over the place. Poor guy. Ty says he's taken it all super hard." She cocked her head. "So you think he's cute, huh? A little nerdy for my tastes, but I dare you to go over there and talk to him."

"No way! I can't just—" Emmy's objection was cut off when the DJ cued up a horrid song that made Vicky's sorority sisters scream and rise as one.

As they swept Vicky away in a tornado of pink tulle, she called, "Go over there. What have you got to lose? You'll never see him again anyway."

There was so much more she wanted to ask Vicky. How old was Evan Winslow? What was he studying? Vicky's new husband knew him from the University of Miami, where they were both grad students. Tyrone was doing his MBA, but she had a hard time imagining this guy in a business school. He seemed like more of an intellectual—a humanities type maybe. His hair, though currently slicked back, seemed like it was a little too long for him to fit in with the would-be capitalists, and his nerd-chic horn-rimmed glasses seemed more Buddy Holly than business. She started to make up a story. Something from the point of view of a sensitive guy forced into business school by his conniving, greedy father. The chorus could be the dad talking, but by the end of the song, the lyrics would be turned around, the guy defiantly using the father's words against him.

Well, hell. Emmy wasn't generally an assertive sort of person. She tended to hang around on the sidelines and make up little snippets of songs about what she saw unfolding around her. But Vicky was right. She was flying back to Minneapolis tomorrow, and she'd never see this guy again. In twenty-four hours, she'd be back doing battle with her parents, facing their perpetual and poorly disguised disappointment over her barista job and her "childish dreams." So why not put an end to their little mutual staring society and go say hi to the infamous Evan Winslow?

Gathering about a thousand yards of pink polyester in her arms, she hiked up her skirts and set off. He must have felt her approach, because he looked up from his cake while she was still a good twenty feet away, an expression of surprise seguing into another of those magnetic, self-deprecating grins as she got closer.

"Hey," she said, trying to make the greeting seem casual.

"Hey," he echoed. Then he added, "You're here," as if all this time he'd merely been waiting for her arrival, as if *she* had been the point of his attending the wedding.

He picked up a wedding program and slid it across the table to her.

"Ha!" She laughed in delight. If she'd been making up a story about him, it seemed he had done the same thing, in a way. Except where hers was coming together from turns of phrase and snippets of melody, his was composed of ink—garden-variety ballpoint from the look of it. He had drawn her on the back of the program, right on top of the Shakespeare sonnet that Vicky, who Emmy was pretty sure wouldn't know a sonnet if it bit her in the ass outside the context of wedding planning websites, had artfully placed on the otherwise-blank heavy-gauge paper. The funny thing was that Emmy wasn't wearing the god-awful dress in his portrait. He'd put her in shorts and a tank top, which was pretty much her uniform when she wasn't performing bridesmaid duties.

"You drew me! You're an artist?" She'd known his dad was an art dealer, but she didn't know that much about the rest of the Winslow family—she'd read the headlines but hadn't really followed the details of the trial.

He paused for long enough before answering that she started to fear she'd offended him somehow. "I used to be a painter."

"What does that mean?"

"It means I used to paint, but now I don't."

Okay then, that was clearly not a topic he was keen to discuss, so she tried another question. "Vicky said you're in grad school with Tyrone?"

"We're both at the University of Miami, but I'm doing a PhD in art history. Ty and I met in a campus running club."

Yes. The satisfying ping of having uncovered the truth in her proto-song echoed in her chest. An artist *and* an intellectual. She'd been spot-on.

"Are you from Minnesota?" he asked. "You look like you're related to Vicky."

"Yeah. She's my cousin. I'm Emmy."

He stood and stuck out his hand. "Hi, Emmy. I'm Evan."

She was on the other side of the table—too far away to reach his hand—so she walked around. Wanting to pretend that she was in control, she slowed her steps. But that was only because she wasn't entirely comfortable with the truth of the matter, which was that in her haste to reach him she'd *had* to slow her steps. She was a stupid, powerless fish he was reeling in.

He didn't let go when the handshake would normally have ended, just hitched his head toward the door. "Want to go for a walk?"

Of course she did.

♫

"Aha!" Evan said, pushing his shoulder against the heavy metal door at the top of the stairwell. "Unlocked!" He held it for a laughing Emmy to precede him onto the roof of the banquet hall. She had her voluminous skirts gathered in one hand and her high heels dangling from the fingers of the other. "Be careful of your feet. Who knows what's up here."

She paused at the threshold and peered out. He looked over her shoulder. Yeah, the gravel that lined the ground was going to require shoes. Or...

"Eeee!" she shrieked, laughing as he swung her into his arms. "What are you doing?"

What *was* he doing? He was acting like the hero of some lame made-for-TV romantic comedy. Not his style at all. But there was something about being in limbo, teetering on the precipice between one life and another, that made every decision this evening seem less important, every action less imbued with its potential future consequences.

"If I'd known that 'go for a walk' was code for 'break onto the roof,'" she said, "I might have thought twice about accompanying you."

The roof had been the only place he could think to escape, where he could be sure there would be no photographers. But he didn't want her to feel uncomfortable, so he paused, wondering if he should turn around.

But then she craned her neck to get a better view and said, "It's gorgeous up here!"

So he crossed the roof and deposited her on some kind of ventilation structure that would do as a bench.

"Beautiful," she said, still talking about the view.

It was. The buildings of the Miami skyline he knew so well were jewels against the otherworldly pink sky of dusk. But so were the shining sapphires of her eyes.

And that was another made-for-TV thing he didn't do: compare women's eyes to gemstones. *What the hell?* There was limbo, and there was losing control of himself.

"Give me that," she said, grabbing the stolen bottle of champagne he had tucked under his arm and setting to work on the cork. When it popped, she squealed and held the fizzing bottle away from her for a moment before tipping her head back and drinking directly from it. The slanted pink light caught tendrils of blond hair escaping the pins that anchored an elaborate updo. He watched her throat undulate as she drank. Then she lifted her head, used her forearm to wipe her mouth, and grinned as she handed him the bottle, perfectly framed by the blazing sunset.

He was cursed with a painter's eye. He saw things other people didn't. He was never going to get over not painting her.

"What's your last name?" he asked, thinking, irrationally,

that if he knew it, he could somehow find her later. Put a bookmark in this meeting and come back to it, even though he knew that he was going to have to draw a sharp line between what he was already starting to think of as his "old" life and whatever was going to come next.

"I'm moving to Los Angeles in two months," she said.

"So it's Emmy I'mMovingToLosAngelesInTwoMonths?" He couldn't help teasing. "That must have been a mouthful when you were a kid."

"No." She laughed. "I'm moving in two months, and I'm going to change my name when I do, I think. I haven't decided to what. So it's just Emmy for now."

Ah, so he wasn't the only one on the verge of reinventing himself. Perhaps that's why he felt this strangely, strongly compelled by her. They were of a kind. "If that's how you're going to be, I won't tell you my last name, either." She likely already knew it, but she hadn't brought it up, so he wouldn't either.

"Don't tell me," she said. "Let's just be Emmy and Evan. E and E." She took another swig of the champagne. "Like e.e. cummings."

"I will wade out till my thighs are steeped in burning flowers," he said. He wasn't sure how his brain had produced that obscure line, but he knew now how he would have painted her.

She'd been looking at the skyline, but the cummings snippet snagged her attention, and she turned, eyes suddenly glazed with moisture.

"What's the matter?"

"I'm a songwriter," she said. "Or at least I'm trying to be."

Ah. The impending move to L.A., the name change—the pieces were coming together.

"Sometimes when I hear a line like that, it makes me

despair of ever writing anything worthwhile," she said, shaking her head.

"Don't despair. You can do it."

"How do you know? You don't even know me."

He shrugged. She had intelligent eyes that looked intently at the world. That's what storytellers needed. That's probably what he had seen in her, why he had picked her out from the row of identical puffy pink dresses. "I have a feeling you're going to make it."

"You're the only one who thinks so," she whispered.

"I have a good eye," he said, struck with the urge to reassure her. "I see things other people don't." He turned so they were side by side, both facing the now rapidly darkening city —which was why he didn't have any warning when she leaned over, grabbed his cheeks, and kissed him.

Her lips were soft, and pressed so lightly against his it almost tickled. His first instinct was to push her away, because what could come of it? They were both headed for new lives, both making a break with the present.

But he couldn't make himself do it. What was so wrong with kissing a pretty girl on a rooftop? It was the perfect coda, actually, to his Miami life. So he surrendered, letting his whole body relax into the soft hunger of their kiss, forcing himself to attend to every nuance of the experience, to savor the bittersweet finale, as if he could file it away somehow, and take it out and examine it again later, like he would a memento from his past.

And, oh, he hadn't felt this alive for months. It was like she was filling him with energy he thought had been drained permanently by the police raids, the meetings with lawyers and PR people, the endless court proceedings. He sipped at her lips, letting his hands frame her face, wanting to anchor her there forever. As he deepened the kiss, testing the seam of her lips, she opened for him, but there was a tentativeness there, a hesitation.

It was like she didn't really know what she was doing.

The rogue thought entered his mind as her tongue slid along his, ripping an involuntary groan from his throat as he gently pushed her away.

"How old are you?" God, how could he have missed that? Hadn't he just been bragging about how good he was at seeing things?

Her brow furrowed. "Does it matter?" She was flushed, her pupils dilated, her breath short.

She was gorgeous.

It didn't matter how old she was, not in any elemental way. But it *did* matter here on this roof, in the clumsy corporeal world. It meant the difference between continuing this spectacular goodbye-to-his-old-life kiss and *not* continuing it.

"Tell me."

She pulled back and scooted farther away from him on the bench, confirming his fears even before she spoke. "I'm nineteen."

Right. It might be perfectly clear that this was merely a casual kiss, but he wasn't going to be *that* guy. He eyed the nearly empty champagne bottle on the ground at their feet. That was all he needed—the story of Evan Winslow, Jr. getting a nineteen-year-old drunk and seducing her.

So much for enjoying his bittersweet Miami coda.

"How old are *you*?" she countered, a challenge in her voice.

"Twenty-six."

"That's not so bad," she said.

"Not so bad for what?" He was teasing her, but only because teasing was all he could do now. "You're right," he said. "A seven-year age difference is not bad at all for sitting on the roof talking about everything under the sun until someone notices we're gone and sends out a search party." He patted the seat beside him, shrugged out of his suit jacket, and held it out to her.

He wasn't a *total* saint, though. He liked the disappointment that washed across the striking angular face he wanted to paint so badly his fingers ached.

"Talking," she said, pouting a little but sliding back over to sit next to him and letting him slip the jacket over her shoulders.

"*Talking*," he confirmed, emphasizing the word for himself as much as for her.

"Okay, uh, what's your favorite TV show?"

"I don't really watch TV." He didn't tell her that he didn't even own one. Or that the glimpses of his family's sordid drama that he'd caught on CNN at his brother's house had been enough to reinforce his desire to never get one.

"Last concert you saw?"

He thought—hard—and came up with nothing. He had been to a few shows on the last cruise he took with his parents. His mother dragged Evan and his brother and their father on an annual luxury cruise and made them dress for dinner and generally fulfill her fantasy of the perfect Ralph Lauren family. But probably cruise ship bands playing Neil Diamond covers weren't what Emmy had in mind. "I'm not really one for live music," he finally said.

"Okaaay," she said, screwing up her face like she was trying to think of a new topic.

"It's no good," he said laughingly. "I'm completely pop-culturally illiterate."

"How come you don't paint anymore?"

Whoa. If her previous questions had been rubber-tipped darts that pinged easily off their targets, this one was a razor-sharp axe that sliced right through him.

"I don't want to talk about that," he said, which was the absolute truth, even if it didn't answer her question.

"Okay," she said, and he was surprised that she was going to accept his evasive answer. Maybe it wouldn't be so hard to upend his life after all. Maybe he could get used to being not-a-painter. "So what should we talk about?"

"You. We should talk about you." She was the most compelling person he'd met in a long time. And she was the *only* person he'd met recently who hadn't said a word about his father. "I want to know everything there is to know about you, Emmy NoLastName. Tell me about moving to L.A. Sing me a song." He turned to face her head-on. He would listen to her for as long as he could get away with it. He would listen and watch. Then he would say goodbye.

To her, and to himself.

CHAPTER TWO

Seven years later.

It seemed like a good idea at the time.

How many of Emerson's misadventures in the past few years could be summed up that way?

She eyed the graceful Victorian as her assistant Tony slowed to a stop. With its overgrown garden, giant shade trees, and huge wraparound porch—complete with swing—it looked like a postcard from Anne of Green Gables Land. Like a place where a catalog family would pose for their Christmas card picture in front of an adorably lopsided snowman.

In other words, something out of another world. As far from her life in L.A. as it was possible to get.

Which, she reminded herself, was exactly the point.

This time it will be different.

Except, yeah, she always said that. And it never was. But to cut herself some slack, when she said that, she was usually talking about a boy. And those days were done for a while—a good long while. No matter how much her romantic misadventures seemed to translate into hit songs that made her managers swoon as the tabloids speculated over which ex-boyfriend could be matched with which song, she wasn't going there anymore. This was the beginning of a new era. Emerson Quinn: single, independent, mistress of her own emotional and creative destiny.

There was also the part where the person inside the postcard house was most decidedly not a boy.

He was a man. Just not a man who was going to have any sway over her.

"I still don't like this, Em," Tony said. "They're going to find you. You busted out, yeah, but you can't hide indefinitely."

Emerson pivoted to face her longtime assistant. Despite his tendency toward melodrama, she adored him. Hell, as her first manager, he'd been the only person in the world who'd looked at the gangly teenager and seen past the combat boots and false bravado. Who'd listened to her demo and heard something bigger than the Neko Case wannabe who hadn't quite mastered the Garage Band app on her Mac.

And when she'd insisted she was going to be a singer-songwriter despite the fact that her parents had vowed to disown her over it, Tony had shrugged and said, "Well, why the hell not? Someone gets to do it."

More importantly, Tony was the only person in the world she could really, truly trust.

"They're my managers, Tony, not the Mafia. Don't be so sensationalistic. I wasn't in prison." No, it was just a hotel suite, fully stocked with snacks, keyboards, and middle-aged Swedish songwriter dudes who were inexplicably talented at churning out pop songs designed to capture the inner life of the modern American twentysomething.

It felt *like prison, though.*

Okay, now *she* was being melodramatic. It was just that the last tour had only finished two weeks ago, and she was *done* with hotel rooms.

She simply needed…a break. People did it all the time. That it was an unscheduled one that would throw a wrench into the well-oiled machinery that was the Emerson Quinn hit machine? Well, she was choosing to make that not her problem for a while.

But she was faking all her bravado. Tears prickled behind her eyeballs. She pressed her lips together and forced them back. Emerson was *not* a crier. Emmy used to cry; Emerson did not. "I'm just taking a little vacation, Tony," she said. "Catching my breath."

"And you couldn't catch your breath in, say, New York? London? Or even back in Minneapolis? You know, somewhere with *civilization*? Lattes. Newspapers. *Homosexuals.*" His lip curled. "From what I can tell, all this place has is corn."

"You heard Song 58," she said. Song 58 was the temporary title of a tune she and a co-writer had banged out yesterday at the Beverly Wilshire, thus named because it was her prolific co-writer's fifty-eighth song of the year. The guy was a machine, and he was currently on loan to her.

"Yes," he said. "It was…"

She knew what he meant. Song 58 was fine. It was good, even. With some work in the studio, it could be totally catchy. It just wasn't…

Ugh. She didn't even have words for what was wrong with her right now. All she could think to say was, "I'm not writing the next album in that hotel room, Tony." Goddamn it, her voice had hitched a little. *And I'm not writing it with them at all.* But she didn't tell Tony that part. That part was a half-baked notion pricking at the edge of her consciousness, the idea that she could...drop out and come back a couple months later with an entire album in hand. She didn't dare voice that out loud.

"So let me tell Brian and Claudia you're taking a well-earned vacation, and you don't have to go anywhere at all. You can hide away at home in your PJs. Just you and the Hollywood Hills. I'll have food delivered daily."

They'd been over this and over this on the flight. "You know that wouldn't work. As much as you think you can just call them and..." She didn't have the heart to tell him that he didn't have a say in the matter; that whatever credit he deserved for discovering Emerson, managing her career for those critical early years, he didn't get a vote anymore.

"I know, sweetie. I know." That was the thing about Tony —he heard what she left unsaid.

The hint of sadness in his eyes was a punch to the gut. They both knew that, theoretically, he could suggest that her managers Brian and Claudia send the co-writer away and leave writing the next album for later. Or she could suggest the same thing. Insist, even—she was the "artist," after all.

But they wouldn't listen. Not for long, anyway. They never did. She and Tony had made their devil's bargain when they'd decided her career needed the power of a big creative management company behind it and left Minneapolis for California, and now there was no escaping.

Except maybe in Dane, Iowa, population 14,581. And, according to the town's Wikipedia entry, half of those were college students.

"I get it. But Em, you don't even know this guy." Tony

nodded at the falling-down Victorian. "And now you're going to hole up in his house? What is this? *Notting Hill?*"

She *did* know Evan Winslow, though. It might be irrational. It might have been one night seven years ago. It might have been one night seven years ago in which *nothing happened*. But she knew him. And he knew her in a way that went beyond the brand. Hell, he was possibly the only person on the planet who hadn't heard of the brand.

And he'd offered to help. *Let me know if I can ever do anything for you*, he'd said as they'd parted ways after their night on the roof in Miami. He was the only other person in the world, besides Tony, who had ever done that. Who had believed in her.

Of course, the offer hadn't been serious. It was one of those things people said but didn't mean. He hadn't even told her his last name. She'd known it, of course, as everyone had, but officially, he'd kept it from her.

But she'd never forgotten those words: *Let me know if I can ever do anything for you*. The phrase had become a mantra during her impulsive flight from the Beverly Wilshire, a lifeline.

And today she was here to call in her chips.

So she hoisted her purse and flashed Tony a smile that belied the fluttering in her belly as she got out of the car. "Pop the trunk, and I'll get my stuff."

"At least let me come in and meet him," Tony said, ignoring her instruction and hopping out to retrieve her suitcase himself.

Slinging her guitar over her shoulder, she tried to take the handle of her bag, but he wouldn't surrender it. "You're my assistant, Tony, not my father. I'm twenty-six, for God's sake. I'm not a kid anymore."

"I know." He rolled his eyes. "Do I ever know—it was a hell of a lot easier when you *were* a kid."

"Easier, maybe, but platinum records pay several orders of magnitude better than First Avenue," she said, naming the Minneapolis club where, with Tony's help, she'd broken into the local music scene, paving the way for their move to L.A. and her first major-label deal.

He laid his hand on her arm. Tony wasn't the affectionate type. If he didn't knock it off, she really was going to cry. And that was *not* happening.

"I just think it's a little sketchy that this guy you met once seven years ago has agreed to let you stay here."

Emerson didn't bother telling him that Evan had not agreed to any such thing. That he didn't know she was coming. That he might not even remember her.

Because if she told Tony any of that, she'd be on the first plane back to Los Angeles, and by nightfall, she'd be ensconced in her hotel suite, the lock clicking into place on her gilded cage like thunder in her ears.

Before he could object again, she air-kissed him, yanked her suitcase from his grip, and rolled it up the cute-as-a-button cobblestone path that led to Evan Winslow's front door.

And crossed her fingers and rang the doorbell.

The doorbell rang.

Perfect. Nine midterms down, twenty-eight more to go, and what Evan really needed right now was Mrs. Johansen on his porch bearing yet another casserole destined to join the growing collection in his freezer. What on earth had possessed him to agree to teach a summer course?

The answer, of course, was Larry. The chair of the art

history department at Dane College had the power to make or break Evan's tenure bid in September—and since he'd made it clear he was currently leaning toward "break," Evan needed to ingratiate himself as much as possible, to be a good citizen of the department. If teaching Intro to Renaissance Art to thirty-seven undergrads in Dane College's questionably air-conditioned humanities building during the summer term was what it took to lock down his peaceful, hard-won Iowa life, he would expound upon the wonders of the Sistine Chapel until he and his students were blue in the face.

Besides, Michelangelo rocked.

It was important to remember that in addition to being optimally located in the middle of nowhere, his job at Dane College was a pretty sweet gig. Much better than he'd ever imagined all those years ago when he'd stepped in front of the cameras after his father was sentenced to thirty years and panicked as a CNN reporter asked him, "How does it feel to have lost everything?"

The doorbell rang a second time.

He sighed and set down his pen. As tempting as it was, he couldn't not answer. Mrs. Johansen would only come around to the back door, and he didn't want her struggling with his half-broken gate.

He padded to the door. Probably he should put a shirt on, but it was hot as hell, and it was almost certainly just Mrs. Johansen, so screw it.

He swung open the door.

It was not Mrs. Johansen.

Holy shit.

He was like a cartoon character, utterly flattened when a grand piano fell from the sky. It was Emmy. With a guitar and a…huge suitcase?

"Hi," she said, like she was paying a routine social call.

"Hi," he echoed, frankly shocked that his voice worked.

She had changed. Her face had thinned out, making those angular, sharp cheekbones even more prominent. Her hair was different—still blond, but instead of a solid color, it was streaked with lots of different shades ranging from light ash to golden honey. And it was shorter now, chin-length with bangs, choppy, messy-on-purpose. Instead of the regulation insipid coral lipstick she'd worn at the wedding, her lips were painted a bright scarlet, which made for a stark contrast to her pale skin.

There was something else different, too. Something harder to articulate, but it was there just the same, lurking beneath the surface. It was what he would try to draw out if he were going to paint her.

If he still painted anymore.

It was a weariness. Not that she looked overtly tired—there were no rings under her eyes, and her skin glowed in the bright afternoon sun. No, it was a hesitancy, slight but definitely there. As if the nineteen-year-old who'd been so guileless, who had told him with shining eyes about her musical dreams in the hours after their ill-advised kiss, had been knocked around a little by the world in subsequent years, had some of her soft, rounded edges hardened off. It was subtle, but enough to change her whole demeanor.

But her eyes were the same. He would know those eyes anywhere. Blue, but not the clichéd blue of milkmaids and Barbie dolls. A deep, dark, soulful blue, with the tiniest ring of yellow around the pupil on one side that you had to look closely to see.

And he *had* looked closely, back then when she was nineteen and he had to take the high road, back when they were both about to embark on new lives. Looked close, as they talked through the night, then forced himself to look away.

She cleared her throat, pulling him from his trance, reminding him that he was standing shirtless on his porch in front of Emmy NoLastName, seven years and fifteen hundred miles from the wedding at which they'd met.

She shifted from one foot to the other. "So, it's too bad about Vicky and Tyrone."

Who? Oh, right. The bride and groom. Her cousin and his friend Tyrone. Though they had occasionally exchanged emails in the year or so after Evan left Miami, he hadn't seen Ty since the wedding. He now belonged squarely in the box in Evan's head marked "Before." Evan didn't like to overlap with "Before."

"Too bad?" he echoed, his mouth having gone dry from the adrenaline spike her appearance had caused.

"They got divorced?" She cocked her head, no doubt astonished that he hadn't heard the news.

All right. He'd been standing there like the proverbial deer in headlights long enough. "How did you find me?" he asked, his voice coming out sharper than he'd intended.

"Google."

"But—"

"I asked Vicky to confirm your last name, and then I *typed it into a search engine*." She grinned. "It's almost like I'm a *spy* or something."

Right. He sometimes forgot that Dane wasn't an invisibility cloak, though it often felt that way, the miles and miles of corn that surrounded it in every direction buffering him like a verdant moat.

A horn honked. "Woo-hoo, Professor Winslow, looking go-oo-od!" A car full of girls squealed down his otherwise-sleepy street, a couple of them half hanging out the windows. They must have startled Emmy, because she ducked her head and shielded her face with both hands—kind of like his father had done every day on his way in and out of court, hiding from photographers and angry crowds alike. Kind of like he had learned to do in the weeks that followed, before he'd gotten his shit together and left town.

His face heated, and he smiled awkwardly. "One of the downsides of a small college town."

She let her hands fall back to her sides. She was looking at his chest.

A shirt. A shirt would be a good idea.

"Did you, ah, want to come in?" he asked against his better judgment. He had never had anyone from his old life in this house. When he saw his mom and brother, it was always at his mom's place in Atlanta, where she'd started *her* life over with Husband #2.

But Emmy was apparently the exception.

Also, some ill-advised part of his brain whispered, *she's not nineteen anymore.*

He gestured into the house behind him, and she whipped her eyes to his face. A slow smile blossomed, like she knew she'd been caught ogling but didn't care. It reminded him of the way they kept catching each other looking at the wedding, except this time, the look was...more heated.

"I was hoping you'd say that, and I would love to come in." Then she sighed, and her shoulders slumped a little—in relief? Defeat? He couldn't tell. "I'm in a bit of a bind, actually."

As Evan disappeared down the hallway, calling, "I'll be right back—make yourself at home," Emerson let out a breath and peeled off her T-shirt, leaving only the tank top she had layered underneath. The Minnesota summers of her childhood had been hot and sticky, but that was nothing compared to the blast furnace that was this town—and Evan's apparently un-air-conditioned house. Other than the odd stint on her terrace perched in the hills, Emerson couldn't think when she'd spent any time recently in an environment that hadn't been artificially heated or chilled.

It was hotter than sin in Dane, Iowa.

But also: Woo-hoo, Professor Winslow. Looking go-oo-od.

He'd been handsome at Vicky's wedding all those years ago, but handsome in the way that really dressed-up men are. In their suits and tuxedos, with their close shaves and careful smiles, men like that flipped the "Prince Charming" switch that girls like her, raised on Disney princesses and graduated to Netflix rom-coms, had socially conditioned into them. Hell, hadn't she spent the last half decade going from one potential Prince Charming to another, telling herself each time that she had finally found "the one"?

But seven years later, shirtless, barefoot, with a pair of jeans sitting low on his hips, Evan was a completely different kind of handsome.

Handsome wasn't even the right word. Because who knew about the bodybuilder's chest that had been hiding under that suit and tie? The dark brown hair that, freed from gelled-back wedding guest perfection, flopped across his face, almost at man-bob length?

There was one thing that hadn't changed, though, and that was the way he looked at her with those eyes so brown they were almost black. Like he was studying her. Memorizing her. Surrendering his grasp on the material world for a moment in favor of…her. Even those nerd glasses he still wore couldn't mute the effect. In the years since she had last seen him, a *lot* of people had looked at her. She'd played arenas of tens of thousands of people and live awards show broadcasts viewed by millions.

None of that was like this. Like the way Evan looked at her.

She was immune, though, she reminded herself. That wasn't why she was here on this ridiculous Hail Mary mission. He could look all he liked, but she was not in search of a prince, charming or otherwise. She was in search of a haven, and if the only one she had access to had a hot guy as its gatekeeper, well, she was just going to have to build a deflector shield around her heart.

She looked around for something to distract herself from thoughts of his gaze, to tip her back into the real world. The world where she had a problem that needed solving. From the entryway, she could see into a sun-drenched living room, its walls covered practically floor to ceiling with art. Photographs and paintings hung on the walls, which, she could see from the cracks between the frames, were covered in a faded floral wallpaper. More pieces sat on the floor, resting against the walls two deep in some spots. It was like a museum—a messy, willy-nilly museum with no theme.

She was drawn to it, despite the fact that she didn't really know anything about art. It was exuberant and hopeful—exactly the way Evan had made her feel at the wedding. Exuberant as they'd sneaked up to the roof, laughing, her heart as fizzy as the champagne they'd stolen. Later, hopeful when he'd asked her question after question about her musical ambitions, making her laugh when he denied having heard of any of the bands or singers she'd invoked to compare herself to stylistically.

"Hey."

"Oh!" She jumped. That was another side effect of life in the spotlight: every moment of her life was scripted. She was never surprised—unless Claudia was shoving a birthday cake in her face unexpectedly so one of the PR people could capture the "surprise" for Emerson's social media feeds.

"Sorry." He scraped a hand through his hair, and she was more disappointed than she should have been that he'd put on a T-shirt. A faded forest green, it was worn and soft-looking. She was seized with an inexplicable desire to rub her cheek against it, to curl up with it like a security blanket. "So what can I do for you?"

Take off your shirt and give it to me for a blankie?

When she didn't answer—she was trying to think of something a little less creeptastic to say—he tried again. "I can't imagine what brings you to Dane."

You told me seven years ago to let you know if you could ever be of any help, and now I'm here? That didn't sound any better than the more specific version, which was that as she'd been on the elevator last night up to her suite at the Beverly Wilshire, floors ticking by like a bomb timer, she'd been overcome with the wild idea that she could maybe find somewhere to hide out and write a renegade album that did not contain Song 58.

Which was obviously insane.

Some people had a devil on their shoulder, or an angel, or some combination of the two. Emerson had a fatalistic imaginary friend who could envision, in extraordinary detail, all the different ways disaster could strike in any given scenario. Maude—yes, she'd named her fatalistic imaginary friend—was good for songwriting. Being slightly obsessive about details, following ideas along to every possible conclusion: this was what made good songs. In fact, the only reason she was here today was that she had told Maude to shut up. She'd gagged her and stuffed her into a closet while she made her dramatic escape from L.A. But she probably should have spent less time on the flight here arguing with Tony and more time figuring out what the hell she was going to say to Evan.

She hadn't gotten much further with her plan than a vague hope that the art history nerd who didn't watch TV would remember her—the real her. That maybe, if she was lucky, he'd had his head in the sand deep enough that he hadn't heard of Emerson Quinn the brand.

But Maude wasn't having it. She'd busted out of the closet.

Of course he's heard of you. He's probably heard all about the scene with Jesse and that model in Central Park. He saw you fall down at the Oscars. Or those horrible paparazzi shots when you were sneaking out of Kirby's house—there wasn't a corner of this earth that picture didn't penetrate.

She cleared her throat. "I, ah, needed a little break from my life. I just wrapped a tour. I'm supposed to start working on my next album, but I...couldn't face it." There. That was true.

"So you did become a musician, then?"

"I did." Saying so made her flush with pride. Even though she wasn't necessarily thrilled with the way things were going right now, she had made it, and she was proud of herself.

"That's great. What kind of music do you do?"

Oh my God, he *hadn't* heard of her. On the one hand, she was a little disappointed. On the other: *Take that, Maude!* Maybe this insane stunt, this idea of trying to find somewhere to hide where someone actually knew *her*, wasn't so crazy after all.

"I needed a break, see," she said, ignoring his question. "Things have been...extremely busy, and I wanted to, well, hide for a while, really, and see if I could put together some new songs."

"So you came to Dane."

You said to let you know if you could ever be of help? She still couldn't make herself say it quite like that. "It, ah, seemed like a really out-of-the-way place where I might be able to lie low for a while, get some writing done."

Then he was coming toward her, his brow furrowed. He reached a hand out, and her pulse quickened. Oh my God, was he going to *kiss* her? Because as gorgeous as he was, that was *not* what she was here for, so she was just going to have to—

"Mrs. Johansen! Be careful on the steps."

Oh. Okay, then.

Brushing past her and letting the screen door bang behind him, she heard him scolding the visitor. "I told you one of my steps is loose. You've got to use the railing!"

Emerson's body automatically went into stealth mode. She didn't even have to think about it—hat on head, hair jammed up into hat. She was fumbling in her purse for her sunglasses when they came in.

"Midori Johansen, this is my…" Evan's brow furrowed.

"Emmy," Emerson said, sticking out her hand even as she avoided eye contact with the visitor, supplying the nickname primarily because giving her full first name would risk exposure…but also, now that she was here with Evan, she *felt* like Emmy again.

Evan cleared his throat. "Emmy, this is my neighbor, Mrs. Midori Johansen."

"Where are you visiting from?" Mrs. Johansen asked.

"L.A.," she answered, but then mentally kicked herself for not making something up.

"I used to live in L.A.!" Mrs. Johansen said.

"How did you, ah, come to settle in Iowa?" Emmy asked, coaching herself to produce normal conversation.

"My husband was a professor at Dane College," Mrs.

Johansen said. "He was at UCLA for his graduate studies, which is where we met. We moved here in 1964."

Emmy allowed herself to relax a little. If Mrs. Johansen had moved here as a young wife in 1964, she had to be in her seventies at least. And anyway, if she'd been going to say, "Are you Emerson Quinn?" she would have done so by now. That was usually the first thing out of people's mouths when they spotted her in an unlikely place. And sometimes, if the place was unlikely enough, she could get away with the "No, but I get that all the time" deflection.

"Dr. Anders Johansen, whom I didn't have the pleasure of knowing," Evan said, "was a world-renowned linguist. He was a Swede, and he came here to study the Scandinavian linguistic traditions of the Midwest."

Mrs. Johansen, based on her first name and appearance, seemed to be Japanese. Emmy wondered how she had met her Swedish husband in L.A. in the middle of the last century. What had their courtship been like? There was probably an interesting story there, and suddenly she wanted to hear it. She felt its pull physically, like her body was starved for the normalcy of a "how we met" story that didn't involve publicists and paparazzi.

"Oh!" Mrs. Johansen exclaimed, pulling Emmy from her thoughts. "I have to go back home. I forgot my money."

"Don't worry about it," Evan said. "Tell me what you want, and I'll drop it by later."

"I couldn't do that." She started to shuffle away. "I'll be right back." Then she chuckled. "Who am I kidding? At the pace I go, I'll be back in twenty minutes."

"Mrs. Johansen, you keep me in casseroles. The least I can do is buy your veggies."

She looked indecisive, so Emmy, though she didn't quite know what was going on, said, "Mrs. Johansen, if a handsome guy like Evan was offering to buy my veggies, you can bet I'd take him up on the offer." *Buy my veggies.* Wait. Did that sound dirty?

Mrs. Johansen grinned. "You do have a point. No one has bought my veggies in a very long time."

Emmy laughed. Mrs. Johansen reminded her of her grandma, who'd been a kindred spirit to Emmy in their family of accountants.

"Just this once, then." Mrs. Johansen thrust a piece of paper at Evan. "I'll make you an extra casserole this week."

Evan smiled. "I can't wait." When his neighbor turned to go, he followed, gave her his arm, and escorted her down the steps.

Emmy waited on the porch while the pair shuffled across their adjoining lawns and up Mrs. Johansen's porch. After he'd seen Mrs. Johansen safely inside, Evan paused on his neighbor's porch, looking at Emmy like he was trying to figure out what to do with her.

Finally he called across the yards, "Fancy a trip to the farmers' market, Emmy NoLastName?"

Did she? Probably the farmers' market in Dane, Iowa, was a world away from the West Hollywood Whole Foods. But wasn't that the point?

He started back across the lawns. "Then I can drive you to wherever you're staying."

Ouch. Okay, message received.

Time for Plan B. Except she had no Plan B.

"I hope it's not the Cornflower Inn," he went on. "Rumor has it they have bedbugs. But even so, there are a few other inns in town, so I'm sure you can find somewhere else if need be. The only time the town is booked up is the first week of classes and homecoming."

Humiliation bloomed on her cheeks as he brushed past

her, scooped up some keys from a table in the entryway and...
a bike helmet?

"I have an extra bike you can ride, and you can use my helmet. It's adjustable."

"Whoa." The farmers' market was one thing. *Riding a bike* to the farmers' market? "No way."

"It's a ten-minute ride. Too close to bother with the car, and parking there is a pain."

"I haven't ridden a bike in..." God. How long had it been? "Fifteen years, probably."

"It'll come right back to you." He grinned. "It's like riding a bike that way."

Emmy imagined herself pedaling down a country road under an impossibly wide blue sky, the buzzing of cicadas the only sound. Not only no security detail, no Claudia and Brian hovering, but no engine, no gas. Nothing but Emmy, propelling herself through space. Suddenly, the notion of getting somewhere under her own steam was incredibly appealing.

Then Maude cleared her throat. *Picture this: a bike mangled in a row of corn. You, in the middle of freaking Iowa surrounded by people, flashbulbs popping, without the protection of a car.*

For the second time today, Emmy told Maude to shut up.

AN EXCERPT FROM HIS HEART'S REVENGE

This standalone novel is part of the 49th Floor series. Read on for an excerpt

Twenty years ago, I was too smart and too poor to be cool. Now I'm laughing my way to the bank—the bank I'm CEO of. Nothing can touch me.

Except maybe him.

We met at summer camp. We made out under the stars. Then he stabbed me in the back.

They say revenge is a dish best served cold. But I'm gonna go with hot.

Alexander Evangelista is a millionaire with all the trappings: houses all over the world and hot guys lined up whenever he's in need of some no-strings-attached company. He's on his way to world domination.

A CEO in his own right, Cary Bell is competing for a major client with his boyhood crush. He's never forgiven himself for betraying Alex. But with his professional reputation on the line, he's going to have to find his inner cutthroat if he wants his new company to succeed.

Alex isn't about to let his nemesis steal a client out from under him. It's time to break Cary's company—and his heart.

CHAPTER ONE

Cary Bell woke with a start when an alarm went off in his head.

No, wait, it was just his cell ringing. And seeing as how he'd fallen asleep at his desk with his face resting on the phone, it felt like the ringing was coming from inside his skull. He fumbled for it. It was a FaceTime from Rose, his cousin Marcus's fiancée. He sighed and accepted the video call, bracing himself for Hurricane Rosie.

"Happy New Year!" she shouted. Then she squinted at him. "Why do you have a dent in your forehead? Wait. I see a printer in the background. Are you still at work?"

He rubbed his head. "I fell asleep on top of my phone." He didn't answer her second question.

She furrowed her brow. "I was going to yell at you for not coming to meet us like you promised. But maybe I should yell at you to go home to bed, instead."

"I meant to come." He really had. He'd begged off dinner with his cousin and Rose and their friends, but had planned on meeting them before midnight at Edward's, their regular watering hole. He'd been working flat-out the past couple of weeks nurturing his fledgling business, but even so, he hadn't planned to stay past midnight because the turn of this particular year was symbolic, and he had wanted to mark it.

This was going to be the year he got out from under his uncle's thumb, took his skills, and parlayed them into something new. Something his. Following the footsteps of his older cousin, Marcus, Cary was in the process of extracting the silver spoon from his mouth and getting on with life on his own terms. He was going to be successful, and this time it would be because he deserved it, not because he was a lucky kid who had everything handed to him.

It was going to be a great year.

If he could just get this dent out of his forehead.

Twenty minutes later, Cary was hoisting a Manhattan and clinking glasses with Marcus and Rose and their friends. Better late than never.

"I got you a client," Marcus said, pulling him into a corner after everyone had exchanged New Year's greetings.

"I have clients," Cary said. It was true. He'd walked away from his job as manager of the investment firm his great grandfather had founded three generations ago, but he left with a handful of loyal clients who had followed him. He had a staff of two and a small, swish office in a corner of his cousin's ad agency in Toronto's prestigious Lakefront Centre. He wasn't playing in the big leagues yet, but he had a nice pool of capital invested already, and his returns, so far, were stellar. The question was, could he keep it up? Could he truly start over and make something of himself without the Rosemann family name behind him? Could he succeed without the backing of his powerful uncle? He sure as hell hoped so.

But whether he succeeded or lost everything—he'd sold his

house and poured all of his personal wealth into his funds—he was going to do it on his own. He was already letting Marcus give him free office space, and that was enough. He didn't need his successful cousin handing him clients on a silver platter, too.

"You have clients, sure," said Marcus, "but you don't have Eleanor Southam."

Cary fought back against the impulse to press Marcus for more information. Eleanor Southam was the heir to a mining magnate and was a local tastemaker who could probably bring others in with her. Southam would be a coup.

When he didn't say anything, Marcus said, "Listen, I of all people support your decision to go out on your own, but no one does everything themselves. Success in business is about networking, leveraging connections. If you don't realize that, you might as well give up now."

"I'm not going to take a huge client because you just hand her to me," Cary protested, as much as it pained him to do so. But he had to. If this all went belly-up and he lost everything, he needed to make sure he still had his pride to cushion his fall. Because nothing else was going to.

"We're doing an ad campaign for her, and she was mentioning she was looking for some new investment avenues," Marcus said. "So I'm not *handing* her to you. I just had a conversation with her. This is how rich people stay rich, Cary. They talk to each other." He shook his head. "For an alleged financial genius, you can be kind of an idiot."

Cary sighed. Maybe he *was* cutting off his nose to spite his face here. "Who is Southam with now?"

"Dominion's private wealth management arm."

Cary tried not to flinch, but every time he heard Dominion Bank referenced, it was like an invisible hand probing at a wound that never quite healed.

"So you wouldn't be taking her from me," Marcus went on. "You'd be taking her from Dominion—the Goliath to your David, if you like."

No, I'd be taking her from Alex.

And he liked to think that he'd screwed over Alexander Evangelista enough for one lifetime.

But that was stupid. Alex was the CEO of Dominion Bank, Canada's largest, oldest, and most prestigious. He wasn't worried about individual clients on the private wealth side. There were probably half a dozen layers of management between Alex and Eleanor Southam. And in the two decades that had elapsed since Cary and Alex had gone to summer camp together, Alex had become one of the richest, most successful people in the country. There was no way he even remembered what Cary had done to him back then.

Except Cary knew that was a lie.

He thought back to all the times he'd seen Alex from afar at parties or industry events in recent years. They never spoke, but Cary felt the freeze. The disdain. Alex was known for being a cool customer, a smooth operator, but his attitude toward Cary was more than that.

The man was holding a grudge.

And Cary didn't blame him.

Marcus handed him a business card. "I don't know what your problem is, but here's Southam's info. Call her. You'd be an idiot not to."

Marcus's fiancée Rose bounded up dressed to the nines in a yellow sequined mini-dress. He tried to muster a smile. She would be expecting his usual bantering, pain-in-the-butt persona, which, unlike other members of his conservative family, Rose actually seemed to delight in. Everyone else was always telling him to grow up, but not Rose. Or maybe she was just as immature as he was.

"Who's an idiot?" Rose asked, slipping her hand into Marcus's.

"Cary," said Marcus without hesitating. "He's being stubborn for no reason."

"I must have learned from the best, *cuz*," Cary said, flashing a grin he hoped looked less hollow than it felt and trying to play his role. He turned to Rose. "You look stunning as always. You'd better be careful, or you'll lure me over to the breeder team." He pretended to shudder.

Rose, who normally would have gotten right into it with him, tilted her head. "Don't be an idiot, Cary."

"You don't even know what this is about," he argued, feeling petulant—feeling a little like the teenager he had been at Camp Blue Lake, in fact. Maybe his family was right, and he *was* immature. God knew, he certainly spent enough time reliving the summer he was fifteen years old.

"It doesn't matter," said Rose. "You're not an idiot, so don't act like one."

Then she smiled her great big smile that practically lit up the room. Cary generally made a point of razzing Rose—she was so very razz-able. But he had no doubt that when she'd exploded into his cousin's life last summer, Marcus had hit the jackpot.

So he mustered a smile—a genuine one this time as he kissed her on the cheek. "I'll try not to."

"Happy New Year, Cary," she said. "It's gonna be a great one for you. I can just tell."

CHAPTER TWO

Four months later

"You're going to have to be quick. I have a flight to catch," Alexander Evangelista said as his assistant ushered Sara Gable, the head of Dominion's private banking group, into his office for their bi-weekly catch up.

"I have good news, and I have bad news," Sara said. "Which do you want first?"

Alexander did not give a shit which came first.

Sara must have sensed his impatience, because she sighed and sat down on the other side of his desk. "We lost Eleanor Southam."

"It happens," Alexander said tightly. It did. Clients went elsewhere for all kinds of reasons. It didn't mean it didn't irritate the hell out of him, though. And God knew he paid Sara enough to make sure millionaires like Southam stayed happy at Dominion. "Do you know why?" He stood and started loading his briefcase as she spoke. He was hopping a flight to New York for a Knicks game. David, his latest arm-candy, was on a shoot there, and somehow, Alexander had succumbed to the "all work and no play" argument.

"Apparently she started throwing some cash at a new firm just after the new year," Sara said. "Now she says she's moving everything over by the end of the month."

Alexander sighed. This wasn't the way he wanted to start the weekend. "And who's won her?"

"Some upstart. Bell Capital. I don't know it, do you?"

His briefcase clattered to the floor. *Bell* Capital? His jaw locked. "Cary Bell?"

"Oh, that must be it!" Sara exclaimed. "I heard he left Rosemann Investments at the end of last year. He must have started his own company. Well, good for him. To hear it told, he was always the brains behind his uncle's—"

"Cary Bell left Rosemann?" Alexander ground out through clenched teeth. "*Months* ago? Why the hell didn't anyone tell me?"

Sara looked at him strangely and said, "I'm not sure. I

guess we thought it wasn't really relevant because..." She trailed off, and he knew what she was thinking. Rosemann Investments, though respected, was more of a boutique firm. Technically, it competed with Dominion's private wealth management division, but Dominion was a behemoth. What Sara wasn't saying was that as its CEO, Alexander shouldn't care about personnel changes at a firm like Rosemann Investments.

But he cared very much about Cary Bell, as much as he tried not to.

He sat, mind churning. He'd spent two decades trying not to let Cary Bell affect him. Maddeningly, it never got any easier. "What's the good news?"

Sara, clearly a bit thrown by his intensity, swallowed. "Don Liu is moving to Canada. Moving over the management of everything—his private accounts and all his companies."

That *was* good news. Don Liu was the world's twentieth-richest man, head of a Hong Kong-based empire that included diverse holdings in several different sectors. He had sent his kids to college in Toronto, and word on the street had been that he was thinking of relocating the entire clan. So far, Alexander had put it all down to rumor, but if it was true, and if Dominion could snag even a fraction of Liu's business, it would be a huge victory.

"He wants to meet tomorrow," Sara said. "I'm driving up to his house, but probably at some point you'll have to wine and dine him."

"Who else is he meeting with?"

"I spoke to his son on the phone, and I tried to probe a bit," Sara said. "They're meeting with us and First Canadian, but he also said his father was considering a few smaller outfits." She paged through her notes. "He mentioned Evergreen and..." She looked up, and he knew.

To her credit, she gazed at him evenly, showing the balls that reminded him why he had hired her. "Bell Capital."

He pressed the intercom button on his phone. "Derek, change of plans. I'm not going to New York."

"All right," his assistant said. "Do you want me to order dinner in, then?"

"No," he said. "But call David, will you? Tell him something came up. Maybe send something to his hotel room." He returned his attention to loading his briefcase. "We're done here," he said to Sara. "I'm doing the Liu meeting myself."

"Oh, he won't expect you at this point," she started, but fell silent when he held up a palm.

"Send me everything you have as soon as you can. If you need to courier anything, I'll be at my place." He left Sara sitting in his office, which was probably a little rude, but, hell, he hadn't gotten where he was today by worrying about people's feelings.

Cary Fucking Bell. He hadn't been able to avoid seeing him all these years, of course. Avoidance was impossible given that Alexander had risen above his former station so dramatically that he now ran in the same circles as Cary's old-money family. And they worked in the same industry, though Alexander had more occasion to run into Bart Rosemann, Cary's uncle and the Rosemann family patriarch. Bart's father had founded Rosemann Investments, and Bart had been grooming Cary to take over—though word on the street was that although Bart was technically in charge at Rosemann, Cary had always been the actual brains of the operation. Alexander didn't doubt it. Cary had always been smart.

The point was, Cary was around. So Alexander had just made sure the bastard knew the score. They didn't speak, limiting themselves to curt nods when forced into proximity. And, to be honest, Alexander also made sure Cary knew the score in other ways. If he flashed his Rolex a little too overtly —or flashed whatever hot guy was his flavor of the month a little too overtly, or flashed the bank's last quarter's financials a little too overtly—it was just to remind Cary of what Alexander had become.

And, more importantly, to remind himself. Money really could buy happiness. And it could buy other, more important things: respect, security, freedom. Power.

Alexander Evangelista had made himself into a titan.

And a titan could tolerate a man like Cary Bell.

Correction: A titan could tolerate a man like Cary Bell as long as he stayed where he belonged, in his box. In his box that was beneath Alexander's notice.

But if that fucking upstart thought he was going to steal clients out from under Dominion? If he thought he was going to use that honeyed mouth of his to sweet talk the twentieth-richest man in the world out from under Alexander?

Alexander rolled his wrists like he was warming up for a sparring session with his jujitsu master.

Bring it.